Franklin
Rock

Franklin Rock

a novel by

Mark E. Klein

Greenbriar Publishing, LLC
Potomac, Maryland

Published by Greenbriar Publishing, LLC. First Edition January 2021
For information contact: info@greenbriarpublishing.com

All of the characters and happenings in this book are fictitious. Any resemblance of any character to a real person, other than those few from history who are used solely—and loosely—to advance the tale, is coincidental.

Library of Congress Control Number: 2020916065

HARDCOVER: ISBN 978-0-9761684-6-1
PAPERBACK: ISBN 978-0-9761684-4-7
EBOOK: ISBN 978-0-9761684-5-4

Book design by Janice Benight

Manufactured in the United States of America

For Ellie, Sam, Jack, and Lucas

Franklin Rock

Prologue

"IT IS AN INDESCRIBABLE HONOR to meet you, Professor Einstein."

"Thank you. I don't believe we have been properly introduced," the professor replied.

"Sorry. My name is Franklin Rock. Please, call me Franklin."

"Nice to meet you, Franklin. What can I do for you?"

"Are you familiar with the Manhattan Project?" I asked him.

"Should I be?"

"It was a secret U.S. government project to develop the atomic bomb," I revealed to him, then held my breath.

"Would you please repeat what you just told me?" Einstein asked me in a quiet but deliberate voice.

"It was a secret U.S. government project to develop the atomic bomb," I repeated. "The bomb was eventually dropped on Japan to end the Second World War."

Professor Albert Einstein, who was seated at his paper-strewn desk in his office at Princeton University, leaned forward and stared intently into my eyes.

"So, if I understand correctly you have just told me that there will be a second world war, that Japan will be an adversary of the United States, and that a weapon based on the harnessing of the nuclear forces will be created, and worse, actually used. As far as I can remember it was 1937 when I awoke this morning," Einstein said as he turned to look out his office window. "And it still looks like 1937. So unless this is a hoax or a joke, you are telling me that you have seen the future."

"Yes, Professor Einstein, I have seen the future. I am from the future."

"How did you get here, Franklin?"

"That I am not quite sure about. I have always wanted to meet you. That might have something to do with it."

"Is there a specific reason you wanted to come to see me?"

"I think I'm here to prove to myself that time travel is possible."

"Are you convinced?"

"I am, Professor. How come you don't seem surprised by my visit?"

"Why should I be? Aren't I the one who discovered that all time is contemporaneous?"

"Yes, but I don't recall ever reading anything you wrote about time travel."

"That, Franklin, is because I did not. I thought it should be my little secret, at least for a while."

"Have you traveled to the past?" I asked, now fascinated by his disclosure.

"I have. And to the future. When I told you we had not yet been properly introduced, I meant those precise words—properly introduced."

"I don't understand."

"I have seen you once before, Franklin. I was watching you."

"Why were you watching me?" I asked incredulously.

"Eventually everyone will be watching you. Oh, I see that you are about to leave. We will likely see each other again."

"How do you know I'm about to leave?" I asked him, but it was too late. I felt the shift and I was gone.

PART ONE

In the Beginning

1

Franklin and Henry

"EVERYTHING ONE WRITES IS AUTOBIOGRAPHICAL. Maybe it all happened. Or maybe you just imagined that it happened. Perhaps you wished that it had happened, or you feared that it might happen."

"Which is it in your case?" I asked Franklin.

"All of the above, Henry."

"Excuse me for being a bit dense, Franklin, but what in the world does that mean? How can they all be correct? Things either happen or they don't. They are either real or fictional. You can't have it both ways."

"Ah, but you can, Henry. You can have it infinite ways."

"No one is going to understand that, Franklin."

"Perhaps not yet, Henry, but explaining how that is so will just be another part of my job."

My name is Henry Clay King, and I have the privilege to call Franklin Rock my best friend. Allow me to first address my name. Students of American history will have already recognized my first and middle names as those of a famous nineteenth-century United States Senator from Kentucky. Henry Clay is remembered—by those same students of American history, and few others—as the Great Compromiser, the man who brokered important laws in the early years of the new republic. My mother wanted to name me John, but my father could not stand that name. Too pedestrian he insisted. Instead, he wished to name me Daniel. My mother felt about Daniel the same way my father felt about John, so they compromised on Henry. My father, who never missed a chance to offer up a terrible pun, then inserted Clay as my middle name to immortalize their spousal compromise.

When Franklin first learned the origin of my name, he laughed uncontrollably.

"What is so funny?" I demanded to know.

"Your dad is so cool. That is such a great name!"

"You're not laughing at my name?"

"No, Henry, I am not laughing at your name. I love your name. I'm laughing at your dad's genius. I have to meet him one day."

Which Franklin did not too long after that conversation, and the two bonded like hydrogen and oxygen. That was no surprise to me. Franklin bonds with everyone.

On the day Franklin decided to tell his story, we were sitting together in a public garden on a beautiful spring day.

"I'm ready now, Henry."

"Why the change of heart?"

"I wouldn't call it a change of heart. My story was always going to be written."

"Fine, but why today?"

"You worry too much about the order of things, Henry."

After a brief pause to sort his thoughts and reach a decision—something I have witnessed repeatedly over the years—he continued.

"I think that you should be the one to introduce our story."

Our story. It's almost all his story. But I accepted the compliment, which is for sure how it was intended. I had no idea when that blustery, gray winter morning arrived during our final year of college that it would have any significance in my life, and most importantly Franklin's life, let alone that it would mark day one. Of course, it's only in retrospect that I recognize it as day one. Which is true of so many events in our lives that reveal their meaning only when viewed in the light of the future. For Franklin, as you will learn, the future means something far different than it does to the rest of us.

Franklin and I have been in each other's lives for a very long time. I can't recall exactly how we grew so close, but that's what happens over the years between best friends. One day you throw a ball around or move a piece of furniture together, and somehow in what seems like an instant you end up irreversibly entwined in each other's reality.

Franklin's story is a tale of hope and redemption, but he is not the beneficiary of that hope and redemption. He is the source.

Franklin Rock is here for us, for all of us. And I thank God that he is.

2

A Winter's Day

"FRANKLIN, ARE YOU LISTENING?" The professor's bark snatched me back from where I had been and deposited me in the current moment.

"Yes, sir," I instinctively replied. I rapidly recognized that I was in a classroom, a college class, literature I surmised by the professor's notes on the whiteboard at the front of the room. Years of education have trained me to automatically respond to any address directed at me from any instructor, without hesitation, with some affirmative retort indicating that I am completely in the moment. Most often I can quickly return from my reverie and summon up a credible response. On this particular morning, I was completely unprepared.

Fortunately, Professor Sorrens became distracted by lovely Joanna fluffing her hair and seemed to have forgotten that my attention was even an issue. The fact that I recognized Joanna was of some significant comfort; little else seemed familiar at that moment. It was as if I had experienced some type of cerebral accident, a stroke perhaps, but I seemed able to move my extremities, to swallow, to blink my eyes, and to think, at least enough to know that something was amiss.

I glanced down at the desk at which I was seated. *Siddhartha* by Hermann Hesse was open to page one hundred forty-three. My eyes swept over the written words. Some of the sentences had been underlined and marked with hand-drawn stars at the beginning and the end, which I recognized as my personal method of flagging important points. My star system is hierarchical; the more stars I assign, the more worthy I believe the sentence to be.

In the margins alongside the underlined and starred sentences were notes obviously of my making—the handwriting was unmistakable. Some of the words were nearly illegible, reliable evidence that the work was my own. Since childhood, my handwriting has been abysmal. Vowels are typically omitted, consonants scrawled as if by a playful toddler, some accurately representing their phonetic intent, others seemingly of a language unknown to this planet. But my notes adjacent to the page's final paragraph were different. Here my penmanship was markedly better. I had taken extra time with this entry, making certain that whenever I returned to review it there would be no doubt of the significance of its content.

That final paragraph was completely underlined; five stars marked each end of the sentence. In the adjacent margin I had written, "This is it!" My note referenced a quote by the protagonist of the book open before me, Siddhartha, speaking with his old friend:

> Time is not real, Govinda. I have realized this repeatedly. And if time is not real, then the dividing line that seems to lie between this world and eternity, between suffering and bliss, between good and evil, is also an illusion.

And just beneath those words, also underlined and bordered by five stars at either end, was a second note, also in my handwriting, though I had no recollection or sense that it was I who had written it:

> You were there. What you imagined is true. It will happen. That's a promise, and you know you never promise anything you can't deliver.

I had no idea what I was supposed to remember; at the moment I recalled nothing. My mind was vacuous, receptive but empty of thoughts or memories. Somehow I knew that this was likely temporary, that soon enough the internal tides would rise and bring back with them whatever memories they had taken.

I closed my notebook and got up from my seat, collected my only two currently known belongings, and quietly exited the room from the back of the class as Professor Sorrens, his back to me, scribbled an assignment on the board.

Soon I was enveloped by a gray late February day. An empty bench beckoned. I sat and looked around. Like the unclothed trees before me, I was barren of thought. Only minutes ago, I had awoken from some deep and unintended slumber. As my awareness slowly grew, I barely recognized the terrain of my life. Though my surroundings were familiar, it was with new eyes that I saw them, as if the previous images of that scene had been permanently erased.

As disoriented as I was, and with no reason at all obvious to me, I was suddenly overwhelmed by a thought, or more accurately an image, of my future. This life—my life—was destined to be a journey previously uncharted. Just why I was consumed by this sense of uniqueness I cannot say, but it was undeniable. It dawned on me—that's how my mother might have phrased it—that at this particular, unique moment everything was about to change. I had no idea what that would entail, but the excitement that had been generated by that thought was palpable. While exhilarating, it was simultaneously unsettling. I knew where I needed to go.

3

Mentor

CHARLES NIEMEYER, professor of English, lifted his head as I knocked on his open door. Last semester I had taken a class with him on German authors. That class was small: only twelve of us. This was not unusual for a senior seminar in a college of only two thousand students. Professor Niemeyer knew us all; we had all had him for one class or another over our college years. We had chosen this class precisely because we had.

"Hello Franklin," he said, removing his reading glasses. "What can I do for you?"

"Excuse me, Professor. Are you busy? I don't mean to interrupt you," I replied, still standing just outside his office.

"No, that's fine. Come in. Have a seat." He motioned to one of the two spartan chairs that sat politely matched in front of his desk. I did as directed. He leaned back in his large, mahogany-colored leather chair. "Yes?"

I hesitated. I had just experienced something so strange that I was unsure where to start.

"It's about Siddhartha," was all I could think to say.

"Siddhartha. The book by Hermann Hesse?"

"Yes, sir. That Siddhartha."

Professor Niemeyer scrunched up his face, obviously confused. "Franklin, are you referring to our class last semester?" he asked.

"Yes." *Get on with it Franklin. He's going to think you're an idiot.* "I happened to be reading it again." I must have been, I realized. It was the only explanation as to why it was open in Professor Sorrens's class.

"OK, and so you have a question?"

"I do. It's about when Siddhartha is talking to his friend Govinda about time."

At the end of that sentence, the professor pulled himself upright in his chair and moved slightly but noticeably towards me.

"Keep going," he added.

"Siddhartha says that time is not real. What does he mean by that?"

"Well, I have two questions for you, Franklin. What do *you* think it means? Or maybe you should answer my second question first. Why are you suddenly so interested in Siddhartha months after we read it?"

"Something happened to me today," I blurted out. I could see concern in Professor Niemeyer's eyes. "I'm not sick or injured," I rapidly added. *Now what?*

The professor saw my hesitation and filled the void. "You came to see me for a reason. It's OK. Just tell me," he said softly, recognizing my angst.

"I was in Professor Sorrens's class. I don't know how to explain it. One moment I was my usual self listening to him, and then after some time—I don't know how long—my mind was blank. I mean completely blank."

"Professor Sorrens's short story class?" he asked.

"Yes."

"You are not reading Hermann Hesse in his class," he confirmed.

"No, we're not. That's why I was confused when I looked down and saw Siddhartha open on my desk. I realized that something was wrong. I looked up and for a second or two had no idea where I was until I saw Professor Sorrens and my friend Joanna."

He prompted me for more. "So then what happened?"

"I looked down at the book and the page it was open to. That's when I saw my highlights and my note."

"You were on the page near the end of the book where Siddhartha talks about time not being real. Is that correct?"

"Yes. And then I saw what I had written in the margin, and I don't recall writing it. It was the strangest sensation, as if someone had written it for me but used my handwriting and markings."

"What did you write?"

I had Professor Niemeyer's attention. *Why is he so interested?*

"I wrote 'this is it' with an exclamation point. And below the paragraph about time I wrote something even stranger."

The professor nodded for me to continue.

"I wrote: You were there. What you imagined is true. It will happen. That's a promise, and you know you never promise anything you can't deliver."

Without any obvious response to what I had just told him, Professor Niemeyer continued his gentle interrogation. "Tell me exactly what happened after that. What did you do?"

"I decided I should leave the class. I got up quietly and left from the back of the room. I went outside."

"Did things start coming back to you? Did you recognize where you were?" he continued.

"They did. You know, it's funny but even when my mind was blank I wasn't worried. Somehow I felt confident that my memory would return." *Should I tell him the rest? It will make me sound even crazier.*

Once again Professor Niemeyer sensed my hesitation.

"You have some more to tell me. Please, Franklin, don't worry. I want to hear what you were thinking."

Still, I paused. Professor Niemeyer then leaned even closer. In his calm, soft voice, the one every student of his remarks on at some point during a semester because it fills him or her with the confidence to answer his question, he said, "If you didn't want me to know you wouldn't have come here this morning."

He was right. I knew immediately after the episode that he was the person I needed to talk with. So many times during his German literature seminar he would reference the unknown, the unknowable, and the mysterious. His selection of works for us to study, including Thomas Mann and Herman Hesse, focused on the unseen and rarely explored aspects of life. Class discussions took us to places within our minds that most of us students had never visited, and involved concepts we had not previously considered. Very often during these exploratory insights, he would reference time. He would do so in a way that always struck me, as if he knew something about time that we did not. The past would come alive in his discussions; in fact, he treated events in the past as if they were the present. I'm not sure if my fellow students took note of this, but it was always obvious to me. Professor Niemeyer seemed to be making a statement about time, as if it were his secret friend, his confidante.

"I had the strangest feeling about my future. Like it was all laid out in front of me, and it would be an adventure. I could see it as all happening simultaneously. I can't explain it. I guess that's obvious," I added with a smile.

Professor Niemeyer lifted his arms off his desk, sat back in his swivel chair, and turned towards the window to his left. His office was on the second floor of the Humanities Building and faced the Science and Engineering Center. The Center's exterior walls were all glass; the building had been built only a year before. Students were easily visible at lab benches, some peering into microscopes, others with protective eyewear working with beakers and pipettes. The scene changed from floor to floor. Professor Niemeyer seemed to be scanning them as he sat silently.

My mind went to this: He has decided that I need urgent mental health intervention and he is trying to figure out how to get me to the hospital without frightening me.

He turned back to me.

"Franklin, has this ever happened to you before?"

"I don't think so. I mean, not that I can remember." *I was right. He thinks I'm crazy.*

"I have one more question."

I nodded my consent.

"Were you frightened by the whole thing?"

I thought for a moment. Fear wasn't the emotion I felt. "No. I guess I should have been but honestly, I wasn't. I actually felt a little excited. I had the feeling that my life was going to be…" I paused and tried to relive the feeling I had had just a short time ago. "Like my life was going to be very cool." As soon as those words left my lips I looked for his response. That sounded like a very strange thing to say, even to me. Professor Niemeyer's expression, though, did not change.

"Anything else you want to tell me?" he asked, but he seemed to already know that there wasn't.

"No, I think that's pretty much everything," I answered. And then I waited.

Professor Niemeyer got up from his chair and walked around the desk towards me. He motioned for me to get up and follow him. *Oh, God, where is he taking me?*

"Let's take a walk."

I followed him out of his office and down the hall. He didn't say a word, but I did notice that he seemed buoyant. He had a slight hop in his step, like he was excited about something. I, on the other hand, was completely confused. I didn't know where we were going, or what he was thinking. I just assumed that whatever was in front of me was not likely to be good. Was I going to be admitted to the hospital? Was he taking me to see a psychiatrist?

We soon reached the entrance to the faculty lounge. Professor Niemeyer stopped at the door and motioned me to enter. He followed me in and closed the door. The faculty lounge was a large room with floor to ceiling windows that overlooked the quad in the center of campus. It faced south, so the midday sun was pouring through those windows and warming the room. Professor Niemeyer walked over to a pair of large upholstered chairs.

"Sit, Franklin," he said, pointing to the chair to his right. He sat in the chair to his left and swiveled so he was directly facing me. The brightness and warmth of the room were both comforting; I felt my muscles involuntarily relax, and I took a deep breath.

"Much better," Professor Niemeyer began. "Sometimes my office seems a bit claustrophobic. I thought you would enjoy being in a more comfortable place while we talked."

"Yes, thanks, this is very nice. I've never been in this room. I thought it was only for faculty. Is it OK for me to be in here?"

At that moment Professor Niemeyer gave me a look that I would come to understand. The look said: "Franklin, if I say something you should believe it." Then he laughed. "It's quite all right. There is rarely more than one person in here at a time. Seems the humanities faculty doesn't believe in taking many breaks to socialize. I highly doubt we will be interrupted."

I remained silent. Although I had no idea what was coming next or where this was going, it was pretty clear that Professor Niemeyer was currently driving the bus I was on.

"First, I want to tell you that you're fine. You are not crazy and I doubt you have a brain tumor or other medical problem," he assured me.

I wasn't going to a psychiatrist or the hospital. So far, so good.

He continued. "I have an idea, actually a pretty good one, about what happened to you. Are you familiar with the word prodrome?"

"No, sir. I don't think I've ever heard that word."

"It's a medical term, Franklin. When someone gets the flu, they might experience some fatigue before the fever and other symptoms come. It's analogous to a preface in a book, or the word preamble, as in our Constitution. All of these words refer to the introductory event that precedes the main event. I think what you experienced might be a prodrome."

"To what?" I rushed to ask. "Do you think I have some disease that made me lose my memory and forget where I was?"

"You didn't lose your memory. You noticed your mind refilled quite quickly after you left the class. It's more like you were somewhere else for a while," he explained.

That was true. Things did come back quickly. "But I did not go anywhere else."

"Technically that's correct. I meant somewhere else in your mind."

"I don't remember anything like that either. So what would the prodrome be related to if it's not an illness?"

Now it was Professor Niemeyer's turn to hesitate. "That's hard to say."

"But you're telling me that since you think this was a prodrome, you believe that something will follow." It had not previously occurred to me that whatever it was that I experienced could recur, or represent the beginning of something. "That is a bit scary, Professor," I said with a touch of panic in my voice.

Professor Niemeyer quickly responded. "Franklin, I am quite certain that you do not need to be frightened. You're not sick; nothing bad is going to happen to you. Look, you undoubtedly experienced something very unusual today. And I can't tell you how happy I am that you came to see me. You did the right thing. When it happens again—I'm pretty sure it will, or something like it—I'd like you to call me immediately."

Despite his reassurances, for the first time since this entire episode began, I became anxious. I could feel my heart pounding. I began to get light-headed and for a moment thought that I might pass out. Professor Niemeyer saw what has happening. He quickly rose from his chair, took my arm, and directed me to the couch next to where we were seated. "Lie down and put your feet on the armrest."

As I stood I became even more light-headed, but Professor Niemeyer had me on the couch with my head down and my feet up within seconds. He stood next to me still holding my arm; he was taking my pulse.

"You should feel better in a minute," he said quietly. He was right. My sweating stopped and the light-headed feeling began to abate. Professor Niemeyer saw that I was attempting to sit up and stopped me. "Not yet. Let's give it a couple of minutes," he said, still hovering over me. "You had a vasovagal episode. You got nervous, and something called the vagus nerve slowed your heart rate. When your heart rate slows, there is less blood to your brain. That's why you felt—and looked—like you were going to pass out. It's very common," he said matter-of-factly, "and as long as you don't lose consciousness and whack your head it's no big deal."

I stayed quiet as instructed, and with each passing second I felt better. After a few more minutes I looked up at him, my eyes requesting permission for the rest of me to rise. He nodded. I sat up; I felt fine.

"Is that part of the prodrome?" I asked him.

"No, Franklin, that's just what happens to some people when they get really scared. It's my fault. I'm sorry."

"No, I'm the one who should be sorry. I'm so embarrassed."

"You have no reason to be," he began, now in his most reassuring Professor Niemeyer voice. "It's very common. Some people experience this when they are about to receive a vaccination, or, like you, when they get anxious. Don't think about it for a moment. I'm glad I was here." Then he laughed. "It seemingly happened *because* I was here. Are you ready to continue our discussion?"

I nodded.

"I believe that you are at the beginning of a process. It's a good thing; a very good thing. To be honest, Franklin, it is possible—even likely— that you will experience something even a bit stranger next time. When I mentioned that you might have gone somewhere else when your mind went blank, you said you hadn't. I'm not quite sure that's true. I think you did go somewhere else but had no recollection of it."

"Wouldn't someone else have noticed if I had left and returned?" I asked. That seemed to me to prove that I hadn't.

"That's only if you physically left the room, which you didn't. What I am talking about is a bit harder to describe." He paused to gather his thoughts. "OK, let's say that you and I were outside the window of this room on a scaffold like the window washers use. If we were to stay there from early in the morning until sunset we would see the same room with the same furniture the entire time. But during the day faculty members would enter and exit the room. The chair you were sitting in could be empty, for a short time it would be occupied by Professor Ames, and then later the same chair might welcome Professor Dowling. Same with the other pieces of furniture. Same set, different actors. What is changing?" Professor Niemeyer looked at me and awaited my response.

"Time," I immediately responded.

"Exactly! You and I are fixed on that scaffold. We are not moving through space, but we are moving through time," he explained. "Everything moves through time, except light, but that's a discussion for another day. What I am trying to tell you is that we all move through time without necessarily moving through space."

I had no idea where this was going. "Professor, I'm not sure I understand what this has to do with what happened to me? We all know that time flows."

"Are you sure that time flows? If so, which way?" Now he was Professor Niemeyer employing the Socratic method. He seemed to have me just where he wanted me.

Am I sure time flows? Of course it flows, and it only flows in one direction. Eggs don't fly up from the pan and go back into their shells. We don't get younger.

"Yes, I am sure time flows, and it only goes in one direction, from present to future." I repeated my egg and aging analogies.

"Just about everyone would agree with you, Franklin. It does seem as though time flows, and only in one direction. As it turns out, that's not accurate."

"Which part? The flow part or the one direction part?"

"Both," he responded. "And you will soon see what I mean."

"What? I don't understand. What do you mean, I will soon see?" Now he had me at the edge of the couch.

"That prodrome we discussed. It implies another step. I'm pretty sure you'll be taking it soon. That's when you'll understand my answer about time."

"How will I know when I'm taking that next step?" I pressed him.

Professor Niemeyer leaned forward and rested his arms on his knees. Now we were only a few feet apart. "You will know, Franklin, because at that moment you will find yourself in another time. Make sure you call me when it happens because I'm one hundred percent certain it will."

4

Revelation

FOR THE NEXT COUPLE OF WEEKS, nothing happened. Days were normal; I was able to return to my studies and fulfill my usual obligations. Even so, I waited for the next shoe to drop. Professor Niemeyer seemed certain that the prodrome meant that another episode was imminent. I had no idea what that would be or what to expect. I scanned every thought that traversed my brain for an indicator that something was happening.

Ever since I was a child I have recalled my dreams upon awakening. On many occasions, I was what I would describe as wide-awake during the dream, conscious of being a character in a very detailed play. Sets were vivid, the other characters distinct in their actions and dialogues.

This did not seem unusual to me, but once I made the mistake of sharing one of my dreams with my older sister. She eyed me as if I had told her I had robbed the candy store. "I'm going to tell mommy," she threatened.

As we got older and the chill between us thawed, I mentioned that episode. "Do you remember me asking you about other dreams?" she asked.

I thought for a moment. "No, I don't."

"Well, I did, at least several times. And every time you told me some crazy story. I even asked my friends about their dreams. No one had dreams like you, Franklin. That's why I never said anything to Mom. I didn't want to get you in trouble."

I just assumed that what Professor Niemeyer was anticipating was a dream. He never told me that specifically, but what else could he be referring to? Each night as I lay in bed over those two weeks, I wondered whether that would be the one when I took the next step, when

Professor Niemeyer's prophecy would be fulfilled. Each morning I quickly checked my mental reservoir for evidence that something had occurred. Nothing registered.

On the fifteenth morning after my prodrome, as Professor Niemeyer referred to it, I awoke and instantly had a recollection that I had had a dream of significance. No details were available; I was simply aware that something had transpired. Instead of getting out of bed, dressing, and beginning my day, I remained motionless. I was hoping that whatever that dream was would reveal itself. There seemed no good reason to go anywhere. My conscience attempted to cajole the rest of me into rising; my body would have none of it. I remained immobile, awaiting something to flash into my mind, but nothing came.

I finally rose, dressed, and left my room with no specific goal or destination. I raised the collar of my jacket as high as possible and shrugged my shoulders upwards to shield my ears from the elements. Thoughts were swirling through my mind, mimicking the whipping March wind. They were all moving too fast for me to hold any one for more than a few seconds. *What am I waiting for?*

In the distance, I could see the top of the College Memorial, the sixteen-sided building that marked the center of the campus. If this were May hundreds of students would be congregating on the lush open spaces between the Memorial and me. But not today. A few heavily bundled human forms were fighting the wind as they traversed the distance between academic buildings. Their heads were down, hands in pockets. No one stopped to ask, "What's up?" No one stopped to admire the intricate design and architecture of the Memorial.

Except me. I can't explain why I am mesmerized by this structure. Like a paper clip to a magnet, no matter my intended destination while crossing the campus, I am perpetually drawn to the Memorial. Despite my almost four years here, I had yet to learn the origin of the Hebrew inscription around the dome. Considering its hold on me, I knew surprisingly little of the building's significance or its secrets. Soon I was standing alongside it and yet again admiring its grandeur.

"Aren't you freezing?" I turned towards the voice. It was the manager of the college bookstore that was housed in the basement of the Memorial. Ms. Constantine is how I knew her, how every student referred to her.

She wasn't much older than the seniors; at least that was my impression. Judging a woman's age has always been difficult for me.

"No, I'm fine," I replied, suddenly conscious of the cold.

"That wasn't very convincing. Come inside the bookstore and warm up for a minute." I followed her through the double glass doors. Like the campus, the bookstore was essentially empty. Not a soul was browsing the rows of hanging jackets and sweatshirts. It made me think of Parents' Weekend when the store is jammed with students and their families filling their arms with logo-laden paraphernalia. The contrast struck me. Same setting, yet such incredibly different scenes separated only by a few months. *Time is so interesting.*

Ms. Constantine pulled her hood from her head. She shook her long red hair like a dog coming in from the rain. Her green eyes fixed on me.

"Franklin Rock. That's correct, isn't it?"

Her recognition took me by surprise. "Yes."

"That's quite a look. Don't be shocked. I have a good memory for names, and you've been buying books here every semester. It's not that hard."

Her smile relaxed me. Funny that I had not previously noticed how pretty she was. I wondered why.

"It's the hair."

Once again she caught me by surprise.

"You're trying to figure out why I look different, right? It's my hair. I usually wear it up in a bun when I'm at work. Sorry. I didn't mean to embarrass you."

"No, I'm sorry. I didn't mean to stare." That wasn't completely true. Her hair was incredible. *Why would she ever hide it in a bun?*

"Do you have classes today, Franklin?"

I was struck by her question. Since I awoke this morning I realized that I had not thought of myself as being in any specific place or in any specific time. I more resembled a tourist visiting an unfamiliar place than the long-term resident of the college that I was. Being in the bookstore at this particular time seemed almost random, just one choice from infinite options. Rather than being shackled to the present, I had the strangest sense that I could choose to be anywhere, or more accurately, in any time. All of the moments of my life seemed equally accessible, like choosing a single 45-rpm record from the rack in a jukebox. For some reason I had chosen this specific moment in the bookstore with Ms. Constantine to be the moment I was in. I felt certain that I could just as easily have chosen another.

"Franklin?" Ms. Constantine's voice returned me to the present. "Are you all right?"

"Oh, sorry. Yes, I'm fine. I was just thinking about where I had to be. Do you know what time it is?"

"It's one fifteen."

"Thursday, right?"

"Yes, Franklin, it's Thursday." Her wrinkled forehead exposed her concern. "You sure you're OK?"

"Yes, I'm really fine. I have to go to a meeting." I was about to leave when a thought occurred to me. "Can I ask you something?"

"Of course."

"I was wondering how much you know about the Memorial."

"I know a lot about this building. It would be impossible for me to work in such an incredible structure and not want to know everything I could about it."

I considered blowing off the meeting I had only at that moment remembered. Ms. Constantine preempted me. "I know you have to go. Listen, Franklin, why don't you come by sometime and we'll talk about it."

"I will. Thanks so much."

I zipped my jacket, turned, and exited through the glass doors, only to find the same wintry blast still awaiting me. I started to jog towards the administration building several hundred yards across the campus from the Memorial. After I had gotten a third of the way, I stopped, turned back towards the Memorial, and thought for a minute about time and Ms. Constantine. Both had gotten my attention.

Dr. Miles Vincent, the provost of the college, had already begun the meeting. My strategy to enter quietly and with as little disruption as possible was immediately thwarted as I realized that taking the only open seat required me to walk three-quarters of the way around the table, directly across Dr. Vincent's line of sight.

"So we will need to invite community leaders to address the entire faculty Senate sometime before the end of spring semester. And it's so nice of you to grace us with your presence, Mr. Rock," the provost added.

Probably better to say nothing. I displayed the most contrived sheepish grin I could imagine.

"Mr. Rock, most adults would now apologize to the group for entering late." He turned to his left. "Professor Nichols, were you touched as much as I by Mr. Rock's sham smile of helplessness?"

All fourteen of the faculty laughed, as did Henry Clay King, the only other student on the Faculty Committee of the Senate. That would be my best friend, Henry Clay King.

"I am very sorry, Dr. Vincent. I was a bit ill this morning. I won't be late again," I said.

"And how are you feeling now, son?"

"Embarrassed, sir. Otherwise much better."

"I am sure I speak for all assembled as I thank the Lord for your recovery." Without a pause, Dr. Vincent continued the meeting from precisely where he had temporarily detoured into his gentle but intentional chastisement.

It was all I could do to feign attention during the meeting. Dr. Vincent ignored Henry and me for the duration of the hour-long session, so fortunately my task was made that much easier. I noticed Henry staring at me every time I looked in his direction. There was no humor in his eyes. He looked concerned, and regarded me as one would a victim just removed from a serious auto accident. When the meeting adjourned, Henry rapidly navigated around the table to my location. He put his hand on my shoulder, leaned down, and whispered, "C'mon. Let's go."

I followed him out the door of the conference room, down the two long perpendicular hallways leading to the exterior door, and soon I was once again engaged with the same frigid temperature.

I had assumed Henry would want to talk to me once we had escaped the building, but he kept right on walking for another fifty yards before he abruptly stopped. "What the hell is going on with you, Franklin?"

"'What do you mean?"

"What do I mean? Are you serious? You didn't answer last night, then no sign of you in class this morning, and now you turn up late for the meeting. Where have you been?"

The insensitivity to the winter wind that I had possessed earlier while outside the Memorial had vanished. "I am really cold. Can we go inside somewhere?" I pleaded.

Henry stared at me for a moment, then turned and headed towards the student center. When we arrived, I followed him to a table at the far end of the nearly empty dining area.

"What's with you, Franklin? You look weird."

"I feel weird."

"Did you smoke something last night? Or take something?"

"No, of course not. You know me."

"Sometimes, Franklin, I'm not sure I do. Sometimes you seem far away. You want to tell me what's going on with you?"

Henry's question was the same one I had been asking myself all morning. Something had happened to me; that I knew. Intermittently I was experiencing short flashes of unfamiliar thoughts and even a few unexpected visual scenes, but these were like the three or four letters a contestant is given in a TV game show and then challenged to guess the entire idiom or quotation from just those few clues.

I closed my eyes and felt a subtle movement.

I was on a long curved staircase. Elsa, my childhood nanny, was by my side holding my hand. I couldn't tell what, but something was frightening me. I was frozen, unable to move.

"Don't be afraid, Franklin. Just keep walking," Elsa instructed me. But I could not keep walking. I felt her pulling my left arm to the point of pain.

"Franklin. Franklin!" Henry's shouting startled me.

I looked up at my best friend standing over me. He had both of his hands firmly on my shoulders and was shaking me. I was soaked in sweat, but the liquid I felt on my cheek was not perspiration. I was crying.

"I'm a little scared, Henry. Would you do me a favor and call Professor Niemeyer?"

"Why Professor Niemeyer?"

"Because about two weeks ago he told me to call him the first time I believed that I was traveling through time. And I'm pretty sure that's what just happened."

5

Past, Present, and Future

ELSA AND I WERE MAKING OUR USUAL stroll down the gently curved marble staircase on our way to the playground two blocks away. Our building's wide double-panel glass front door afforded a panoramic view of the neighborhood. I stopped. Elsa sensed the abrupt change in me and held my hand tightly. "Everything's fine, Franklin. We'll just stay to the right, and go down to the bottom one stair at a time."

"No, Elsa. I don't want to go down. Let's go home," I heard myself say in a child's voice.

I tried to let go of her as I turned back up the stairs, but Elsa would not release me. She held me fast by my left hand.

"Let me go, Elsa!" I struggled to free myself but her grip was too strong. I felt pain in my arm as I worked to get away. She pulled me closer and wrapped her free arm around my right shoulder.

"No, Franklin, stop. You must stop. It will be all right, I promise," she whispered into my ear. "We will just wait a moment longer." Elsa's firm hold on me spoke much louder than her words of assurance.

What I saw through the glass of the front door confused me. There were horses with men on them. I saw women with large hats and long dresses. Children ran by in strange costumes. Boys had on pants too short for their legs. Their shoes looked nothing like mine; they rose high onto the backs of their calves, and they had strange laces like none I had seen before. It wasn't until I saw the cloud of dust that I realized that my street was gone. No pavement, no sidewalk, no signs instructing when and where to park. All that remained was a dirt road.

NO POSTAGE
NECESSARY
IF MAILED
IN THE
UNITED STATES

NYRJ1CS1B

BUSINESS REPLY MAIL

FIRST-CLASS MAIL   PERMIT NO. 107   BOONE IA

POSTAGE WILL BE PAID BY ADDRESSEE

THE
NEW YORKER

PO BOX 37617
BOONE, IA 50037-2617

THE NEW YORKER

Subscribe and save up to 66% off the cover price.

Plus get a free notebook with your paid subscription.

☐ 23 issues for just $3.49 an issue
($80.27 total)

☐ I prefer 47 issues for $2.99 per issue
($140.53 total)

Name		PLEASE PRINT
Address		Apt.
City	State	Zip
E-mail		

Bonus: *To get 5 additional issues FREE, order at newyorker.com/go/5reissues3B*

☐ Payment enclosed

"Elsa! Look!" I said, again in my childhood voice. I pointed to the view I just described. Elsa said nothing. She remained calm and continued to hold me close. Her embrace comforted me. We stood together, motionless, in the middle of the staircase.

"Can you see the horses? And look, Elsa, our street. It's just dirt!" I yelled while pointing to the front door. Still, Elsa just held me close.

"It's all right, Franklin. Don't worry, the street will come back soon. We will just wait a bit longer. You just tell me when it does."

And indeed, just as Elsa promised, it soon did. The horses with the men on them, the ladies in the huge hats and long dresses, the boys in the funny pants, all vanished. Once again I saw my paved street with its sidewalk and signs and cars just as it had been before.

"Oh, Elsa, it's all here again. You were right. Our street is back. You are so smart, Elsa."

"Are you ready to go down now, Franklin?"

"Yes, Elsa, we can go now." We continued down the stairs and through the front door and out into a beautiful spring day. I felt the warm breeze blow my hair over my forehead. I heard the birds chirping. I looked up and saw the sun. The bright sunlight made me close my eyes; I could feel the sun's warmth. It felt wonderful. Then I opened my eyes and saw Henry standing over me, his hands on my shoulders, shaking me, calling my name.

"Is that everything you can recall, Franklin?" Professor Niemeyer asked me. "What were you thinking about before this happened?"

"I was thinking about what Henry had asked me. He wanted to know what was going on with me, and I think I told him I had been wondering the same. I closed my eyes and that's when the vision came."

"You mentioned that you think this wasn't the first time something like this happened to you as a child. Why?"

"I remember being in the kitchen later the same day that I had that vision, and I heard Elsa talking with my mother."

"What did she tell your mother?"

"That it happened again in the same place. She told my mother I was very scared and tried to get away, but that this time it passed more quickly than the last few."

"Franklin, do you have any idea how many times this happened to you as a child?"

"Well, it's hard to be sure now. When I think about it there were probably lots of times. I remember in the beginning telling my parents what I was seeing. My dad would laugh and make believe he saw the same, but I knew he didn't because he would describe things that weren't there. So soon I stopped telling anyone, except Elsa. She would just listen and hold me until it passed. I always felt better if I was with her when I had one. My mother took me to my pediatrician once and he asked me to describe what I saw. I remember trying to explain, but it was so hard to do. It wasn't just what I saw. I didn't just see things. I *felt* them. It was all so real."

"You told me that for a while they stopped. How old were you when that happened?"

"Ten or so, I think. I remember one day realizing that I hadn't had one in a while. I can't describe how happy I felt."

"So this is the first time something like this has happened since you were ten?"

"No, I think I have had a few since then, but I assumed they were dreams. They all happened at night, and when I awoke it took me a few minutes to decide what was real and what was a dream. At the time I didn't associate them with the ones I had years earlier. But now I'm pretty sure at least a few of what I thought at the time were dreams were not."

"Franklin, what happened last night? Did you go somewhere?"

"You mean off-campus?"

"No, Franklin, I mean somewhere else in time."

I leaned back in my chair and closed my eyes. I was hoping I could go back to where I had been the night before because I was certain Professor Niemeyer was correct. I had gone somewhere, but I had no idea where. The shift was noticeable; I opened my eyes.

"Ah, so finally you are awake. Lydia, come, the boy has awoken!"

"Franklin, are you all right? What was it that you ate? How many times must I tell you not to eat the berries right from the bush? You're not old enough to know which are safe and which are not. Maybe in a couple of years when you are nine. How do you feel?"

Uncle Len removed the cool cloth from my head. The sweet scent of Aunt Lydia's perfume filled my nostrils.

"I'm fine, Aunt Lydia. I just need to use the bathroom." *Why did she say I could pick the berries when I am nine?*

"Len, help the boy."

"I don't need help, Aunt Lydia. I'm not a boy anymore."

"Oh, right you are, Franklin. You're not a boy; you're a big boy!"

I saw Uncle Len wink at Aunt Lydia.

What is going on here? "What time is it? I have to get back for class."

Aunt Lydia's smile vanished. "Oh, no, not again. Franklin, oh, Franklin. Len, you'd better call right away."

I watched Uncle Len head towards the telephone on the wall. Suddenly I felt the familiar motion. The scene abruptly changed. Now standing before me was Professor Niemeyer. Henry was next to him, his mouth agape.

"Are you back now, Franklin?" Professor Niemeyer asked.

For a moment I wasn't sure where I was. I took a breath and looked around.

"Yes, I'm back."

"Where were you?"

"With my Aunt Lydia and Uncle Len, I think at their country house."

"How old were you?"

"Aunt Lydia said I would be nine in two years, so I must have been seven. At first, that confused me, but soon I realized that time was out of sync just for me. For them, everything seemed normal. It was very strange. I didn't feel seven. I felt twenty-one. I felt like I do right now."

"Who is your Aunt Lydia?"

"She's my mother's younger sister."

"You're smiling, Franklin."

"She was my favorite as a child. She always wore the same perfume, so I would know when she was near. As soon as I recognized that scent I felt instantly happy. I loved Aunt Lydia like my own mother. My visits with her were magic for me. She would be the first to wake up in the morning, and by the time I wandered downstairs, she had made me pancakes with syrup. And she would let me drink all the chocolate milk I wanted."

"Have you seen her recently?"

"She died when I was fifteen."

"Henry, would you please give Franklin and me a few minutes?"

"I'll wait in the lounge for you, Franklin." Henry looked at me. He was visibly upset as he turned and left.

"Franklin, you are aware that you are time traveling?"

"Now I am. It's a bit unsettling. Am I in danger, Professor? Should I be worrying about this? Because I have to tell you I am worried."

"Listen to me, Franklin. Don't be frightened. You should be excited. You have a gift. A wonderful gift."

"It doesn't feel like a gift. I'm scared to death. I'm afraid to even close my eyes."

"It's all right to be afraid, Franklin." Professor Niemeyer reached over and grabbed a tissue from the box on his desk and handed it to me. I dried my eyes.

"But you have to trust me. Your gift will turn out to be a blessing, and not just for you."

"What does it mean that I'm having these? Why now? Why have they returned?"

"It means that you are coming of age. It means that you will soon be ready."

"Ready for what?"

He was about to speak, then paused to consider his words. "What do you know about the theory of relativity, Franklin?"

"I'm embarrassed to say, nothing."

"Then we must begin there."

"Why relativity, Professor?"

"Because, Franklin, this world in which we find ourselves is a strange place, much stranger than you can imagine. For you to understand why you are having these experiences you must first understand how the world, especially time, works. And for that, I need to introduce you to Albert Einstein."

6

A Block of Ice

WHEN IT BECAME CLEAR TO ME that Franklin wouldn't be leaving Professor Niemeyer's office for some time, I left. I didn't hear from him for the rest of the day or that evening.

The following morning I walked across campus to Franklin's dorm. Franklin had elected to stay on campus as a senior, as did I. The two of us were so involved in campus life that we only briefly entertained the thought of moving into an off-campus apartment. Franklin selected one of the large singles reserved for seniors in the north end of campus, while I remained in the south end as a resident advisor to underclassmen.

Not that it mattered much where I lived. Our friends all knew that I spent almost all of my time with my head in a textbook, ensconced either in the library or in my room. In retrospect, I probably suffered from at least a mild case of obsessive-compulsive disorder. At least I enjoyed some benefit from my neurosis. I would end my undergraduate studies as class valedictorian.

"Bad trade, Henry," Franklin said to me when the class rankings were revealed.

"What is that supposed to mean?"

"You traded four years of experiences, great adventures, and a lot of fun for something no one, including you, is going to care about twenty years from now."

"Congratulations would have been a better thing to tell your best friend, don't you think?"

"Congratulations, Henry. It was still a bad trade."

For years Franklin had tried to drag me out of my room and away from my books to one event or another. Sometimes it was a concert, sometimes a ball game, or sometimes a trip in search of girls. He would beg me to join him and our other friends.

"Henry, you'll still get good grades. You can't stay in your room forever. This is our time; this is college. Meet people, have different experiences, have some fun. It's OK, I promise. Just let go."

But I could not let go. As much as I wanted to, and as much as I knew he was probably right, I could not let go. So I was the valedictorian, and I often wonder if it wasn't my friends who got the superior education.

I knocked on his door. After a few seconds, it was clear that Franklin wasn't in, so I decided I would return to my room and wait for him. He knew that I would be concerned and I was certain he would find me. As I opened the main entrance door of his dorm to leave, there he was, standing in front of me. It was immediately obvious that something had changed. Franklin was smiling. Heaviness had been replaced by lightness.

"You look much better, Franklin."

"I have so much to tell you, Henry. Let's go upstairs."

We climbed the two flights to Franklin's floor and entered his room. Although I was anxious to hear what he had to say, just seeing my friend in this improved state relaxed me. Franklin remained silent.

"So, what happened?"

"Hold on a second, Henry." Franklin held up his right hand. He didn't look at me but instead lowered his head and stared at the space in front of him. This was nothing new. I had seen this many times. An idea, a thought, a problem—something needed to be addressed before he could speak with me. As usual, after a moment, he lifted his head. Focus had replaced the smile that had greeted me just minutes ago.

"It's all about light, Henry. It's different from everything else in a very strange way."

"I have no idea what you are talking about."

"Sorry. You had already left when Professor Niemeyer told me that I had to understand Einstein's theory of special relativity before he could begin to explain what was going on with me. So we spent the next few hours talking about Albert Einstein and his theory. It took a while—this is crazy, complicated stuff—but eventually I began to understand. And Henry, once I realized what it meant, I almost started to cry."

"That's not exactly unusual for you, Franklin. You cry at television commercials."

"Henry, these visions, or whatever they are, are scaring the crap out of me. I haven't been able to sleep. I never know when one will start or where I'll be."

"So let me guess. It's my turn to learn about relativity."

"Do you mind?"

We have been through this drill before. Franklin learns something that he finds fascinating, and then can't wait to practice his new knowledge. Of course, Henry Clay King, the loyal friend, is most often the recipient of this fresh education.

"Go ahead. But just remember I don't share your affinity for all things physics." I sat down on the side of Franklin's bed. I figured this would take a while.

"Light, Henry, is very strange. No matter how fast you are going, if you try to measure its speed it's always the same."

"And this is important because?"

"Nothing else is like that. If you and I are riding next to each other on our bikes at the same pace, and I measure your speed from my moving bike, it will measure zero, since relative to me you are not moving. But if we did the same thing on light beams instead of bikes, you would always seem to be moving at the speed of light relative to me no matter how fast I was going."

"Like I said. Why exactly should I care about this?"

"Because it means that time is different for each of us if we are moving. There isn't just one 'now.' What you and I would say happens at the same instant will be different if one of us is moving."

"I can hardly catch my breath, Franklin. This is so exciting."

Franklin didn't say a word. He didn't need to. His facial muscles produced a look that reflected his thought. "You are an ignoramus, but since you are my best friend I will try again."

"What this all means, Henry, is that time does not flow. It's not like the past is something that happened and is gone, or that the future is a blank sheet of paper. It means that all of time exists simultaneously, like a block of ice with each moment permanently frozen in that block. Not just the past or the present. The future too. Now think about what's happened to me recently."

The light went on. Franklin had time-traveled. It was either that or he was psychotic, and the latter was an impossibility.

"So you're telling me that traveling in time is possible because all of time always exists, each and every moment is forever in that block. And since they always exist, it's possible to visit them."

Franklin's smile exploded onto his face.

"This is why I love you, Henry. Just when I think you are a hopeless loss, you come through."

"Gee, Franklin, that's the nicest thing you've ever said to me."

"OK, you're right, I'm sorry. But I do love how you always get it. All of this would be so much harder for me if I didn't have you to share it with. I am sorry, Henry. I know I can be a jerk sometimes."

"Now there's a sentiment we both share."

We looked at each other for a moment, then simultaneously began laughing.

"So now what? What else did Professor Niemeyer tell you?" I continued once I caught my breath.

"That the visions will probably go on for a while. He said I should call him when I go somewhere new."

"Why does he want you to do that?"

"I asked him. At first, he just told me it was important."

It wasn't like Franklin to not pursue a line of reasoning. For him understanding the cause of something, the fundamentals of how something works, is part of his nature.

"You didn't leave it at that," I told him.

"No, I didn't. But he didn't want to tell me anymore. So I had to convince him," Franklin said.

"And you did that how?"

"By giving him an analogy about how I preferred to learn. I told him the story about a discussion I had had with my music teacher when I was a kid. I wanted to know why the composer had chosen the notes he did when writing the music I was playing. He told me the composer thought they sounded good together. Fine, but what made them sound good? It was only when I began to study music theory that I could answer my own question."

"Sorry to interrupt your train of thought, but what's the answer to your music question?"

Another look. This one combined a bit of typical Franklin exasperation with a realization that he had already been a jerk once and didn't wish to repeat his mistake.

"Notes sound good in particular sequences based on their frequency. Music is mathematical. Composers put notes and chords together in a specific manner because our brains prefer certain progressions of frequencies."

"So what happened? Was Professor Niemeyer impressed by your music analogy?"

"He might not have been impressed but I'm pretty sure it had an effect. He seemed to get that I would feel a lot better if I knew why it was happening and if I had some idea of what to expect. "

"What did he say?"

"I could tell he was conflicted. He sort of paced around the room for a minute. Eventually, he stopped, sat down, and explained what he was thinking."

"And? Franklin, you're killing me. Just tell me already." I realized that Franklin was going through the same process Professor Niemeyer had. He wasn't sure whether he should share that information with me or not.

"It's not that I don't want to tell you, Henry. You know I share everything with you. I just don't want to worry you." Franklin looked at me, obviously allowing me to make the decision.

"I appreciate your concern. Now just tell me, you dope. You think I'm going to let you go through all this by yourself? C'mon, Franklin, you know me better than that."

With my approval, Franklin began. "First he assured me again that I would be fine, that I shouldn't worry. He said it might be better to wait to discuss this until we saw what happened next, that it might make me more anxious. I told him that I was already worried all the time. After I said that I could tell that he was changing his mind and that he had decided to go with my request. He explained to me that even as a young boy I had made trips only to the past. He was pretty certain that sooner or later I would end up in the future; that's why he wanted me to let him know where I end up."

"Why is he concerned about that?" I asked.

"Because that would indicate that the next phase would soon begin."

"The next phase of what?"

"The next phase of me becoming Franklin Rock."

7

A Friend of a Friend

"YOU KNOW IF MARIJUANA WERE LEGAL we'd never have another war. Everyone would be laughing too hard to pick up a weapon."

"You're right, J Bob. And everyone would be too fat to move."

"Brilliant, Henry. The munchies are the path to peace."

I listened as Henry and our good friend J. Robert Smithson—known to just about everyone as J Bob—discussed the merits of marijuana use while J Bob took a hit from the fattest joint I'd ever seen.

"Franklin?" J Bob leaned over and offered me the joint. He knew better than to even look Henry's way.

"No, not anytime soon. It might send me over the edge."

"Right. Henry told me you're having some weird hallucinations. Like you actually travel through time. Way cool, Franklin. I wish I could do that. I got so high on that Asian weed last summer I'm pretty sure I went prehistoric." Henry looked at me and rolled his eyes.

J Bob was responsible for my first encounter with marijuana. Also for my first encounter with hashish, and my first—and only—encounter with some hallucinogenic that may have been LSD but we were never actually sure. I admitted all of this to Professor Niemeyer. I was afraid that my indiscretions might have been the cause of my visions. Professor Niemeyer assured me that although there were many reasons not to smoke marijuana and even more to avoid hallucinogenics, he was certain they were not to blame for my situation.

J Bob was known campus-wide as "The Source." Students sought him out, not just to acquire weed, but to benefit from his knowledge and expertise on all things smoked and swallowed.

"J Bob, have you ever seen one of these?" Hook Whelan asked him one Saturday night. In his hand Hook held an unlabeled deep blue oval pill.

"Yeah, man, and if I were you I would pitch it. It's evil, and you will not like what happens. Tell you what. Just give it to me and I'll dispose of it for you." Hook gratefully thanked J Bob for saving him from some harrowing experience as he handed him the little blue pill.

"What is it?" I asked J Bob after Hook had departed. "Is it really dangerous?"

"Hell no," J Bob said, "it's great stuff. I tried it last month and I've been trying to find more."

"You lied to him?"

"Hey, if he's dumb enough to not know what he had it's not my problem. I probably did save him. I'm pretty sure Hook couldn't handle it. He would have freaked out and probably turned himself into the campus police. It's wicked stuff." All was fair in the soft drug business as far as J Bob was concerned.

Although I did not condone his frequent marijuana smoking nor his incessant sarcasm, I found J Bob incredibly interesting. His mind was as quick as a cheetah. Like an audiophile identifying a particular piece of music from the first few notes, he was on top of whatever issue you wished to discuss almost before your first words were revealed. Now, when I most needed people to talk to, J Bob proved to be perfect. He lived on the edge of the common and accepted, and frequently tipped over into the bizarre and forbidden. My visions fell across the line separating usual from unusual, and this was a place J Bob, unlike most people I knew, was most at home.

"You know, I'm not making up this time travel story," I told him. "I know it all sounds crazy, but it's really happening to me."

"Franklin, my man, I get it. I know you think I waste my time and who knows what else smoking pot, but I have to tell you it has opened my eyes. It's a strange world, man. I know it. I believe you've been time-traveling. Are you having fun?"

"No, I wish I were. It's a bit upsetting not knowing when it will happen or where I will go."

"You're looking at this the wrong way, Franklin."

"What do you mean?"

"I mean you shouldn't be scared. If it were me, I'd think it was fascinating. I'd be wondering, why me? And I'd be trying to figure out why it was happening now. Maybe someone or something is trying to tell you something."

"Like what or who?"

"I don't know. Look, Franklin, it's pretty clear that something is going on. This kind of stuff does not happen to everyone." J Bob thought for a moment, then looked at me in what I knew to be his serious mode. "I think you've been chosen."

"Chosen? C'mon."

"Oh, most definitely. I've read about stuff like this. There's this guy I know that you should meet. He calls himself Govinda. It's not his real name, but hey, that's his deal if that's what he wants people to call him. Anyway, you should meet him. He's way cool, and he's into time and stuff like that. I'll bet he'll tell you something similar."

Govinda. In my mind I saw a flare shooting into the night sky. J Bob had just heightened my attention. "So how do I meet him?"

"He'll probably be at the coffee house on State Street tonight. I'll take you."

Henry had been listening to our conversation while stuffing J Bob's munchie-satisfying corn chips into his mouth. J Bob heard the crunching and turned towards him.

"Yo, Henry, those are for stoned folks. You'll be back in the library in ten minutes. Go to the vending machine and get your own," J Bob said with a laugh and feigned tackling Henry.

J Bob's comments struck me. I had not told him about Professor Niemeyer so he couldn't know that Professor Niemeyer had implied the same, that I was on some type of journey towards something. "I'd be trying to figure it out." Easier said than done.

I left Henry's room and walked back to mine. We wouldn't be heading over to meet J Bob's friend Govinda until later in the evening. *Try to figure it out.* Those words hovered the entire way to my dorm. How? Even if I conquer the fear, where do I even start? Thank God I wasn't going to have to do this alone.

I lay down on my bed, arms folded under my head, and stared up at the ceiling of my room. *Try to figure it out.* My eyes slowly closed; I felt the shift.

◆◇◆◇◆

"HEY, FRANKLIN, the matches."

I was sitting in a group with three other boys. I estimated their age at about twelve. Each had a cigarette in his hand. We were on a concrete path between old wooden buildings. I had no idea where I was. Overhead a blue sky loomed. It was hot. I looked down; I was wearing shorts and a T-shirt, as were the others. Then the smell registered; saltwater. We were at the beach! Those buildings were changing lockers for guests.

"Matches, Franklin. Hello! C'mon, we're waiting," the same boy who had originally spoken yelled.

The matches were on my lap. I opened the cover, pulled out one of the paper matches, and struck it against the roughened edge of the matchbook cover. I lit the talking boy's cigarette first and tried to light another's, but the flame was fast approaching my fingers so I threw it down.

"Here, give them to me," another of the boys said as he reached over and grabbed the matchbook from my hand. He then proceeded to light the third boy's and his own.

"Are you smoking?" he asked, turning towards me.

"No. Not now. I don't feel like it," I told him. "Maybe later."

I stood up and looked into the open locker to my left. A mirror hung on the back wall. I was momentarily stunned; looking back at me was twelve-year-old Franklin. Panic nearly overtook me. *Try to figure it out.* I took a deep breath and looked down at whom I assumed were my friends. One of them I remembered, the one who spoke first. Last name Smith: what was his first name? I could picture his parents; they were friends of my parents. I didn't like them, and I'm pretty sure I didn't like him. Ricky! His name was Ricky.

"Why are you staring at me, Rock?" he asked.

"Oh, sorry, Ricky, I was just seeing if you guys were done smoking."

"Does it look like we're done smoking?" Ricky laughed, as did the other two who deferred to him. One of them began to cough.

"Too much for you, Doug?" Ricky asked mockingly.

Doug didn't answer and kept coughing. He could not catch his breath. I watched as it became clear that Doug was in trouble. His entire chest was now heaving, trying to get air into his lungs.

"Asthma," Doug said in a barely audible voice, working harder and harder to get air.

Doug was having an asthma attack. I looked down at Ricky and the other boy whose name I could not remember. They were both frozen. Of course they were; they were only twelve. I knelt next to Doug.

"Do you have an inhaler?" I whispered in his ear. He nodded. "Where is it? Do you have it with you?" He nodded, pointing to the locker with the open door. I stood, turned, and stepped into the locker. Under the mirror was a shelf, but it held only a comb and brush. I was looking for a current type of inhaler until I realized it was a decade earlier. I scanned the entire locker. A bench traversed the three walls. There on the bench, just under a hanging towel, I saw it. It was larger than current inhalers, but it was unmistakable. I grabbed it, stepped out of the locker, and handed it to Doug. Immediately he shook it, placed the opening in his mouth, and took two puffs.

Within a minute it was clear that it was working. Doug's gasping diminished; his chest heaves dissipated. Soon he was breathing near normally. During the entire episode, Ricky and the other boy were silent and motionless. Shouldn't they have run for help, I thought? What would I have done at twelve?

All three boys were now staring at me. Ricky and the other boy's eyes were as wide as if staring at a ghost. Maybe they are, I thought, and smiled.

"I think you saved my life," Doug said softly to me, his gratitude implied in his tone of voice. As I was about to tell him I was glad I could help, I felt the shift.

◆◇◆◇◆

I LOOKED AROUND. I was still in my room, on my bed. I hadn't moved.

My entire body shook with a passing chill. I searched my memory. Had I saved Doug's life? Did any of that happen? I could recall a day hanging out with Ricky and other kids at the beach; I was probably around twelve, so that made sense. And I remembered the cigarettes. I didn't tell my mother about it. I never liked Ricky and those boys and I was angry that she had arranged for me to spend time with them at the beach while she spent the day with their mothers. I had no recollection of any episode of saving anyone from an asthma attack. *Try to figure it out.* Easier said than done, I said to myself again. A wave of fatigue overcame me.

J Bob's knocking woke me.

"Sorry, I must have fallen asleep," I told him as I opened the door and let him in. Time travel seems to tire me, or maybe it's just the anxiety of the whole thing that saps my energy. Another thing to figure out.

"It's OK. No hurry. Govinda and his friends will be there until late," J Bob assured me.

It took no time to traverse the five blocks to the State Street Coffeehouse. We entered through the windowless wooden front door and crossed the vestibule that separated the front door from the main room. I had not previously been in this much-heralded local shrine of rhythm and blues. First of all, I didn't smoke, and the place was rancid with the smell of discarded cigarettes. My musical tastes were also more traditional, the typical rock of the college scene. Here was another way J Bob separated himself from his peers. His musical tastes ran the gamut, and he was frequently drawn to the deep melancholy of R&B.

Within seconds J Bob spotted his target.

"There he is. Follow me."

I noticed the music had stopped. The band was putting down their instruments and getting up. We must have arrived just after a set, I thought.

We maneuvered through the smoky haze, around the closely spaced tables, and made our way to a rectangular wooden picnic table along the far right wall. Seated on the benches were five people, three guys, two girls. The interior of the State Street Coffeehouse was barely illuminated by low-level lights scattered about the room, so judging the ages of those at the table was difficult. They all appeared older than me. J Bob addressed the one in the center.

"Hey, Govinda."

"J Bob. Welcome. Who's your friend?"

"This is Franklin. Franklin Rock."

Everyone else at the table turned towards me. They didn't just take a quick look, smile, greet me, and then return to what they were doing. All eight eyes remained fixed on me. J Bob also noted the attention.

"Why are you guys staring at him?" he asked. No one answered him.

"Govinda, what gives? They're looking at him like he's a cop."

"Oh he's not a cop, I know that," Govinda responded.

"Sorry, Franklin. Here, sit down." Govinda motioned for the two seated across from him to scoot over to make room for me. "Let me introduce you. This is Terri, Andy, Jane, and Rich," Govinda said as he moved clockwise around the table.

I nodded to each of them. They were all still looking at me. Terri, who I had assumed was the girlfriend of either Andy or Govinda based on her location at the table, was staring more intently than the others. I began to feel uncomfortable so I turned to face Govinda.

J Bob began to speak.

"Govinda, I brought Franklin to meet you. I'm pretty sure you'll enjoy talking to him. He's had some interesting adventures lately."

"So, Franklin, what are these great adventures?"

I looked at J Bob. His nod was meant to encourage me to speak.

I leaned closer to Govinda, and in as quiet a voice as I thought would be audible I began. "This is going to sound strange, but I have been moving around in time lately. At least I think that's what's happening. I have these strange visions."

Govinda put down his beer and looked first at J Bob, then at Andy. He mouthed a word that I was pretty sure was an expletive.

"Will you share some of them with me, Franklin?"

"Sure, if you want. They are weird, though."

"They probably won't sound weird to me."

"Oh, just wait. They will. Until you've had one of these it's impossible to understand."

Govinda leaned closer. I could see his eyes were tearing, which surprised me. He reached over, gripped my shoulder, and gently pulled me towards him.

"I know exactly what you mean, Franklin. I've never been able to explain it to anyone either."

8

Govinda

Though no one else could hear what Govinda had whispered to me, it was immediately obvious to everyone at the table that something important had just occurred.

"We're leaving," Govinda announced.

"Just like that?" Terri asked.

Govinda didn't respond. He merely nodded at Andy and motioned to J Bob and me to follow.

"Go ahead, Franklin," J Bob said. "I'm gonna hang with these guys." And allow me private time to talk with Govinda, he might have added but instead winked.

Govinda's dark blue sedan was parked half a block away. He got in and reached over to unlock the passenger door. I collapsed into the passenger seat, still in disbelief since learning that I was not alone, that someone else, someone right here right now, actually understood.

We both remained silent as Govinda did a u-turn down State and headed south. I cared as much about where we were headed as a spinning roulette ball cares about the number it chooses to make its home. Once you have left your own space and time, destinations become far less significant. One seems no better than another.

Govinda pulled into an empty outdoor parking lot and cut the engine. Huge overhead lights illuminated the entire area. As if in a championship boxing match, I expected an announcer to bring us to the center of the ring and introduce us. "In the white trunks, the young challenger, Franklin Rock. And in the red trunks, the champion, with all the knowledge and experience, the mysterious Govinda."

The champ spoke first. "Did you notice my friends staring at you, Franklin?"

That was not the question I expected. I had noticed, and it had made me uncomfortable.

"Yes."

"It's not the first time, is it? I'm guessing people stare at you all the time." *How did he know?*

Govinda continued. "You're in a group, maybe at lunch or in a friend's room. You notice that whoever is speaking is talking directly to you. Right?"

That was almost always my experience, no matter the group, no matter the speaker. It was just as Govinda described.

"It's been this way as long as you can remember. You're embarrassed by the attention. You try to divert the focus of the conversation to someone else, and it works for a minute or so. But the speaker always turns back to you. Am I right, Franklin?"

"How do you know this, Govinda? Is it the same for you?"

"Yes, but I'm sure it's much more so for you. Even I felt the pull, even I was obligated to look at you tonight. Can I ask you a personal question, Franklin?" Govinda did not wait for my response. "Women also seem drawn to you, am I correct? Not all women, of course. Only the ones tuned in, only the ones paying attention and looking for something other than big muscles and blue eyes. It's true, isn't it?"

For so many years I wondered why women found me interesting. I have never considered myself handsome. Even when it was crystal clear that I was not nearly the best-looking or most successful male in the group, inevitably there would be a girl—sometimes more than one—who fixed me with her eyes the moment I began to speak. For me, it was much more confusion than flattery. I never understood the attraction. I confided all of this to Govinda.

"Franklin, you can't see it yourself. It's invisible, like pheromones. But pheromones have substance. This is different. This is a sixth sense. It's hard to appreciate, but it's absolutely real."

Why my eyes were tearing at this moment was unclear. Perhaps it was the knowledge that I was not alone or unique. Everyone likes to think that he or she is in some way special. But the truth is that no one wishes to be that unique. We want to fit in. It is when we find ourselves completely outside the box that sadness makes its presence.

Govinda, without any need for explanation, instantly understood me. Trying to explain my visions to others had been like trying to describe yellow. Yellow has no shape or texture. Yellow has no mass or volume. Yellow just is. Govinda already knew yellow.

"Can you tell me about your visions, Govinda? Where have you gone?"

For what was probably an hour Govinda described his experiences. They began when he was eight years old. At first, his parents thought he was having fevers. And just like me, when it became clear that no one either believed or understood him, he stopped telling anyone about them. Mostly he saw family members in his visions, some dead a long time, some who lived great distances from his home. On what he called "special occasions," he was in the future, part of an event or a happening. He had only vague recollections of these moments, but he recognized them as momentous. Large crowds were gathered during these visions, and these events were always celebratory. Govinda did not know the exact context of these events, only that they brought incredible joy to those participating, and he felt elated. But there was something peculiar about these special dreams and visions, something that made them very different from my own.

"I'm never the main character in my visions, Franklin. Never. I am always the friend, the accomplice to another. Sometimes I merely observe the goings-on. Other times I have a major role, but never the lead role. Long ago I realized that the main character, the focus of these special times, is always the same person. The setting changes but the protagonist remains constant. I can never quite see his face; his back is always to me. But I hear his voice, and I know that voice like my own."

Govinda paused as if he was recalling a favorite song. Then he returned to me.

"It's your voice, Franklin. Once you began to speak this evening, I knew immediately. Oh my God, I thought, oh my God. A thousand volts went through me. I have spent so many hours with that voice, and to suddenly hear it from a live person was beyond what I can describe to you." Govinda shook his head. "I still can't believe that you are here. It's almost too much for me."

I had no idea what to say. All that came into my head was his name, Govinda.

"Why do you call yourself Govinda?"

"Have you read Siddhartha, Franklin? It's a book by Hermann Hesse."

"You won't believe this, Govinda, but I just finished it. And something very strange happened just after I did." I told him about Professor Sorrens's class and the events that followed.

"So you know that Govinda was Siddhartha's lifelong friend and confidante. We learn a great deal about Siddhartha through their relationship. I know from my visions that I am not the central character of whatever this story is that I am in. I am the friend, the catalyst. So I took the name I felt most appropriate to my life. I'm fine with being the catalyst, Franklin. At least I know my role, which is far more than most people ever figure out." Govinda leaned closer and placed his hand on my shoulder. "Tell me something, Franklin. Tell me what you know."

"What I know?"

"What you know about your mission."

Govinda was inside my head; somehow he knew. But it seemed fine. I wasn't frightened or upset. I felt relieved, as if the chaos of the city had been magically replaced by the calm of acres of green rolling country hills.

"I have never told anyone what I am about to tell you, Govinda. Not my parents, not even my best friend Henry. No one."

"You can trust me, Franklin."

"I'm not concerned, Govinda. I'm pretty sure that I am supposed to tell you."

"And I am equally sure that you are."

"As long as I can remember, even before the dreams and visions, I have had this recurrent feeling that I am here for a reason. I can't shake it. I can't rationalize it or suppress it. It's always there, reminding me, encouraging me, demanding something of me. Probably lots of people feel this way."

"I don't believe that, Franklin. But go on."

"So many times in my life I have an idea of something I want to do. But inevitably I am derailed. Something happens that prevents me from following that path, as if some invisible hand is forcing me from my desired direction towards one not of my choosing. Does that make any sense to you?"

Govinda wiped his tears.

"I have seen this moment, Franklin. This very moment that we are in. I have seen it before. I have listened to the faceless character describe his sense of purpose. I have heard his confusion, and I have witnessed his frustration. He described it to me as if he were driving a car whose direction and destination were not his to control."

"Yes! That's exactly what it feels like. There is a dream I have had many, many times. I am the driver of a car. It begins to speed up. I try to step on the brake but it's missing. I try to turn the wheel, but still nothing happens. Faster and faster I go, certain that a crash is imminent and that I will be killed. But I never crash. Every curve is negotiated, and every obstacle is avoided."

"And you wonder what it means?"

"I do. What happens to your faceless character, Govinda?"

"He too never crashes. He too is never injured. You know, of course, Franklin, that although you are in the driver's seat, someone else is driving the car."

"Don't tell me it's God."

"I have no idea who it is. A true religious believer will try to convince you it's Jesus or God. It doesn't matter."

"Why do you say that?"

"Because who is driving the car is not the point."

"What is the point?"

"That your destiny is already determined. That you are on a mission."

"Which is?"

Govinda's quizzical look surprised me. "You don't know, Franklin?" Govinda studied me for a moment. "Of course you do. But you're still too embarrassed to speak it. Or more likely petrified to speak it. I don't blame you, Franklin. I'd probably be scared, too."

I had instinctively grabbed the passenger seat bottom with both hands as if steadying myself for impact. But Govinda was correct. I have always known. Unconsciously I let go of the seat. My course had been set for me, I knew, and I was not going to crash.

9

The Morning After

GOVINDA DROVE ME HOME. The car was silent as we made our way back to the campus. Something surreal had just occurred; that was clear to both of us. At a moment such as this, where the climax of the story hits like an avalanche, the dénouement is often vague and uneasy. What happens next? Only in Hollywood are the answers obvious. In this world, the real one, the protagonists are far more likely to be disoriented and directionless, uncertain of what will or should transpire. So it was for me and Govinda.

As we neared my dorm, Govinda spoke. "You OK, Franklin?"

"Yeah, I'm fine. Stunned but fine. You?"

"The same. A lot is going to happen."

"I know, Govinda. But you'll help?"

"I most definitely will."

As I climbed the two flights of stairs to my room, I yearned to close my eyes, to leave all of it behind—the visions, the time travel, and the immense burden I suddenly felt. But the questions, uninvited and unwelcome, still came. Who am I to be so presumptuous to presume that I had been singled out, one of what, billions? I am no hero. I have never in my humble life demonstrated any special courage. And what accomplishments do I have to promote my place? None.

My door was slightly ajar when I arrived. I pushed it open. Joanna was sitting on the floor, her back to me, with Henry directly across from her. They were engrossed in conversation and at first did not realize that I had returned. Henry finally looked up and saw me standing in the doorway. Joanna turned her head to face me.

"Franklin," she said in a concerned tone, "you look exhausted."

"I am. Not that I'm not glad to see you two, but why are you here?" It was immediately obvious that, just before I entered the room, they had been discussing me. Joanna returned her focus to Henry. My best friend wasn't smiling.

"Franklin, Professor Niemeyer..."

Before Henry could finish the sentence, I already knew. He was gone. Professor Niemeyer was gone. I felt it from inside my marrow; there could be no other explanation for this knowledge that suddenly filled me.

"He died, Henry, didn't he? Professor Niemeyer died tonight."

I heard Joanna's gasp as background, like the bullfrogs and crickets on a summer night.

"This morning, Franklin. They said he must have been ill for a while. I don't even think most of his friends knew." Henry paused, not out of grief but to plan his next sentence. But he needn't have worried. That too I already knew.

"What did he leave for me?"

Joanna was lost, as if trying to follow a conversation in a language in which she possessed only a rudimentary facility. She seemed unsure of which way to turn, to whom to pay attention. So instead she silently excused herself, slid back towards the couch, and laid her head on a fallen pillow.

Henry got up and walked over to the kitchen table. Under his blue down jacket was a thick yellow envelope.

"His teaching assistant brought this for you an hour ago. He said that Professor Niemeyer had given it to him last week and told him to deliver it to you after he died. He must have known that his time was short. Did you know, Franklin?"

I was embarrassed to admit that I did not. Like a child in a one-way relationship with his parents, I never once considered Professor Niemeyer's well-being. I knew almost nothing about him or his life, other than his standing in the college. I had no idea if he had any children, what his hobbies were, or if he loved his wife. I had never asked. I became very sad that I did not, that I had not taken the initiative to learn anything about the man.

As I was temporarily lost in guilt, Henry had walked across the room with the envelope. I took it from him and turned it over in my hands. On the front, written in the Professor's elegant cursive, was my name. It was sealed, and the flap reinforced with clear plastic tape. Its contents were obvious—a book, and something small made of hard plastic that was easily palpable just under the surface.

"Are you going to open it?" Henry inquired.

For a moment I contemplated his question.

"Not tonight. I'm way too tired. I'll explain everything in the morning, Henry." The thought of rehashing the evening's events was just too much. My curiosity about the envelope's contents was far superseded by my exhaustion. I needed sleep.

Henry, the great, great friend that he is, recognized my state.

"Joanna, we better let this boy go to bed." He took her hand, helped her up, and within a minute they were gone.

"You'll be out like a light," my mother used to tell me at the end of a long day of play as she hustled me into my bed. She was always right: at those times sleep came before my head hit the pillow. No sleep is like the deep sleep of childhood. Children escape into a blessed land of invulnerability, where the sounds of night cannot reach them and disturb their peace. Every parent knows that place, where the challenges and dangers that will confront that child in the years to follow are kept at bay by a force forged of love and God's good grace.

"Let him sleep," my mother would insist whenever my father approached his dormant son. "He never admitted why he wanted you awake. But I knew that he simply couldn't wait to see your eyes open and to snatch you into his arms and hug you," she told me years after he had passed away.

A hug would be nice now.

Sleep did come rapidly. Sometime later when my mind was again ready, the dream began.

I was airborne, back to the wind in a semi-reclined position. All I could see was a brilliant blue sky, void of even a cloud. The only sound was the wind. "Heaven. I am in heaven," I said out loud.

"Are you sure?" a voice answered back.

"Isn't it?" I asked the voice. "What else could it be?"

"What do you think it could be?"

"Peace. I think maybe peace in the world would feel like this. Or love. Or both."

"It's nice, isn't it?" the voice continued.

"It's perfect. Will it last?" I needed to know.

"It can."

"So how do I make it last?"

"You get everyone else to want it as much as you."

"Will they?"

"Why wouldn't everyone want it as much as you? You just told me it's perfect."

I couldn't imagine that everyone wouldn't. So why are love and peace so elusive, I wondered? And then I started to drop like a stone, and within a moment I was awake.

My room was dark; it was still the middle of the night. How long had I been sleeping? It felt as if only moments ago I had closed my eyes, yet I felt refreshed. Whatever sleep I had had was sufficient.

The envelope. "He's gone," I reflected as I lifted it from my desk. But for some reason I wasn't morose, as if word of his death was for others to hear and to say, "Isn't it sad that Professor Niemeyer has died?" That message was meant for them; not for me. I still felt very much connected to him, as if he were but a thought away.

When Henry gave Professor Niemeyer's envelope to me I hadn't noticed that it was in two parts. Taped to the front of the larger envelope was a letter-sized envelope. Written in large bold print were the words "OPEN THIS FIRST." As instructed, I removed the top envelope, tore open the seal, removed and unfolded the letter as I placed the larger envelope on my bed. In Professor Niemeyer's hand was written the following:

> Franklin, if you are reading this I must be dead. Not to worry, it's not all that important that I have died, as you will one day understand. I am sorry I had to leave you so early in this process. Make no mistake; it is a process in which you are now engaged. You have much to learn, and you will. How am I so sure? I have seen it. By now you understand what I mean by that. You have lived time in the truest sense, and you will undoubtedly continue to do so.
>
> I asked my assistant to deliver this letter and the contents of the large envelope upon my death. Since I could not

guarantee that it would reach you in the future I wanted it to be in your possession. However, I ask that you not open the large envelope at this time. You are not quite ready to review its contents, or more accurately it won't have the same significance now as it will in the future. I have not specified a specific date on which you should open it. You will know when the time is right.

I had unconsciously unsealed the larger envelope as I read the letter. By the time I had reached Professor Niemeyer's instruction, it was too late; the deed was already done. The contents of the envelope had already easily slid into my hand. First to exit the envelope was a clear plastic case within which was an unlabeled cassette tape. Just beneath the tape was a sheet of paper, folded in half, its contents concealed. At the bottom of this threesome was a book, its back facing up, binding to the right. I laid the contents on my bed, then read his second note:

Franklin, if you are reading this you have decided that the time is right. I struggled with when would be best for you to hear this. I likely shouldn't have concerned myself with such a question. You are Franklin Rock; anytime would have been fine. Listen to my tape recording before you open the book—then follow along with me as you do so.

As instructed by my now-deceased mentor, I opened the plastic case that housed the tape, lifted it, placed it into my small red Panasonic recorder, and hit the play button.

"Hello, Franklin. Since you are playing this tape I have died. It's a bit strange to talk about the fact of one's death while still very much alive. But as you will learn the line between life and death is no line at all.

Lift the book, cover facing you. As I am recording this, I am trying to anticipate the look on your face as you read the book's title. Are you shocked, fascinated, fearful, perplexed? Most likely a bit of them all I would guess. Now open the book to the table of contents. Notice that the page is blank. A table of contents should list chapters. As you can see there are none. That is because you have yet to write those chapters, so they cannot yet be numbered and named. And when I say you have yet to write them, I don't mean that you will necessarily be the author who pens the pages. Your choices and actions will determine their content, and only then will they be written. There will be as many chapters as is necessary, or as many as you decide will be necessary. Confusing, I know, but you'll eventually understand. How many chapters are eventually written is not important now. That will take care of itself.

I tried to teach you so many things in the limited time we had. Remember, all outcomes are possible until a choice is made. Everyone makes choices, literally billions upon billions are made every day. It is through our choices that each of us participates in the creation of reality. Each of our choices initiates a cascade of events that leads to innumerable possible outcomes as they intersect with the other billions of choices. With each of these interactions, a new chapter is written and reality unfolds. That is how the world works. I tell you this so that you know not to worry about any single choice you make. There is no such thing as the right choice. And don't worry if what I am telling you doesn't quite make sense; you will hear all of this again.

One more thing. You will find the future in the present— and the past—if you pay close attention. Don't worry if this seems odd. Eventually, you will see what I mean. It's quite thrilling to behold, and I had only a small taste of it. You will have far more. Don't fear the future, Franklin. Fear nothing. You don't need to. Recall that I told you all works out as it must. You know things, Franklin. That's important; this too will become clear as you move on.

I will see you in time, Franklin. Godspeed.

I looked again at the blank table of contents. Why did he give me a blank book? I flipped through the pages from back to front looking for something. It was only when I reached the very beginning of the book that

I saw it. On the backside of the title page, I saw the following: *Publication date: December 31, 2020*, almost thirty years from the present. Why that date? What would fill those pages? Thirty years of events and experiences. Thirty years of history. Thirty years of relationships sure to rise and fall. These were all mine to create, all mine to discover. Such a great weight of responsibility should have cowered me, but it did not. I felt exhilarated, elevated by the possible.

"Why wouldn't everyone want it as much as you?" The words from the voice in my dream returned to me. I shook as if suddenly within a deep freeze. Govinda was correct; I was already aware of my mission. Which explained the title of the book that lay before me:

Franklin Rock: The Man Who Fixed the World

10

Ms. Constantine

ONCE THE EXHILARATION I FELT after listening to Professor Niemeyer and seeing the book waned, I returned to my bed to reflect on it all. Despite the predawn hour, I did not anticipate falling asleep, but I did.

Aging Venetian blinds lost the battle against the streaming sunlight from the eastern exposure of my room, so unlike my fellow students who rarely arose before noon on a Sunday, I awoke shortly after sunrise. As soon as my eyes recognized the arrival of the new day, my mind was inundated with the events of the recently concluded night.

Did Professor Niemeyer die? Those first minutes of wakefulness are often incomplete. Fiction and reality overlap, and it is often impossible to be certain for a time which recalled events are true and which remain from an early morning dream.

I threw on a pair of jeans and a turtleneck, grabbed my coat, and headed out into the cold morning air. After a few minutes, the mental fog began to clear. Yes, it was true; Professor Niemeyer had passed on. His letter, the tape, and the book all thrust themselves back into my consciousness.

So much had transpired in so little time, I thought. Just weeks ago all was as it had always been. Coursework and other recurring responsibilities took turns in demanding my attention. One of those recurring responsibilities was reading applications for prospective students.

Henry and I had been selected as the only two students on the college admissions committee. This was a great honor and both of us were grateful for the opportunity. We would spend a few hours a week together in the admissions office. Each of us would scoop up a pile of applications and retire to one of the soft chairs in the designated reading area of the building.

I remembered that I had promised Henry we would meet at the administration building Sunday morning to fulfill our application-reading commitment. By the time I arrived, Henry was already ensconced in his lounge chair of choice.

"Good morning," Henry greeted me. "I see you recovered from last night. I'm sorry about Professor Niemeyer."

"Thanks. I still can't believe it. I woke up this morning hoping it was a dream. I feel terrible that I didn't know he was sick." I knew what was coming next.

"What did he leave you in that envelope?" Henry inquired. I had already decided that if he asked I would not tell him. That too made me feel bad, but I couldn't see how I would possibly be able to explain this all to him, at least not yet.

"A book he had told me about, and a nice note. It was kind of him," I answered, hoping there would be no more questions if I made it seem like no big deal.

"Well, I am sorry. I picked up a pile of applications in the office and brought them in here. They're over there." Henry pointed to the corner table across the room. "Let me know if you get a good one."

Crisis averted. I took a deep breath, picked up a few applications, and sat down in a plush easy chair opposite my friend. Students from all fifty states and many countries annually applied to the college. That was the fun part. Reading high school senior essays, on the other hand, was often tedious. Why colleges ask students to write about themselves I have no idea. It's like asking a short-order cook to prepare three-day coq au vin. What do you expect you're going to get? Most of the essays were the equivalent of undercooked chicken in a brown-colored flavorless sauce.

After six applications I was done. My mind had too much to process to give the applications their due.

"I'm leaving, Henry."

"Where are you going?"

"I have laundry to do, and some other stuff. I'll see you later."

Soon I was in front of the Memorial, its sheer mass a counterpoint to the recent and ongoing chaos in my life. I loved this building, but if asked to explain why I would be at a loss. Its beauty, its symmetry, and its permanence as the center of the campus, which represented the center of my world, all probably added to my affection.

Recently I had been hurled into an unknown and unpredictable vortex. Uncertainty had replaced the normal rhythm of my college life. At any moment I could find myself years in the past. The massive Memorial, unchanged for over a hundred years and immovable, rock-solid and stable, seemed a friend and anchor to the world I knew best.

Her motion across the glass doors caught my attention. The campus bookstore, housed on the lower level of the Memorial, was closed on Sundays, but a woman was inside, crossing from one side of the store to the other. I watched her unbox some apparel, sweatshirts, I presumed from their bulk. She placed them on a shelf across from a ceiling-to-floor bookshelf. By her location, I was pretty certain that bookshelf housed Chemistry. After almost four years, I knew the orientation of the bookstore by heart, with Archaeology at the southern end and Zoology twenty yards to the north.

I reflected on all of the books I had purchased during college—probably twenty or more a year. It's not their content or their cost that struck me as I considered those volumes. It's the juxtaposition of all of the components of the set that was my life at the time that I purchased them that intrigued me. Who was dating whom when I bought Calculus I? What was happening in my life when I pulled the anthology of American short stories from the stack? Time, always time. Those snapshots sped through my mind like a slideshow at speed.

Ms. Constantine was no longer visible. She had probably returned to the stock room for another box to unpack and prepare for the next wave of students who would arrive the following morning. I watched her reenter, her left elbow pushing the swinging door in front of her as she exited the storeroom sideways. She looked up, still half in and half out of the storeroom, and a broad smile returned my fixed gaze. She rested her armful of books on a counter, instinctively reached down and straightened her sweater, and walked towards the front of the store. As she turned the key in the door she motioned me inside.

"Well, the wandering student mysteriously appears again," she began, her dazzling green eyes fixed on me and inducing a not altogether unpleasant paralysis.

"You do seem mesmerized by my hair, Franklin. Perhaps I should cut a few locks and give them to you as a present."

She was right. My gaze had shifted to her thick, flowing red hair. It was down, instead of in the bun all of the students, and I, associated with Ms. Constantine. That was how she had worn it on every single day I had entered the bookstore, except on that one day she had rescued me from both the cold and from my vacuous mind. Today was Sunday, the store was closed, and no customers were expected. Her bun had the day off.

"Sorry, Ms. Constantine." I blushed, with no earthly idea of how to respond. Without a pause, she came to my aid.

"If I recall Franklin you had the same problem the last time you turned up unexpectedly. I would think that seeing my hair down the second time wouldn't be that surprising." She laughed, "I guess I was wrong. The last time you were here you seemed a bit distracted. Don't tell me here we go again."

At our last encounter, I was more than distracted. It was the morning that I first realized that something significant had happened during sleep that previous night. I could not recall what, and my mind was furiously attempting to recreate that episode when I ran into Ms. Constantine. Confusion reigned that morning; now I was on far more settled ground.

"No, I'm fine today. Sort of."

"Something happen, Franklin?"

"It's Professor Niemeyer. I don't know if you've heard but he died last night."

"Oh, my, no, I hadn't heard. What a nice man. What happened?"

"Evidently he had been sick. I didn't know, and my guess is few people other than his family knew."

"Were you taking a class with him this semester?"

"No, but he had been helping me with something."

"I didn't realize you were an English major."

"It wasn't like that. He was sort of a mentor. It's hard to describe."

"Well, I can see from your reaction that he meant a lot to you. But don't be too sad, Franklin. He's not gone."

My head jerked up. "What did you just say?"

"I said that he's not gone. You will always have the memories of your time together."

"Oh, right, yes thanks." For a moment after she had said those initial words my heart raced. Did Ms. Constantine know what Professor Niemeyer, Govinda, and I knew about time? But then she had added, "You will always have your memories."

Now I wasn't sure.

"Don't think so hard, Franklin. It will give you a headache. Would you mind giving me a hand while we chat?"

"Of course," I replied. What I wanted to say was "Thank you so much for asking."

We walked behind the checkout counter, past the three registers at which I had laid down scads of dollars over the years. I glanced at what had previously been invisible to me during all of those many visits to the store. Shelves ran end to end under the register counter. Paper bags were neatly stacked, all stamped with the college insignia. Mound after mound of sheets of the thin white tissue paper used to wrap the coffee mugs and other fragile college artifacts that parents bought for their kids on visiting days filled the lowest shelf. I never once, in four years, witnessed any student buy one of those for himself. Considering all of that paper, someone was doing so in quantities. I was struck by the orderliness of it all, not one bag or sheet of paper askew.

Ms. Constantine noticed my eyes rolling over the precision of the shelves. She stopped, smiled, and gave her shoulders a brief shrug.

"OK, so I'm a bit obsessive. But it does make checkout faster and more efficient. God knows you students are perpetually in a hurry, late for one thing or another. C'mon," she added as we continued our walk until we reached the end of the counter. We were now next to the door that led into the back storage area.

"We're headed behind the scenes now Franklin, into the bowels of the bookstore. All secrets will be revealed." She pushed open the door and led me into the storeroom. After a minute surveying the scene, I began to laugh. I was expecting chaos, partially unpacked boxes of books, piles of college clothing, and scattered miscellaneous supplies. Instead what faced me was the most orderly stockroom I could ever imagine. Tall metal shelving units ran from floor to ceiling, each standing straight and tall together resembling a column of highly-disciplined soldiers.

Some were labeled with the name of a college academic department. Upon these identical copies of textbooks lay perfectly arranged, one upon another.

In large bold letters, the signs announced the contents of each shelf. The listed items were piled in tightly organized stacks, perfectly aligned, proving that the world, at least Ms. Constantine's, was not the least bit random.

"Why are you laughing?" she asked me most playfully, clearly anticipating my response.

"Whoever saw a storeroom this neat?"

"It's a girl thing, Franklin. We tend to be a bit more organized than you boys."

"Wow, Ms. Constantine, you are amazing," I instinctively said without thinking. Her precise organization and her stunning beauty were both more than worthy of my feeble compliment.

"Thank you, Franklin. Ready to help? Oh, can you wait here for a minute? I need to get a marker from the front."

While she was gone I made a loop around the storeroom looking at the massive piles of books. As I turned the corner, I saw that she had already returned and was checking her reflection in the poster of the college hockey team that hung on the wall over the counter. She flipped her hair back from her face and adjusted the collar on her blouse, and ultimately seemed satisfied with what was looking back at her. My pulse quickened. I finished my tour as she turned to find me.

"I have some new stock to put away. Would you mind helping? That would save me a lot of time," she asked with a look that eliminated any possibility of my refusing.

"Of course, I'd be happy to," I replied as if I had a choice.

"So, Franklin, tell me something," Ms. Constantine instructed me as she unloaded a box of pens emblazoned with the college logo.

"Like what?"

"Here, take these to the end of the counter if you would, please," she politely commanded, handing me six boxes of the pens, then continued. "Anything. Tell me why I have the feeling that you know something I don't."

My sudden turn toward her caused the top box of pens to slide off and hit the ground.

"Damn! Sorry, Ms. Constantine," I said as I quickly knelt and grabbed the fallen box.

"Oh don't worry, Franklin, it's nothing. They're just pens. I'm sorry if my question startled you."

"I am pretty sure there is a whole lot more that you know that I don't."

"I wouldn't be so sure about that, Franklin. Can you take another load?" she asked as I gently placed the pile on the counter.

"Sure." I walked back and she reloaded my arms.

Ms. Constantine opened another box. "I can't imagine we need all of these," she commented to herself, then continued her original thought.

"I first noticed it the last time you ended up outside the bookstore. I sense that you are passing what you hear through some sort of, what's the word, filter? Like when you first arrived and informed me about the passing of Professor Niemeyer. I mentioned that he was not gone, that you would always have your memories of him. You froze as if I had said a secret word. Why did you react that way?"

No quick answer occurred to me. It was either blow her off—and I knew I did not wish to do that—or try to explain my recent life. And even if I wanted to, where would I begin? Was she a person I could trust? I hardly knew her.

"Goodness, Franklin, take a breath."

"What?" Her proclamation jolted me out of my jumbled collection of thoughts.

"You'd think I'd asked you for the nuclear codes." Her laugh carried her words towards me. She stood up with her arms now laden with pen boxes. "I'm not trying to embarrass you or put you on the spot. I work in a college bookstore. I've seen thousands of students. You're different, interestingly different."

I was now positive my heartbeat was so loud that she might wonder if a thunderstorm was imminent.

"Thank you, Ms. Constantine," was all I could come up with.

"Please, call me Lori. I should insist that all of the students call me Lori. I only graduated from college two years ago. When you all call me Ms. Constantine I feel so old."

Only two years, I thought. That creaking sound I heard in my head was a door opening.

"Thanks, Lori. What else can I do to help?" Still not stellar conversation on my part, but it was better than continuing to say nothing and looking like an imbecile.

"Nothing, Franklin. I really appreciate your help. I think I'm done for now."

"You were going to teach me about the Memorial," I reminded her.

"You are right. I did tell you I would, and I will. I'm excited about that. You know you are the first student I have met since I began working here who has ever shown any interest in this building."

"To me that is unbelievable. The Memorial is the center of the campus. It's incredible. Even your friends don't have an interest?"

"Even though I am barely older than most of the seniors, I haven't found many friends among the students."

"My guess is that they look at you more like a grown-up since you have a real job. Plus you act a lot more mature than most of the people around here."

"I was thinking the same about you. So maybe we can get to know each other and I can finally have a mature student friend," she offered with a big grin.

"That would be great. I can learn about this building and make a new friend." A bit stilted, I thought, but mature-enough sounding.

She was now standing in front of me, her eyes focused on mine.

"We don't know each other, Franklin, so this might sound a bit strange. I have a special gift. I see hearts. Don't roll your eyes; I do. I can share a few moments with someone and know almost instantly. Yours is a good one."

Rarely is a moment so utopian that the universe pauses. A window miraculously and unexpectedly opens into another world, one that until that moment had been hidden. In that world there is peace, kindness, and especially love. It is a tease; the window remains open only briefly, just long enough to make you want more of what was momentarily offered.

"Come, Franklin, I'll take you on a tour of the Memorial." The sound of her voice dragged me back to our lesser world.

She held onto my hand and led me through the storeroom door back into the bookstore.

"We have to leave the store and enter the Memorial by the front door. We can dash just around to the front so I don't think we need coats. You OK with that?"

"Of course." I was, but really what was I going to say? No, I'm a pansy, I need my jacket?

"OK, then let's go!" She yanked my arm, and like a dog on a leash, I jolted forward.

"Ooh, wait, Franklin, I have to lock the door." She dropped my hand, turned, and gave me one of those "oops" expressions. Back through the door she went, leaving me freezing outside in the cold for the minute it took her to fetch her keys and lock the door.

"Sorry!" She took my hand, and with me once again securely in tow, zipped around the corner of the sixteen-sided building, led me up the stairs and through the ten-foot-high solid mahogany front doors.

"Wow, it's cold!" With a sheepish grin, she added, "Guess we should have taken our coats. And I left you standing out there! Will you forgive me, Franklin?"

Forgive her? I would have given her every worldly possession I owned at that moment. Anything, I thought, ask me for anything Lori, and it will be yours. Such is the power that women have over men. Women erroneously believe that what men want most is sex. A kind word, a held hand, an embrace, and loving eyes; these are what convert grown men to puppies, loyal, faithful, and forever.

"Franklin?"

"Sorry, Lori."

"You are sweet, Franklin," she said, as if she knew precisely those thoughts that had traversed my mind.

"So here we are, dead center in your favorite building, and mine. Sixteen sides. I don't think there are more than a few other sixteen-sided buildings in the country. And this one is over one hundred feet tall. Look at the windows, Franklin. Almost three hundred stained glass beauties. Incredible, isn't it? All because many years ago one man had a vision, and then made his vision reality."

My head was almost at a ninety-degree angle to my neck. Each window depicted a different scene. Light flowed through each, bathing the open atrium in a full rainbow of color. This downpour of vitality conjured up a memory from, of all places, my high school physics class. It was there that I had first learned about wavelengths, that each color represented a component of the visible spectrum, all equal and integral parts of the totality that is white light. Quite unintentionally, I was gripped by a metaphor and reminded that humanity, just like white light, is the homogeneous result of markedly heterogeneous components.

Lori was standing to my left, also with neck extended and eyes to the heavens. I turned to her and was certain that at that moment we shared the same sense of humility. Neither of us uttered a word or moved an inch for several minutes.

"You haven't yet asked me the question I thought most interesting to you," she said breaking the silence.

"The inscription on the outside. You distracted me with the beauty of the windows," I answered out loud—and with your beauty, I said silently to myself.

"It's freezing, but of course you already know that," she laughed. "So instead of walking the perimeter of the building, how about I just tell you what it says?"

"Great."

"It's Hebrew, from a book called the Talmud, specifically a portion known as the *Pirkei Avot*, loosely translated into English as *The Ethics of the Fathers*. Unfortunately, Franklin, I don't read Hebrew so I can't tell you how the inscription is properly pronounced."

"But do you know what it means?" I inquired, the tone in my voice communicating the disappointment I would experience if she answered that she did not. But my concern was unnecessary.

"Of course! You think I would promise you that I knew a good amount about this building and not know that?"

"And?"

"And what?" she answered coyly.

"And what? Are you going to tell me?"

"I could give you an assignment and make you look it up." That mischievous smile again perched on her lips.

"That would be cruel."

"I don't know. We could make it a game, and if you get the correct answer maybe you would get a reward."

At that moment I was certain I would faint. My legs nearly buckled. Anger at my weakness fortunately overcame my imminent physical collapse. I regained my composure.

"All right, I'll play. But I don't read Hebrew either, so how in the world can I possibly solve the riddle?" I responded, now solidly back in the land of the living.

"I suppose it wouldn't be fair without a hint." She paused, assuming the pose of Rodin's thinker, hand under chin, faraway gaze.

"The quote can be translated into a four-phrase sentence. I will give you one of the phrases. Your mission is to find the other three and assemble the phrases in the correct order. Here is the free phrase: "The reward is much.""

With those words uttered from this magnificent red-haired, green-eyed beauty, I once again flirted with sudden unconsciousness. The reward is much! Fireworks were going off in my head; my heart raced like a Ferrari.

"Franklin, are you all right?" The tone of her voice signaled her real concern that she might have gone too far.

Recovery number two. "Yes, I'm fine. Just thinking," I lied. "But I have two questions. How long will you give me to find the answer?"

"Twenty-four hours. And the second question?" she asked, those wonderfully delicious eyes effortlessly penetrating my thoughts with no regard for my privacy. As if she didn't already know.

11

Pirkei Avot

Sometimes desire itself—even if the object of that desire is unobtainable—is simply delicious. I relived each luxurious moment of our time together and wallowed in the entirety of the encounter.

When blessed with some beautiful vision—lush mountain vista, sun dipping into a crystal clear ocean, or stunning green-eyed redhead—I endeavor to form a lasting mental image, one I can recall at will. Lori's image was now fixed on my retina. Had I attempted to cross a street all traffic would have been rendered invisible and tragedy probable.

I briefly considered finding Henry and sharing the details of my time with Lori. I pictured our encounter. "Are you insane?" Those would be the words he would instantly offer up upon the retelling of my story, followed by, "You have enough happening in your crazy life. Get real and concentrate on what's going on." I knew Henry well enough to write both sides of the conversation that would evolve. His practical, sensible self would first chastise, then attempt to educate, and ultimately dismiss my opposing irrational, impetuous, and passion-driven actions.

Instead, I knew where I must go: the library. Among the many thousands of volumes that filled the near two-hundred-year-old college library, I was sure to find the Talmud. Although she had not given me the translation of the Hebrew inscription atop the Memorial, I was quite certain that she had given me what I needed to solve the puzzle.

Nearly four years of constant residence among the library's shelves had acquainted me with the location of most of the school's collection. Religious books occupied the far western section of the third floor. Although the college had gained possession of some very old and valuable bibles and other religious texts, those were secured in a separate, locked climate-controlled room. Fortunately, I did not need one of those; a mass-produced copy would suffice. Within a few minutes, I had located my prey on an upper shelf labeled "Judaic Texts" and pulled it from its home.

Although I had located The Talmud, I had no idea of its composition. I expected it to resemble a Bible, a chronological story with distinct chapters. As I opened the large text I was surprised and soon confounded. What I found instead was a collection of rabbinic laws and commentary, with no obvious organization. It was as if I had picked up an international law book written in its original foreign tongue. Lots of information, but at the moment completely useless. I could find no index in this particular volume. This was not going to be as easy as I had thought.

I stared at this tome on my lap, wondering how I was going to discover its secrets. Then I looked up and sitting next to the now open space on the third shelf from where I plucked this copy of the Talmud was a more contemporary looking book titled, *Unlocking the Babylonian Talmud*. My eyes continued skyward as the words "thank you, Lord" sprang joyously from my lips.

I had no idea if the Talmud I currently possessed was Babylonian—*how many flavors does the Talmud come in*? I turned it over to see if any more information was available on the binding or back, but these were blank. Oh well, I thought, I guess I'll know soon enough.

Like an arriving ambulance siren, voices rapidly rose in volume as they approached my position. Instinctively I turned my head in their direction. The male voice was not that of a student. Its pitch and tone were those of someone older. The female voice was less distinctive.

"We're in the library, for God's sake. Keep your voice down," the man insisted.

"No one comes up here; it's all religion stuff," the female responded, now more obvious that hers was a younger voice, a student I assumed. She continued. "You told me not to worry. You promised! Now what am I supposed to do? My parents will kill me! And what about college?" Her voice was replaced by sobs.

I was inadvertently privy to what was obviously a very personal conversation. After a brief review of my available options, I decided that the best strategy would be to remain silent and wait for the two of them to move on. *Unlocking the Babylonian Talmud*, the route to my highly anticipated reward, lay several feet above me, but it might as well have been a thousand miles away. I was not going to risk being discovered, and so sat still and quiet.

"Barb, it will be all right. First of all, you're still not sure, right? It could just be that you are a couple of days late. Has that ever happened before?"

"I don't know, yes, maybe a couple of times," she responded between sobs.

"See? So I think we should just wait a little more. And don't say anything to anyone. You haven't yet, have you?"

"No. Oh, Dennis, I am so ashamed."

I heard the man, Dennis, take a couple of steps. I imagined he was now embracing Barb, a few sniffles the only audible sound for a minute or so.

"You have nothing to be ashamed of. If anyone should be ashamed, it's me. I'm the professor, I should have known better." He paused for a few seconds, then continued. "You know, Barb, the moment you walked into class that day you had me. That entire hour was a struggle. Here I was responsible for guiding fifteen juniors through the thesis process, and it was all I could do to remember what I was supposed to say. I found myself staring at you every chance I could." Silence, then a minute later, "I promise you everything will be fine, Barb, I promise. C'mon, let's go. I'll walk you back to your room."

More sobs, but the volume was diminishing. They were leaving. I stayed still for a few more minutes until I was sure they were no longer nearby, then stood up, walked to the end of the aisle, and peered around the corner. No one was visible.

Suddenly I experienced the strangest thought, that the book I needed had vanished, that when I returned to the stack and looked up it would be gone. It wasn't only that thought. Something had changed, as if two adjacent tectonic plates had shifted ever so slightly. My eyes darted up to the third shelf and scanned its contents. *Unlocking the Babylonian Talmud* was nowhere to be found. I looked down at the floor where I had placed the other text—the Talmud—but that too was missing. I must be in the wrong aisle, I told myself. I rushed to the end of the stack, then raced from aisle to aisle looking down on the floor for the Talmud, but it was nowhere to be seen.

My heart was now beating at what seemed an unsustainable rate. I became light-headed, nearly losing consciousness, just as I had with Professor Niemeyer. Now seated, I crossed my legs and put my head on my arms for support.

"Hey, are you all right?" I heard a voice ask.

I looked up. A girl was standing over me.

"Are you? Do you want me to get help?" she continued.

That voice. I didn't recognize her face but I knew I had heard that voice.

"Oh, sorry, no, I'm OK. Thanks."

"You don't look like you're OK. Did you fall or something?"

"Do I know you? You sound so familiar to me," I asked, as I stood back up.

"That's a strange thing to say, that I sound familiar. I don't think you know me. I don't think I know you," she answered.

"Hi, I'm Franklin Rock," I told her, extending my hand.

"Hi, I'm Barbara Lance. Everyone calls me Barb."

Barb! The girl I just heard crying with Dennis, the professor. Worried that she was pregnant.

"Are you alone?" I asked.

"Yes, why do you ask?"

"I thought I heard someone else, that's all. What year are you in?" I asked for no good reason, already aware from my eavesdropping that she was a junior.

"I'm a graduate student. And you?"

A graduate student? I was certain hers was the voice I had just overheard with her professor-lover Dennis. He said that he had met her in a class of juniors planning their senior thesis.

"Are you sure?" I stupidly asked.

"Am I sure?" she laughed. "Yes, I'm pretty sure that I know what year I'm in. Maybe you're not OK. We should get help."

"No, no, I'm sorry. I just thought I might know you. You remind me of a girl who's a junior. My mistake," I explained, hoping she would be content with her theory that I was not quite myself.

"Well, I have to go. Look, I can walk down with you to the first floor to make sure you're all right."

"That's kind of you, but I'm all right, and I have some books to get up here."

Barb smiled, turned, and left. What in the world is going on, I thought?

I looked down at the floor and there in front of me, just as I recalled leaving it, was the Talmud. I looked up, and sure enough once again on the third shelf I saw it: *Unlocking the Babylonian Talmud.*

I sat down on the cool tile floor. "Holy crap!" I shouted out loud. The volume of my own voice startled me. I looked around to confirm that no one had heard me. Holy crap, I repeated to myself, far more quietly the second time. There was a single explanation for this phenomenon. I had briefly time traveled. A minute ago Barbara Lance, graduate student, stood before me, and only a few minutes before that I had overheard Barbara Lance the junior. No doubt about it: I had moved in time. The rub—for the first time I wasn't certain in which direction it had occurred.

The Talmud was with me when I heard Barb and Dennis, then suddenly vanished. But when did it vanish? Before they arrived or after? And when did it return? When graduate student Barb showed up, or just before, or just after she left? I tried to recall what action accompanied what event, but I could not be certain. If the book had vanished exactly when graduate student Barb appeared, then for the first time I would have traveled forward, into the future. I could not be sure.

During our conversations, Professor Niemeyer had mentioned that he was fairly certain this would happen, that at some moment I would find myself confused in time. Profound sadness engulfed me, like a tsunami swallowing the unsuspecting. Professor Niemeyer was gone. I could not discuss this with him. He would have wanted to know every detail of the story, like a famous fictional detective identifying clues obvious only to him. Even if he had been here, I could not be sure of the sequence of events.

The Talmud lay next to me on the floor. I looked up, and thankfully its previous neighbor, *Unlocking the Babylonian Talmud* was still awaiting me. I stood, reached up, and lifted it off its shelf. This was no small work; I gently lowered it with both hands.

Unlike the Talmud, this book was far more contemporary. The inside title page was followed by a standard table of contents, which I rapidly perused. Chapter sixteen, *Pirkei Avot.* My eyes scanned to the page number, 221. Chapter seventeen began on page 419. Almost two hundred pages. I reviewed the entire table of contents and was relieved to see that this book, unlike the Talmud, had an index. Even better, though, was Appendix B—*Quotes.*

I picked up both books and headed over to an empty carrel. Appendix B was the target. Each chapter was represented separately; I had been hoping that the quotes might be alphabetical. At least it was clear that none of the sections were very long. First I looked for quotes beginning with the word "reward," but there were none. Stupid, I thought. She said there were four phrases; "the reward is much" could be in any position. I needed to keep my eyes out for the entire phrase. Within a minute I had found it. "The reward is much" was the third of the four phrases. The full quote: *"The day is short, the work is great, the reward is much, the Master is urgent."*

I had assumed that when I found the answer to Lori's riddle I would be euphoric. There was innuendo in her choice of the phrase I was tasked to find—the reward is much. Instead of euphoria, I experienced a sense of awe. *"The day is short, the work is great, the reward is much, the Master is urgent."* This was no random quote. This one was undoubtedly meant for me to find. It was as if the Memorial and its inscription had been constructed for this very moment, to speak directly to me, to instill in me a great responsibility.

Here, in an infrequently visited portion of the college library, I became conscious of something massive, something completely overwhelming. My chest began to heave. Unrestrained tears rained down as if a storm cloud had released its payload. The stopper had been blown from the top. Everything I had been holding in for so long now erupted.

After a few minutes, I regained my composure. My good cry over, I once again took control. Yes, I had lost my mentor, but Professor Niemeyer had every confidence in me. On multiple occasions, as I sat confused and scared, he would remind me that I had a gift, that my time travel was nothing to fear but something to embrace.

"Well, if the day is short and the work is great, I'd better get going," I told myself. I replaced the two books where I had found them. As I did so I experienced a small shiver, a reminder that I was in the presence of God.

12
Serendipity

By THE TIME I HAD CONCLUDED my research, evening had arrived. Even though I knew the bookstore closed at 6 p.m., I was hoping that I would still find Lori closing up. No such luck; the bookstore was dark when I arrived with no sign of human activity. I admit I was deflated, like a child opening a birthday present only to find clothes instead of a toy.

I headed back toward my room across campus. With all that was going on in my life, classes and homework had taken a back seat. Although my grades from exams earlier in the semester were probably adequate to carry me through to the end, the compulsive student within me— although admittedly of far less devotion than the obsessive Henry—made an appearance and encouraged me to get some work done.

My growling stomach, however, halted my progress across campus and instead directed me to the local Italian dive for a quick bowl of pasta. Twenty minutes, I thought, and I'll be ready to get down to work.

Few tables were full. It was just on the latter end of the dinner crowd and early for those, like J Bob, who would need something to eat after an evening of smoking weed. I sat facing the door, a habit inculcated by Henry, who insisted that James Bond would never sit with his back to the door and neither should we. I ordered, and ten minutes later the linguine arrived, steam wafting off the top of the generous mound covered almost completely by Vesuvio's famous marinara.

"God am I hungry," I unintentionally said out loud. Maria, Vesuvio's longest-tenured waitress, turned and smiled. With barely a breath between forkfuls, I consumed the contents of the large, white ceramic bowl. Marinara addiction is how I often referred to Vesuvio's specialty, that final sensation of taste that begs for more.

I sat back in the booth, eyes closed, and lingered in the moment, warm, and content.

"Looks like you ate too much, Franklin".

My pulse immediately quickened as I recognized the voice and simultaneously met the green-eyed gaze. I jumped to attention like a recruit on his first day of boot camp.

"Lori! Hi. What are you doing here?" *What a stupid thing to say! It's a restaurant genius. Why do you think she's here?*

She wasn't going to let me off the hook.

"Let's see, I was looking for a dress for the alumni dinner." She feigned a visual scan of the room. "Hmm, don't see anything appropriate. Probably should try another store." And with that, she turned and began to move towards the front door. She stopped and turned back to me. Those gorgeous eyes and stunning hair slammed me to breathlessness.

"Oh no, not again Franklin. How come every time I see you I have to tell you to breathe?" She laughed as she approached me.

Because your presence paralyzes me every time would have been the honest response. Instead, I said, "It does always seem that way. You just caught me by surprise. I wasn't expecting to see you here."

"Why not?" she responded. "I do eat, you know."

"I don't know. Vesuvio? I just thought…"

She interrupted. "What, that only poor students eat here? Everyone loves this place. Especially that sauce."

"Yes! I love that sauce! Do you want to sit down? I mean, join me?" *Oh God, I am such a loser!*

"Sure, but haven't you finished eating?"

"No. I was considering getting another bowl of the linguine with that awesome marinara. I haven't eaten much today." *I'd eat ten bowls just to keep you here.*

"OK, great. I'd love to." And with that, she slipped into the booth across from me. Slip is the correct word, or maybe glide. Such a simple movement yet so impressively elegant. As I took my seat across from her, I began to tremble ever so slightly, and I hoped imperceptibly. I lowered my hands onto my lap beneath the table to conceal the involuntary motions. *Settle, Franklin.*

Lori picked up the menu that Maria had left with me earlier.

"Let's see. What should I have?" she purred as she perused the menu. To be that menu, I imagined, and be free to stare into those eyes. I would make my pages stick together, do all I could to prolong the time.

"I don't know why I even look at this menu. I know it by heart. It hasn't changed since I can remember. Right, Franklin? Do you even look at it?"

"I don't. I am a little embarrassed to tell you that I order pretty much the same things every time. If I'm not having pizza with my friends then it's almost always the linguine with the killer marinara. Or the lasagna."

"Lasagna! Great idea, Franklin. That's exactly what I'm in the mood for."

Maria left the table behind us and immediately greeted Lori.

"Loretta, love, so nice to see you," Maria began.

"You know, Maria, besides my mother you're the only person who calls me Loretta. That's what happens when you stay in the same place you grew up. I'm great. How are you? And the family?"

"We're all fine. You remember my brother Jake? Just had a baby. Cutest little guy. You can imagine my big Catholic family going insane over this child."

"Congratulations! Please tell your brother and parents I am so happy for them," Loretta Constantine answered.

"So what can I get you, hon?"

"Lasagna tonight, Maria. Franklin, are you going for another bowl?"

"Sure, why not? Thanks, Maria."

"You got it." And with that Maria snatched the menu and headed off to the kitchen.

"Your name is Loretta, but no one, or hardly anyone besides Maria and your mother calls you that. How come?"

"Really, Franklin, you have to ask?"

"Can I call you Loretta?"

"Very funny. No, you cannot," she immediately responded with a stern but playful look.

"OK. Lori it is. I assume from what you said to Maria that you grew up here," I asked, hoping small talk would give me some time to get more grounded.

"I did. I went away to college but I decided to come back. I'm pretty close to my family."

"Do you have brothers or sisters?" I continued the friendly interrogation.

"Both. I'm the middle child. I have an older brother James—he's three years older—and a sister Elaine two years younger."

"Do they all live here?" The small talk plan was working. I imagined myself hooked to one of those hospital monitors you see on TV. Pulse and respiratory rate were returning to normal.

"My sister is in graduate school in Boston. So not too far. James lives in Chicago. He got married two years ago and his wife is from there. She's pregnant so that's been exciting."

"Did you think about moving somewhere else? A bigger city, or some-place warmer at least?"

"I went to college in Chicago. Not exactly warmer. I thought about staying there. I like Chicago. The people are great, and there is a ton to do all of the time. I accepted a job offer right after college. But then my dad got ill. He's fine now," she added, quickly closing any further line of questioning on that topic. "I just decided that I would rather be closer to my family. So, here I am. Now, what about you?"

"Me. There's not much to tell. I have a sister; it's just the two of us. To tell you the truth my childhood was pretty boring."

"Are you close to your parents?" Lori asked leaning forward as if she might need to reach out and grab my words if necessary.

"My dad passed away while I was in high school," I replied.

"Oh, I'm so sorry to hear that, Franklin."

"Thanks. It was a tough time. He had cancer."

"I bet you miss your father."

"I do. We spent a lot of time together when I was young so that was good. I do miss not having had a chance to have a more adult relation-ship with him."

"At least you have some good memories."

"It's funny, but for the longest time my only memories of him were of when he was sick. It took a while for those to be replaced by the happier ones when I was a kid. I still sometimes regret not spending more time with him before he got sick. I barely talked to my parents once I became a teenager."

"Same for me. I was just horrible."

"Too bad we don't get a chance to revisit those times once we finally get old enough to appreciate that time with them," I said, but Lori seemed to be off in thought revisiting her adolescence. I don't think she even heard me.

"My mom still reminds me of those days. 'You could be so nasty,' she would tell me. She was right. I was. But now we are very close and we laugh about it."

I wish I had that chance with my father, I thought.

Maria arrived with Lori's lasagna and another bowl of linguine smothered in marinara for me. All I could think about was not making an absolute mess of myself eating the stuff. At that moment I felt more like a three-year-old than a twenty-one-year-old. Ravioli, I realized, would have been a much safer choice.

"I admire your bravery, Franklin. I don't think I have ever eaten Vesuvio's linguine without wishing I was wearing a raincoat. You should have seen me a few weeks ago. I was covered in marinara sauce. My older cousin was with me and told me I wasn't any better at eating spaghetti now than I was when I was five."

I looked up from my bowl; Lori was smiling at me. I wasn't sure if that story was true or if she had concocted the tale to put me at ease; I suspected the latter. What a sweet thing to do, I thought.

I was overwhelmed every minute of that meal. Like every other person on the planet who has been smitten by another, I have no words to explain what was going on in my mind during the time we spent together in Vesuvio. For me, every second was whizzing by far too quickly. As best I could I tried to savor each one. But as delicious seconds so often do, those precious moments skillfully evaded my attempt to freeze them.

"Franklin, are you all right?" Lori's words pulled me back.

"Sorry, yes, I'm fine. Just thinking."

"About the riddle I gave you?" Her smile taunted me, daring me to rise to the occasion.

"As a matter of fact, I solved your riddle," I answered triumphantly.

"Oh you did, did you? Well, I'll be the judge of that."

Maria was now standing between us at the end of the table. "Sorry to interrupt. Do you two want anything else?"

"Not for me, Maria. Two bowls. What was I thinking?" I laughed. "I'm stuffed. Would you like anything, Lori?"

"No, thank you, Franklin." She turned to Maria. "Thank you, Maria. Just the check."

I quickly jumped in. "Maria, please give me the check."

"That's sweet, Franklin, but I'm the only one at this table getting a paycheck. Dinner's on me."

"Dinner's on me," Maria joined the fray. "It's just so good to see you, Loretta. And Franklin spends enough money here. Tonight is on the house."

Simultaneously Lori and I rushed in. "You don't have…"

"Don't be silly. It's not a problem. Now get out of here so I can clean up and get ready for the late crowd."

Lori rose and hugged Maria. "That is so kind of you, Maria. And it is so nice to see you. Congratulations again to Jake. Please send my best to your family."

"I will, Loretta. And please say hi to your parents."

"Thanks, Maria. I'll order three bowls next time in gratitude," I added. Maria left me another of her famous winks and walked towards the kitchen.

"So, where were we? Oh yes, you think you've solved the riddle. Pretty impressive. Here's an idea. Let's head over to the Memorial and you can show me." Lori paused. "Do you have time, Franklin? We can do it another time if you don't?" Her eyes dared me to decline.

So much for catching up on my work. "Seems to me you don't believe I could have solved it so quickly. Let's go," I responded, full of confidence that I had, and near bursting with anticipation for the reward.

13

Cashing In

"BRRR, IT GOT A LOT COLDER since before dinner, don't you think?" Lori said, putting her arm through mine as we headed up Mott Street.

Winter was never a better friend, I thought. If it would keep her close to me for even a minute more I would have welcomed plunging temperatures and howling northeast winds.

"Maybe it's all of that pasta we just ate," I replied.

Lori pulled herself even tighter to me. "Then next time I'm having a salad. I am freezing! Want to run?"

Of course not, I silently responded. The last thing I wished to do was hurry.

"Sure," I answered instead. We immediately crossed the street, and with an impish glance, she was off, no longer jogging but instead in high gear. I took off after her.

Lori made it to the door of the Memorial just ahead of me. Truth is I could have easily caught and passed her, but the thought of doing so never crossed my mind. I was enjoying having her in my line of sight. I reached across her and completed the opening of the door she had begun. She turned as I did so.

"Thank you, sir," she said, then quickly slipped through the door into the Memorial with me a breath behind. Lori stopped, turned, and lightly kissed me on the cheek.

"You are sweet, Franklin."

Now hand in hand we walked towards the center of the Memorial. Lori stopped directly under the dome that marked the center of the structure.

"So the last time we were here…" She paused and looked around. "The last time we were here," she continued, "exactly here in this spot, I challenged you to answer the riddle of the inscription around the top of the Memorial. So, how did you do?" Her head was tilted in the way a woman does when toying with a man whom she knows is completely under her control. He is the marionette, she the puppet master, but in lieu of strings, she employs the coy smile and the subtle licking of her upper lip. The poor man can only hope she will be kind and gentle and not pull a string too suddenly or too tightly and emotionally topple him.

"I did quite well," I responded. "I nailed it. Beat the twenty-four-hour time limit easily. Are you ready?"

Lori placed her folded hands in front of her like a grade-school teacher preparing to hear one of her small minions recite the ABCs. She nodded for me to begin.

"As you know there are four phrases. Here they are, in the correct order." I paused, for some reason a bit nervous, although I knew I had it right.

"The day is short," I began, and immediately looked up to check that I was indeed on the right track. Her head nod reassured me and I restarted. "The day is short. The work is great. The reward is much. The Master is urgent," I slowly and humbly recited. Even though I had read the phrases previously and had thought a great deal about their meaning, hearing those words moved me yet again.

The two of us stood still as wooden soldiers. I was not the only one affected by the simple but powerful statement. After a few moments, Lori took a step towards me, grasped my hand, and led me across the open expanse in the center of the building to a table with two chairs under one of the second-floor walkways. She sat first; I followed.

"You know Franklin. I have read those phrases almost daily for so long. I hear them in my mind as I do so. I think this was the first time I had heard another speak them out loud. They are so moving."

I began to speak, but as I uttered her name I felt an abrupt shift. "Lori" faded, and I was gone.

◆◇◆◇◆

First thing I saw was the wire hanger shaped like a basketball hoop on my closet door. As I scanned my childhood room it was evident that everything was as it had always been. Above the bed was the lamp I made in shop class in junior high school. Well, the lamp I sort of made. After many days of drawing, sawing, and sanding it was time to drill the center hole through which the wires would run. As Mr. Kim lowered the drill press—students were not permitted to work the press—it happened. The neck of the lamp broke like a dried twig. My heart immediately sank, but it needn't have. Mr. Kim turned to me. "Don't worry, Franklin, we will make another." What had taken me days to fashion Mr. Kim recreated in minutes. Unsurprisingly his output was far superior in quality to my initial efforts. That lamp hung over my bed until my mother sold our house.

My door was closed, so I could not see down the short hallway to my parents' room. Their discussion, however, was easily audible.

"Can we keep the house?" my mother's voice inquired.

"Yes, I think so," my dad answered.

"Elyse's college?" my mom continued.

"Fortunately, she's almost done. We put away enough to get her through."

"And Franklin?"

"We've got a few years to recover before we have to worry about that. He will go to college Martha, that I'm sure about. And so are you."

"You mean because he told us about it when he was a little boy? You think that means anything?"

"Of course. He described everything about it. He described all of the buildings, the classes, even eating meals. No way he made that up. Do you doubt that Franklin could see the future when he was young? He hasn't done it for a few years now. Maybe he can't anymore; that I don't know. But he certainly did when he was younger. He's going to college, Martha. That's for certain."

My desk was tucked under the window just next to my bed. I walked over and opened the top drawer on the left, the one that secured my most precious belongings. As I opened it, there they were. Two red horseshoe-shaped magnets, clinging to each other like twins as they had since I was six years old. Just as I was about to lift them from their long-standing home, the shift occurred. Two green eyes were inches from mine.

"Franklin!" Lori was calling my name, her hands firmly shaking my shoulders just as Henry had done.

"Oh, God, Lori." I paused to make certain of where I was. "I'm back," I instinctively said out loud. I realized that she had witnessed the entire event. "I'm so sorry, Lori. I was somewhere else for a bit," I tried to explain, but as usual I had no idea how long the episode had lasted.

Lori was visibly shaken by what she had just witnessed. "Do I need to call a doctor?" she asked, her tortured expression manifesting her concern.

I leaned forward and took her hands. "No, you don't need to call a doctor. I'm fine, I promise. What you just saw, it's part of what's been happening to me recently. It's not a health thing. I'd like to tell you about it. I just hope you won't be scared away."

"I won't be," she answered with a reassuring look that instantly lifted concern.

"What I am going to share is kind of out there. But I promise you I am not crazy. I'm a very sane and rational person. I just don't want you to think I'm mentally ill."

"That's not what I was thinking, Franklin. Since that first time we talked outside the Memorial I have sensed that there was something special about you." With one elegant motion, Lori placed her arms around my neck, pulled me closer, and kissed me. If I could control my time travel, every trip would end in the moment of that kiss.

"That was lovely," she said softly.

"That was lovely," I repeated back to her. I could think of no better words.

"Who is he? I keep asking myself? Why am I so drawn to him? And I am drawn to you, Franklin Rock. There's just something about you. I can't explain it. Do all women react to you this way?"

"Hardly."

"Then they aren't paying attention," she whispered.

"Are you ready for the story?" I asked her, thoroughly embarrassed by her flattery. "It might take a while."

"Yes, but we can't stay here. Are you all right coming to my apartment?"

If she had asked me that an hour ago, I likely would have once again found myself at the brink of unconsciousness. But now everything was different. A door had been thrown wide-open and we had stepped through together to another place. In this place I was calm and peaceful. In this place perfection dwelled.

14

Laying It on the Line

"**W**HY ARE YOU SMILING?" Lori asked me as she took my coat. We had just entered her apartment and as we did I had taken a quick panoramic view.

"It's exactly what I would have imagined," I answered.

"What does that mean, *exactly?*" Lori inquired, mimicking my inflection.

"It's immaculate. Nothing out of place. It reminds me of the bookstore."

"OK, so maybe I'm a bit obsessive. I like a neat place. Don't you?"

"Yes, but wow. You are super neat. Plus I don't have anywhere near what you do," I added, looking around now with greater awareness. Lori had a plethora of knick-knacks. Every surface had some accoutrement, like a candy dish or a miniature. Both windows in the main living area had blinds and drapes. Her apartment was what another woman might call "lovely." I was searching for another word to describe it.

"Finished," I blurted out.

"What?" Lori turned and asked.

"It's what my mother would call finished. That's what your apartment makes me think of. Like it's done, put together, complete. And clearly a girl lives here."

"I'm not sure if that's a dig or a compliment. Do you like it?" Lori asked.

"Of course. It's lovely; it's finished," I said with my own head tilt.

"So you're making fun of me, is that it?" Her face had gotten just a bit more serious.

Uh, oh I thought. Don't blow this, Franklin.

"No, of course not!" I quickly replied. But my fear had been unnecessary. She took a step towards me, now wearing an honest smile.

"Don't worry. I know you're just playing." She guided me toward the sofa in front of the two perfectly finished windows. We sat simultaneously. "I want to hear everything."

When we were in the Memorial, in the midst of that emotional connection, I was certain that I wanted to tell her all. I wanted us to be wrapped in each other's lives and histories as well as each other's arms. Now that some time had elapsed a seed of doubt appeared. Perhaps it was too soon. Maybe I shouldn't. I hesitated.

"Franklin," her soft voice began. "If you don't want to talk now, if you feel you're not ready, it's OK. But don't think for a second that I don't want to hear, or that I will judge you, or that I won't understand. I do want to hear, and I will understand. You are not the only one who feels a connection to something bigger."

I was reminded of the feeling I had the first time talking with Govinda, back in his car in the brightly lit parking lot. Govinda had understood. And now Lori's words: "You are not the only one who feels the connection to something bigger." Perhaps she did, too.

"What do you mean by that?" I asked.

"I think I told you that I grew up in a Catholic home. Faith was very important. I learned all of the prayers and followed the rules. But for me, there was always something more. I'm going to share something I have not told anyone other than my mother. When I was still a child, I was sure that I could feel God. At least that's what I assumed I was feeling. I had no other explanation. In my world, the only choices for me, the only possible explanations for what I was experiencing were Jesus or God. What I felt, really what I guess I heard in my head, was not a man, so in my way of thinking at that age, it couldn't have been Jesus I was hearing. I just assumed, then, that it must be God. That feeling has become more infrequent as I have gotten older, but it has never completely left me. Now if I had to describe it I would probably say that I'm just certain that there is something else. Maybe it is God, but whatever it is, I'm sure there is something more to this world than just what we can see."

There it was: my confirmation. I was already head over heels from her beauty and kindness. Now, this. For a moment I was afraid I would explode. My heart and mind were both racing. I knew I had to calm myself. I sat on my hands to keep them from fidgeting. Lori noticed.

"Give them to me," she insisted, extending both of her arms towards me. I did as she asked. The softness of her slender fingers triggered an immediate sense of calm as if a quart of endorphins had been poured into my blood.

"Better?" she asked me with kind eyes.

"Much," I answered. "How could I not be?"

"I hope what I said didn't upset you, Franklin."

"No, just the opposite. I don't think you could have said anything more important. Now I know I need to tell you everything. I'm ready. You?"

"I am," she responded.

And so I began. I told Lori about my visions. I told her about Professor Niemeyer. I told her about Govinda. And although I did hesitate for a moment, I decided to tell her about my previous time-traveling; she had after all already witnessed it live. Everything I could recall I shared. Lori never interrupted me, nor did she glance away. Her eyes remained trained on mine during the entire recounting of my experiences.

When I had finished I leaned back on the couch and waited. Lori sat quietly. Her gaze had released mine and she was looking down, clearly in thought. For a moment I became anxious. Had it been too much? Did I make a mistake telling her all of this?

"Did you leave anything out?" Her question surprised me. There was indeed one part I had not shared. I decided not to mention the mission that Govinda and I had discussed. The concept embarrassed me. Despite Govinda's assurances to the contrary, the whole idea of a mission sounded presumptuous.

"What do you mean?" I feigned ignorance, though probably not convincingly.

"I mean, why? Where is the why? Why is this happening to you? Why was Govinda so taken with your story? Why was Professor Niemeyer so insistent on teaching you? There must be a 'why' Franklin. Do you know what it is?"

Damn, this woman is smart. She knew that I knew. So now I had to decide what to say. If I told her what Govinda had told me, what I had already known in my bones to be the case, what would she think? Lots of people have dreams she might say. Lots of people feel a purpose. "What makes you so special, Franklin?" I could imagine her asking me. And how would I then respond? I would have to agree with her, confirming to myself that this is all some foolish act of self-importance.

"I'm not sure," I answered instead.

"Really?" Her eyes betrayed her attempt at innocence. "Look, I know we don't know each other for that long, but I want to believe, I *do* believe, that you trust me and that you know I would never hurt you. Don't you think we are together at this time for a reason?"

Unlike an interrogator pushing and threatening, Lori was instead pulling. She was the cool air drawing in the warm, the low pressure enticing the high. She was the irresistible.

I folded. "Lori, you have no idea how difficult this is for me to say. I'm not the kind of person to take myself too seriously. I have done nothing of note so far in my life. I'm nobody, no one of any importance." I still was unable to answer her, to lay the "why" squarely on the table.

"Want to know what I think?"

Before I could answer she continued.

"Well, I'm going to tell you. You're one-hundred percent wrong. You are not nobody. All of what has happened to you speaks just the opposite. You don't get a magical mentor if you're nobody. You don't get to travel around time if you're nobody. People don't respond to you, people like Govinda, or even me, like they do if you're nobody. I told you, Franklin, I know there is something else. There is a deeper story. I am not wise enough to know what it is, but it's there. And then I meet you. You are my proof. I am sure of that. You are my proof. You are somebody, that is for sure. It's extremely exciting and wonderful, and I cannot tell you how much it means to me that you have shared it with me. And I am also quite certain that you know the 'why.'"

"I have a mission," I began without argument. "That is what Govinda called it. He told me that I must recognize and accept that I had a mission. I am not feigning modesty when I tell you that I am extremely uncomfortable with the whole concept. It's so hard for me to say, even to you, someone I know I can trust."

She waited patiently for the next line.

"I'm supposed to fix the world," I quickly said before my brain stopped my lips from speaking. I looked directly at Lori and awaited her response.

"I'm not sure if I read your mind or was praying for that to be the case, but I was fairly confident that was what you were going to say."

"What? How could you have known that?"

"Franklin, while you're running around in your own head, you can't see what is pretty obvious to others, at least those who care to pay attention. It wasn't that hard to guess."

"It sounds crazy, doesn't it? I keep coming back to the same thought, Lori. Who am I? I'm no one special. How can I even presume for a minute that I can fix the world? I'm embarrassed just to hear those words or let those thoughts into my mind."

"Who was Moses? Who was Gandhi? Who was Martin Luther King? They were all just people like you. It's what you do with your gifts that count, Franklin. You have been granted some special ones. It's OK to feel like this now. It just would not be OK to squander those gifts. So what's next?"

"I haven't even thought about that yet," I responded, now cognizant of just how ridiculous I must sound claiming that I am supposed to fix the world with no idea what that meant. I wouldn't even know where to start. And the only person who might guide me, or at least offer me a clue, was now gone.

Once again Lori sensed my angst.

"Franklin, it's all right. I'm pretty sure you're not supposed to know how just yet."

"Why do you say that?" I asked her.

"Goodness, Franklin, it's obvious. How could you know? It's clear that you are somewhere near the beginning of this whole process. You just need to let it come to you. I'm sure it will. You are not a very patient person, are you?" she added.

"It's that obvious?"

Lori laughed. "Very. Well, if I were you I'd start practicing. I'm pretty sure you're going to need some patience to accomplish your mission. Everyone needs patience. The more the better."

"No kidding. Impatience is my Achilles heel. At least one of them. I don't have enough heels for all of my shortcomings," I admitted.

"Goodness, you are hard on yourself. That's another thing you're going to need to address. Go easier on yourself. I'm sure that's part of your patience issue," she added.

"You are so kind," I replied. And so sweet, and smart and beautiful I added silently.

"You might not agree with this, Franklin, but I don't think much of life is random. People don't just run into each other. We meet for a reason. Things happen for a reason. You and I are here for a reason."

"I have never been one to believe that stuff. I kind of favor the random theory of the world. I mean, there's no evidence to the contrary," I said.

"My grandmother once told me something that I have never forgotten. When I was a young teenager I told her that I wasn't sure if I believed in God. Truth is that before telling her that I had never even contemplated the question. My Catholic upbringing left little room for doubt.

"I was hanging out with one of my friends and her older sister just the day before. Her older sister was trying to impress us and made the statement that there was no proof of God and that she didn't believe He was real. She said to us, 'I'll prove it. Have you ever seen a real miracle? If God were real we would have seen them for sure by now.' So I repeated that same 'grown-up' idea to my grandmother. Here is what my grandmother then explained. 'Lori, darling, people who say that simply haven't noticed all of the miracles God has placed right smack in front of them. He makes them every single day.' I don't know if there is a God, Franklin. But as I told you earlier, there is doubtless something else. And you, Franklin Rock, are Exhibit A."

15

Henry's Dilemma

I HADN'T SEEN FRANKLIN for a couple of days. That wasn't unusual, but considering his recent history I was getting a bit concerned. As I walked the campus I asked some of his other friends if they had seen him. No one had. Most of them were surprised that I was even asking them.

"Henry, why are you asking me?" was the reply I got from one of our mutual friends. "If you don't know where he is why would you think I would?" It was true. If anyone had any reason to seek out Franklin and couldn't find him, I was the guy to ask.

There were a limited number of places he could be, and I had checked them all. His room, the library, the campus center—those were his most frequent stops. The college was compact. There were just not that many places one could hide.

I made one final trip back to his dorm room. Franklin wasn't there, so I left a note on the door imploring him to find me and headed back to my place. I climbed the stairs to my third-floor residence. As I opened the stairwell door, seated right across the hall on one of the common sofas was Franklin. He was waiting for me.

He looked up when he heard the door open. A smile appeared instantly; he was anxious to talk.

"Where in the world have you been?" I asked him.

"Waiting for you, Henry. See? Here I am," he replied as if nothing at all had transpired that warranted my question.

"Yeah, really, you've just been sitting here for days, obviously invisible since no one had noticed you. I'm gonna guess more crazy stuff has happened to you and you want to tell me about it. You want to go to my room or somewhere else?"

"Let's go to the Gardens," Franklin answered.

The Gardens is shorthand for Johnson's Gardens, a delightful oasis in the middle of the academic buildings. I doubt that many students know that it happens to be the oldest cultivated garden on a college campus in the United States. Even if they did, they wouldn't care. What they care about is the beauty, peace, and tranquility it offers. A gentle brook babbles along its edge. Numerous varieties of trees, flowers, and even herbs reside within its boundaries. Strategically located benches provide students and faculty solace and often solitude unless it's an early, perfect April day when winter-weary students flock to picnic as they welcome spring.

Franklin and I discovered the Gardens the first week on campus. We had become acquainted with each other just before college began, so it was natural for us to spend the first weeks of our higher education together before our circle of friends expanded. Together we wandered about, getting our bearings, figuring out how we had arrived at this specific place at this specific point in our lives. That sounds a lot like something Franklin would say. Sometimes I'm not certain where my thoughts end and his begin.

"Let's go." I waved my arm in the direction of the stairwell.

We exited the building and began the short walk to the entrance of the Gardens. I looked at Franklin. "So, you want to start spilling the beans?" He shook his head.

"Let's wait until we get there."

We reached the statue of the only U.S. president who had attended the college. Some thought he symbolically guarded the Gardens. Some said he represented wisdom inviting those who sought meaning from the earth to enter solemnly. Franklin disagreed. He said it was the only place they could put the statue of the guy where students were unlikely to cover him with graffiti.

Behind the statue were the wrought-iron gates guarding the single entrance. Simply passing through the gates with Franklin was not an option; a stop was always required. Franklin looked them up and down as if admiring a famous work of art.

"Again?" I asked. "Why do we always have to stop for you to check out the gates? You have seen them a thousand times."

After concluding his assessment, Franklin turned to me. "Because they change," he responded.

"C'mon, they do not. They have been here for over a hundred years."

"You don't notice it, but I do. You know why?" Franklin had no interest in my opinion and did not wait for me to respond. "It's because I have seen them at different ages—not mine, theirs. For some reason, I end up at these gates in some of my time travels. I have no idea why. I never got to talk with Professor Niemeyer about it. Anyway, I do, and they do look different at different times. It's like one of those games where the illustrator alters a few subtle things between pictures and you have to find the changes. A character has a different hat. A baseball is on a table. A dog has appeared behind a tree. Here it's a new marking on one of the gates. Someone tried to scratch his initials. Rust has appeared where none had been before. The tilt is slightly different because a bolt needs tightening."

I vowed at that moment to never ask him any question about why he did a particular thing ever again. My assumption would forever be that Franklin had a reason, and that turned out to be forever true.

"Where do you want to go?" I asked Franklin as we passed through the gates and headed down towards the back of the Gardens and the creek.

"You choose," he answered. Johnson's Gardens had many small sanctuaries hidden among small groves of trees or behind tended flower and herb beds. Alone or with Franklin I had been in them all. I preferred to sit brookside, away from the bulk of the manicured areas, among the grand old trees, so that is where we headed. Franklin remained silent until we arrived.

"Good choice" were his initial words as we arrived at one of the benches nestled among a small collection of tall river birch, just a few yards from the creek's edge. Although it was still winter, we were experiencing a fortunate warming, what locals called a winter thaw. The absence of any significant wind made it comfortable in the sun.

"You're up," I said as I turned towards Franklin. He did not respond immediately. That classic Franklin Rock look was upon him, eyes down, head tilted towards the ground, brow slightly furrowed. Like a computer sorting files, he was organizing his thoughts, deciding on the sequence of events he was about to present before he began. Franklin never did anything random; that is not how his mind worked. He had explained the process to me several years earlier.

"Franklin, how is it you seem to predict what is going to happen in just about any situation? Not that you're always right," I added as a reminder.

"Scenario playing, Henry. Haven't I ever told you about that?"

"Not that I remember. Or I wasn't paying attention when you did," I told him. "Sometimes it's a bit much listening to you." Franklin ignored my friendly insult.

"You just play out the options in your head before deciding on a specific course of action. If I do this, what will happen? OK, that won't work. How about this? No, that's worse. And so on until you find an option you like. If not, then forget what you were planning to say or do; only bad things will happen."

Simple but brilliant: don't do random. Franklin's advice has helped me avoid more than one unpleasant outcome. But this is his story, not mine. Franklin was back in the moment having turned away from the brook, now directly facing me.

"After Professor Niemeyer died, everything seemed so up in the air. I was confident that he had a method to help me interpret what was happening to me. Then all of a sudden I'm on my own. You know me. I don't stay scared or worried very long. So I just wandered a bit to let all of the recent events sift through my brain. I'm sure you can guess where I wandered."

"The Memorial," I instantly answered. Long ago I had learned of the appeal of that structure to Franklin. He said he found it interesting, but I always felt there was something more. It drew him like a mouse to cheese.

"Right, the Memorial. And what is inside the Memorial?"

"The bookstore," I dutifully responded like a grade school student to his teacher. Then the college student in me took over. "So you went looking for a book on time travel, and you found one that explained your situation," I added with an air of exceptionalism. I was certain that I had already solved the riddle of his story.

"No, Henry, I don't think they, or any bookstore, have any books explaining time travel." Another condescending glance was tossed my way before he continued. "You know who Ms. Constantine is."

"The lady in the bookstore? Yeah, why?" Franklin kept his eyes on me and waited. Seconds later the light went on. "Wow! You and Ms. Constantine?"

Franklin's grin was a giveaway. "She's amazing, and beautiful with her hair down."

His face was now one huge smile. Here we go again, I thought. When Franklin is smitten, it's a big deal. He becomes helpless. The thoughtful, strong, resilient and solid Franklin Rock is gone, replaced by the liquid version that is ready to take the shape of whatever container has lured him her way.

Scenario playing, Franklin Rock style, now took over in my brain. I weighed the options of what I could say to him. None seemed to end well as I rapidly worked through each of them, and so I chose to remain silent.

Franklin could see that the floor was still his. He continued.

"I know what you're thinking. I'm a sucker for a pretty face. Which is of course true. But this is different, Henry."

It's never different, I thought to myself.

Franklin continued. "It started with the inscription at the top of the Memorial. I have always wondered what it said. Are you curious to know?"

"What inscription?" I instantly asked, but as soon as those words left my lips I knew I would regret it.

"What inscription? You have lived here for almost four years, walked by that magnificent edifice a zillion times, and you never noticed that there is an inscription in Hebrew that encircles the top?" He paused, thought for a moment; a revelation had occurred. "You're pulling my chain, aren't you?"

Sometimes you have to weigh full honesty against revealing yourself to be a dunderhead. I had no idea there was an inscription at the top of the Memorial, let alone that it was in Hebrew. One of Franklin's shortcomings is assuming that everyone shares his level of curiosity and interest in a broad set of topics. He sets the bar high for others, and I admire him for that. Unfortunately, he ends up repeatedly disappointed when he learns that most people limit their concerns to the mundane. I feel fairly certain that among the many thousands of students who have walked past the Memorial over the many years that it has been at the center of campus, relatively few have taken the slightest notice of its inscription.

I decided there was nothing to gain by admitting my ignorance on the inscription matter. I smiled and shrugged my shoulders, with that response neither lying to my friend nor admitting culpability. Franklin bit, then continued.

"I had no idea what the inscription said, but for the longest time I wanted to know," Franklin, continued. "So I asked Lori if she knew. Of course she did, and we made a game out of me figuring it out."

Lori? If Franklin was calling the person in charge of the campus bookstore by her first name something had transpired between the two of them. My initial inclination was to tease him about this, but I caught myself. Franklin was about to tell me something that he felt to be of great importance.

Over the next hour, I learned about the Talmud, specifically something called the Ethics of the Fathers, the meaning of the inscription, and a lot about Lori Constantine.

"I had another time travel episode while we were in the Memorial."

"Lori witnessed it?" I asked.

"Yes, and she was great about it," Franklin added. "I also had a previous episode. It happened when I was in the library researching the inscription. I had been looking for the Talmud when it happened." Franklin then told me the story of the possibly pregnant college student and her professor lover. Sad to say, that was the part of his entire soliloquy that interested me the most. My ability to dismiss gossip and scandal was far inferior to that of Franklin's. But I managed to refrain from asking any questions about the two protagonists and instead focused on what mattered most to Franklin—his time travel.

"How long did it last? Where did you go?" I asked.

"I don't think I went anywhere. I mean, I was still in the library."

"I don't understand. Are you sure you time-traveled?"

"I am. The problem is I don't know in which direction I went. I couldn't recall the exact sequence of events. It's possible I traveled into the future," Franklin concluded, his uncertainty and concern visible in his eyes. He looked at me. I interpreted his silence as a question.

"You want to know what I think?" I accidentally asked before I had decided whether to comment at all.

"Sure," he answered.

Now that I had implied that I had an opinion, especially one that might add value to the situation, I had to come up with something. I didn't want to encourage Franklin's flights of fancy. I remained unconvinced that his visions were actual examples of time travel. I didn't believe time travel was possible, even though Franklin Rock, the one person I held in the highest regard, claimed it to be. I was sure, however, that getting involved roman-tically with Lori Constantine was not a good idea just now.

We were at the end of our undergraduate careers. Graduation was looming, and I knew that Franklin had done pretty much nothing academ-ically in the recent past. His mentor, Professor Niemeyer, had just passed away. I was also unsure whether Professor Niemeyer was the prophet Franklin claimed him to be or a bit of a nut. I dared not mention *that* to him. Franklin had neglected just about all of his responsibilities since that first episode in Professor Sorrens's class. As his closest friend, I wanted to drag him back to our reality, or at least to my reality.

But then I opened my mind to all the possibilities, to all of the scenar-ios as Franklin would do. Maybe I'm wrong; maybe he is time traveling. Maybe Professor Niemeyer was a prophet. Maybe discouraging him from a relationship with Lori Constantine would be an error.

"So Henry, what do you think?" he asked again.

"I think there is a lot on your plate." Before I could continue, even though I had no good idea of what should follow, Franklin saved me.

"You're right. There is. And I know you want to say the right thing; you want to help. But you're not sure what to say, Henry, are you? You can't possibly be. I have no idea what to say, and I have a huge head start on you. I'm the one who has been living this craziness. I have to figure this out by myself."

And with that Franklin arose and began to walk out of Johnson's Gardens. He turned back to me after he had gone about twenty yards. "Don't worry about me, Henry. Everything will turn out as it should. Professor Niemeyer assured me that it always does." He resumed his ascent of the path out of the Gardens. This time he didn't turn back to me as he added, "Professor Niemeyer was not a nut. He was the real deal."

16

All Good Things

Lori and I had suddenly and rapidly arrived at a new set point in our relationship. Most often it takes some period for two people to converge. As they spend time together, they discover similar interests. Endearing traits become evident, and through shared experiences, they move closer and closer. Instead of discovering one commonality at a time, like teeth in a zipper, Lori and I had slammed together like two pieces of Velcro.

The day after I revealed everything to her, I felt as if I was carried along by an invisible cushion of air that prevented my feet from ever touching the ground. I walked the campus and allowed my mind the luxury of reliving each moment again and again. "We were meant to meet," she had told me. It was hard for me not to agree. Life often resembles a giant jigsaw puzzle. You guess where to put the first pieces; none of the shapes mean much. But as you get closer and closer to the end the overall pattern is revealed and you see that each piece is constructed exactly as it should be. It all makes perfect sense.

Lori had told me that she would be with her family for the next two evenings. What if the symmetry I had felt between the two of us was imaginary, merely wishful thinking? As each hour passed I became less confident and more anxious. By the second day, I had become a psychological mess.

Three days after our conversation, at 5:30 p.m., I walked to the bookstore. Closing time was 6 p.m., and I did not want to take any chance that I would miss her. I lingered outside for a minute. Doubt yet again seeped into my thoughts. I had convinced myself that our evening together was a singular event; perhaps the stars had aligned one time and one time only.

Lori saw me through the glass. The instant explosion of her smile reassured me that my worst-case scenario was to be replaced by a victory lap. We met at the door.

"I am so happy to see you!" she said before I could state the same. "I'll be closing in half an hour. Can we have dinner?"

"I was hoping you'd say that. Do you want to go out somewhere?"

"Do you mind if we eat at my place?" she asked, well aware I am sure that she knew she needn't have.

"Should I wait or meet you there?"

"It would be great if you could stop at the store and pick up a few things. We can cook together. Whatever you get is fine. Surprise me."

As I traversed the aisles in the supermarket, I grabbed anything I thought might work. What we made and ate could not have mattered less to me. My mind was focused elsewhere. By the time I arrived at Lori's apartment, she was already inside and gearing up for our first culinary endeavor.

"Let's see what you got," she said while emptying the two paper bags I had set on her kitchen table. In her left hand she held a bag of potatoes, in her right a box of spaghetti. "Franklin, did you realize these are both starches?"

"Hey, I know that. I just wanted to give you a choice."

She had nearly emptied both bags. "Hmm. So it looks like we might be eating both, considering I don't see anything that resembles a protein," she said, turning her smile towards me.

"Oh, God, I am such a dope. I didn't even realize I hadn't gotten any meat or chicken. Sorry!" was all I had to offer.

"I see you bought some lettuce and a cucumber, plus this red thing that's advertised as a tomato. Oh, well, good enough. Pasta and salad are great. We can satisfy ourselves in other ways," she added, assuring me all was more than well.

Celebratory gongs were going off in my head. Nothing is as delicious as anticipation of desire guaranteed to be fulfilled. *God, if this is all there is in my life I will still be forever grateful.*

Cooking next to her was blissful. I observed her every movement. As her lithe fingers scooped up a handful of salt and released it gently into the pot of water I was transfixed, a simple act made nearly holy. I was well aware of my hyperbole, but it seemed that if anything I was understating the elegance of her actions.

"I thought you were going to help," she said over her shoulder as I stood behind her.

"I thought so, too, but I didn't expect to be frozen by just being close to you," I admitted.

She turned to face me. "That's so sweet. Now can you unfreeze yourself and set the table—and get us something to drink, please?"

I hardly remember eating the meal. I felt full at the end, but I had no recollection of even a single bite as if magically the food had invisibly passed through my body and filled my stomach. I recall wiping my mouth and looking at my napkin for any evidence that food had passed my lips.

We talked well into the evening about our childhoods, our friends, our victories, and defeats. I could not learn enough about her. After each story she told, Lori would say, "Your turn, Franklin," but all I wished to do was listen to her. I loved her voice. Its pitch was like a harmonic on a guitar, pure and uncluttered by extraneous noise. Why, I thought, would I ever wish to interrupt its flow with the tinny clang of my voice? Still she persisted, and I was forced to comply.

"What do you want to know about? You already know all about my current life. I can't imagine you would want anymore," I told her, hoping she would concur.

"Tell me about your mother."

My mother. Images of her raced through my brain at various ages of my life.

"Well, I guess I would start by saying she's a character. There is nothing subtle about my mother. When I look at pictures of her when she was young she is always smiling, always the life of the party."

"What does she look like?"

"Blonde. Small. She always wears high heels and an ankle bracelet. For some reason when I think of her, I see the ankle bracelet. When I was a kid, I just assumed every mother wore one. It wasn't until I was a teenager that I realized it was my mother's special thing."

Lori waited. "You want more?" I asked. She nodded. "OK, let's see. She worked off and on when I was young. I was too young to understand what she did but I knew it had to do with women's clothes. For a woman who never attended college, she's pretty educated. She reads a lot and loves politics. God knows why."

"She sounds interesting. I'll bet she's pretty."

"Why would you bet she's pretty?" I asked innocently.

"Because you're pretty good-looking and you had to get it somewhere."

I blushed. Compliments and gifts are two things I don't accept graciously. I moved closer to her on the couch. "Enough about my mother," I said, and kissed her.

If we are lucky enough, there are times in our lives that surpass good or even excellent. They are perfect. My time with Lori Constantine was that. I could not identify even the most minimal of imperfections in the days, evenings, and nights we spent together. Her lips delivered perfect kisses, her long, slender fingers perfect caresses, her words perfect peace. As the world sped madly through time, we existed separate and apart, immune from all that existed outside of our perfect sphere.

Over the next couple of weeks, we spent whatever time we could together. Lori had her job at the bookstore, and I still had a semester to conclude. We did not make plans; neither of us was sure what any day would hold. Instead, in the evenings I could, I would make my way to the bookstore just before six. If she were free, we would spend the evening together.

On a Thursday evening, I arrived at about five forty-five. I looked through the doors, but I did not see her. After a few minutes of waiting outside, I went in. A few students were inside looking for assigned books. No one was at the register. I walked over to the door that led to the store-room and looked through its window. Lori was not visible.

"Can I help you?" a male voice asked from behind. I turned and saw a gray-haired gentleman dressed in a corduroy sport coat.

"Oh, yes, thanks. I'm looking for Ms. Constantine."

"She had to leave early today. Something I can assist you with?"

"No, she was going to help me with something. I can come back tomor-row," I told him.

Funny, I thought, Lori hadn't said anything about working less today. During the five-minute walk to Lori's apartment, my mind covered a lot of ground. Was she sick? Did something happen in her apartment that made her leave early to meet a repair person?

I knocked on her door. Tear-filled green eyes greeted me. "What's wrong?" flew from my mouth.

"My sister-in-law has cancer." She began sobbing and fell into my arms. I wasn't prepared for her catastrophic response. She didn't have a cold and all of her appliances were in working order. My naive college-student brain had not made it past the insignificant to have conjured far worse possibilities for her absence. We found our way to the couch, the one where the romance began just a few weeks ago. As I sat down, I could feel the change. It no longer welcomed me with the promise of delight. Now it was the crucible of sorrow.

Lori collected herself. "I'm going to go to Chicago to help my brother. I don't know if I told you, but Elizabeth, his wife, is also pregnant. The baby is due in a month. They are going to deliver the baby early—I think next week—so they can start treating my sister-in-law."

I remained silent. I wasn't sure what to say. In retrospect, it should have been easy. So often people don't know how to respond when presented with bad news about another's life. Instead of running away the correct action is to run directly into the fire. "I am so sorry to hear that. Do you want to talk about it? I'm not going anywhere." But that night I was still too inexperienced in the world to know. I waited.

"She has Hodgkin's disease. Do you know what that is?"

"No, I don't. You said she has cancer so I assume it's some form of that," I replied, finally able to speak.

"Yes, it's a type of cancer of the lymph nodes. It's very treatable, thank God. They think she will be fine, but she's going to have to have chemotherapy and maybe something else. Anyway, it will take a while, and they will need help with the baby."

They will need help with the baby. Oh, God, she isn't going just to visit.

"So you're moving there?" I asked, terrified of her response.

"Yes. Sorry, I guess maybe I didn't make that clear."

I swallowed hard. Lori noticed but said nothing.

"It's wonderful of you to do this for them," I told her after a long enough pause to catch my breath.

"I can't imagine not doing it. It's my family."

"When are you planning on leaving?" I asked, hoping it would be some time well into the future. Selfish as that question was, it was the only one I needed answered.

"This weekend, Franklin," she said sadly, knowing how devastating those words would be for me, and from the quality of her voice, for her.

Sometimes one is confronted with a fait accompli; no words or actions have any possibility of altering the course. What had happened was not reversible, nor was Lori's selfless decision. "I am going to miss you," escaped my lips with no thought behind them.

"And I am going to miss you," she answered as she rested her head on my shoulder.

I closed my eyes. Instantly I was offered a glimpse into my future. A sharp pain caught me beneath my breast bone and caused me to gasp. Another woman was standing beside an adult Franklin Rock. Her face was turned away, but for certain that woman was not Lori Constantine.

"What?" she asked. "Are you all right?"

"Nothing. Just thinking. At least you'll get to spend time with your new niece or nephew." She is not the one, I thought, unable to ignore the future I had just seen.

"It will be wonderful to be an aunt and to have the baby know me. I just wish the circumstances were better." Lori wiped her eyes.

"It sounds pretty optimistic from what you told me, that they think she will be OK after her treatment."

"Our family doctor had us speak with an oncologist here who specializes in Hodgkin's disease. Seems it is pretty common among young people. Nowadays, he said most patients are cured and live normal lives. So we're praying that's what happens with Elizabeth."

I reached around Lori's shoulder and pulled her closer. My sudden knowledge that we were not to be together in the future had momentarily seared me, but this wasn't the future. This was now, and I wanted to capture every moment with her that I could.

"What can I do? I can help you pack. Anything. Just tell me," I pleaded. I needed all the contact I could squeeze from our short time left together.

"So sweet," she whispered, then kissed my cheek. "I'm not sure yet, but it means so much to me that you are here. We have a few days left. We certainly don't want to waste them."

We didn't. Lori had quit her bookstore job upon learning of her sister-in-law's illness. By day we packed up her apartment. Moving illuminates the extent of one's possessions. Each delicate miniature, each fragile candy dish required attention. Intermittently, I would stop and watch Lori. I began a mental photo album, recording everything she did so that I could recall them whenever I desired. Sometimes she would catch me staring, to which she would respond with alternating smiles and looks that said, "OK, lover boy, back to work." Never before had I been immersed in a "labor of love"; I would never again misunderstand the concept.

Every few hours, Lori would walk over to me, take some object out of my hand, throw her arms around me and kiss me. We would embrace for a minute or two, and then she would return to whatever had been occupying her before that delicious time-out. She would leave me frozen, for unlike her I could not simply release the moment and return to the mundane chore of packing. "C'mon, Franklin, you said you wanted to help. Now get back to it," she commanded. "The sooner we're done..." Her wink finished the sentence and accelerated my packing effort.

We spent day and night together, paradoxically growing closer while separation loomed. I refused to envision her day of departure, nor would I do so even hours before it was to occur. Our last night had arrived.

"We should go to Vesuvio tonight," I suggested.

"Absolutely. I believe that is where you fell for me," Lori surmised.

"Nope. I fell for you the moment I saw you with your hair down in the bookstore."

"Oh, yes, my hair. Every time you saw it down I thought you were star-struck."

"I was starstruck, by everything. Your eyes, your hair, your voice, your hands. I still am," I admitted.

Dinner was sublime. We both had linguine with Vesuvio's famous marinara. I was fearless, unlike that first time together.

"I have a question for you," I said. "That first dinner in Vesuvio. When you saw I had ordered linguine with marinara, you made the comment that you always got the sauce all over you. Was that the truth or did you just say that to put me at ease in case I managed to make a mess of myself?"

"Yes," she answered.

"Yes? Yes what? Which is it?" I pressed her.

"It's one of those two."

Oh, God, how I am going to miss her.

We had been long finished with our food when it became clear to both of us that we had to leave. As we exited the restaurant, we turned simultaneously to take one last look. For Lori of course that made sense. My last look was different. I was certain that I would be back both in the future and in the past.

Lori's dad's best friend was in the moving and storage business. He had arranged for a team to come early the next morning and take her furniture and those belongings she would not need in Chicago. Since she would be staying with her brother and sister-in-law at their house, all she required for now were her clothes and other personal items. Everything else would be stored locally.

Pray as I did during every waking moment of that night, I could not prevent the sun from rising and the new day from arriving. The movers came as scheduled. We held hands as the truck was loaded, both of us staring straight ahead. That moment we both were avoiding with all of our might was bearing down on us, as relentless as a freight train barreling down the tracks towards its destination. I could feel her grip on my hand tighten as the final pieces were shoved into the truck. A minute later we watched from her window as the men slammed the rear door, jumped into the cab, and drove away with Lori's tangible life. Her "finished" apartment had suddenly vanished. Still, every moment we had shared there remained perfectly in place. A changing set does not displace what has occurred in that set. Every emotion experienced in that space still floats in the air, available to be inhaled and re-enjoyed.

Lori and I held each other, or more accurately held onto each other.

"I will call you," she said.

"I will call you, too," I replied.

"Can I tell you that I love you?" she softly asked, her lips caressing the edge of my ear.

"I love you, too," I said, working with all my energy to suppress the heaving in my chest and the flood of tears that awaited permission to flow. "You know what Professor Niemeyer would say now?"

"No. What would he say?" she asked in a voice begging for a last-minute reprieve.

"He would say, 'Franklin, don't be sad. Remember that every moment lives forever. You and Lori will be together in every one of those days and nights you spent together for all eternity.'"

"Will we, Franklin?" Lori asked as she pulled away, checking to see if my eyes confirmed what my lips had just uttered.

Of course they did. That is how our world works.

17

A Chance Encounter

"**H**EY, FRANKLIN!" I HEARD AS I crossed the campus and headed towards my room. I looked up and saw my friend Danny Benson.

"Hi, Danny."

"Where have you been?" he inquired. "I haven't seen you in weeks."

Danny Benson and I had met in the first few months of college. During those early days, most of us spent time with the people who lived on the same floor in the dorm. Danny lived on the fourth floor, Henry and I on the second, so our paths didn't cross much in the beginning. One day in the late fall, Danny wandered down to the second floor and approached Henry and me.

"You two planning to join a fraternity?" he asked us.

Henry and I looked at each other. I don't think either of us had considered the option up to that point.

Danny continued. "You should come with me to a party this weekend at Phi Sigma Delta. I'm thinking about pledging there. "

"What do you like about it?" Henry asked.

"Very nice guys. And best-looking girls at a party that I've been to," he added with a grin.

That got my attention. I looked at Henry. "We should go," I told him.

"So that we can get ignored by better-looking girls than the ones that ignore us at other parties?"

Danny laughed out loud. "Henry, I think Franklin is just suggesting that if you want to eventually have a good-looking girlfriend you'd probably have a better shot if there were good-looking girls where you're looking. Plus, if you guys like it we can get a group of us to join together."

Up until that conversation, Danny and I had probably not exchanged ten words. Maybe he included me in the invitation because I was Henry's friend. It's a question I never asked Danny. If I asked him years later he would have had no recollection of the event. The past seemed to shun Danny; people and places didn't stick in his mind.

Henry and I took Danny up on his offer, went to the party, and along with a handful of other freshmen joined Phi Sigma Delta. Our friendship grew rapidly. What I most admired about Danny was his steadiness. He approached every challenge with the same equanimity. Most college students rode the typical emotional roller coaster from euphoria to dejection. Not Danny. I never saw him lose his cool. Imperturbability was a trait that, though foreign to me up to that point in my life, was one I wished I possessed. I recall early on trying to emulate Danny, and I told Henry about it.

"Franklin, forget it; don't even try. The guy has ice in his veins. You have syrup in yours," Henry reminded me. "Sorry, it's true. And so do I. Danny and Jimmy are a different breed than you and me." Henry was referring to his childhood friend Jimmy Gardener. The first time we got together with all of our high school and college friends in one place, it was clear that Danny and Jimmy were two peas in a pod. Their dads were both doctors, the old-fashioned general practice kind of doctors who had dedicated their lives to their patients. The more that Danny and Jimmy talked, the more they bonded. Their life experiences were near carbon copies. Dinnertime for both of them was often mother and children with dad off to care for an ill patient. Their fathers were serious men who routinely dealt with illness and death. Small things would not receive any attention from either of their dads. Both fathers set the bar high for their sons, and both sons had decided they would not simply jump but leap over it.

When I told Henry that I wished to emulate Danny's steadiness, I knew what I was doing. It had long been obvious to me that I needed some additional personal assets, and I was in search of the best. Each of us can invent ourselves, and even reinvent ourselves if an earlier iteration is unsuccessful or undesirable. None of us is stuck.

"Sorry, Danny, I've been a bit distracted with crazy stuff. I'm fine. You?"

"I'm fine," he responded. If I wished any more information I would need to interview him. Danny was a person of few words; he was unlikely to

spend much time talking about himself and would volunteer scant information unless specific questions were asked.

'Where you heading?" he inquired.

"Back to my room. I'm behind in just about everything," I answered,
and realized how true that was. I prepared to say goodbye and get back
on my way.

"C'mon, whatever it is can't be that important. Why don't you come
with me? We could get something to eat, talk about girls, you know like
we used to do. It will be fun."

My immediate instinct was to say no and to beg forgiveness, but almost
immediately I reconsidered. Friends have always been important to me.
If you don't make time for your friends, they won't be friends for long.
When that happens, something valuable is lost. You might not appreciate
it at the time, but it is loss nonetheless. Every relationship leaves a mark.

"Sure, that would be great," I told him instead.

"I need to drop off a tennis racket I borrowed at the fraternity house
and then we can head off and get something to eat."

On the way to the car, we talked about our upcoming graduation and
the speed with which our college days had flown by.

"Can you believe it, Franklin? Four years! It's like we just got here.
Remember that football game on the first day. You made *the* catch. A ton
of kids playing defense and you manage to grab that pass. What was that
quarterback's name who threw it? I don't think he stayed here after that
first year."

Although the set didn't change at that moment—I felt no shift—my
mind returned to the event to which Danny was referring. It was our first
day of college. More than thirty of us spontaneously decided to begin
a game of touch football on the lawn in front of the dorm. We were all
new; most of us were complete strangers. No one was going to insist on
culling the sides to eleven each as in a real game. We just cleaved like the
Red Sea, half on offense, half on defense. It happened that the recruited
quarterback of the freshman football team was on my side of the field. On
each play, he simply told us all to run a pass route and try to get free. I did
as instructed, and when I looked up I saw his long pass coming directly
towards me. Here was a critical moment in a young man's life. A singular
thought was about to simultaneously traverse the mind of the thirty-plus

freshmen on the field. If I drop the ball, the thought is this: "Loser." Catch the ball, and instead and a reputation is born.

We had reached Danny's car. As we got in I pondered how much to tell him. Despite our friendship, we had never talked much about anything other than the mundane activities of college life. In all fairness to my friend, I had never pushed the envelope, and it was not his style to burden another with his thoughts unless specifically prompted to do so. I had no idea how he would respond if I shared my recent history with him.

We began to drive towards our old fraternity house so Danny could make a brief stop and return the tennis racket. As Danny began his left turn onto the street housing the fraternity, a black pickup truck accelerated from behind the lead car on the other side of the street. The driver was attempting to beat the light at the intersection. By the time he realized that Danny was already heading into the intersection the truck was on a trajectory to hit us head-on. Without flinching, Danny reflexively jerked the steering wheel sharply to the right and somehow avoided the collision. As he did so our right front tire smacked the metal portion of the road drain. Within seconds it was obvious that we had a flat tire.

As Danny brought the car to a stop, with my heart racing, I turned and looked at him. "You do have ice in your veins," I said with obvious admiration and gratitude. Danny smiled at me. "Well," he said, "at least we're not dead. But it looks like we're about to change a tire."

As we exited Danny's car a blue sedan pulled up behind us. Danny was first to exit the car and noticed before I did.

"Seems like someone is going to help us," he surmised as I turned to see what he was referring to. I recognized the car immediately. Govinda opened his door and got out. We saw each other simultaneously.

"Franklin! You know how close you just were to getting killed?" Govinda yelled to us as he approached.

"You know this guy?" Danny asked as he swung around and looked at me.

"I do. Govinda, this is Danny."

"Hey man, that was one nice piece of driving you just did. You saved at least two lives," Govinda said holding out his hand to shake Danny's. "Very impressive."

"Sorry, I didn't get your name," Danny asked as he shook Govinda's hand.

"Govinda. That's what my friends call me." Govinda nodded towards me. "I'm sure Franklin will explain it to you." Govinda kneeled and looked at the now completely flat tire. "Can I give you a hand with this? I have a sweet jack we can use." Govinda walked to the rear of his car, popped his trunk, and took out a tripod. He carried it around and stood it up next to the rear of Danny's car. "You cannot believe how many flat tires I have gotten over the past couple of years. I got tired of fooling with the toy jack that came with the car. I assume you have a spare, Danny?"

"I do. And that jack is going to make this a whole lot easier," Danny responded, flashing his mellow smile.

Within ten minutes the three of us had the tire changed. While Danny was putting the flat in his trunk, Govinda approached me and quietly asked, "How are you?"

"I have a lot to tell you," I answered softly.

Danny noticed our exchange as he closed his trunk. I could tell he was sizing up the situation. "Hey, if you two need to talk, I'm fine to get on my way," he told us. Classic Danny Benson. He reads a scene and responds; there is never drama.

Govinda looked at me inquisitively. I turned to face my life-saving friend.

"Danny, I didn't get the chance to tell you but some pretty crazy stuff has been happening to me lately. That's why you haven't seen me. Govinda knows a part of it. I'm happy to share it with you if you want, but I don't want you to feel like you have to."

"It's not that I'm not interested. But I don't want *you* to feel like you have to," he answered. I wondered why it always took me so many more words than Danny to convey my thoughts.

I looked over at Govinda. "You have time now?"

"Sure," he answered.

I returned to Danny, but before I could say another word he said, "Franklin, this is not a big deal. You two have some stuff to talk about. Not a problem." He pulled his car keys from his pocket. "I'll check on you in a couple of days if that's OK," he added, then got into his car and drove off with a wave out his window.

Govinda motioned for me to get into his car. Just after the two of us were seated, Govinda turned to me. "I want to hear what's been happening since the last time I saw you," he began, "but I also have something to tell you."

"OK, why don't you go first?"

"You won't be surprised to hear that I had a dream." Govinda paused. "I just realized how easy it is to say that to you as compared to anyone else. Remember I told you that occasionally I'd have what I call special event dreams? Most of the time they are in the future. The one I had the other night was especially real. In it, I meet someone who is from another time. That person has no idea where he is. Turns out he is famous in my time, the future time of the dream, and he doesn't know that either. In the dream, I'm the one that tells him that he is famous."

"So you think I'm the person from another time that you meet?"

"For sure it's you. The voice. It's you," Govinda confirmed.

"In your dream, am I from the past or the future?"

"From the past."

Govinda stopped talking. I could tell he was trying to recall the details of the dream.

"You were clueless about where you were. I remember that I had to explain lots of things to you."

"So what happens?" I was at the edge of my seat.

"The last thing I recall is telling you about how famous you are in my time, and that I am going to show you. Then I woke up. I remember sitting up abruptly; the visions were so real."

Govinda's dream was another jolt. The recurrent clues were getting difficult for me to ignore and I told him so.

"Franklin, you have to accept your fate. You're already drowning with evidence. You're going to keep meeting people like me who are repeatedly going to reinforce what I've told you, and really what you already know."

I then told him about Lori Constantine, about the inscription on the Memorial, about the strange brief time travel in the library, all of it.

"See, I'm telling you, Franklin, stuff is happening to you."

"That's what Professor Niemeyer said. But I can't get away from the thought that this is all insane. Govinda, I cannot shake my conviction that I am not anybody important. I've never done anything that special. I still feel like an idiot sometimes," I insisted.

"Well, you might still be an idiot sometimes. We're guys; we all are. But you are special, and it's a lock that you won't be an idiot for long," Govinda graciously replied. "You have to be more open. You have to start accepting your responsibility. That means you have to pay ever attention to everything that happens to you. And you have to start r nizing your powers."

"What powers?" I asked incredulously.

"You have certain powers, of that I'm sure," Govinda stated unemotionally.

"I don't have powers. I can't bend steel in my bare hands or leap tall buildings in a single bound."

"Of course you do, Franklin. You travel through time. You have glimpses of the future. What do you think those are? Remember how we talked about people always picking you out in a group and staring at you? That's another power. People will listen to you. You have insights that you take for granted. You see things; you know things," Govinda concluded.

You know things. Those words struck me more strongly now than when I first heard them from Professor Niemeyer on his tape. I had always thought that I somehow mysteriously "knew things" about life and the world. From an early age I knew time was strange. The idea that time was simply a line extending from past to future did not sit well with me; I *knew* that concept was incorrect. I *knew* that the world we see is only a part of the story and that there was more, much more, that remained hidden.

I took a deep breath and looked at Govinda.

"Oh, and you have even more powers in my visions," Govinda continued.

"Like what?"

"This one I admit is a fantasy power. But you have it."

"So what is it?"

"I hesitate to tell you because you may decide that all of my visions are fiction."

"C'mon Govinda. What is it?"

"You can fly."

"That would be fun. So now I do have to weigh what you tell me."

"Look, I'm not saying that everything that happens in my dreams is an accurate predictor of your future. But I am certain that you do have a mission, that you are going to be somebody really important, and that you will do great things. Flying might be a stretch, but the rest I am sure is true. Plus, didn't Professor Niemeyer tell you a lot of the same things?"

was afraid to tell me too much. He knew I was
˙ he didn't want to make it any worse."

my shoulder. "This is going to be great Frank-
˙t for you. It's going to be great for a lot of

...d looked out his window, scanning the landscape, then
...ck towards me. "I just had a sense that all of those people out
...re will one day turn to you."

"Fine, you just put the entire world on my shoulders. That's not exactly what I need from a friend right now."

"That's exactly what you need from a friend, and I promise you I will be your friend every step of the way." Then Govinda added, "Remember: The day is short, the work is great, the reward is much, the Master is urgent."

18

The Boys

MIRACULOUSLY, WEEKS WENT BY without a vision, and thankfully, without any dislocation from the present. More than allowing me to catch up on classwork, laundry, and what used to be my life, it gave both my mind and my heart a chance to recover. I found myself standing up just a bit straighter, looking up at the sun instead of at my shoes. Breaths were longer; sighs were shorter. It's only when a weight is lifted—if only temporarily—that one appreciates how light the load had been in more normal times.

Henry and I saw each other off and on during those few weeks. He had his own life to live, and as good a friend as he is, he too needed a break from the Franklin Rock drama. He would stop by every couple of days to make sure I was alive. When I told him that wasn't necessary, he said, "Oh really, how do I know you're not fighting in the Civil War or learning to cultivate seeds in Mesopotamia?"

I explained to Henry that in my version of time travel I never physically left the present, so he didn't have to worry. I had no idea if that was always going to be true. I had not had a chance to ask Professor Niemeyer about physical time travel, although he did hint in our discussion of Einstein's relativity theories that such a thing was not possible. He had rolled his eyes when I told him I felt that I was in the H.G. Wells book *The Time Machine*.

"Franklin, that's a story. Don't confuse what is happening to you with that sort of science fiction. Although Wells was closer to reality than he probably thought. Man was a genius," he mused. That was all he had said on the matter.

My other friendships had suffered during the previous few months. J Bob and I used to talk regularly; it had now been over a month since I had seen him. I felt bad about blowing off Danny the day we ran into Govinda, right after we almost got killed. When we ran into each other earlier that day he reminded me that we had gone a long time, at least for us, without spending time together. I stopped by Danny's apartment a couple of days later on my way to the laundromat but he wasn't around. If I were to apologize yet again he would say something like, "Franklin, get over it. It's nothing. I don't even like spending time with you," and with his characteristic smile and a laugh, off he would go.

My absence from Joanna was another story. She, Henry, and I had shared so much. During our college years, lunches and dinners were often taken together. We didn't schedule them; they just happened, probably because our study habits meshed. As freshmen, the three of us would find ourselves on the same floor in the library just about every night. Soon we began to take simultaneous study breaks, grab a coffee, and chat. It became our routine. If one of us did not show up at break time the other two would scour the library in search of the missing member of our trio.

It was her shoulder-length blonde hair that I had noticed instantly upon entering our freshman seminar on our first day of class. Henry claims I have a special neurologic receptor that signals me when, as he describes it, "blondness" is in my immediate vicinity. It is undeniable—blonde women attract me mercilessly, sapping whatever will power I might attempt to bring to bear to ignore their presence. My mother was blonde and glamorous; that's the easy explanation. As I told Henry when he insisted that was the case, it hardly matters why. I remain incapable of mounting any resistance.

Sadly Joanna was never as interested in a romantic relationship as I was. Nevertheless, I continued to attempt to change that dynamic for the first two years of college. One day Joanna sat with me on the grass outside of her dorm and gently ended my quest. "Franklin," she began, "you have no idea how important you are to me. So many times in the past two years, you have calmed me, supported me, and been such a good friend. I don't want that to change. Can we just be wonderful friends to each other?"

"If that's what you want, Joanna. You know it's not my first choice."

"Of course I know it's not your first choice. You've made that very clear. And don't get me wrong. There is nothing about you I don't find attractive. God, I was about to say 'it's me, not you' like we were in a movie. I want you as a friend, and I don't want anything to change that. I hope I am not hurting you." She paused, then acknowledged the truth. "I know I am, and I am so sorry. It's the last thing I want to do," she concluded as she took my hand.

All I heard during that speech was the final nail being driven into my aspirational coffin. My wish that things would change had not been fulfilled. Was my heart broken? No, by that point I knew my chances were minuscule; I was hardly stunned by her pronouncement.

Since that day of disappointment and acceptance of my reality, Joanna and I have gotten even closer as friends. Only her romantic interests remain off-limits for me. I am certain she would share if I asked, but honestly, I could never be supportive. I could never say, "Oh, you're seeing Sergio? He's such a good guy. I hope you're happy." Joanna knows this, and she is kind enough to avoid that topic. Henry, on the other hand, occasionally jabs me with a detail of that aspect of Joanna's life in which I would prefer to remain ignorant. It's his secret weapon when I get to be a bit too much.

As I was traversing the campus on my way back from the library, she surprised me from behind. "Hi, handsome, been anywhere lately?"

Still, my heart adds a touch of pace when I hear her voice. I turned to greet her.

"No, and that's the way I like it."

"You know you look a lot better," Joanna observed as her eyes scanned me.

"I feel a lot better," I said, as my eyes, as always, scanned her. "You on the other hand look as beautiful as ever."

"Franklin, you are always the flatterer, and always the flirt."

I shrugged my shoulders and smiled. We both knew the game would never end if I had any say in the matter. "How are you? Where are you off to?"

"I'm coming back from the art studio. I finally finished my last canvas."

Among her myriad talents, Joanna could draw. Beautifully. She had given me a drawing of the campus for my last birthday, with the Memorial squarely in the center. Joanna was well aware of my affinity for that building. Recently she had begun to paint. She took advantage of the opportunity to study with an accomplished watercolor artist who was spending the semester as a visiting professor. After the first couple of weeks, she worried that she had bitten off a bit more than she could chew.

"So, are you now glad you took the course? You weren't too happy at first," I reminded her.

"I am, so glad! I have learned so much. I look back at where I started and where I am now and I am amazed. And it's not just the technical part. I am even more amazed by the creative part."

"I'm so glad to hear that. Do you have time for lunch? We can eat and you can fill me in."

"I do. Let's go."

We headed to the cafeteria. It was already nearly two o'clock by the time we had gotten our food and sat. Only a few other tables were still occupied. "So tell me, what about the creative process amazes you?" I asked, reflecting her earlier observation.

"I never know where it comes from. I mean, I can't explain how I know to draw a line here or add a touch of color there. It's sort of magic. When I look at something I've done, it feels as though my hand was guided by something other than me. Plus—and here's the scary part—I don't have any confidence that I could do it again."

Joanna's comments did not surprise me. Just about every artist, musician, artisan, or writer will tell you the same thing. Inspiration is an enigma. A poet pens a lovely sonnet and worries he may never be able to do so again. The musician creates a moving melody, then thinks that this is the pinnacle of her creativity, never to be matched.

"What do you think?" she asked.

"Creativity comes from somewhere unknown on its own schedule," I told her. "Artists of all types have said that they are merely the conduit for the creative work, that it merely passes through them from its unknown mysterious source to the page or canvas."

"Has that happened to you?" she asked me.

I closed my eyes to reflect on my own creative moments. And then, for the first time in a while, I felt the shift.

◆◇◆◇◆

"THEY LOOK REALLY GOOD," Ross Albert said to our group as he watched the baseball team from the opposing camp warming up.

"Hey, Albatross," I heard another of our teammates say. Albatross. I remember that's what we called him, turning his name around. "We're a really good team, too."

My God. I was back at summer camp. Albatross, Jeff, Ben. They were all there.

"Rock, when you get on base you'd better run. Their third baseman has a good arm," Ben said turning to me. "Good thing you're the fastest kid ever!" he exclaimed. Fastest kid ever. I was in those days. I looked around. Everything was the same. The baseball diamond with the poorly cut grass in the infield. I could see the lake just down the hill. I turned around, and there were the bunks I remembered, unchanged in the twelve years since I had been there. I returned my gaze to the opposing pitcher. For a second I didn't recognize him. Danny! Nine-year-old Danny Benson was their pitcher.

As college freshmen, my friends and I had spent hours discovering people and places we had in common. Many of us had attended summer camps in the mountains as kids. Danny and Henry had gone to camps that competed annually with mine. The two of them thought they remembered playing against each other. I had had no recollection, nor did either one recall me. But here was incontrovertible evidence that Danny and I had been in the same place at the same time.

I watched Danny as he warmed up. After each strike he threw he would spin around on the mound like a top in celebration. When he threw a ball, he would simply stare at the catcher, then pound his mitt in frustration. Regular as clockwork, one motion or the other would occur after every pitch.

"You're up, Franklin," I heard my counselor say. My twenty-one-year-old mind walked my nine-year-old body to the plate. God, it felt good to have a bat in my hand. I took off my hat, looked at the camp logo on the front, smiled, replaced it, and stepped into the batter's box. I peered down the line of my shoulder right into the gaze of nine-year-old Danny Benson. Danny was a very good athlete. He starred on his high school basketball and soccer teams and had played on both the first two years at college. Now here I was on the receiving end of his pitches.

I had the advantage. My nine-year-old self had been scared to be hit by a pitch. Nine-year-old Danny would have easily struck out nine-year-old Franklin. Twenty-one-year-old Franklin was smiling knowing that no matter how hard Danny threw it wasn't going to be all that fast. If he hit me with the ball, it wouldn't hurt nearly as much as I had feared it would twelve years ago.

His first pitch was in the dirt in front of the plate. Danny glared and pounded his mitt. His next pitch was closer but still a ball. Again a glare, again the pounding of the mitt. I decided I'd take the next pitch no matter what he offered. Danny threw one right down the middle of the plate. As I had watched him do earlier, sure enough, he spun like a top after the counselor acting as the umpire called it a strike.

The next pitch was another one right over the plate. I swung as hard as I ever recall swinging and made exquisite contact. That ball rocketed off my bat and soared into left field, far over the left fielder's head. I flew around the bases, completing the home run with time to spare. The return throw reached the catcher after my teammates were already embracing me. I stole a look back at Danny. His head was down as he pounded his glove relentlessly.

Three outs later I trotted out into the field as Danny's team took its turn at-bat. Instinctively I ran to play second base, my usual position. I was euphoric. Baseball at summer camp! I put my hands on my knees and awaited the first pitch from Jeff, our pitcher. Sure enough, the batter hit the ball right at me. While nine-year-old Franklin the batter was in constant fear of being struck by the hardball, nine-year-old Franklin the fielder was deft with the glove. I easily stopped and cradled the ball and made the play at first base for the out. My teammates were all hooting and hollering as the hero of our first at-bat also converted the first out. Never in my years of baseball had I ever excelled in both the top and bottom halves of the inning. If I had only known then what I know now.

With every play, I awaited my return to my present time. How long would this last? Long enough for me to get up to bat two more times. As I did in the first inning, I let Danny throw a few pitches. All three were balls, and each one was followed by a glare and the ritual pounding of the glove. Even though his fourth pitch would have likely been called a ball, I wasn't going to pass up the chance to swing. Exactly as before I crushed the pitch, easily rounding third and reaching home well before the ball returned to the infield. My third at-bat mirrored the first two. Three times at the plate, three long home runs.

What a gift this was to recall the sheer joy of playing ball with friends. I loved being nine.

We were now in the fourth inning, and I was back at my second base position. Jeff looked over at me, gave me a nod as if to confirm how much fun we were having, then turned and threw to the batter. With the sound of the ball and bat making contact, I felt the shift and the rotation of scenes occurred. I returned to a vista of blonde hair and concerned eyes.

"Franklin, are you all right?" Joanna was asking, her mouth half-open in anticipation of my first words confirming my healthy return from wherever I had been.

"Wow!" was how I responded.

"Wow?" Joanna asked, her lips back together indicating that her anxiety had receded now that she was certain I was fine.

"I was at summer camp playing baseball. It was so great!"

"So you were having a dream? Is that what happens to you?"

"No, Joanna, it's not like that. I return to something that happened in my past. It's not a dream; it's real." Then it occurred to me. Here was an opportunity to confirm that what I just told Joanna was correct.

"Joanna, I have to go see Danny Benson, and I need you to come with me. Do you have time?" It was imperative that Joanna understand that what she referred to as dreams were anything but.

"Of course," she graciously responded.

Danny's apartment abutted the west edge of campus. Joanna and I were only minutes away. As we made the short walk I explained to Joanna why this visit was so important.

"As I told you, I was at summer camp. My camp was playing Danny's summer camp in what we used to call inter-camp games. Danny was the pitcher on the opposing team. I got to bat against him." I told her about his idiosyncrasies during balls and strikes, and about my three home runs. I thought there was a good chance Danny would remember that game. Athletes of all ages recall their losses and mistakes far more than their great plays and victories. Danny would remember giving up three home runs to the same guy.

I knocked on his door, hoping we would find him home. In less than a minute, there he was.

"Hey, Franklin, Joanna, come on in. What are you two doing here?"

Joanna answered for us. "Franklin has a question for you."

"Sure," Danny replied, motioning us into his living room that lay just inside the front door. Danny shared the small three-bedroom apartment with our friends Simon and Jay. Since the apartment was quite compact, someone in the living room would be easily heard by everyone in the place no matter their location. Simon was home, heard the voices, and joined us.

"Hi Simon," I said. Simon was another fraternity brother. All agreed that he was the most academically gifted of our friends. The joke was that he would be the most likely to win a Nobel Prize unless he was distracted by a good-looking girl or the opportunity to go fishing.

"Hey, Franklin." Simon greeted me quickly, then immediately turned to Joanna. "Joanna, always glad to see you," he said with his endearing smile. I was always surprised that Simon had not tried to date Joanna. My guess is he would have if he had not fallen head over heels with one Ellen Shaker. My infatuation with Joanna paled in intensity compared with the emotional drudging Simon experienced daily from his desire to live forever with Ellen.

I directed my words to Danny. "First of all, sorry I took off the other day with my friend Govinda."

"No big deal," he responded with a shrug.

"Danny, I don't think you and Simon know what's been going on with me lately. This is going to sound very, very strange. And I am sure you guys are going to make fun of me." I was sure because that is what we did constantly to each other. Our deep friendship was manifested in sophomoric put-downs and insults.

"Beginning about a month or so ago, I started experiencing what I can only describe as visions. But they are more than visions." I paused and took a deep breath, having decided to just dive into the story. "I am traveling—I am going back in time." Silence greeted my admission. Simon eventually spoke first.

"Franklin, Danny and I already know that. Henry told us a couple of weeks ago."

I should have anticipated that. We were all so close that now that I thought about it I would have been surprised if Henry hadn't told them, if for no other reason than to share the burden.

Simon then added, "But we told him we didn't believe you, and that he shouldn't believe you, either." Simon looked over at Danny, who immediately nodded his confirmation. "We think you've been secretly taking some of J Bob's pills." Danny again nodded agreement, and then added, "And we think it stinks that you have not been sharing."

"Yeah," Simon joined in, "What's with that? Don't friends share?" he asked rhetorically, again looking at Danny for agreement.

"Absolutely," Danny added, including yet another nod as a flourish.

Normally, I would join the game, allow myself to be made fun of and insulted. It wasn't that I was feeling sensitive; we didn't do sensitive in this group of friends. I needed them to know that I was serious and that this was real.

I turned back to Danny. "You pitched on your camp baseball team, right?"

Danny was surprised by the sudden turn of questioning. "Yeah, I did. How did you know?"

"I just hit three home runs off of you this afternoon," I said. Danny and Simon looked at each other, trying to understand where I was going with this.

"Well," Danny replied," you didn't hit a home run off of me today because I did not play baseball today. Plus you would never be able to hit a home run off me anyway," he laughed, winking at Simon.

"When you were the pitcher on your camp team, you had some habits. If you threw a ball, you'd stare at the catcher and then pound your mitt. If you threw a strike, you would spin around the mound in celebration," I stated with certainty.

Danny's expression changed instantly. "How did you know that?"

"Do you remember an inter-camp game you pitched in when you were nine where the first batter hit a lead-off home run?" I wasn't quite sure that would be enough to jog his memory.

"I do. It only happened once in all the years I pitched at camp," he answered.

"And do you remember what that batter did after that?" I asked.

"Yup. He hit two more just like the first. I never gave up three home runs to the same kid, never before that and never after."

more question. Do you remember what position that kid played?"

yeah. Second base. I had to look at him all game."

"Joanna, can you tell them what happened at lunch today? And what I told you?"

"Franklin seemed to be in a trance or dream," she began. "I couldn't get him to wake up for a while. When he finally did wake up, he told me he was back at camp as a nine-year-old. He was playing a baseball game against Danny's camp." She stopped and looked directly at Danny. "He told me you used to pound your mitt when you threw a ball and dance around the mound when you threw a strike. Then he told me he hit three home runs off of you. Oh, and he said he played second base."

No one uttered a sound; no one moved a muscle. Danny had seen a ghost. Simon was staring at Danny hoping he would deny what was obvious.

"Holy shit" were the next words out of Danny's mouth. The same followed from Simon's. Joanna, already convinced, came over and hugged me.

No one said a word as each of us contemplated the significance of what had just become apparent. Although all eyes were on me, it was Joanna who broke the silence.

"So now what?" she asked.

19

Moving On

Now what? Joanna's words hung around my neck. Like the stock market in volatile times, I was up one day, down the next, uncertainty at the root of both.

I found myself walking the campus with no specific destination, but the magnetic field drew me, as always, towards the Memorial. As I passed by, my head involuntarily turned towards the glass bookstore doors, hoping a woman with lovely red hair—in a bun or set free—would cross my line of sight, see me, smile, and flash her miraculous green eyes my way. Same place at a different time and they would have.

Graduation was only weeks away. I had nothing; nowhere to go, no job, no plan. Danny and Simon were going on to medical school. Henry had been accepted to a graduate program in psychology. Joanna was deciding between an offer to join a large corporation in a management training program or to follow her real desire, design. Months ago Henry had sat with me over a beer. "Franklin, you have to figure out what you're going to do," he warned. "We are going to be graduating before you know it. What are you thinking?"

Even then, before the visions and time travel had taken hold of my life, I was paralyzed by what might have appeared to others to be disinterest. My apparent absence of initiative, however, was not lack of desire, nor was it malaise or laziness. As has occurred at other times in my life, there was the familiar, silent voice, this time imploring me to wait, to be patient, and to remain uncommitted. Looking back it was probably part of the prodrome that Professor Niemeyer had described.

"So now graduation looms, a love has vanished, my mentor is gone, and I have pretty much nothing," I said out loud as I turned my back on the Memorial and headed towards no place in particular. I started to laugh at how ridiculous my situation had become. I sat down on a bench across from the library. Better than crying, I thought.

"C'mon Franklin, think," I said, again out loud.

When I was young my dad once told me that I should always look for the silver lining in any cloud. His words had not been necessary. It was my nature to instinctively always do so. Rather than being a sign of a positive psyche, my optimism most likely was the result of a persistent discomfort with anything sad or negative. Henry once said that he could not recall me ever being down for an entire day. "I can't imagine why anyone would stay that way for long," I told him. "What's the point?"

Today was no different. All that was required was to flip the situation from north to south, to radically change the perspective. I didn't have nothing; I likely already had everything I needed. I had Professor Niemeyer's tape. I had the book. School was over; I now had time. I must be patient, I decided.

Patient. That word reminded me of Lori. "You must learn patience," she had urged me. Lori had also surmised that I was at the beginning of my journey. If that were true, then everything was in front of me. Where would I go and what would I be doing? Whom would I meet? I leaned back, closed my eyes to think through these questions, and the world moved.

◆◇◆◇◆

"Hey, throw it to me!" I heard myself ask, but it was not my brain that had generated the question, and the voice I heard was that of a child, not mine. A tall boy with black hair turned to me. He had a baseball glove on his left hand. His right hand cradled the baseball.

"You want me to throw it to you, Franklin? You can't catch. Why would I throw it to you?" he asked dismissively. Another boy of about the same size answered for me.

"Throw it to him, Jesse. Let's see if he can."

"You think so? OK, let's see him catch this," Jesse said menacingly, and with that, I watched him rear back and fire the ball at my head. I had no time to move. The ball struck my left temple. The pain was searing and I fell to the ground.

"Nice catch, Franklin," I heard the boy named Jesse say mockingly and watched as he turned to the other boy, the two of them now laughing.

I looked around. I was on a field of grass. Kids were playing kickball to my left. A group of girls was sitting on the grass across from me. One of them stood up. "Jesse, that was mean!" she screamed. She walked towards me.

"Franklin, are you OK?" she asked, now standing over me. She looked familiar. I knew her, but I could not recall her name. I looked behind me over my shoulder and saw my elementary school. I was in the schoolyard in front of the school. Judging by the number of kids and the time of day, it must be recess.

"Yes, I'm OK," I answered the girl, with the same prepubescent voice I had already been surprised to hear.

"Don't play with Jesse," she said. "He is always mean to everyone." She turned to the other girls. "Isn't he always mean?" she asked them. All three nodded their heads. "Are you going to tell Ms. Callaway?" she then asked me.

Ms. Callaway was my second-grade teacher. That would mean I was seven years old. Why am I here? I looked up at the girl. "No."

"You should, you know. Otherwise, Jesse will just keep doing it to you," she stated quite authoritatively. I remembered the girls were always more mature than the boys. Although we were both seven, at the moment she was the adult and I the child.

I got up and instinctively walked towards Jesse. As a young boy, I was perpetually frightened. Everyone was bigger than me, including most of the girls. I would never pick a fight and instead did all I could to avoid ending up in one. But this situation was different. Maybe my voice was that of a seven-year-old, but my brain was twenty-one. I had no plan to run anywhere.

"It's OK; I know you're sorry," I said to Jesse intentionally loud enough so all of the other kids who were now intently focused on the two of us could hear.

"I'm sorry?" Jesse asked, moving closer to me.

I contemplated my move. I could simultaneously grab his shirt and kick his legs out from under him. I would have him on the ground in a second, pin his arms with my knees, and grab his throat. But I didn't. Instead, I got even closer so only he could hear what I whispered into his ear.

"Yes, just say you're sorry. I know that you think no one likes you, Jesse, but you're wrong. Everyone wants to like you. They think you're smart and they don't understand why you're mean. You don't have to be mean. The whole class will like you more if you're not. Even Ms. Callaway will like you more. She will be nicer to you. So if you apologize to me now with everyone watching, they will all want to be your friend. I promise. Try it."

Jesse looked at me and whispered back, "Are you sure?"

"Yes, I'm sure. If I'm wrong I'll let you beat me up."

Jesse laughed. He stepped back. He held out his hand to shake mine. "Franklin," he said, his eyes confirming his sincerity, "I'm sorry I threw the ball at you."

"It's OK, Jesse. We're still friends," I answered, and we shook. I looked around. Our classmates were awestruck.

"Jesse, that was so nice!" the girl who had talked to me said. The others chimed in one by one. "That was so nice!" By now they were surrounding him. "See, I told you Jesse could be nice," a tall thin girl said to her friend. My confrontation with Jesse had drawn a crowd. The kickball game had paused to watch.

A man in a shirt and tie approached us. "What's going on?" he asked us.

"Jesse threw a ball at Franklin and they almost got into a fight but Jesse said he was sorry and now they're friends, Mr. Goodson," one of the girls blurted out in a single breath.

"Is that right, Jesse?"

"Yes, Mr. Goodson," Jesse answered, looking at the ground.

"He didn't mean to," I chimed in. "We were just having a catch. It didn't even hurt," I added, trying to mimic seven-year-old diction. I saw Jesse raise his eyes and smile at me.

"OK, have fun and be careful," Mr. Goodson said, then turned and walked back towards the school.

Kickball resumed; the group of girls picked up where they left off. Jesse looked at me. "Thanks, Franklin. Mr. Goodson is always yelling at me for something."

"He won't anymore, Jesse. You're a good kid, and you don't have to get into trouble to get anyone's attention." Jesse's face changed. I realized that those words sounded too adult. "Let's be friends, OK?" I added.

"OK," Jesse said. Once again the set shifted.

I opened my eyes. I was back on the bench, the library in my line of sight. No longer was I surprised or frightened by my hopping through time. So far at least I still landed back where I started. Instead, I was fascinated by these events. Why had I gone back to second grade? Why had I almost gotten into a fight?

"Recognize your powers." Govinda's words filled me. "People will listen to you."

"You don't get a magical mentor if you're nobody. You don't get to travel around time if you're nobody. People don't respond to you, people like Govinda, or even me, like they do, if you're nobody," Lori's words replaced those of Govinda.

I filled my lungs. People will listen to you. Well, at least seven-year-olds will, I thought. Govinda has assured me that in his dreams one day their parents would as well.

◆◇◆◇◆

FRANKLIN AND I SPENT THE ENTIRE DAY before graduation meandering around the campus. As we passed each landmark some apropos story arose from one us.

"How deep was that massive snow we had during our sophomore year?" Franklin asked me.

"All I know is that I was looking up at the top of the snowbanks crossing between Humanities and Social Sciences," I answered. "Do you remember where we were the first time we saw those enormous snow-eater trucks?"

"I do," Franklin answered. "We had walked a mile at midnight to get those nasty hot dogs with the chile and onions on top."

As we approached our fraternity house, I assumed we both experienced the same melancholy.

"Sad," I said.

"Don't look at it like that," Franklin responded.

So much for melancholy. I should have known better.

"Just think of what came out of those years. Remember mopping that filthy floor as freshmen? That seems like so long ago, doesn't it? We had so much fun, Henry. So many great people."

"You're right. It was great. But nothing lasts forever, I guess," I added. Franklin looked at me.

"You know, Henry, that's what people say but it's incorrect," he responded, his eyes checking to be certain that I understood. Franklin was referencing his favorite topic, how every moment of time lives on forever. It was his mantra. I'm not sure I have ever gotten as comfortable as Franklin with that concept, but for the sake of our friendship, I nodded.

We eventually arrived at the entrance to Johnson's Gardens. I paused at the gates for Franklin to make his usual assessment, but this time he did not stop.

"Aren't you going to check out the scratches or something?" I asked.

"No, not this time. No need."

"Why no need?"

"Because I was here last night," he responded.

"What do you mean you were here last night?" I pressed him. "You were with me last night, and I would know if I had been here."

"Well, it was last night when I got here, but I'm not sure when it was from where I left."

"You time-traveled here? When was that?"

"I'm not sure. I don't pay too much attention to the order of things anymore, Henry. Seems that it's not all that important."

We continued into the gardens. It was a perfect spring day, a few scattered cumulus clouds above dotting an otherwise Rocky Mountain-quality blue sky.

"Let's sit, Henry."

We did, and talked about the time as freshmen a kid named Thomas got on a plastic make-shift flotation device and, following torrential rains, rode the babbling brook-turned-river through the gardens and into the drainage tunnel that was submerged under the street. We thought he had drowned when he didn't reappear for many minutes and were all stunned when he miraculously appeared in front of our dorm, completely drenched but with a huge smile on his face. That day was followed by a plethora of memorable college experiences.

"Hi, boys." We simultaneously turned towards the voice.

"Joanna! Do you have time to sit with us?" Franklin asked.

"Of course!" she replied, then added what I was also thinking, "Who knows when we will be here together again."

"You know what I am going to say," Franklin said with a smile.

"Yes, Franklin, we know," I immediately replied. We are going to be here together forever, blah blah blah."

"OK, make fun of me Henry, but you will find that thought very comforting in the future," Franklin added as if he had already seen that moment when I would.

"One more day. I can't believe it," Joanna said, changing the subject. "I'm getting very sad. I'm going to miss you both."

"Don't get him started," Franklin responded looking over at me. "He has been nostalgic for a week now. I keep telling him this is the beginning, not the end. Plus, just think Henry, you will finally be free from your valedictorian-consumed neurosis."

Though Franklin was kidding, his words hit home. I had thought about how much time I had devoted to studying. Becoming valedictorian was a source of great pride, but a part of me kept reflecting on what Franklin had said to me when I told him I had achieved that status. The thought that he was right, that I had made a bad trade, now especially weighed on me as our college days dwindled.

"Well, Henry, I am very happy for you. It's a great accomplishment. Plus an Ivy League PhD will be something else to be proud of," sweet Joanna told me. I looked at Franklin who just smiled and shrugged.

Two hours later, after we had covered many of the high points of our time together these past four years, we headed out of the Gardens. I looked at my two best friends. Joanna's eyes were moving from side to side as if recording every plant, tree, and flower of our beloved natural treasure. Franklin's eyes were straight ahead as if looking directly into his, and possibly our, future. Joanna and I could feel our college days receding into our past. For Franklin, the past had no special significance. "They are all just moments in time, Henry," he had assured me. Maybe for him, but not for me. This would soon all be just a memory for me and Joanna, and the two of us were savoring every single moment.

"Can you guys come up to my room for a moment?" Franklin asked. "I have something I want to show you."

"I can," I answered. Joanna nodded her consent. We followed Franklin to his dorm and were soon in his room.

"Thanks for coming up," Franklin said as he motioned for us to sit. "You guys remember the night you told me that Professor Niemeyer had died. Henry, you gave me that package that Professor Niemeyer's assistant left for me. The next day when you asked me what was in it I wasn't completely honest."

"I had a feeling that was the case. I decided that you would tell me when you were ready," I said. "So I guess we are here because you are ready."

"I am. It's very important to me that I share this with you two. It will help explain why I haven't made any plans for after graduation. I know you're concerned about that, and I appreciate it. That envelope contained a letter, a tape recording, and a book. Professor Niemeyer..." Franklin paused. Joanna glanced over to me to confirm that I too had noticed the tears in Franklin's eyes. "He wasn't sure I was ready to know what my future was going to be. In the letter he told me to read first he specifically instructed me not to open the large envelope and listen to the tape just yet. But while I was reading the letter I just automatically opened the envelope and the tape fell out. At that point, I decided to listen."

Franklin paused again. Whatever emotion had surfaced upon his mention of Professor Niemeyer was now replaced by the analytical Franklin Rock.

"In his recorded message he explained the book he gave me. I'll show you that in a minute. One very important point he made is that the choices we make are not as important as we think. Joanna, you're struggling to decide whether to take a really impressive job or to go into design. According to Professor Niemeyer, you can't get the choice wrong. I know, it sounds crazy, but I think I understand what he means. There is no way to know ahead of time which choice is the right one, but not for the reason that you think. It's because all the other billions of people on the planet are also making choices, and their choices affect your future. It's impossible to predict which path will work out best. The only thing we can know is that each choice will lead us—and everyone else—down one specific path, which will not necessarily be better or worse than another path, only different."

He looked at each of us in succession, judging whether those words had had any impact.

"So according to Professor Niemeyer that implies that our lives are predetermined, right?" Joanna asked. Of all of us, Joanna was the fastest at distilling the essence of a question or discussion and focusing on its logical consequences.

"I had the same question," Franklin answered, now looking directly at Joanna. "He told me I was not yet ready for that conversation. When I asked him when I would be, he smiled and said, 'Sometime in the future. But the short answer for now, Franklin, is that one would only believe in predestination if there were only a single way for things to work out. Which there isn't.'"

"Oh God, Franklin, between you and the Professor we can never get a simple answer," I told him.

"I know, Henry. When I was with him I just wished he'd give me straightforward answers. Whenever I expressed any frustration at the vagueness of his replies, he looked at me with disappointed eyes. For him, it all seemed so obvious. Lately, as I have thought about all that he taught me, I have been understanding more and more."

Franklin reached behind him and lifted a leather-bound book. The back cover of the book was blank. "This is the book that he left me. You are going to find this strange. I certainly did. It's taken me a while to understand why Professor Niemeyer gave this to me."

Franklin paused yet again. I'm pretty certain he was just checking with himself one more time that sharing this with the two of us was the right thing to do.

"This is hard for me. First I have to tell you that I'm humbled, and I'm afraid I am not worthy of the responsibility it seems I've been given. You two are my best friends. I can't have you thinking I'm an egotistical crazy person. I'm hoping that you won't after I show you this."

Franklin turned the book towards us. Joanna's eyes got wide; she did not utter a sound, just remained transfixed by what she saw. When

I read the title I, unlike Joanna, was only mildly surprised. I had known for a while now that Franklin was different, that he had a calling, that there was something he was supposed to do. I will admit that I had not necessarily expected this magnitude of commitment, but neither was I shocked.

"*The Man Who Fixed the World*," I read aloud. I looked squarely at Franklin. "Does that mean that we can conclude that you didn't screw it up?" I asked him, my smile revealing my motive.

"Well, as Professor Niemeyer said, there is more than one way for things to work out. At least in one iteration of the future, I guess I didn't," he replied.

Joanna was still focused and not ready for banter. "What's inside?" she asked. "Can we see that?" she inquired.

Franklin opened the book to the table of contents. It was blank. No pages were numbered, and the remaining pages of the book were also blank.

"I don't understand," she said.

Franklin explained. "Professor Niemeyer said the chapters would be written in the future. He told me that the number of chapters and what's in them would be decided then."

"But didn't you and he both say that all time already exists, that the future has already happened? How can that be if the pages are blank?" she logically continued.

I watched Franklin carefully. He did not seem upset by what I thought was an excellent question and an obvious paradox.

"I think it's because of what we talked about before. The intersection of all of the choices of all people creates the future, or probably more accurately futures. It gets back to Professor Niemeyer telling me that there is more than one way for things to work out. So honestly I don't know. I am pretty certain that will become clearer to me one day."

"Don't forget to share that with us when you do," Joanna told Franklin. "It still seems to me that there is a conflict here, but I guess we—you—will eventually figure it out. So if you're supposed to fix the world, then I guess you have some things to learn. And graduate school I assume is not where the learning is going to occur," she concluded.

Franklin, who had been standing during his short presentation, now sat down on the edge of his bed, noticeably relieved that he had unburdened himself to us. "So now you understand why I haven't made any plans. I have no idea what I'm supposed to do. I'm going to let it come to me," he said.

After we left Franklin, Joanna and I walked through campus one last time. "Henry," Joanna asked, "how worried are you about Franklin?"

"I would be more worried if it were anyone other than him. He's not like the rest of us, Joanna. Whatever is going on I feel pretty certain he can handle."

"Even without Professor Niemeyer?"

"Did you notice Franklin's response to the news that night when I tried to tell him that Professor Niemeyer had died? It was as if he had anticipated it. I have no idea how since he told me he was unaware that the Professor was even ill. If it were you or me I am sure we would not have been as calm as Franklin. It's as if events are never a surprise to him, as if he knows what's coming. So to answer your question, no Joanna, I'm not worried about him."

"I guess I am a little, Henry," Joanna told me as she looked over my shoulder at the Memorial. "I don't expect it will be easy being Franklin Rock."

PART TWO

Evolution

20

When You Least Expect It

"Let it come to you," Lori had suggested. Well, so far it hadn't. Summer after graduation was filled with hot days, long nights, and great uncertainty. Danny and Simon began medical school, both in Boston. Although at different universities, they had decided it made sense to share an apartment. Simon's father had an old friend who owned an older apartment building in downtown Boston and offered Simon and Danny a large walk-up three-bedroom apartment. Simon called me and asked me if I wanted to share it with them.

"I don't have a job yet," I told him, "so I'm not sure how much rent I will be able to afford."

"It's cheap. You think Danny would pay a lot in rent? I have an idea for you. Why don't you think about getting a job in one of the hospitals here? There are a million in Boston."

Working in a hospital had not been on my radar. Unlike my two friends, a career in medicine had not been something I had ever considered. Still, the opportunity sounded appealing; I had nowhere special to go and nothing special to do. If the plan was to let it come to me, a hospital seemed as good a place as any.

Armed with my newly minted college degree, I trudged to several of the renowned Boston hospitals. I made no headway at the first two; my lack of experience in anything was an issue. My third visit was, as they say, the charm.

"Can I help you?" the woman behind the desk inquired.

"Yes, ma'am," I replied. "I am interested in a job in your hospital."

She reached behind her and grabbed a clipboard with a pen on a string that made a semi-circular flight as she whipped back in her chair to face me.

"Fill this out and return it to me when you're done," she said, pointing to the row of plastic chairs indicating where I was to complete the task, and she went back to whatever it was she was doing before I had interrupted her.

The application was pretty straightforward. Mostly demographic information was requested, plus a place to list previous employers with the pertinent details. That wouldn't take me long; I had had no previous job, only summer employment. When I got to the education section, I felt far more confident. At least here I had something of value, or so I thought at the time.

With little to write about, I handed back the form in five minutes. I stood and waited for additional instructions.

"Yes?" she asked, looking up from her desk.

"Excuse me, but what happens now?"

"Now, you leave, and we take a look at your application and let you know if we have anything for you."

"How will I know?" I persisted.

"We will call you."

"I don't have a phone right now."

Another look of disdain followed. "Well, if you want you can come back on Wednesday."

"What time?"

Her phone rang. She picked it up with her left hand and held up her right index finger indicating I should wait while she took the call.

"Really?" I heard her say. "I'm sorry to hear that. He's such a nice man." She paused to listen, then added, "Sure, I'll let you know when we do."

"Sorry, what was your question?" she asked, turning back to me.

"What time should I come on Wednesday?" I repeated.

"What kind of job are you looking for? Are you a nurse?"

"No, ma'am, I'm not. I just graduated from college. I don't have any hospital experience."

"Well, you may be in luck. That phone call was about one of our long-time orderlies leaving us. He's an older gentleman and just found out he could no longer work. Very nice man. So as of this minute we have an opening. Would you be interested in that type of work?" she asked, now far more attentive than she had been.

"I don't know what an orderly does," I admitted.

"It's an assistant nursing position. You would help the nurses care for the patients. You don't need any experience; the nurses will teach you what you need to know."

Let it come to you. "Yes, ma'am, I would very much like the job. Thank you."

Together we reviewed the salary, the hours, and she seemed quite pleased to add that the job included health insurance. I would have to join the union and pay union dues. She then handed me a packet of materials to review and more forms to fill out. Once again she pointed to the chairs. "You might as well do them now if you have time. It will make it easier when you start next Monday."

"Great!" Simon said when I told him that I was now employed and could pay the rent. Over the next few days, I moved in and got organized. It rapidly became clear that my roommates would not be around much. Between classes, labs, and the library, I rarely saw them that first week; this pattern was to continue.

Monday morning I headed out early with absolutely no concept of what was in store. Probably exactly as it should be, I thought, a metaphor for my life during the past months. After the requisite stop at the employment office, I soon found myself on the third floor of the hospital being introduced to the woman who would be my supervisor.

"Welcome to 3 South, Franklin. I'm Ann Forman, the head nurse. This is my domain," she told me while sweeping her hand in a grand gesture of ownership. "If you have any questions or problems please bring them to me. I have assigned Nancy, one of our nurses, to train you. You'll be working directly with her for the next couple of weeks. You just graduated from college, I hear."

"Yes," I answered with a proud smile.

"It's not likely that much you learned there will come in handy here. But don't worry; we will teach you everything you need to know. So let's see if we can find Nancy and I will introduce you." I followed her from the main nursing station down the hall. We passed by a dozen patient rooms. Several doors were ajar and I could catch a glimpse of the interiors. Here was a world with which I realized I was completely unfamiliar. A mild wave of anxiety briefly flowed over me. I took a deep breath.

"Franklin, this is Nancy Sturdivant. Nancy is a registered nurse—one of our best," she added sending a big grin Nancy's way. "She's going to teach you everything you need to know."

"Hi Franklin, nice to meet you," Nancy said, then looked down at her hands. "You probably don't want to shake my hand right now," she added with a smile.

Nancy Sturdivant had shoulder-length brown hair and matching kind brown eyes. My first impression was that she was gentle, exactly what someone would want in a nurse.

"I will leave you two then," Nurse Forman said, then headed back to the nurse's station.

"I'm going to assume you know nothing about being an orderly, Franklin. Am I right?"

"You are. I have only been in a hospital once I think. My aunt was ill and we went to see her. I don't think it's possible to know less than I do," I admitted.

"That's fine. You made it through college. Nothing you are going to do here is that hard. I'll teach you everything. Don't worry. First thing I'm going to show you is how to make a bed. Then I'll show you how to help the male patients dress. We will be going into Mr. Roosevelt's room first. He's my favorite patient now. Wonderful man. Oh, one more thing. I assume you've never changed a bedpan?"

Bedpan? Oh my God. I had not thought of that. I took a deep breath.

"No. I can honestly say I never have, but I'm guessing I will be doing it a lot?" I answered, not anxious to hear what I was certain would be her response.

Nancy returned my smile. "Yes, you will. But you will get used to it. Here's a tip you should keep in mind. Don't think about the bedpan. Think about the person you are helping. As my grandmother told me when I said I was going to be a nurse, always remember they are all God's children. That is in my mind at least once a day. It helps."

"All God's children. Got it," I replied, as I felt those words penetrate deep into me and take up permanent residence.

Week followed week as I performed my limited and routine duties. Nancy, as promised, taught me what I needed to know. The work was humbling. Each morning she and I would get our list of patients. While she recorded—charted, she called it—each patient's vital signs, weight, urinary output, and checked intravenous lines and medications, I did the dirty work. I learned how to change sheets while a patient too ill to sit or stand remained in bed. I learned the correct way to lift patients, to help them in and out of chairs, and to get them in and out of the bathroom. I learned how to bathe the male patients. And as anticipated, I changed and cleaned a pile of bedpans. Each time a chore was about to overcome me either because of a smell—that happened frequently—or the pitiful situation of a patient, I recalled Nancy's words. "All God's children" appeared in my mind as needed, like an antidote to a poison. Those words reminded me that I was there for a reason and that my menial tasks were anything but to those in need.

"Franklin, we got a new patient last night. His name is Maurice Burnside. He's eighty-two. He has lung cancer and congestive heart failure. They admitted him to tuneup his congestive heart failure. Seems there is nothing to do for his lung cancer. On top of all of that his wife of sixty years passed away just last month. Do me a favor and go check on him."

He was lying quietly in his bed when I entered the room.

"Mr. Burnside?" I inquired as I walked towards him.

"Yes, son, that's me," he answered, a big smile accompanied his words.

That smile struck me. He's sick, has terminal lung cancer, and just lost his wife. Yet he's smiling as if I just told him he was cured and could go home and live another twenty years.

"I'm Franklin Rock. How are you feeling?"

"I'd say for an old guy I'm doing just fine. This thing in my nose isn't the most comfortable, but I guess I need the oxygen."

"Let me see if I can fix it for you." I walked to the side of his bed. The tubing was stretched tight and was pulling up on his nose. In a few seconds, I had it adjusted. "Better?" I asked.

"Yes, much. Thank you. What was your name again?"

"Franklin Rock. I am the orderly on this floor, so if you need help I'm your guy," I told him.

"Can't think of anything else I need just now. But if *you* need anything you can ask me," he said with a wink.

"I'll be back later to check on you. You call if you need anything."

"I do appreciate that," he said with a nod. "Maybe you and I can talk later," he added.

"Sure thing. I've got some other patients to take care of but I will definitely stop by later," I said and then exited his room. Nice man, I said to myself.

As so often happened the day got away from me. The end of my shift was fast approaching. Nancy and I ran into each other at the main nursing area.

"So how was your day, Franklin? Any problems?"

"No, just the usual stuff."

"Thanks for checking on Mr. Burnside this morning. He thought you were very nice."

Mr. Burnside! I had promised to go back and talk with him, and here it was already the end of the day. "Thanks for reminding me," I told her. "I had promised him I'd see him again today but I've been so busy."

"Don't worry, Franklin. He's doing well. I was in his room just a short time ago. Tomorrow's fine," she assured me.

But tomorrow wasn't fine with me. I had promised him I'd be back. "I'm just going to stop in for a minute and say goodnight," I told her, then headed up the hallway to his room. I knocked on the partially closed door.

"Mr. Burnside?" I said as I slowly entered the room.

"Hey there, young man. I thought you had forgotten about me," he said with the same smile I had seen earlier.

"I'm sorry. I've just been very busy. How are you feeling?"

"Me? For an old man pretty damn good. And you? You look a bit tired I'd say," he said after giving me a full once over.

"Oh, I'm OK. Is there anything I can do for you?" I asked.

"If you've got time, we could talk a bit. Were you getting ready to go home?"

I had been preparing to leave, but the way he asked struck me. He wanted to talk.

"No, I'm not in a hurry. I can talk for a few minutes," I told him. He motioned for me to sit in the chair under the TV that was hanging from the ceiling.

"Franklin, that's your name, right?"

"Yes, Mr. Burnside."

"And what's your last name?"

"Rock. Franklin Rock."

Mr. Burnside sat up just a little taller in his bed. "I've heard that name somewhere. Was your dad or grandad the same name?" he asked.

"No, I'm the first in my family with the name Franklin. Why do you ask?"

He scrunched up his face. "Hmm. That name is surely familiar." I could tell he was actively searching his memory.

I tried to start up the conversation. "Mr. Burnside, what kind of work did you do?"

"Worked as an electrician for most of my life. When I was your age—how old are you, twenty?"

"Twenty-one."

"Well, close enough," he laughed. "Anyway, when I was about fifteen I apprenticed with a fella who knew my dad. John Davidson was his name. Nice man. He got me started. By the time I was your age, I was already a licensed electrician. Mostly did new home construction. I'll tell you, that's the way to go if you're an electrician. Nobody else's mess to fix. You'd be surprised how many electricians have no idea what they are doing. I'd sometimes go into a friend's house who was having a problem. Man, nothing matched. Wrong color wires, wrong size fuses, just a mess. New construction, you don't have those problems. It's the way to go."

"So when did you retire?" I asked.

"Well, let's see. I'm eighty-two now. Been retired going on ten years. So I was seventy-one, seventy-two, around there. Had to retire. Kept getting short of breath when I was working. Cigarettes. You don't smoke, I hope?"

"No, sir."

"Good for you. Terrible, those cigarettes. Course when I was a kid everyone smoked. Couldn't watch a movie without all the stars holding a cigarette. They were everywhere. We didn't know. So here I am with heart troubles, all 'cause of those things. Cancer sticks. That's why I also have lung cancer. Nothing I can do about it now."

"I'm sorry to hear that." I wasn't sure what else to say.

"Oh, that's OK. I'm just thinking about the wrong things. That's the mistake people make. Thinking about the wrong things."

Now he had my attention. "What do you mean, thinking about the wrong things?"

"Look, I've got heart failure, and lung cancer, and who knows what else? I keep telling the doctors to stop looking or they'll find some other problem," he laughed again. "Don't know if they told you but I just lost my wife. I miss her. When you're with someone for so long you miss them even if you spent half your life trying to hide so she wouldn't make you fix something." Another laugh. "Hell, that's life. Everyone dies. Well, sort of."

"Sort of?" I could suddenly see Professor Niemeyer in the bed instead of Mr. Burnside.

"Sure. You know all those times we had are always right here," he said, pointing to his head.

"You mean the memories," I clarified.

"Yeah, the memories." He paused. "Sometimes I have the feeling that all of those times are still going on somewhere; we're just not there to see them. You think that's possible?"

"You know, I do. You're the first person to ever say that to me, except for Professor Niemeyer."

"Did you say Professor Niemeyer? Would that be Charles Niemeyer?"

The question stunned me. "You know Professor Charles Niemeyer?" I asked incredulously.

"If it's the same one. He teaches at one of those colleges in New York state."

"Taught," I corrected him. "He passed away a few months ago."

"No. Well, I'm sorry to hear that. Great man, Charles Niemeyer."

"But you live in Boston. How is it that you knew him?"

"I've only been in Boston for a few years. My daughter lives here and since my wife and I were getting older, she wanted us closer. So sold the house and moved here. I did a lot of work for the Professor over the years. Sorry to hear he's gone."

"Me, too." My words escaped without thought.

"Good teacher I'll bet."

"Great teacher, plus he became a mentor to me."

"Well son, you couldn't have had a better one. We learned a lot from each other," Mr. Burnside added. "I taught him about wiring, and he taught me about some very interesting things."

"What kind of interesting things?" I asked, my curiosity now piqued.

"Well for one thing, when I told him once that I had this feeling that all the stuff in the past was still going on somewhere, like I just told you, he explained why my feeling wasn't so crazy. Told me some wild stuff about time and how it worked. I hope he's right. I like to think Betsy and me are still together."

I checked my watch. Danny, Simon, and I were going to meet some of their medical school friends for dinner tonight. "Mr. Burnside, I have to go now. But can we continue this tomorrow?"

"Oh, sorry Franklin, here I am chewing your ear off and making you late. I'll be here tomorrow. I'm not going anywhere!"

We said our goodbyes and I left the hospital. My mind was racing as I walked home. Professor Niemeyer! What were the chances I would have a patient who knew him? *Let it come to you.* Looks like it just did.

21

Future in the Past

"So how's the job?" Simon asked me on the way to dinner.

"Humbling. But I like it a lot more than I thought I would," I told him.

"I hear you're the bedpan king," Danny chimed in. "They've got the right guy for the job."

During dinner with Danny and Simon and their friends, I could not stop thinking about Mr. Burnside. What an amazing man. *I've been thinking about the wrong things.* Most of us would dwell on our loss, our disease, and fear our inevitable demise. Yet here was a man from whom a smile did not seem removable.

I arrived at the hospital early the next morning and headed straight to Mr. Burnside's room. I knocked, and hearing no response I slowly opened his door and quietly entered. His bed was empty. I turned towards the bathroom. That door was open; no one was inside. My heart began racing as I helplessly feared the worst. My anxiety was rising rapidly when I heard his voice from behind.

"Hey, Franklin, good morning! Nice to see you, son."

I whipped around. There he was in a wheelchair, the candy striper volunteer wheeling him into the room. "Mr. Burnside. Where were you?"

"They took me down for an X-ray pretty early to see how my lungs are doing. I was awake, they asked me if I wanted to get it over with, and I said sure, why not?"

My heart rate and blood pressure were again approaching normal. "It's so good to see you, Mr. Burnside!"

"Well, it's good to see you, too, Franklin. That's quite a greeting. Did you think I was dead?" he said with a laugh.

My silence was my reply.

"Don't worry, son, I'm not going anywhere just yet. Have time to talk?"

"I have to get to work now, but I have an idea if it's OK with you. How about if we have lunch together and we can talk then? They usually bring your lunch around noon, is that right?"

"If you say so. You know when you're in the hospital you kinda lose track of time."

"I'm pretty sure that's right, but I'll check with the dietary team. And I'll make sure they bring you something good."

"If they do, Franklin, that will be the first time," he laughed.

"You know what? How about if I change your bed while I'm here? You OK in the wheelchair for a few minutes?" I asked.

"Oh, sure. The doc told me last evening after you left that my heart was doing better and I should try to sit up more and take short walks."

"I have another idea, then. How about I take you over to the solarium for lunch? It's a nice sunny day and we can eat together there."

"Franklin, that is real nice of you. I look forward to it."

I finished his bed, waved, and left. The morning flew by as I attended to my other patients. Nancy was fine with my plan to have lunch in the solarium with Mr. Burnside.

"You seem to have developed a friendship with him," she said.

"He is an amazing man. His attitude is something. When I told him I was sorry about his cancer you know what he said? 'Oh, that's OK, I'm just thinking about the wrong things.'"

"I'm not surprised. If we're willing to listen, these patients will teach us a lot. Sometimes they will break your heart. It can be so sad to see these people in pain. And to watch the grief on the faces of their families is sometimes just incredibly difficult. But then you see their gratitude, and you know you at least made it a little better." She paused. "I love this job."

I was beginning to love it, too.

Noon arrived and I hurried over to Mr. Burnside's room.

"Lunchtime already?" he asked as I entered.

"It is. Are you ready?"

"They haven't brought me any lunch yet," he said.

"It's already in the solarium. We had them bring it there," I assured him.

"Well then, let's go!"

The 3 South solarium was located on the west side of the building. Overhead the sun was shining, so the room was warm and bright.

"How's this?" I asked him.

Mr. Burnside looked around, his eyes settling on the sunlit trees visible through the wall of windows overlooking the hospital grounds. Then he turned to me.

"Beautiful. I miss walking outdoors."

"Soon enough, Mr. Burnside. We will have you healthy and out of here in a couple of days for sure," I replied. "For sure."

"I hope you're right, Franklin. I was wondering, do you happen to know what happened to Charles?"

"You mean Professor Niemeyer?"

"I called him Charles. He insisted. When I tried to call him Professor, he would tell me that I taught him at least as much as he taught me, so unless I wanted him to call me Professor Burnside, I had to call him Charles. I liked the idea of being called Professor Burnside," he added with a smile. "How did he die?"

"I don't know. I didn't even know he had been ill. I'm embarrassed to say I didn't know much about his life."

"Come to think of it I guess I didn't either. He didn't say a lot. I met his wife when I was doing some work in the house. Very nice lady. I don't think they had any children," he told me.

"You did electrical work for them?" I asked.

"Oh yeah, lots. I'd go in and add some outlets, lights, that sort of thing. I remember once Charles wanted more light in his office. Beautiful room, walls of built-in bookcases, looked like a real library. He spent a lot of time in there and told me he was tired of squinting in the evening 'cause the lighting was so bad." He paused, then his face lit up.

"Book! It was a book. That's why I recognized your name. Someone wrote a book about a Franklin Rock. I was moving books off of one of the shelves so I could run a line for some lights. I remember because when I moved it, Charles saw it and came to pick it off the pile. He didn't touch any of the others. I remember asking him who Franklin Rock was and what the book was about."

"What did he tell you?" I asked excitedly.

"Don't remember him saying anything. He just took it and left the room. Never mentioned it again. Was it about someone in your family? Or maybe it's just a coincidence. I'll bet there's lots of Franklin Rocks. There sure are a pile of Maurice Burnsides, I'll tell you that. Who would have thought?"

For the rest of our lunch, he told me about his family, the town he grew up in, and stories of how they had to deal with racial discrimination. I was struck by the fact that he was not the least bit bitter. I asked him about that.

"Franklin, we are all born into what we are born into. Can't do much about that. We were poor, that's for sure. But luckily we were never hungry, and I think if you're lucky enough not to be hungry the rest kind of works itself out. Just gotta work hard and make something of your life, no matter what. That's the thing. Work hard and make something of your life."

And think about the right things.

◆◇◆◇◆

THAT NIGHT I WAS LYING IN BED reflecting on our conversation. How little I knew of what people have endured in their lives. My family wasn't rich, but we always had what we needed. Our house was small, but it's only now that I even recognize that. I had friends who were rich and lived in very large houses, but I never recall feeling envious. Maybe that's what Mr. Burnside meant. "We are all born into what we are born into." Made a lot of sense. My mind began to drift, and then I felt the shift.

I looked around. I was in someone's home. To my left I heard voices; I followed the trail of the sound. In a few seconds, I had arrived at the doorway of a wood-paneled room. Bookshelves covered the walls. Two men were in the room. One was bent over; he was placing some books onto an existing stack on the floor. When he was done, he stood, took the remaining books off the shelf, and began a second pile on the floor. The other man standing to his right had his back to me. He was arranging what looked like an antique pipe collection on a shelf. The first man who removed the books took a screwdriver from his belt and began to work on something on the backside of the bookcase where the books had been removed. As he did so he inadvertently kicked one of the book stacks; the top book toppled onto the floor. He stopped, picked up the book, and spoke to the other man whose face I still could not see.

"Professor, who's Franklin Rock?" he asked.

The sound of my name jolted me. The other man then turned to the first. I gasped. Standing ten feet from me, alive and healthy, was a younger Professor Niemeyer. He seemed unfazed by the question.

"Why do you ask, Maurice?" Oh my God. The man with the tool belt was Maurice Burnside. At that moment, I surmised I was in one of my real-world dreams. These were not rare. I tried to wake myself as I usually can do when I find myself in one. This time I couldn't. This wasn't a dream.

"Call me Charles, remember, Professor Burnside?"

"Right, Charles. I accidentally kicked this book off the pile. *Franklin Rock: The Man Who Fixed the World*. I never heard of a Franklin Rock. Who is he?"

Professor Niemeyer slowly walked over, picked up the book, looked it over, then headed directly towards me. As he did so he said to Maurice Burnside, "Don't remember. I must have read it a long time ago. I'm going to check on my tea. I'll be right back. Would you like any, Maurice?" he asked.

Maurice Burnside turned towards the Professor who was now approaching the doorway where I was standing in plain sight. Maurice was looking directly at me. "No, no thanks," he replied and returned his focus to his work.

He couldn't see me! Professor Niemeyer slowed his steps; he was now a mere few feet away. He leaned closer and whispered, "I can; he can't. Remember, Franklin, if you pay attention you can see the future in the past."

My eyes followed him out of the room. I turned back to look at Maurice Burnside. He was whistling, and of course, smiling. Once again the earth shifted.

"Aren't you going to work today?"

Danny's words startled me. "What time is it?" I asked, that well-known pit you feel when you realize you have overslept was already present in my stomach as I awaited his response.

"Seven."

"Crap." I leaped out of bed. So much for any morning routine. I donned my scrubs, flew down the hall to the bathroom which fortunately was free, and was out the door in ten minutes.

As I raced down the 3 South hallway I ran into Ann, the head nurse. "Sorry I'm late. I overslept," I admitted, my eyes pleading my case.

"Relax, Franklin. This is the first time I can remember that you've been late and—she looked at her watch—it's not even fifteen minutes. And I know you often stay late. You have nothing to worry about."

My next stop of course was Mr. Burnside's room. His door was closed, so as I did the day before I knocked and slowly entered.

"Franklin! So good to see you, son." He was seated in the chair next to his bed. He looked so much better than on the day of his admission.

"Good morning, Mr. Burnside. It's good to see you, too. You look great this morning."

"I feel great. Last night the doc said I could go home soon, maybe even this afternoon. How do you like that?"

"Nice," I told him, noticing a bit of sadness in my voice. Be happy for him, I reminded myself.

"Want to have lunch again today, just in case I end up leaving? If you have time," he inquired.

"I will definitely have time. I'll come get you around noon, just like yesterday."

Throughout the morning, my mind was filled with images from the prior night. The more I reflected on the event, the less certain I was. Maybe it was a dream. I saw and heard Professor Niemeyer, and he saw me. How could that possibly be if it wasn't a dream? Lunch was my one chance to confirm that I had indeed been in Professor Niemeyer's house.

Just before noon, I knocked and opened Mr. Burnside's door. He was dressed in street clothes.

"I've been freed!" he exclaimed upon seeing me.

"I'm so happy for you. When are you leaving?"

"Just waiting for my daughter to arrive and fetch me. Sorry, Franklin, I can't have lunch with you. But if you have a minute we can chat before she arrives." He looked at his watch. "See, time and I are back together. I finally gotta be somewhere: my own home!"

"I do have a question for you if you don't mind."

"Sure. What's your question?"

"You told me you did some work in Professor Niemeyer's office, his library. Do you happen to remember that room?"

"I do. I was in that room a lot. Why do you want to know?"

"Professor Niemeyer told me he collected old smoking pipes," I lied. "Ever see them?"

"Oh sure. He had them neatly lined up on a shelf over his desk. He was always fiddlin' with them. Not sure he ever actually smoked one. Did he show them to you?"

Proof. I was there, in Professor Niemeyer's library, invisible to Mr. Burnside, visible to Professor Niemeyer. "No. Just curious since he mentioned them on occasion." Lie number two.

Maurice Burnside's daughter soon arrived. He introduced us, then wrote his address and phone number down for me. "Franklin Rock, I'm gonna miss you. Never thought I would ever say I'm gonna miss something about a hospital. Thank you, son, for your kindness."

"Thank you, Mr. Burnside. It's been an honor to help you. You take care of yourself. I'm gonna miss you, too."

"Well, don't be a stranger. You know where I live, so come on by one day and we'll fix you an iced tea and we'll talk some more. Small world, Professor Niemeyer and all. Small world."

22

More Questions Than Answers

"Ms. Forman, do you have a minute?"

"Of course, Franklin."

"Would it be OK to take next Monday off?"

She laughed. "You do know you get three weeks off every year. If I'm correct, you haven't taken a day off since you got here. Of course. Enjoy your first official day off. I'll make a note of it."

Danny and Simon both had a long weekend from class so the three of us headed back to our college to catch a game and see some friends. We arrived Friday evening and met a few of our fraternity brothers for dinner. I did not need to time travel; just being together again simultaneously transported all of us back to our collective past. As the evening wore on, one of our group suggested that we go to the State Street Coffeehouse to listen to some music. I hadn't been there since the evening I first met Govinda.

Nothing had changed since that visit. Cigarette smoke hung in the air, as did the smell of marijuana. Danny looked at Simon as the scent hit us immediately upon entering.

"We should have brought some," he said.

"I did," Simon answered, a big smile on his face.

"Well done!" Danny added, putting his arm around Simon. "Perhaps a stop in the bathroom is in order." They looked at me. "I assume you're not coming. Is that right, Franklin?"

"Correct." I followed our other friends to a table in the back. As we sat, I checked out the room looking for Govinda. I had no idea how often he came but I was hoping that he might be present. No luck.

Danny and Simon returned with big smiles on their faces. "Look, Danny, they got us beers. Wasn't that nice?" Simon said, his head bobbing to the music. "You guys get anything to eat? We are definitely going to need something to eat," he added, looking at Danny.

"Hey, Franklin," Danny said, "guess who I saw in the bathroom?"

"I give up," I answered.

"That friend of yours we met when we almost got killed in my car. You know, the guy that helped us change the tire. What's his name?"

"You saw Govinda?" I asked excitedly.

"Yeah, Govinda, that's it. He didn't see me, but I recognized him."

"Where is he?"

"I don't know. Here somewhere I suppose." He resumed talking to Simon.

I looked around again. Sure enough, there he was, at a table on the other side of the room. Just then he turned his head, and our eyes caught each others'. I could see him say something to someone at his table, then he stood and walked over to me.

"Franklin, what are you doing here? Aren't you living in Boston?"

"I am. We just came for the weekend. You probably remember Danny," I said as I pointed him out.

"Sure, the evasive driving expert. Good to see you, Danny," he said.

"You, too." Danny turned to Simon. "Guy's got a cool jack," he told him.

Govinda looked at me. I shrugged.

"Anything to report?" he asked quietly.

"Oh yeah." I got up unnoticed. Danny and Simon were laughing, oblivious in their stoned state. Govinda and I headed to the back of the coffeehouse. We ended up in a vestibule behind the coatroom.

"How are you doing? Are you working?" Govinda asked.

"I am, in a hospital. I'm an orderly, basically a nursing assistant. It has been a surprisingly terrific experience."

"Cool."

"You?" I reciprocated.

"Still at the same job. All good," he quickly responded, anxious to dispense with the niceties and get on to the main event. "I've had more dreams."

"Anything interesting?"

"Oh yeah, and guess who is still starring in them."

"Do I need to be worried?" I asked, not completely in jest.

"Of course not. Your future keeps showing up in my dreams, Franklin." Govinda noticed that I barely reacted. "I know, after all you've seen, hardly anything surprises you anymore, right? I've gotten to be the same way."

"So what were the dreams about this time?"

"First let me ask you a question. Is there something going on with you and a book?"

"Why do you ask?" No way he could have seen the book I received from Professor Niemeyer.

"In my dream, you are holding a book with your name on it. Does that mean anything to you?"

Oh my God. "I almost said you won't believe this, but of course you will. I have the book I think you're talking about. Did you see any more?"

"Just your name on the cover. I can't tell you anything else about it. At least I don't remember anything else. What is the book?"

"It's not just my name that's on the book. The complete title is *Franklin Rock: The Man Who Fixed the World*. I awaited Govinda's response. The stunned look I anticipated seeing on his face did not materialize.

"That might explain my other dreams."

"What other dreams?"

"Remember I told you about the dreams I occasionally have where you are standing in front of large cheering crowds?"

I nodded.

"I've had a few more since I saw you last. For sure you are going to be famous, Franklin, in a very big way. I could feel a ton of admiration in those dreams. People are going to love you."

"Govinda, you have to stop saying that," I insisted.

"Look, I don't ask for these dreams. They just come. Once I met you, I no longer questioned their significance. For so long, you were just a character in my dreams. You're real, Franklin, and so are my dreams."

"It's just so uncomfortable for me. I still haven't done anything for anybody. Plus don't you find all of this confusing? If everything is predetermined in our lives then what's the point of anything? I mean, you and I get glimpses into the future, so then how is it possible that we have any control over what that future is? None of it makes sense," I concluded, relieved to have the opportunity to unload all of my angst to someone who would not recoil from my words.

"You once told me that you always had this premonition that time was different than it seemed," Govinda continued, ignoring both my whining and confusion.

"For as long as I can remember."

"Do you have any idea where that came from?

"No. It was just there. Why are you asking me that?"

"Because I have a similar feeling, but not about time. Mine is about what we're talking about; knowing the future. Suppose there is not only one way for things to go, meaning only a single future. Maybe there could be lots of futures. That's the feeling I have. The future you and I see might be only one of many."

"Professor Niemeyer told me that there is not just one way for things to work out. I had no idea what he meant; he never fully explained it to me. Maybe that's what he was referring to."

"Too bad you didn't get to ask him before he died."

"I saw him again, Govinda."

"Professor Niemeyer?"

"Yes." I then told Govinda about my patient Maurice Burnside and discovering his relationship with Professor Niemeyer, followed by the incredible trip I took to Professor Niemeyer's library.

"Here is the insane part," I continued. "While I was standing just inside the door of the library, Mr. Burnside could not see me. He was staring right at me only a few feet away but he looked right through me. Professor Niemeyer *could* see me. He walked by me with the book you saw in your dream and reminded me of something he had told me previously."

"What was that?"

"He told me that if you pay attention you can see the future in the past."

"I believe that, Franklin. I've experienced it."

"You have?" His admission startled me. "When?"

"Sometimes in my dreams I see an event from my actual past. In retrospect, it was a hint of the future, sort of a guidepost to which way to go."

"Are you saying that we have to correctly choose which way to go? I mean, if I or you or anyone has to make a choice, how do we know which option will get us to the right future?" I asked, now totally perplexed by the conversation.

"I don't think it's like that. I don't believe that you have to make the right choice." Govinda paused to consider his next words. "Remember your dream where someone or something is driving your car? I think it's sort of like that. Our choices may not be all that important. You'd think they should be, but maybe they're not."

"How can that possibly be?"

"Haven't you noticed that things just seem to work out?" Govinda replied.

"Maybe, I mean so far. Does all of this make sense to you? It doesn't to me."

"Look, we both know that something is going on. We just don't know what, or how it works. I still believe it very much matters how we behave, and that we have to make something of our lives."

"Mr. Burnside—the patient I told you about—said the same to me. So if that's true, and it certainly sounds true, why?"

"I could be completely wrong, but I think it has something to do with why we are here in the first place, and maybe what happens after."

"After what?" I asked.

"After we're gone."

"You mean after we die?"

"Yes, after we die."

"Something else to worry about."

Govinda smiled. "Not really. C'mon, Franklin, we should get back so your friends don't think the guy with the weird name has kidnapped you."

"So you're going to leave me with a zillion questions?"

"Look, I'm just the backup guy. You're the main guy. If you don't know the answers, why would you assume that I do? Here's what I do know. For sure, Franklin, you will eventually figure it all out."

As we walked towards Danny, Simon, and the others I stopped. "Do you think our lives will keep intersecting like this?"

"Probably. It's worked so far. Let's hope it doesn't take another near-fatal car accident to make it happen."

"No kidding."

Govinda put his arm around me. "Having fun yet?" he asked, then patted my shoulder and headed back to his friends. I returned to Simon, Danny, and the others.

We headed back to the fraternity house a short while later. Danny, Simon, and I stayed up reminiscing about our year living in the fraternity house together. This was exactly what I needed. My head hurt after my conversation with Govinda. It was clear that even though both of us recognized that another level existed beneath our visible reality, neither of us seemed to have a reasonably clear concept of what that was.

As we sat together in the room where so much had transpired, the three of us took a chronological tour of our year in the fraternity. Inevitably, we got around to recounting the night of the infamous inferno: I had just gotten back to the house after a date to find Danny and Simon sitting in the same room with about twenty candles set precariously on a plywood plank in the center of the room. They were both wasted, laughing uncontrollably as they lit one candle after another. I sat and watched my two great friends enjoy themselves as if this was the funniest thing they had ever seen. Since I was the only one in control of my senses, I decided to keep an eye on things.

"Uh, guys, I think you should stop now. You could easily start a fire," I warned, sounding like the parent of toddlers.

"Oh, c'mon, it's fine," Simon said with his wonderfully contagious laugh. "Danny, isn't it fine?" he asked, still laughing.

"Yup, it's completely fine. Let's light a few more." As he reached over to light yet another candle, he lost his balance and leaned on the plank. Candles started tipping like dominoes, and in an instant the plywood began to smolder. "Whoops," Simon said, the two of them now looking directly at each other, the realization that their playtime had suddenly gone amiss.

"Move!" I yelled to both of them as I aimed the fire extinguisher at the developing fireball. I had grabbed it from the wall a few minutes earlier while I watched my clueless friends continue their play. Within a short time the fire was out, no damage done.

Simon looked at me. "OK, so you were right that night. I have to admit, you were awesome getting that fire extinguisher. That should be our permanent rule. One of us should always have a functioning brain."

"C'mon, Franklin, you have to admit that was funny," Danny said. "It all worked out, didn't it? Simon, wasn't that funny?"

"Funny," he replied.

"Funny," I concurred, "once the fire was out."

"So how come you never smoke with us?" Simon asked, abruptly changing the subject. "Is it because of the time stuff?"

"It's because of the time stuff. I am not taking any unnecessary chances."

Danny, Simon, and I had not talked about my time traveling since the day I had experienced and recounted the camp baseball game. I was surprised they hadn't asked any more about my visions. Now the two of them looked at each other deciding who should speak first.

"OK, what's going on with you two?" I asked.

Simon began. "We're just worried about you. I mean, maybe you should talk to someone about all this."

I could see where this was going. "You guys don't believe I'm moving through time."

Another look between the two.

"Simon and I talked about it after you described hitting those home runs off of me. It didn't prove anything. I mean, so you hit them, and you remembered the stuff I did with my glove. You have a good memory. That hardly proves you time-traveled."

"I did."

"Look, we're your best friends. If we can't be honest with you, then who will?" Simon jumped in.

I realized it was time for them to know everything.

"I know you guys are worried about me," I began. "Sometimes *I'm* worried about me. But you have to understand that as insane as it seems, I did travel back to when we were nine that day." I turned my focus to Danny. "It was a twenty-one-year-old Franklin batting against a nine-year-old Danny. You were right when you said I could never do that as nine-year-old Franklin Rock. I was deathly afraid of the ball. For a little kid, you threw a rocket. I would have struck out every time."

I paused to make sure I wanted to do this. It seemed like the right time.

"Do you two want to hear the whole story?" Both nodded.

I proceeded to tell them almost everything. I was embarrassed to suggest I was destined to fix the world so I left that out. At least for now. That could be too much. I told them that it had become clear that I was supposed to do something important in my future and that, according to Professor Niemeyer, my current episodes were preparing me for that.

When I was done the two of them were silent.

"You're not kidding, are you?" Danny spoke first.

"No, Danny, I am not kidding."

"You understand how totally weird, bizarre, insane this is?" Simon asked, more as a statement than a question.

"Yes," I replied. "All of those things."

"So what happens now?" Simon continued.

"I have no idea. I just have to wait and go with the flow."

"I do have another question," Danny asked.

I turned towards him. "Sure."

"If Professor Niemeyer died, but you saw him when he was younger, but he knew who you were from the future and had the mysterious book," he paused. "I don't get it."

"Man, I don't know how you are living with this," Simon added.

"When all of this started I was pretty upset and scared a lot of the time. But I am learning as I go. It's much easier to deal with now. So do you two still think I need professional help?"

"Not anymore," Simon answered for the two of them.

"Thanks. I am not imagining any of this; I am not making anything up. When you see what I have already seen you begin to understand that the world we live in is incredibly strange. What goes on every day is just part of the story, the part that we can see. There is another part. I'm not talking about ghosts or wild stuff like that."

"Then like what?" Danny asked.

"I'm not sure, but I do know we are here for a reason. I don't want to sound religious; I don't mean it like that." I stopped and searched for an analogy. "Imagine you're watching a movie or a play where the outcome is known to the entire audience. You know what is going to happen; everyone except the actors in the play knows what is going to happen. But the actors are helpless. Even though the ending of the play has already been written, they're in the middle of it; they can't see the end. Does that make any sense?"

"Not really," Danny said. "At least the way you just messed it up," he added with a smile. "So you're saying it's like we are all in a play, and we can't see the end of the play because we're in the middle of acting it out, but the end of the play has already been written. We just don't know what it is."

"Yes, exactly," I replied, not quite appreciating the difference between what Danny and I had just described.

"If that's true—I'm not saying I agree—but if that's true, how come it's that way?" Danny asked.

"That is exactly the question I have been struggling with," I admitted.

"And, what did you come up with?" he asked me.

"I have no idea. But when I figure it out I promise I'll tell you," I told him.

"Well, let's hope you don't have to be dead to find out," he said.

"Funny you should say that. I had considered the same thing," I replied.

Danny looked at Simon. "Maybe we shouldn't smoke anything for a while."

23

Words of Wisdom

NANCY GREETED ME AS I REACHED the 3 South nursing station. "Good morning, Franklin. After you left yesterday Maurice Burnside's daughter called looking for you. Have you seen him since he was discharged?"

"No. I meant to, but every time I would think about him, it would be late at night or something came up." Truth was I just never made it a priority to get in touch with him, and suddenly I felt very badly that I hadn't. "Is he OK?" I asked with trepidation.

"His daughter said his lung cancer has taken a turn for the worse. She wanted to tell you herself. She left her number and asked me to have you call her."

I took the number from Nancy and walked to a free phone at the nurse's station. His daughter answered. "Hi, this is Franklin Rock," I said.

"Hi, Franklin, this is Lucille Burnside, Maurice's daughter. So nice to hear from you. How are you?"

"I'm fine. How is Mr. Burnside?" I asked, already aware of the answer.

"Unfortunately my dad isn't doing too well just now. I hate to trouble you but he asked me to call. You made a big impression on him, I can tell you that. He would love for you to come see him if you can."

"Can I come later today?" I couldn't stand the thought of waiting any longer than necessary; guilt was chewing through my soul.

"That would be so nice. He will be very happy to see you." Lucille gave me their address.

"Maybe around 5 or so. Would that be OK?"

"Fine. We will see you then. I'll tell him now. I'm sure he will be very excited."

It was just before five when I rang the Burnside doorbell.

"Franklin. So good to see you, son," a smiling Maurice Burnside said from his chair as I entered the living room. It had been only a couple of months since I had seen him, but he had visibly changed. He was noticeably thinner in the face and looked tired and more frail than that day he left the hospital. Still, the smile persisted.

"It's so good to see you, Mr. Burnside. I am so sorry I haven't been to visit you. I feel terrible about it."

"Don't be silly, Franklin. I'll bet you've thought about me."

He was right about that. He had no idea of the significant place he already held in my life.

"And I have thought about you too," he added.

"Really, why?" I asked.

"Because you have that effect on folks." He looked at me, awaiting my response. Seeing none, he continued. "So you're a modest one. Good for you. First time I saw you I just got that feeling, 'something special about this boy,' I said to myself. I'll bet you've heard that before."

Indeed I had, from both Govinda and Lori. But this was different. Here was an elderly man whose life could not have been more different from mine telling me the same.

"You know why I asked Lucille to call you, Franklin?"

He knew he was getting sicker and that his time was limited. I figured he wanted a chance to say goodbye to people. I couldn't have been more incorrect.

"You think it's because I'm dying, and I just want to tie up loose ends as they say. You don't have to answer. But that's not why. I wanted you to come here for you, not me."

My stunned reaction was evident. "I'm not sure I know what you mean."

"Like I said, there's something special about you, Franklin. I've been around for a good long time, and I've learned a few things. One of those things is that we got a responsibility to teach each other, to look after each other. You looked after me pretty good in the hospital. So now it's my turn to look after you."

I had no idea how to respond. Mr. Burnside's words were so unexpected. He had flipped the script on me. Here I thought I was here to help him at a difficult time, but instead, I was to be the recipient.

"Cat got your tongue, huh?" he laughed. "Don't worry. You don't have to say a thing. Let me tell you what I'd like to do if it's OK with you. Think you can find your way to come over here once a week? Afternoons are best, but not too late. I get a bit tired at the end of the day and I don't want to be falling asleep on you. I know I'd enjoy talking with you, and maybe I could share a little of what I've learned. Never know; might just help. That sound good to you?" He paused, but before I could answer him he continued. "Now don't go feeling like you have to. I'm sure you're busy, you being a young guy and all. Only come if it works out for you. Don't feel like you got to humor an old man," he concluded with his trademark smile.

"I definitely want to," I answered immediately. "Most days I get off around three. Any day?" I asked.

"Yup, any day is fine. You pick."

"OK, how about Monday? I'll come by then."

We talked a bit more about his health and my job. Lucille then reentered the room.

"Time to take your medicine, Dad."

Lucille winked at me; that was my cue to leave.

"Monday then," he said as I went to shake his hand. He gripped mine with both of his. "I'm looking forward to it."

"Me, too, Mr. Burnside."

It was about a forty-minute walk from Mr. Burnside's home to our apartment. Something seemed odd. Why was Maurice Burnside, now sadly nearing the end of his days, suddenly interested in spending time with me? He said he wanted to help a young kid in whom he saw "something special" while he was still able to. Why did he think I was special? None of it made any sense to me. Maybe I was overthinking this, I decided, as I entered our apartment. Sometimes a cigar is just a cigar, recalling that infamous line attributed, probably erroneously, to Sigmund Freud. Nevertheless, I still harbored doubts.

At 3 p.m. on Monday, I was out the door of the hospital and on my way to Mr. Burnside. Lucille let me in, offered me an iced tea, and then left the two of us alone.

"So Franklin, how's it going at that hospital? How are my favorite nurses?"

"All good, Mr. Burnside. How are you feeling?"

"Oh, I'm doing just fine for an old guy, except for the lung cancer part. No one to blame but myself. I've had a good life, no complaints," he answered, his smile still intact. "Wouldn't change a thing," he added, "except of course for those cancer sticks. Can't understand why young kids smoke nowadays. We didn't know any better. They do. Everyone knows they kill you. Anyway, enough of that. What are your plans, son?"

"You mean for my future?"

"Your future, your present. What are you thinking about?"

"Well, I'm enjoying working at the hospital. After that, I don't know."

"So you have no long term plan? Nothing you think you're supposed to do?"

His words hit me right in the chest as if I had been tackled by a middle linebacker.

"You OK, son?" Mr. Burnside asked as he leaned forward in his chair.

"Yes, I'm fine." His question rekindled the doubt I had had when he told me last week that he wanted to help me. Why? I had to know.

"Mr. Burnside, can I ask you a question?"

"Sure, go right ahead."

"When I came to visit last week you said you wanted me to come once a week because you wished to help me. Don't get me wrong. I am very appreciative, really I am. It's just that it seemed kind of unusual to me that all of a sudden you wanted to do this, especially since you haven't been feeling well. Is there something else you haven't told me?" My heart was racing. Maybe I overstepped my bounds. Maybe I just insulted a very kind older man who just wanted to help a young kid.

He nodded his head a few times. "So, you think there's something else going on?"

Oh crap, I thought. I just hurt his feelings. I was ready to plead ignorance and apologize.

"I'm going to level with you. I just hope you don't think I've lost whatever sense I ever had. I guess if you do I could blame it on this damn cancer." Another telling smile. "Did you ever have a dream that was so real that when you woke up it took a while to figure out if it actually happened or not, like you can't tell the difference between real life and the dream?"

Had I ever. "Yes, a bunch of times."

"A few days before I called you, I had one of those. Man, it was so real. I was in Professor Niemeyer's house doing some work. He came into the room. 'Maurice, I want to show you something,' he said to me. So I put down my tools and walked over to him. 'Take a look at this,' he said. In his hands was that book I told you I saw with your name on it. I could read the title. *Franklin Rock: The Man Who Fixed the World.* Then the Professor looked at me and said, 'Maurice, if you ever run into Franklin Rock, make sure you help him.' I asked him how I will know who he is and what to help him with, and he said, 'Don't worry, you'll know. You just teach him what you've learned. He could use your help.' He turned away from me with the book in his hands, then just like that he disappeared. I looked all around the library but he was gone. And then I woke up."

Like a virus, whatever it was that was infecting my life was spreading to everyone I met. It would not let me escape.

"I know. Crazy right?" Maurice Burnside's words returned me to the present moment. "But I tell you, Franklin, sometimes you just have to accept; that's what I think. Just accept. Seems to me that someone was trying to tell me something. I don't know who, but I know when it's time to pay attention. So here we are."

Now what? Do I tell him about my visions and my time travel? Do I tell him the whole story with Professor Niemeyer and about Govinda? Not yet, I decided. I wasn't sure why that conclusion was reached, but I decided to listen to the voice that suggested against it.

"I don't think it's crazy. There are lots of things we don't understand."

"I'm glad you don't think my brain is losing out to this nasty cancer. As far as I can tell I'm still thinking just fine. Maybe it's crazy, but maybe it's not. So I'm going to do what Charles asked me to do in that dream. That's why I invited you to come here once a week. I'm going to try and impart what I've learned to you, one generation to another. Simple as that. Then I will have honored Charles, God rest his soul."

Maurice Burnside now had his own mission: me.

"Seeing as Charles didn't give me any one thing I should tell you, I thought we would just start talking about a topic and see where it goes. How does that sound? I can just pick something, or you can, and we go from there. When we're bored we move on to something else. Look, tell you the truth, I have no idea what I'm supposed to be doing. I'm just gonna accept like I said, and just hope we will get somewhere."

"Sounds good to me, Mr. Burnside. Where do you want to start?"

"Let's start with this. It's something I think about a lot. Maybe it's because I have cancer and I won't be around all that long. What do you suppose is the most important thing in life?"

Honesty, being successful, helping others, and being true to yourself all ran through my mind. I rattled them off in no particular order.

"OK, that's a fine list to start. So how do you pick which one is the most important?" he asked me.

Only a couple of minutes into this and already I'm stumped. "I'm not sure."

"I've got another question for you. Do believe in a purpose to life?"

"You mean like why are we here?"

"Yes, exactly, Franklin, why are we here? Do you think there's a reason each of us is here?"

"Are you asking me if I believe in God?"

"No, son, I'm not. I just want to know if you think there's some purpose for each of our lives or are we just like every other living thing. We just were born and whatever happens happens, no real plan or nothing."

"I think there's a reason."

"Why do you think so?"

"Too many coincidences. I just can't see how it's all random."

"You mean like you taking care of me in the hospital, and my seeing your name on a book, and then me having that dream? Now that would be some coincidence, huh?" He sat back in his chair. "I'm with you. Too many coincidences to believe something's not going on. So let's get back to the first question. How do you pick the most important thing?"

"I honestly don't know. Do you?"

"I'm not the most educated, but like I said I've been around a while. What I'm trying to say is that I think I have a pretty good idea, but I'm not gonna sit here and tell you I've got it all figured out 'cause, believe me, I don't. So I can give you my opinion is all."

If Professor Niemeyer thought I could learn from Maurice Burnside, as I'm pretty certain he did, he must have believed that Mr. Burnside had a good deal figured out correctly. For me, that was the ultimate endorsement.

"Franklin, I can just say that I'm pretty sure it's all about the people in our lives. You know, what people call relationships these days. Funny, I had never heard that word growing up. Relationships. We had family—

parents, brothers and sisters, aunts and uncles and cousins—and neighbors, and the man who sold the seeds and the farm equipment, and the man and woman who owned the hardware store, and the mailman. These were the people we had relationships with, but no one ever thought of it that way. They were just people in your life. So I think that's what the story is all about. The people in your life."

"I'm sure that's true. But that can't be all of it. How about what you do with your life?"

"You mean like a job, or being something like a lawyer or doctor or a teacher? That what you mean?"

"Yes, like what you make of your life. Isn't that important?"

"Whoa, son, I think we just found your first mistake." Maurice Burnside stopped and a big grin appeared signifying his realization that this get together might indeed be useful for me. "I think you're confusing a job with making something of your life. Let's say you're a politician, a successful politician. You win a bunch of elections, maybe get money for your community, help pass some laws; stuff like that. But you treat your staff terribly and cheat on your wife. Have you made something of your life?" He awaited my response.

"I don't know, maybe. I mean you probably did a lot of good things for your community. Doesn't that count, even if you were mean to your staff and family?"

"That depends, now, doesn't it?"

"On what?" I asked.

"On what you think the purpose of a life is. Look, if the purpose of a life is to rack up wins, then I guess you're right. Same thing for making lots of money, or becoming a famous movie star or athlete. Maybe you even invent something that people love. You could be a horrible father and husband—probably same guy would be a lousy friend—and still have that record of success. That's only a winning hand if the purpose of life is to be famous or rich. Now suppose there's a different purpose." He paused and waited for me.

"So you think there's another purpose."

"Could be," he continued. "Could be that the purpose has nothing to do with that sort of stuff. How about if the purpose is to learn to care about people, look after them, be a friend, and love your neighbor?"

I could easily see the flaw in his logic. I did not wish to be impolite; I had too much respect for him to even consider that. But he wanted this discussion, so I was going to assume he wanted my honest opinion.

"What would be the point of that? I mean, I think we should all be nice to each other no matter what, and look after each other like you said. But how can that be the purpose? Where would that get us?"

"Where would that get us? It would certainly make us feel good about ourselves, and for sure it would make many others happy. But I can see your point that it wouldn't necessarily get us ahead. But what if there's another life after this one? And what if the whole point of this life is to get us ready for the next one? Then everything would look a lot different, don't you think?"

Govinda had suggested the same. I was long since done with coincidences.

"I know lots of people believe in an afterlife. But don't you think it's a bit much to base everything you do in your life on an unproven theory that there is something after this life? That's kind of a big risk," I told him.

"I don't know. Doesn't sound like a big risk to me. I've tried to be a good person. Not saying I'm perfect, no sir. I've been a rascal in my time. But most of my life, especially as I've gotten older, I've tried real hard to treat people right and to do the right thing. It's made me very proud and very happy. Never wanted to be famous. More money would have been OK," he said with a chuckle, "but wouldn't have changed my life. Money might get you some respect from others, but it will never get you respect from yourself. That's the one that counts the most."

I had to think about that. Respect from others versus self-respect. "Are you sure about that?" I asked him.

"Oh, that one I'm sure about. Hundred percent. Let's say a patient you took care of gets out of the hospital and forgets his wallet. Now you find it, you look inside, and see a bunch of twenties. You figure, I'll just take one, no one will ever notice. Then you give the wallet to the nurses, they call the man, he comes and gets his wallet. The nurse tells him young Franklin here found your wallet. He thanks you, and then gives you a twenty as a thank you. All the nurses, that patient, his family, they all think you're a great guy. But you know you stole a twenty. You got their respect, but you know you're a thief. That's gonna make you feel lousy, believe me. Maybe not right then and there, but eventually it will."

It was obvious he was talking from personal experience. He changed the setting for my benefit, but somewhere down the line he had metaphorically stolen a twenty. And he was still sorry he had.

"Can I ask you about the 'next life' question?" I asked, prior message received.

"Of course, son, ask me anything. If I don't know the answer, I'll just make something up." Another chuckle.

"Other than reading the Bible, where is there any proof that there is anything other than this life?" Now we had entered an entirely different realm. Here we would get to the what-ifs. My recent life was all about a different realm of unknowns and what-ifs.

"For me, it all gets back to those coincidences we talked about. There's just too many. There's just too much that is hard to explain. I'm not talking about science stuff. I'm talking about things we can't see."

"OK, but that isn't something that everyone appreciates. I mean, if it works for you that's great, but I'm not sure that works for most people."

"So you want proof? I don't have what you might call proof. But here's something to think about. Look at me and you. You've been to college, got a degree and all. But I got eighty-two years of experience. I pretty much know what's a stupid thing to do. I know how most things are gonna work out, 'cause I've seen most of them before. Now I'm getting near the end, we both know that. So what good to me is all this wisdom I've collected all of those years? How come I'm finally smart when it don't make any difference? Unless."

"Unless the whole point is to get the wisdom to use in the next life."

"Exactly."

We had been at it for a while. He was beginning to tire.

"I gotta run, now Mr. Burnside. That was great. Same time next Monday?"

"You bet. See you then, son."

He sat back, his eyes closing. "I guess I really can help him, Charles," I assumed was the thought that brought the wide smile.

24

Loss

"Monday already? Time is picking up speed for me, Franklin."

I had just arrived at Mr. Burnside's house. Lucille greeted me with another iced tea—this was to be the ritual—and left us. Mr. Burnside looked the same as last week; that was a relief. I was concerned that he might be fading quickly, so to see the same man was reassuring.

"I thought about the things we talked about last Monday. In fact, I hardly thought about anything else," I admitted. "Can we talk about the self-respect thing again?"

"Anything you want. I've got all the time in the world," he told me, then smiled and added, "Guess that's not true anymore."

He could see that I was struggling with a response.

"It's fine, Franklin. I'm not sad and you shouldn't be, either. Now, what was it you were about to say?"

"You explained that there is a difference between what other people think about you and what you think about yourself, like with the wallet story."

"You can't give someone self-respect. They have to earn it. Especially kids. Lucille will tell you, I never told my kids they were so great and all that. Hell, no. Now if they did something good, like in school or around the house, I would tell them I was proud. Or if they did something for a neighbor or the church I'd do the same. You can go on and on to a child about how wonderful they are, but they're not stupid. They know if they've acted right or done something to be proud of. A person's got to earn respect; you can't just give it to 'em like a gift."

"Got it. So what's next?" I asked.

"Here's something I was thinking about during the week. I told you that I thought it was peculiar that by the time you reach my age and finally know some things it's too late for it to do much good. I gave that one some more thought. You know how teenagers do dumb things, right? Like smoking, or driving way too fast. Or taking drugs, or getting pregnant. Which of course works both ways. The teenaged girl is stupid for spreading her legs for her boyfriend who is equally stupid for doing it without taking any precautions. Either way, it messes up a lot of young lives. All of those things fit into the same bucket that I call major stupid."

"Major stupid. I love that!" I told him.

"I'd tell my kids, don't do anything major stupid. After hearing it a million times they would look at me and say, 'Dad, don't worry. I'm not gonna do anything major stupid.' Problem is not enough parents tell their kids that. Hey, Lucille," Mr. Burnside yelled over his right shoulder, "come here for a moment, would you?"

"You OK, Dad?" Lucille asked.

"Yes, I'm fine. I was telling Franklin about what I would say to you kids when you were about to go somewhere or do something. Do you remember?"

"Do I remember you telling me every time I was going anywhere with my friends don't do anything major stupid? Yes, I remember. We all remember."

Lucille rolled her eyes. "I'm telling you, Franklin. *Every* time any of us went anywhere, those were the last words we heard. 'Now remember, don't do anything major stupid.' You need anything, Dad?" she asked. "Franklin?"

"No, thank you. I'm fine."

"So the point is that it would make a lot more sense if we knew more stuff when we were younger, right?" he continued after Lucille left. "No one would have to tell a teenager not to do anything major stupid if we were smarter when we were young. 'Course now at this age, I couldn't do anything major stupid if I wanted to. See how it's all backwards? That's why I think we're just here getting prepared for the next life. Otherwise, it makes no sense to be so dumb when we're young and get smart when it's hardly worth it. All right, I think I've beaten this horse to death. Let's move on."

"No, don't feel that way. That was very interesting. I would never have thought about that if you hadn't talked about it. It is peculiar that we get smart when we need it less and we're kind of dumb when we need it more." I wondered why that was not obvious to everyone.

"Franklin, are your parents alive?"

"Just my mother. My dad died when I was a teenager. I have one older sister. That's it."

"Losing your father was a big deal I'm sure. Always is. Sorry to hear that. Did it toughen you up?"

His question surprised me. That was not something to which I had given any thought. "I don't know. I was very sad, of course, but it's been so long I don't think about it much anymore. Tougher? Maybe. I guess I know bad things can and do happen."

"Hard times make you stronger; that's for sure," Mr. Burnside said. "Truth is the more you go through them, the more mentally strong you get. Makes it easier to deal with the next hard one. I don't wish anything bad to ever happen to anyone, but I know that it will and it's best to be prepared for when it does."

I had always wished to be mentally tough. As a kid and even a young adult, I was anything but. My dad's death hurt, but I was probably just too young to recognize that it was my first real challenge. I wouldn't count my current situation as a tough time.

"How do you get prepared for tough times?" I asked.

"Like most things. You gotta practice."

"How do you practice for something bad happening? It seems like the first time you're just never going to be ready."

"What you're practicing is how to deal with a new situation."

I could tell Mr. Burnside was searching for an example.

"Here's a good one. When you started in the hospital you'd never done that kind of work before, right?"

"Right."

"OK, so what was the first thing you had to do that you'd never done and never imagined doing?"

"That's easy. Cleaning a bedpan."

"Now how do you feel about it?"

"Now I don't even think about it. I just do it," I answered.

"See what happened? You ran into something you didn't expect to have to do, and then you did it. One thing that could have happened is that you could have said I can't do this and quit the job. But you didn't. How come?"

"Why didn't I quit? Because that would be giving up. I try not to give up."

"Good for you. You met something difficult, but you decided you could do it and you refused to quit. That, Franklin, is being mentally tough. You don't think it's a big deal. You didn't jump on a hand grenade, I get it. But you did something you didn't want to do and didn't think you could do. And when the next thing like that comes along, you just need to remember that you learned to clean a bedpan. See?"

"So how do you practice? I assume you don't start hoping bad things will happen."

Mr. Burnside smiled. "That's a good one, Franklin. No, but you don't need to. When you get a chance to take the easy way to do something or take the harder way, take the harder way. Better yet, look for challenges. You can find them everywhere. Like in the hospital. I'll bet you can always do something for a patient, or for one of the nurses, that you don't have to do but it would make someone else's situation better. Look for those and then do them. The more you do, the more you take on your shoulders, the more you can do. Then when something hard shows up, you got the confidence to know you can do it."

"And that works? It prepares you for the tough stuff?"

"Hundred percent. You know what the real definition of mental toughness is?"

"I think I do," I answered. "It's being able to persevere through something difficult."

"It's more than that. It's knowing that when you do take on something hard you're going to succeed. Failure would be the surprise."

Three o'clock Mondays became the focus of my week. We covered a lot of ground. Friendship, honesty and integrity, work, and the need for a sense of humor were all on the agenda. He was insistent that I learn to never take myself too seriously, no matter what I ended up accomplishing. "You want to have close friends, Franklin. Not much more important than that. If you get a swelled head no one will want to be your close friend," he warned me. On the flip side, he also told me to never get too down on myself. "Everyone makes mistakes, Franklin. You will too, maybe even big ones. Just like you don't want to get too full of yourself, you don't want to beat yourself up too much, either. It's good to expect a lot from yourself; I'm all for that. But you will mess up. When you do, just correct your mistake, try not to make the same one again, and try harder."

On our fifth Monday, I noticed a change in him. His breathing became more labored, and he seemed to tire more easily. When I arrived for the sixth session, he was on oxygen. Still, he insisted on having our time together. The following Wednesday Lucille called me at the hospital.

"Franklin, hi, this is Lucille."

My heart stopped. I gripped the phone as tightly as I could. "Hi, Lucille."

"My dad isn't doing too well. Maybe you should come see him in the next day or so if you can."

"Can I come this afternoon?"

"Of course. Anytime. See you then."

I did not possess the skill to hold back the tears. Ms. Forman, the head nurse, had been listening. She came behind me and put her hand on my shoulder. "It's all right to cry, Franklin. In this job we all do sometimes."

It was not lost on me that this might be my final walk to Mr. Burnside's house. Every few minutes I had to stop, take a deep breath, and consciously instruct my muscles to raise my stooping shoulders. Lucille answered the door; no iced tea was in her hand.

"How is he doing?" I asked for want of something to say.

"Not good," Lucille replied quietly. "But I know he will be very happy to see you." This time we did not stop in the living room. No Maurice Burnside occupied the comfy upholstered armchair that he preferred. Lucille instead directed me into the bedroom. He was propped up on a few pillows; the semi-upright position aided his labored breathing. He looked so much more emaciated and weaker than he had only a few days ago. How could he slide so quickly?

"Franklin, so good to see you!" Even terminal cancer could not displace his trademark smile.

"Hi, Mr. Burnside. It's so good to see you, too."

"Come, have a seat here next to me," he instructed me, pointing to the armless folding chair by the side of his bed.

"So, here we are Franklin. I know it's not Monday. I hope that's OK," he said with a wink. "Anyway, when Lucille told me you were coming by today, I asked myself if there was anything we hadn't talked about that I wanted to make sure we did. I did think of one thing that I don't think I've had a chance to tell you. Remember when we talked about hard times in life, and practicing getting mentally tougher?"

"Of course," I replied.

"There's one more piece to it. When times are hard there's a trick to making yourself feel better. Most people don't know this, because they're so focused on their own problems. Here's the trick: when you begin to worry more about other people than yourself, when you place their troubles ahead of your own, the burdens of your own life instantly lighten. When things are tough, go help someone else. Works every time."

Tears were now clearly visible on my cheeks.

"No need to be sad, Franklin. I've had a wonderful life. We all gotta go sometime. It's my turn; nothing more to it. I just want you to know that these visits have meant a whole lot to me. I'm very grateful that we had this time."

"Oh, no, Mr. Burnside. I'm the lucky one. I can't thank you enough. You have taught me so much. I wish there were something I could do to thank you."

"There is. Go fix the world, like the book said. I'm guessing I was right; that book I saw at Charles Niemeyer's house is about you?"

"I think so, yes."

"Isn't that something," he said, shaking his head. "I told you I could see there was something special about you right from the start. I'm not smart enough to understand how all this works, Franklin, you know time and some of the other things we talked about. But I'm fine with not understanding. Maybe I'll learn more when I see Charles. I just hope he thinks I did a good enough job teaching you."

His funeral was packed. I had no idea how many people's lives he touched. It should have come as no surprise. I too had grown to love him. One person after another eulogized him. I learned a great deal about his life and his family. Simple man, so many said. They had no idea. There was nothing simple about him.

As I walked out of the church I felt a hand on my sh
neously heard a woman's voice say, "You're Franklin Ro

I turned to see who it was. I did not recognize her. "E
I know you?" I tried to ask politely.

"Sort of," she answered. "I am Gloria Niemeyer."

My stunned silence forced her to continue. "Charles N   . _ ъ wife."

"Yes, hello, I'm so sorry. It's nice to meet you," I finally managed to say.

"I understand from Lucille that you spent a good deal of time with Maurice over the last few months. That must have been special for both of you."

"Especially for me. He was a great man. I'm going to miss him."

"I only met him a few times at our home. He was an electrician. Did you know that?"

"Yes, ma'am. He told me he had done some work for you and your husband."

"Very sweet man. Charles was very fond of him. And very fond of you as well."

I had no idea how to respond. What did she know about me? Had he told her everything?

"I'm so sorry, Franklin. I'm sure running into me has probably caught you off guard. We never met, and you're wondering what I know about you. You might even be wondering what I know about Charles," she added, clearly teasing me. "My husband is an interesting figure, don't you think?"

"I guess. I mean, sure." Truth is, I didn't know what I meant.

"Dear, I won't keep you. You have a lot on your plate, that I know. Don't worry. You will be fine. Charles has assured me of that. Oh, and he told me to tell you he will be seeing you again soon." She offered a royal wave as she walked away.

Let it come to you. In waves, I thought. It's coming in waves.

25

Reflection

I N THE WEEKS FOLLOWING Mr. Burnside's death, I decided to focus on my tangible, real, non-time-traveling life. My hope was that doing so would ground me, allow me time to reassess all that had happened, and perhaps even prevent any new temporal adventures. It would also provide me an opportunity to practice the lessons I had received from Maurice Burnside.

He had given me a crash course in life. Did I smile enough, I wondered one afternoon on my way home, as I recalled his indelible smile, ineradicable even in the face of his terminal cancer and the hardships he had endured throughout his life? At that moment, I made the quite deliberate decision to adopt a smile as my default appearance to the world. In the months to come, I would randomly check myself throughout the day: was I smiling? If not, I would force the issue. It became my standard, and with it my interaction with the remainder of my fellow humans changed forever. I soon learned that a smile given uniformly elicits a smile in return. Like Pavlov's dogs, we fortunately seem unable to respond in any other way.

Project number two was to make myself more prepared for adversity. "Take the harder way when possible," Mr. Burnside told me. "That's how you practice mental toughness." So each day at work, I added something extra to my list of duties. I would surprise one of the nurses to whom I was not assigned by changing the bedding on one of her patients. I made certain the stockroom was complete and neatly organized, not one of my official duties. I came a bit earlier and stayed a bit later.

Nancy commented. "Franklin, all of the nurses have been discussing you. Do you know why?"

"No, I have no idea." I was honestly concerned that I had committed an unknown error.

"It's because you're doing all of this extra work. Don't get me wrong. It's terrific and admirable. I'm just wondering; what's the motivation?"

"Maurice Burnside," I said, and proceeded to explain what he had shared with me.

"He meant a lot to you. You're a good guy, Franklin Rock," she told me and gave me a hug.

This wasn't about being a good guy. It was about being a more mentally prepared guy. My target was to fulfill Mr. Burnside's definition of mental toughness: when confronted with a difficult situation, I would assume that I would succeed. I wouldn't know how successful my efforts would be until tested. I was sure that eventually I would be, so I kept practicing every chance I got. I never liked getting stuck with a needle, so I volunteered to give blood. Horror movies were just that to me; a nightmare to be avoided. So I watched a few on TV and even went to see one at the theater. Keeping my eyes closed, my previous strategy if forced to watch this genre of entertainment, was now barred. Eyes open, I made it through them all. Now at least I could be in the room with friends who enjoyed them, although why they do remains a mystery.

Mr. Burnside's example of the stolen twenty-dollar bill also stuck with me. We had subsequently talked about honesty and integrity. Honesty, he said, is more about what we think of ourselves than what others think about us. "You can't fool yourself forever," he told me. "Integrity," he added, "oozes from a person, like sweat from an athlete. You can almost smell it. That's one smell you want," he added with his trademark wink. I now demanded complete honesty for myself. I would only tell the truth, and if for some reason I could not in order not to hurt someone's feelings, I would stay silent. If I could do so, I hoped, that smell of integrity would follow.

My ego needed work. That was also clear from his lessons. Even though what I had experienced over the past year was challenging, learning that others think that you have special gifts will inevitably raise one's opinion of oneself. "Don't take yourself too seriously, Franklin," he warned. I became tougher on myself. So far I had accomplished little, certainly nothing worthy of admiration. What I needed to do was to work harder, be kinder, and make certain I did not unconsciously stick a pedestal under myself.

Of all he taught me, the one piece of advice that occupied the majority of my waking thoughts was the benefit of putting others' welfare above your own. Mr. Burnside called it a trick to lighten your burden. For me, there was nothing intuitive about this concept. It would never have spontaneously occurred to me; its brilliance soon became crystal clear.

Nancy had casually told me a few months earlier about the food bank she volunteered in one Sunday a month. As I reflected on Mr. Burnside's advice, I thought joining her there would be a perfect place to put his words into action.

"I'd love to have you come, Franklin. It's a different experience from the hospital. Most of our patients come from good homes and will return there after they recover. What you will see at the food bank is totally different. These people are by and large healthy, but they are poor. What you and I take for granted, walking into a supermarket and filling a basket, is something they just cannot do."

So I went on Sunday, and for most Sundays after that for months to follow. Some people came alone, some came as families. Some were there for the first time; some were regulars. Some were just down on their luck, a job lost but hopefully soon to be replaced. Some had chronic illnesses and could not work. Few enjoyed getting a handout, and many were embarrassed that they needed to ask for this kind of help. At the end of every one of those Sundays, I felt grateful and energized.

My new regime was like a New Year's resolution to exercise more, only the exercises I chose were designed to build a different kind of muscle. Each week I felt stronger. I had never been one to habitually lie, but I wasn't guaranteed to always tell the truth. My commitment to honesty cleansed me as if I showered every morning in a downpour of humility. Adding additional work to my load and volunteering at the food bank burnished my self-respect without feeding my ego, precisely what Maurice Burnside had predicted. I stood straighter, and coupled with my new permanent smile, I felt exhilarated.

"You working out?" Simon asked me one morning.

"Why do you ask?"

"I don't know. You look healthier."

I was on the right track.

"Franklin, there's a phone call for you at the nurses' station," one of the ward secretaries called to me as I was walking out of a patient's room. I followed her back and picked up the call.

"Hello, this is Franklin Rock."

"Franklin, it's Lori."

"Lori! Wow. It's so good to hear your voice. Where are you?"

"I'm in Chicago, but I'm coming to Boston this weekend. Think you can find time to see me?"

"I would drop everything to see you. You know that."

"I'm glad you still feel that way, Franklin. I miss you."

"I miss you, too. Why are you coming to Boston?"

"I don't know if you remember, but my sister is in graduate school there. She's getting an award and wants me to come. So I'm busy with that for most of the weekend. Saturday night I'm free. Is that OK?"

"As long as I don't have a heart attack in anticipation before then, it's great. I am so excited to see you."

"Me, too," Lori replied with a warmth that made me sad for her absence from my life.

For the rest of the week, I could think of nothing else. That I had to wait until Saturday night added to the torture. Lori's sister shared a small apartment with two other women who also had guests arriving and space was therefore at a premium, so she had decided to stay in a small hotel downtown. The plan was for me to meet her there at six.

Her brilliant red hair was the first thing I saw as I scanned the lobby on arrival. I stealthily made my way around the perimeter of the room and came up behind her. "You look more beautiful than I remember," I whispered.

She spun around and threw her arms around my neck. I held her just a little too firmly, unconsciously not willing to take any chance that she would get away.

"God, I've missed you," I said. Instead of responding she kissed me.

"I don't even know where to begin," she said. "Let's go to a restaurant. We can get an early dinner and talk. Any suggestions?"

"Sure, let's go to Little Italy and get some Italian food. We can pretend we're at Vesuvio."

So that's what we did. We held hands as we walked. I looked at her every few seconds to convince myself this was real.

"I'll bet you have a lot to tell me," she said.

"I do, but first I want the hear about your family. How is your sister-in-law? Elizabeth, right?"

"Yes, Elizabeth. She's doing great. It looks like her treatment is working. She's had some tough days, but now she's feeling much better. And the baby is so cute! That part has been a lot of fun."

We arrived at the restaurant. It was early so we were seated immediately.

I filled her in about the details of my job at the hospital.

"OK, now tell me about the important stuff. Have you traveled?" she asked me.

"Only back to the college."

"No, Franklin, I meant to other times."

"As a matter of fact, I have. Twice I think." I told her about going back to second grade and the experience with the boy named Jesse.

"Why do you think you went there?" she asked me.

"I think I was practicing," I responded.

"Practicing what?"

"This is going to sound ridiculous, but I think it has to do with convincing someone to see a situation in another light. That's the only reason I can think of."

Lori was laughing. "So do you think you convinced that boy? What was his name?"

"Jesse."

"Do you think you convinced Jesse that he didn't need to be mean to get attention and have kids like him?"

"I think I did. I don't remember anything more about Jesse as an older kid, so I have no evidence. But it seemed like he got it. Anyway, he was seven. I don't think that's going to cut it with adults."

"You have to start somewhere," she graciously replied.

"Thanks for not making fun of me. You easily could have done that. I probably would have made fun of you."

"I'm nicer than you, Franklin," she reminded me as if it were a known fact. "You said you made two trips. Tell me about the other."

"I met this man," I began. "His name was Maurice Burnside."

"You said was. Does that mean he is no longer with us?"

"It does."

"Oh, my. What happened?" she asked.

"I have to start at the beginning." And so I did. I told her about my first encounter with Maurice Burnside in the hospital. When I got to the part where he said he knew Professor Niemeyer, she sat straight up and grabbed the edge of the table.

"Oh my God, Franklin, when he said that you must have been shocked!"

"Stunned. But wait, that's not the craziest part." I told her about how he saw the book with my name on it.

"Was that the book Professor Niemeyer gave you?"

"Yes. I know, it's crazy, but it gets even more incredible. That's where my next time travel comes in." I then told her about being in Professor Niemeyer's house and seeing Mr. Burnside, Professor Niemeyer, and the book, all of it.

Lori released her grip on the table and sat back. "Is there more?"

"No more hopping around in time. But there is more to tell you about Maurice Burnside." Over the next few minutes, I shared our Monday visits. "That's it, Lori. You're caught up now in my insane life."

"Wow. You must be exhausted. I am just listening to it all."

"Just the opposite. I feel better than ever. I've been working on the lessons Mr. Burnside taught me."

"He sounds like a wonderful man. You were lucky to get to know him and spend that much time with him."

"I was. I think about the things he taught me just about every day. He has changed me for sure."

"Oh, you were pretty good already," she said, her magnificent eyes assuring me that I had not been forgotten.

We finished dinner and headed back to Lori's hotel. "Can you stay?" she asked.

"Forever?"

"How about we start with tonight?"

As we lay in bed together holding each others' hands, Lori turned to me.

"Sounds like you're getting closer, Franklin."

There was some truth to that. Like an athlete training for the Olympics, I had designed a regimen and was following through on it, in preparation for who knows what.

"You still have doubts, don't you?" she asked me.

"Tons. To you and Govinda, what's happening to me seems obvious. It's still not to me."

"That's because you are humble, and your Mr. Burnside has made you even more so. It's a wonderful part of your personality, and I'm sure that will never change. Yes, it is obvious to me. Soon it will be obvious to you, too."

"I don't have to dream tonight, I thought," as I drifted off to sleep, now next to the one person I would have wished to star in my dreams.

I awoke before her and watched her sleep. Lori's eyes opened and caught me in the act. "How long have you been staring at me?" she asked, her sweet smile assuring me that I had committed no crime.

"Not long enough. What time are you meeting your sister?"

"About ten. What time is it now?"

"Eight thirty," I answered, wishing it were still the middle of the night.

"Good. Time for breakfast together." She leaned over and kissed me, then turned and hopped out of bed. I watched her walk towards the bathroom, my heart pulling from my chest as if attached to her by a rope. Saying goodbye yet again was going to hurt.

"My life is getting a bit less hectic now that Elizabeth is doing so well," Lori told me over a croissant and coffee. "I think I have a job lined up with a college placement agency."

"That sounds like fun. When do you start?"

"Not sure. We still have to finalize all of the details, but probably in a couple of weeks. I'll let you know."

The conversation had turned to the mundane, a sure sign that we were about to separate.

"You will call me?" she asked.

"You will call me?" I asked in return, and we both laughed.

"Better than nothing, don't you think?" she said, recognizing our mutual sorrow that the time together was so brief.

"You know I pay attention to every minute we have together, Lori. I'm not exaggerating."

"I know you're not. You wear your heart on your sleeve."

As I turned to walk away after one last embrace, she called to me. "Hey, Franklin, maybe you could stop at my place on one of your travels?"

"I'll put it on the agenda." As soon as I figure out how to do it.

26

Forward

I KNEW I SHOULD HAVE BEEN GRATEFUL for those hours with Lori. Instead, a hunger for her prevailed. Even the knowledge that she was not to be the one, that some other woman would be my partner in the future, could not mitigate my emptiness. My default smile attempted to abandon me; only great discipline on my part kept it from succeeding. Sunday's remaining hours were spent listlessly. Simon and Danny were at the hospital doing whatever medical students do on a Sunday afternoon, so I had no one to distract me from my self-pity. I lay down on my bed, my mind refusing to do anything other than wallow in loss. My eyes closed, and the shift occurred.

◆◇◆◇◆

"IT'S NOT HALLOWEEN; that's for certain. I'm not too good with dates these days," he admitted, "but this one I'm clear on." The old man was smiling and standing behind a smooth, rounded structure that I assumed was some sort of lectern. He reminded me of a greeter at a department store, an elderly retiree looking for something to occupy his free time. He was grayed, quite thin, but very healthy-looking and robust for what I assumed was his fairly advanced age. His eyes were a brilliant blue, the color of a Canadian Rockies lake, and just as crisp and alive.

"Excuse me? Are you talking to me?" I turned to face him directly.

"No, son, I'm talking to the twelve-foot tall invisible man standing next to you. Of course I'm talking to you. Just admiring your costume." His sapphire eyes were scanning me. "Why are you dressed like that? You get those clothes from an old movie set or something?"

I looked down at my clothing. Nothing unusual about it. My jeans and leather coat, though hardly new, were neither worn nor distressed. I assumed the old man was toying with me.

"Son, I'm not looking to harass you. Just curious, that's all. You look a bit confused. Can I help you with something?"

I had no idea if he could help me. Once again, I found myself in a strange place with my mind devoid of thought. I had time-traveled; that was clear. Panic no longer followed my arrival. I had become accustomed to arriving lost and clueless. It would take a bit of time to figure out where I was. I had learned that after many similar trips. Still, the unknown always delivered some level of concern.

"Excuse me, sir. Can you tell me what place this is? I have this amnesia problem and I sometimes forget where I am."

Once again he studied me. I assume he judged my demeanor non-threatening, so he walked around his lectern and approached me.

"So you *are* an actor. And no doubt we are being shown on a teleson somewhere. Am I right?" He looked around in search of some indication that he had correctly deduced that this was some sort of reality TV show.

"No, I'm not an actor. Teleson? Did you mean television?"

"Television? C'mon, this is one of those throwback shows, isn't it? Am I supposed to play along?"

"No, really, it's not a show. What's a teleson?"

His perplexed look concerned me and made it obvious that I should have known the answer to my question. For a minute neither of us said a word, both of us trying to dissemble our mutual discomfort.

He spoke first. "Son, where do you live?"

"I can't remember. It's that amnesia thing. Sometimes I forget everything for a while."

"Do you live near here? Can you remember that?"

My blank look conveyed my hopelessness.

"Do you at least have somewhere to go?"

I had no idea where I was, so could not imagine that I had somewhere to go. "No, I don't," I admitted.

"Well, then come with me. I can take you someplace we can wait until your memory returns."

He immediately sensed my fear of his intentions.

"I'm not going to hurt you. I'm not even a Sentry. And I could use something to eat. It must be about lunchtime so I can leave the A-station for awhile."

Sentry? A-station? More words I didn't know. He seemed sincere, and I had no better option. Once again I found myself in a strange place, and I assumed a strange time, with no idea of how I had arrived at this point. My only option was to go with the flow. This elderly man was now my flow.

He had gone behind his lectern—what he had referred to as the A-station—to retrieve something. As he was doing so he slipped and barely caught the edge of the lectern with his free hand, enough to cushion his fall. Slowly he raised himself from his now recumbent position. He was struggling to get his legs under him. I offered my hand to help him, but he shook me off. "I'm fine. Maybe not quite as agile as years ago, but still pretty damn good."

I could see that he had a device in his hand.

"Would you mind holding this for a second?" He handed the object to me. It was metallic, about the size of a small pack of cigarettes, and hardly weighed anything at all. No markings were visible; I had no idea what it was.

"Thanks." Now upright and stable, he reached out his hand and I placed the metallic object into it. He must have seen the puzzled look on my face.

"You have no idea what this is, do you?" he asked, holding the object vertically in front of him.

I shook my head. It was then that I noticed his clothing. His outfit was one piece, tight like a leotard. There were no buttons or zippers, nor a belt. I wondered how he got it on.

"Communicator," he offered. "For speaking with other people?" his inflection rising as if talking to someone who had been stranded alone on a desert island for years.

"Like a phone?" I asked.

Once again his eyebrows skewed down, his lips no longer smiling but in a neutral position as he contemplated my response. He noticed me staring at his clothing.

"I know it's old and not the most fashionable, but it still works. All of the electronics are perfectly functional, though you wouldn't know to look at it." My astonishment must have been indistinguishable from confusion.

"Son, you are either lost, disoriented, or both. You are perfectly safe with me. Now let's go."

He motioned me to follow him and pointed to the edge of a building one hundred feet to his left. It was only then that I noticed them. All of the buildings were a stark white. None had windows. Not one. Most were the same height, about fifty stories I estimated, but without windows, it was just a guess.

He moved far more quickly than I had expected considering his age and his difficulty in arising off the ground after his fall. He stopped and turned to me.

"You have elevars in those shoes?" he asked.

"What are elevars?"

"Really? What are elevars? Son, where *are* you from?" his tone reflecting his obvious consternation. "You're not a big guy. I think mine might get us high enough for the entrance. When we get there, you'll just hang on to me."

My stomach began to churn. Oh my God. Teleson. Sentry, A-stations, elevars, huge all-white windowless buildings. No question now; I was sometime in the future. The past was one thing. I had been there and back numerous times. But the future was a whole other order of magnitude. I froze like a child caught with contraband.

"Son, we need to get going." The old man could see that I was nearly catatonic. He gently tapped my right shoulder, then took my forearm. "We need to go."

We were off, and in a minute had reached the edge of the building he had pointed out as our goal. Before us was a long, stark lane, not quite an alleyway as I would think of one. This lane was flanked by the window-less sides of the white buildings that framed the lane. The buildings were immense in length, at least five times what I had anticipated from the front. I looked up. I noticed for the first time that the buildings were covered by a transparent dome. I could not determine its size nor whether it covered only the two buildings on either side of the lane or extended further.

The old man gave my arm another short tug. "No time to stop and look around now, son. We'll be there in a minute." He hustled me down the lane.

"OK, now we elevate." He wrapped both arms around me from behind, as if about to do the Heimlich maneuver. "Hold on."

Suddenly we were moving up, slowly, as if on an old elevator. Soon we were hovering in front of what appeared to me to be an alcove carved into the side of the building to our right. Our trajectory changed; we were now moving horizontally towards the alcove. Within a few seconds I realized that like the building itself, the alcove was another optical illusion. It was more like a floor-less tunnel that extended well into the building.

Slowly we moved ahead into this tunnel. Two, maybe three minutes passed as we continued to glide forward. Then we stopped, and together we slowly rotated clockwise ninety degrees.

"Here we are." And as the old man said those words, a portion of the white wall slid open revealing what looked to me like the lobby of a fancy office building. He released his hold of me and for a moment I was certain I would drop like a stone, but I didn't. I was standing quite solidly on a floor that seemed to appear out of nowhere. I turned behind me to watch the door close, but all I could see was a wall that seemed no different than those that stretched out in front of me in this lobby.

"Well, that turned out just fine, I'd say." He added a quick wink before he nodded to our right. Once again he motioned me to follow him. I looked around as I trailed behind. People were milling about talking. I wouldn't say it was crowded since the lobby was enormous. I looked up. The ceiling of the lobby soared above. I could not even hazard a guess as to how high it was. The dome I had observed when outside allowed the light to pour in and brightly illuminate the lobby.

I had stopped to take it all in and soon became aware that the old man had not noticed my dawdling and had moved quite a bit ahead of me. As I started walking towards him, he suddenly vanished. I quickened my step and then broke into a trot. My heart began to race. Although I didn't even know his name, he was my only current contact in this time. Like a small child who had lost his mother in the supermarket, I began to panic as I raced ahead.

"Whoa, son, slow down. You almost zoomed right past me." He caught hold of my jacket and held on as I came to a stop. "Sorry, I didn't realize I had lost you," he offered in an apologetic tone. He could tell by my clear sense of relief that I was frightened. "We need to get you something to calm you down."

He turned me around one hundred eighty degrees. I was now facing a cafeteria with probably two hundred tables. He steered me past all of them into a room filled with what looked to me like floor-to-ceiling electronic walls.

"You hungry?"

I realized I was. "Yes, sir, a bit."

"Me too." He fumbled with his left arm sleeve. "It's here somewhere." He walked over to one of the electronic walls and spoke as if chatting with a friend. "Good day. Durning 4-11-12," he spoke out loud. A panel opened. The old man stepped forward, moved his forehead towards the panel, and held still.

"Authorization confirmed," I heard. A portion of the electronic wall then instantly transformed into a menu of sorts.

The old man again spoke to the wall and ordered what sounded like turkey sandwiches and some type of drink, though I either could not hear him clearly or it was some beverage with which I was unfamiliar. He didn't bother to ask what I wanted to eat. As soon as he was done talking to the wall, he again took hold of my arm and directed me back into the dining area. Soon we were seated at a table for two, a good distance from the other diners.

He held out his right hand.

"My name is Doranto Durning," he began, then quickly added, "but don't tell me yours just yet. If you're a fugitive, it's better if I don't know it. Then I can honestly deny any knowledge of you."

"I'm not a fugitive," I quickly replied. He waved me off.

"I was only kidding. We don't have fugitives here."

His response intrigued me. "What do you mean by that? You never have a fugitive? No one ever escapes the law?" I asked.

"Are you being sarcastic?"

"No, sir."

Doranto seemed confused. "Why would you think we would have fugitives? We hardly ever have a serious crime; haven't for years. Do you have a problem where you're from? I've not heard about another place that still had a crime problem for as long as I can recall."

Doranto paused as if trying to decide if what he was about to say next was a good idea. "Son, it's pretty obvious that wherever you are from is a long way away. I am going to go out on a limb and surmise that you are not of this time. Your clothes, the way you look around at everything as if it's the first time you've seen it. Am I correct?"

"What year is this?" I asked, afraid of what I might hear in response.

"2095."

My heart almost stopped.

"What year was it where you came from?"

"1989."

Reflexively Doranto leaned back away from me. "Oh my, son, I'll bet you're a bit disarmed by all of this, then. Any idea how you got here?"

"I wish I did. I've traveled to the past for short periods, but this is the first time I have ever traveled forward in time."

"Well, one hundred-plus years seems like quite a first-time trip." He was smiling.

"Mr. Durning,".

"Please call me Doranto."

"Doranto, you don't seem all that shocked to meet someone from another time. I seem more surprised than you."

I turned my head to the sound coming from behind me. A black and red machine was making its way towards us with a basket of sorts perched on top. This was a robot, but not like the ones depicted in the 1980's science fiction stories. It more resembled a moving file cabinet. As it approached us, it slowed and came to a halt just at the edge of our table. A front panel retracted and a tray extended with two pretty normal-looking sandwiches on it. Doranto lifted them both. As soon as he did, the tray retracted and a second tray extended. It had two glasses and two cups, some sort of metallic vessel, and a metallic box. Doranto removed them all. The tray then retracted, the panel closed, and the robot turned and moved away.

"I thought I heard you order turkey sandwiches. At least these haven't changed much in a hundred years," I said, examining the plate laid in front of me.

"It's not what you probably would think of as turkey. We don't eat real turkeys. This is synthesized from organic vegetables. I'd be interested to know what you think of it."

I took a bite. "Wow, this tastes exactly like turkey! It's delicious!"

Doranto laughed. "Of course it does. The replication of taste is quite simple. Oh my, I can only imagine your reaction to lots of other things that are pretty normal for us."

I hadn't realized how hungry I was. Although I had a million questions, they were now going to have to wait until I finished this terrific sandwich.

"You eat, I'll talk." Doranto noted my delight with the lunch he had ordered me. "About your time travel question. Yes, we know it's possible. At least some scientists have concluded that. But no one has yet figured out how to do it. There have been reports of a very few individuals who have been documented to move between times. It's not something we spend a lot of effort on. Maybe we're no longer as curious as you were back in your time."

I finished my sandwich and realized that I had forgotten to thank my host.

"Thanks so much for the sandwich, Doranto. It was incredibly good. I'd offer to pay you, but you probably already figured out that I have no money, at least money that would work here."

"My pleasure," he replied, a genuinely warm smile gracing his face. "You gave me something to do. It's my job to help people like you. Well, not exactly like you. The people I normally help live here and aren't zooming around time. So tell me, what is it like moving through time?"

"Sometimes unsettling. Like today, I often find myself in a strange place with no idea where I am, how I got here, or why I am where I am. Today is the first time, at least that I can remember, that I ended up in the future."

"Except for the initial shock you seem pretty calm now," he observed.

"I guess it's because so far I have always returned home from wherever I have been after a short while, and nothing bad has happened to me. Plus your kindness is so comforting. I can't thank you enough. I'm a total stranger, and yet you just dropped what you were doing and helped me. That means a lot."

"You are more than welcome. May I ask you something?"

"Of course."

"You said you have no idea where you are in time and place when you time travel. That seems to be the case right now. You also said you don't know why you are in a specific place in a specific time. Is there a why? Do you end up in certain places for a reason?"

"I think so. At least it seems that way to me. But I can't say for sure. Professor Niemeyer and I never discussed the 'why' of my travels."

Doranto's head jerked upward. "Just to make certain I heard you correctly. You said Professor Niemeyer."

"Yes. Why?" I couldn't imagine why that name had struck a chord with my new friend.

Doranto focused his sapphires right at me. "Son, I know who Professor Niemeyer is. Everyone does."

"No, Doranto, this is a different Professor Niemeyer. He is from my time. He died a very long time ago. Much too soon as it turns out. For you, that would be over one hundred years ago."

Doranto leaned closer. "I'm pretty sure we are talking about the same man."

"It can't be the same Professor Niemeyer. My Professor Niemeyer died long ago. He was my teacher, my mentor. He died during my last year of college. So we must be talking about two different Professor Niemeyers."

Doranto moved even closer. His voice softened as he spoke. "You haven't told me your name, son, but I'm pretty sure that I know who you are." He hesitated. His smile vanished. I thought he was about to cry. Words suddenly became difficult for him to utter.

"Are you…" he paused, needing to catch his breath, then continued. "Are you Franklin Rock?"

I began trembling. "Yes. Yes, that's me. But how could you possibly know that?"

"Every child knows that Professor Niemeyer was Franklin Rock's mentor."

"Why would they know this? How would they know? I don't understand."

"Franklin. May I call you Franklin?"

"Yes, of course." I could barely stand the second or two before he replied.

"Franklin, you are famous and have been for many years. Your name is known worldwide."

"What? I'm famous? Are you sure it's me you're talking about?"

Doranto was almost laughing as he replied. "Oh yes, it's you I'm talking about. You are a certified hero. You honestly mean you don't know that?"

"Hero? What are you talking about? Me? Why would I be a hero?"

Doranto stood and held out his right hand. "Franklin Rock, it is an incredible honor to meet you."

I had no idea what to do, so I stood and offered my hand in return. What in the world is going on?

"Speechless. I understand. This is all new to you coming from so long ago. Franklin, I can take you to a place where it will all become clear."

Not a thought, not a word came to mind. I simply stood there and stared at Doranto. There could be no doubt that Doranto, the unfamiliar technology, and the strange building were all real. This was no dream. And so what he had told me must also be real.

Doranto stood placidly in front of me, his smile that of someone who had just unexpectedly met his lifelong idol. He placed his hand under my upper arm and began to lead me out of the cafeteria.

"Where are we going?"

"To the Franklin Rock Museum."

And with those words fading from my world, I felt the shift and I was gone.

27

Mixed Up

"FRANKLIN, ARE YOU with me?"

Like a patient waking from anesthesia, I became aware of those words as I opened my eyes. Professor Niemeyer was standing over me, his gracious smile spread across his lips. At first, it all seemed so natural, until I remembered that my mentor was dead.

"Professor Niemeyer! You're alive!" I yelled as I sat bolt upright. I looked around. I was on my bed in my room, no one but the two of us present. My heart was racing.

He laughed. "Of course I'm alive. Why shouldn't I be?"

Was I just in the future? Did I imagine Professor Niemeyer's death? At that moment I had no idea what was real.

"You died. You left me the book. I saw you in your house with Maurice Burnside, and I met your wife." I grabbed my head in my hands. In an instant of clarity, I looked directly at Professor Niemeyer.

"What day is today?"

"Tuesday," the Professor replied.

"No, I mean the date. What is today's date?"

"I'm not sure," he responded in a completely unconvincing manner.

"What do you mean you're not sure?" I pressed him. "What year?" I was now glaring at him. His previous response seemed designed to dismiss me.

"I was afraid that might be your question. That's not quite clear either."

"How could it not be clear? What year is this, Professor? You're scaring me."

"Franklin, I'm sorry. Don't be scared. I'm always conflicted about what is best for you to know at any one time. Seems my desire to make certain that you are not frightened too often results in just the opposite. The proper answer is of course that it is any day and every day simultaneously."

"Is this the 'all moments of time exist forever' speech? I get that. But…" Suddenly my fuzzy thoughts coalesced and crystalized. "I'm not dreaming. And your death was not a dream. I've traveled back again from where I was, but I haven't landed back from where I started. I'm right, aren't I? I was just in the future. That I know for sure. And now I'm not, that's also for sure. So where exactly am I?" Before he could respond, a second thought gripped me, and the words escaped before I could corral them. "Oh my God, Professor. You are going to die. I am so sorry!"

"Franklin, don't be silly. Don't you think I know that? Remember I told you that death is not what you think. No one 'dies' as everyone assumes. How could they if each moment of time is eternal? Now, let's get to the important issues."

"You haven't answered my question, Professor. Where am I? Where are we?"

"Franklin, you can see that you are in your room. Now as to when, that is a tricky question. Your assessment is surprisingly accurate. We will go with your guess that you haven't landed in any particular time. That's not quite accurate but for now it will do. Don't worry; you're not in some purgatory or time warp. You are in a definite time—there is no way not to be. But neither of us will be in this particular time very long."

Professor Niemeyer paused and subtly leaned away as if expecting me to leap at him. I was too busy processing what I knew for sure. Before when I time-traveled it was always finite and into the past. Except for the incident in the library with Barb and her professor boyfriend—and I am still not certain which event preceded which—my travel had been unidirectional. Always I went backward, and always I returned to a recognizable present. This time was different. First I found myself in some bizarre future, then suddenly here with a living Professor Niemeyer somewhere in the past. It was as if I had missed the present stop on the train. Past and future were difficult enough, but an unknown time was a concept I had not previously encountered. Professor Niemeyer awaited my conscious return to the moment.

"Franklin. Where did you go?"

"Sir, I don't know where I was, just that it was the future."

"I assumed so. Well, it was inevitable. Did you talk with anyone while you were there?" he asked.

"Yes, I met a nice older gentleman. His name was Doranto Durning."

"I don't know that name," Professor Niemeyer commented.

"Well, he knew you—and me!" I was almost shouting.

Professor Niemeyer began to chuckle. "So," he said, "I'm assuming then that the cat is out of the bag. You know."

"You mean that you and I are famous in the future and that I am some kind of hero? That's what Doranto told me. Is it true, Professor?"

My mentor turned his back on me, his right hand rubbing the tip of his nose as he always did when contemplating a reply to a question. He turned to face me, his head now up, eyes forward. "The short answer is yes," he eventually answered me. "But it's a bit more complicated."

"What does that mean?"

"You recall our discussion of relativity, Franklin."

"Yes, Einstein and all of that," I acknowledged.

"So now we need to throw in a bit of quantum physics."

"Oh God, Professor. Now? I have no idea where I am, I have no idea if I'm talking to a dead person, if this is all real or a dream or even something else. And now you want me to learn quantum physics?"

That look, the one I had seen on more than one occasion when a student seemed so dense that the Professor wondered how he had made it past adolescence to college, was now focused on me.

"You think I could teach and you could learn a topic that enormous in a few minutes as if it were a cake recipe? No, Franklin, you just need to know some basics so that you can understand what is going on with you. I assume you would want to know that?" his voice rising, implying that only a moron would disagree.

"We think of our world as precise and certainly predictable. Let me use an analogy that might help you understand, even though it is not technically correct. If we know, for example, the trajectory and speed at which I throw a ball, we can safely assume that with some calculations we can determine precisely where it will land. But suppose I told you that once in a very, very, very large number it might end up somewhere else, like on Mars or maybe on a star light-years away. You would of course tell me that I was crazy, and almost every single time you would be correct.

But not one hundred percent of the time. Franklin, quantum physics has proven that the world is not as certain as we might think. Even things that you would bet your life are completely predictable are not. They usually are—the ball will just about always end up where you think—but nothing can be predicted with guaranteed certainty. Our world, Franklin, is probabilistic, meaning that it is never one hundred percent that any action will result in a definite outcome."

I understood how Henry must feel when I insist on sharing some insight with him. I neither understood the Professor's explanation nor at this moment of temporal confusion cared a whiff about what he was trying to teach me. My expression revealed my attitude.

"Franklin, this is important," Professor Niemeyer snapped. "You are quite bright, certainly bright enough to understand that I'm telling you all of this for a reason. Please, pay attention.

"You know that atoms consist of a nucleus in the center and electrons that float around the nucleus. Let's say we wanted to know the precise location of any single electron as it circled the nucleus. That doesn't seem hard to do. That electron must have a specific location, right? It has to be somewhere. But quantum physics has proven that to be untrue. Until we look for the electron, it has no specific location. It could be circling that nucleus, or zooming around in another galaxy, or under your bed. Only when we try to look at it does it have a single precise location. So far so good?" he asked.

"Yes, I think so."

"OK, good. That electron could be anywhere in the universe until we look for it. As I just told you—and I am repeating this because it is very strange indeed—it does not have one single location until we try to find it using some experimental technique. It not only can be anywhere, but it is likely everywhere simultaneously. Meaning it behaves not as if it is one single particle, but infinite particles. That implies that the universe we know is only one of an infinite number of possible universes. That electron is actually in different locations in each universe. Electrons are particles; they are things. What I am telling you does not only apply to tiny things like electrons. It applies to everything. Imagine, in one universe you might be in your dorm room as we are here. In another you might be somewhere else, doing something else, with someone else."

Like a muscle attempting to lift an unexpectedly heavy weight, my brain was struggling with the ideas Professor Niemeyer was throwing at me. He paused to allow me to reflect on the mystery he had just revealed.

"Nothing is one-hundred percent; our world is about probabilities. So is any outcome always possible?" I asked him.

"It's not just that, Franklin. It's that *every* possible outcome happens in one of the infinite universes that exist. You are now wondering why I am telling you all of this."

"I am, sir."

"Good. Because you need to know this, and I think you will feel a lot better about all of this after you do. Let's assume that you are indeed in different places with different people right now in different universes. You and I are now here in this one. The fact that you are in a specific place at a specific time means something; it implies purpose."

"How does it imply purpose? I don't understand. If all time has already occurred, what difference does anything make? Hasn't everything already happened? For that matter, why are any of our choices important?" Here was my chance, in one fell swoop, to unburden myself of all the questions that Govinda and I had discussed.

"Those are excellent questions. You know of course that we are all constantly moving through time. The idea you have, and that most people have, is of linear time and space; you are in one time and one place, then time advances and you are in another time. Seems pretty simple, but that's not how the world, or I should more properly say worlds, work.

"Time, you have already learned, is quite different. It is not the timeline most people think it is. You and I have already dispensed with the incorrect notion of past, present, and future. So what happens then? What creates what we think of as reality? Reality is determined by the intersection of the innumerable choices made by billions of people. Here's the really interesting part. Those choices, like switches on train tracks, are continually doing something remarkable. They are moving us from one universe to another, or more precisely creating one universe after another. Life can seem quite random, Franklin, but when you understand that there are infinite universes with infinite Franklin Rocks, the fact that you are who you are in this particular universe is enormously significant. In this particular universe you have a purpose. We all do. Yours just happens to be incredibly special."

"I will be famous in this particular universe, the one you and I are in right now, but you're telling me that in some other universe, or maybe all the others, I am not famous. Is that right?"

"Yes, Franklin, that is correct."

"Is it possible I will move to another universe from this one, one where I won't do anything important?"

"No, the branch at which it became determined that you would be who you are and will be occurred long ago. You are long past that. Additional branch points will arrive that will determine the outcomes of other events, that will bring other Franklin Rocks to other places. But for now, it's enough for you to know that you are on a path toward the destiny you just had a glimpse of on your trip to the future. That part is a certainty."

Professor Niemeyer eyed me, awaiting any emotional reaction. He had correctly assumed that my head was about to explode so he kept talking.

"Look, no one of us can control the way the world works. But the beauty is that we don't have to. The universe, or more accurately, universes unfold based on the billions of choices we each make. It seems random, I know, but it is not. It's not frightening; it's fantastic. I'm going to ask you to trust me that there is a plan. And as you are beginning to learn, you are a big part of that plan."

"Just to confirm, I am going to be famous? I am going to do good things?"

"Yes. You will be quite famous, and you are going to do great things."

"I'm not sure I'm ready for all of this. Am I?"

"Probably not," Professor Niemeyer replied with a wide smile not meant to offend. "But that's just fine, Franklin. Rarely are any of us prepared for what we are called to do. Every one of us reaches the day, the specific moment when he or she crosses the threshold and realizes that dependency is no longer necessary, and transitions from one whom must be cared for to one who can care for others. Welcome to the other side, Franklin."

"We will see each other again, won't we Professor?"

"I see you have already figured that one out. We will, Franklin."

"Is there a way that I can find you when I need help?" I asked, actively praying that the answer was yes.

"Let me answer your question with another," he began. "You now appreciate that all time is accessible, correct?"

"Yes, sir. But I still have no idea how to get where I want to go."

"There are several ways to do that, and you will figure it out before too long. I'm not sure you are ready for that, but on the other hand, I seem to be quite poor at determining just what you are ever ready for. Don't worry about finding me. I tend to keep an eye on you, and so far you are doing just fine. You feel better now?"

"I do. So when do I start doing, you know, the important stuff?"

"You already are. You can't see the whole picture."

As one often is after any fierce emotional experience, I was suddenly overcome by fatigue.

"Goodbye for now, Franklin. Oh, and Maurice Burnside sends his best wishes. He did a nice job, don't you think?" Those were the last words I heard before I found myself once more in motion, on the way to where and when to be determined.

28

Another Farewell

THE PREMONITION AND THE RINGING of the telephone were simultaneous. *This isn't going to be good.*

"Franklin, it's Lori."

"Lori! I miss you," I whispered into the phone.

"I miss you, too. I have some news to share."

The premonition was about to be fulfilled.

"I'm moving."

"To Boston?" I asked, as if my question would magically alter her reply.

"No, unfortunately not. To Germany. My brother has been asked to run a division of his company. He and Elizabeth asked me if I wanted to join them."

My heart sank faster than an anchor. For a few moments, I was unable to speak.

"Franklin, are you there? Oh, I am so sorry."

"It's all right. I'm happy for you. It sounds very exciting," I replied, breaking my vow of total honesty.

"That's what you say to an acquaintance. You think I don't know how you feel? I dreaded calling you. Maybe I shouldn't have," she added, her voice trailing off.

"No, I'm glad you did. At least I get to hear your voice. When are you going?" I asked as if it mattered. The deal was done.

"In two weeks. I was hoping to get to Boston one more time to see you, but I won't be able to. We have to pack and make all sorts of arrangements. I need to help them, especially with the baby. I'm so sorry," she repeated. Lori had no other tools available. Sorry was all she had to offer.

Our conversation continued for a while, but in effect, it had ended with her news. I filled her in on my travel to the future, but I left out the part about me becoming famous. When I practiced saying those words in my head, they seemed absurd. Maybe if we were together in person I would have told her, but not now over the phone as we were about to be separated by an ocean.

Just before we hung up she told me she loved me. She told me this was a very difficult decision for her because of me. I told her I loved her too, and we concluded with the promise that we would stay in touch. But I knew at that moment that even if we did, it would only be to let each other down gently, to avoid an end too painful to contemplate. Lori had thrown one of those switches on the track; she was in effect shifting to another outcome. I should have known, should have expected something like this to occur. I had already seen my future; the woman I would be with was not her. Wishful thinking could not alter that fact.

At the moment she informed me that she was moving, the bond of intimacy was in my mind instantly and permanently severed. When we were together, I saw no reason to withhold anything. I could not wait to share. Now everything would be different. We would become memories to each other, sweet but distant.

Why does that happen to us humans? Why do we give ourselves to each other in the most intimate way only to see the relationship dissolve for one reason or another? Are we supposed to learn from these experiences? If so, and I suspect that is the case, can't there be a better, less painful way to acquire that knowledge? What good can come from love lost?

Like the song that you suddenly and mysteriously hear in your mind that perfectly fits the situation, Professor Niemeyer's words arrived. "Time is like a block of ice, Franklin. No moment ever dies." With that thought, I was released from the bonds of despair. Lori and I would be together in perpetuity in those glorious times we were together. I closed my eyes to recall a few of them, and the world once again shifted.

◆◇◆◇◆

"GOODNIGHT, FRANKLIN. I will see you tomorrow." I recognized Elsa's voice. We were in the apartment we lived in until I was four. My mother was behind me. She waved goodbye to Elsa, then talked directly to me.

"Franklin, I'm making dinner. You can play with your Lincoln Logs in the living room."

Lincoln Logs! As a child, I loved that toy. They came in a cardboard cylinder with a metal top that I remember prying off with my fingers and always enjoyed hearing the pop as it came free. Then I would turn the cylinder upside down and spill them all out onto the floor. Logs of different sizes intermingled. Long ones were for making the walls, the smaller were connecting pieces. Every time I built the same house. Seems I was never curious enough to imagine different ways they might go together. As I marveled at my favorite toy, I heard my parents talking in the kitchen.

"Ray, it happened again. Elsa and I were fixing lunch and Franklin began talking about someplace in such detail you would swear he had been there. He talked about buildings covered by what he called a big dish. When I asked him what he meant, he pointed to the glass cake dome over there on the counter. 'It looks like that, Mommy. It goes way over all the buildings. You can see through it to the sun.' I asked him if that was his dream last night. He told me it wasn't, that he had seen it and described other people being there. I asked what else he saw there. He said people could go straight up into the air by themselves and move around."

"Did he tell you how he knew this?" my father asked.

"He just said he was there and then came home."

"Look," my father said to my mother, "we both know Franklin is different. We've known it since he could talk. Don't you remember all those things he said he could see that you and I couldn't? I used to think he just had a vivid imagination. When I would try to play along, it was obvious that it wasn't a game to him. He knew I wasn't seeing what he did. I think that's why he stopped telling us. He's a special child, Martha."

"What are we going to do?" my mother asked him.

"Nothing. I don't think there is anything we can do except watch him. It will be interesting to see what happens as he gets older. You know," he began, then stopped.

"What?" my mother asked. "What were you going to say?"

"I was going to say that I've had this feeling for a while now that Franklin has a destiny. I know," he continued, "it sounds crazy. He's only a small child. It's just the things he talks about, the way he sees people and places; they're not what you hear from other kids his age. He seems to understand so much. I don't mean things we tell him. I mean things about the world, about people. I know you see it, too."

"Elsa says the same thing you do," my mother responded. "She says he's gifted."

"She knows him the best. He loves her," my dad added.

"He does. He trusts her. He tells her things he doesn't tell us."

"Like what?" my dad asked.

"Elsa told me he said something very strange the other day. He told her he was going to be very important when he was older. Elsa of course just assumed he was talking like any kid would, wanting to be the center of attention. When she asked him what he was going to be, she thought he was going to say a policeman or something like that. Instead, this is what he said, word for word. Elsa was sure to get it right because it was such a surprise to her. Franklin said, 'Oh Elsa, it's not like that. I saw that people were clapping and saying my name and were very happy to see me.'"

I listened to see how my father would respond.

"I'm not all that surprised, Martha. I have the same feeling about him. There's something more. It's hard to put my finger on it."

"What do you mean?"

"C'mon, we've both said it. Sometimes you forget he's a child. He's so directed. He doesn't get distracted by things like most kids. It's almost like he's on a mission."

My head whipped around. I could hear the two of them mumbling something as they came around the corner from the kitchen to the living room. "Franklin," my dad began, "you love those Lincoln Logs, don't you? I like the house you built. Mom and I have a question. Can you tell us about the place you saw with the big dish over it?"

Was he asking his young Franklin or me, his twenty-one-year-old son? How was I supposed to respond? I put down the long Lincoln Log I had been holding and turned to face my parents. I should have expected that the world would then shift again, and it did.

◆-◇-◆-◇-◆

No LONGER SHOULD I QUESTION my destiny. My trip forward to meet Doranto and to learn of my future was no fluke, nor was this trip to hear my parents discuss their unusual child. Past, present, and future were all pointing their fingers directly at me.

29

Joanna

THE NEXT SEVERAL MONTHS PASSED rapidly and uneventfully. It had now been one year since I began working at the hospital. My duties were still limited to the blocking and tackling of patient care, but despite the unchallenging routine I continued to enjoy taking care of and spending time with the patients. No second Maurice Burnside had appeared, but asking for that would have been pure greed.

I had watched families experience the joy of good news and recovery and sadly witnessed sorrow and loss. What surprised me was my reaction to each. I would have imagined that the happy times, where patients and their families celebrated a good outcome, would have been much more memorable to me than the moments of despair, but that is not what I experienced. Holding the hand of a dying patient, or offering words of comfort to his or her family member was unexpectedly fulfilling. As I watched a tear dry or received a hug or words of appreciation from someone at a time of deep sorrow, I knew that my presence was import-ant. Maurice Burnside had been, as usual, right on the money: "When you begin to worry more about other people than yourself, when you place their troubles ahead of your own, the burdens of your own life instantly lighten."

As I entered 3 South the following Monday morning, I found myself reflecting on my work. Being a nursing assistant wasn't going to be a career for me, but as I walked past the patient rooms I realized how comfortable I had become in this setting. We were a team, all of us dedicated to taking care of our patients. Each day I felt that I was doing something worth-while. I liked that feeling.

On the way home that afternoon, I thought about a possible long-term career in the hospital. Danny and Simon were becoming doctors, but that didn't interest me. Perhaps hospital administration would be good. I didn't know much about it but decided I would look into it over the next few weeks.

"Reunion weekend is coming," Simon announced as I walked through the door of our apartment, bringing me back to the present.

"You guys want to go?" I asked the two of them.

"Absolutely!" Danny replied. "Don't you? J Bob told me a few weeks ago that he was going. Have you heard from Henry?"

"You're asking me that? Does anyone hear from him? I'll bet he comes. I don't know anyone more nostalgic than him."

"You think he'll just show up without telling anyone?"

"I'll try calling him again. Eventually he has to answer his phone. Maybe."

"Maybe," Danny agreed.

Two days later I reached Henry.

"Finally you answered your phone," I said.

"Yeah, sorry, I've been real busy," he responded.

"Ensconced in your room, I assume. Why you ever thought going to graduate school right after college was a good idea for you…" I left out the rest. "You OK?"

"I'm fine. You're calling about the reunion, right?"

"I am. Are you going? Danny, Simon, and I are. Danny says J Bob is, too. Am I going to have to come drag you out of your room like the old days?"

No," he laughed. "I'm coming. Are you thinking of going Friday afternoon?"

"That's our plan. I'm glad you're coming, Henry. I was worried about you."

"Franklin, you're always worried about me. I'm still alive, I think."

"We can talk when we're together. I have a lot to tell you."

"I can only imagine. Have you been moving around in time at all?"

"Yes, and it's been something."

"I'm sure. Have any physics to teach me?"

"As a matter of fact, Henry, I do."

"Maybe I won't come after all."

"Yes, you will. But I promise I'll keep the physics to a minimum."

Two weeks later Danny, Simon, and I piled into Danny's car and headed back to our college. It had only been a year; everything was still fresh. We met up with Henry who had beaten us there by an hour. Danny and Simon headed to meet some other friends. Henry and I preferred to remain outdoors; it was a beautiful day.

As we walked around campus, the magnetic field still pulled me towards the Memorial.

"You're thinking about Lori, I assume?" Henry asked me, catching me staring at the entrance to the bookstore.

"Yes, but not the way you think."

"You didn't tell me what happened."

"How was I supposed to tell you if you never answer your phone?"

"Well, we're here now. So what happened?"

"It's not important. It's been months since we've seen each other," I responded. Just hearing my own words confirmed their veracity.

"I know, but I'm still interested if you want to tell me."

"I'm not sure what the last thing you knew was. She was living in Chicago helping her brother and sister-in-law with the baby because her sister-in-law Elizabeth had cancer. Had I already told you that?"

"Yup. I knew all of that."

"Lori came to Boston for a weekend. We got to spend an evening together."

"You must have been a basket case."

"Not really." I decided that Henry did not need to know about my vision of my future, the one that did not include Lori Constantine. "But it was great to see her."

"It doesn't sound that way. Did you have an argument?"

"We never once raised our voices to each other. I don't remember even disagreeing about anything. She knew all about my time travel, about Professor Niemeyer, everything."

"So, what happened?"

"She moved to Germany."

"What? Why did she move to Germany?"

"Her brother got transferred, and she went with them."

"I'm sorry, Franklin. I bet you were crushed."

"I was when she moved away the first time. Not the second time."

"Franklin, that doesn't sound like you. Is there something you're not telling me?" Henry persisted.

That's the problem—or benefit—from having a best friend. They know you too well. My initial omission had been a mistake. I changed my mind and told him about my future vision.

"No wonder you didn't go insane. It sounds like it was great while it lasted."

"It lasts forever, Henry."

"Oh, yeah, I forgot. All moments of time in ice or something like that, right?"

"Something like that."

"What time is it, Franklin?"

I checked my watch. Four thirty. "Why?"

"Just curious. C'mon, let's head over to the Gardens."

So we did. As we got to the gates Henry paused.

"Stopping or not?" he asked me.

"Not. Haven't been back here for a while," I said with a wink as I walked through them.

Every bed had something blooming, fulfilling the plan of the gardeners who dedicated many hours so that the denizens of the College could luxuriate in their presence. The place was packed. Henry and I weren't the only ones for whom the Gardens were a paradise. As I looked around, I saw men and women of every age. Days like this, where former students return, are magical. It is as if all of time's component parts make a simultaneous appearance, reminding us of what permanently exists within its boundaries. I never tire of that mental picture.

"Let's head down to the brook and over to the clearing," Henry suggested. As we headed around the bend of the brook, we heard a woman's voice calling our names.

"Joanna!" I yelled before even turning toward the voice. She looked more beautiful than ever. Sunlight illuminated her blond hair; her smile illuminated her lovely face. She hugged Henry, then me. Just seeing her reminded me that the pilot light was always lit.

"That's why you asked me what time it was Henry. You two had a plan."

"We did, Franklin," Joanna answered. "Well done, Henry. You got him here right on time."

"It is so good to see you, Joanna," I told her.

"It's so good to see you, Franklin."

What did I just detect in her greeting? Something was different. She could see me thinking.

"Oh my, that Franklin Rock brain is working already. Don't hurt yourself, Franklin. We all just got here. You'll have plenty of time to think."

"You know me, Joanna. It's hard to keep my brain quiet."

"So the last time we spoke you were about to start fixing the world. How's that going?"

"I knew I shouldn't have told you two. Now I will never hear the end of it," I said, only half-joking.

"No, you should have, and I'm glad you did. And I'm sorry. I shouldn't have said that. It was stupid."

"Joanna, I have never heard you say anything stupid. Am I right, Henry?"

"Never. Franklin and I are in charge of stupid."

"I want to know all about what you are doing," I told Joanna, hoping to remove myself from the center of the conversation.

Joanna turned to me. "You might not remember what you said to me last year. I think we were here in the Gardens. You told me to do what I wanted to do, so I did. I passed on that job training program and instead went to work in a design company. It's been fantastic. I get to do all sorts of different things, all creative. I love it. So thanks, Franklin. That turned out to be the right choice."

That's not exactly what happened. I did not tell her which choice to make. I just told her that there was no way to know the outcome of any choice, so she should feel free to choose whichever path she wanted. But I wasn't going to tell her that now. Henry would have glowered at me for preaching, and rightfully so. I was glad she was happy; that's all that mattered.

"Henry, what about you?" she asked him.

"Me? You could just replay the movie of college. Graduate school is no different. I'm working pretty much all of the time. I don't think I've made much progress in that way," Henry said, looking towards me.

"Are you glad you're doing it?" she followed up.

"I think so. I mean, it's interesting. I'll like it more as I get to see patients. Right now it's pretty much like every other psychology course I've ever taken."

"You know you don't have to stay if you'd rather be doing something else," I told Henry. But I realized that wasn't true as soon as the words left my mouth. He had made a commitment. To his credit, Henry always finished what he started. He would just keep his head down and grind it out.

"No, I'll keep going. It's fine," he said, indicating that the topic was now closed.

After a bit more chatter, we headed out of the Gardens to meet up with Danny, Simon, J Bob, and some other friends who had also decided to return for the reunion. As we got to the student center, we could see the group of them out in front awaiting us. Henry waved and continued towards the group. Joanna grabbed my arm and held me back.

"Franklin," she said, "Can we find time to talk? Just you and me," she said quietly.

"Is everything all right with you?" I asked, now a bit concerned.

"Yes, everything is fine. You know how hard it is to talk when we're all together."

"Why don't we meet early tomorrow morning? These guys will drink too much tonight and I'm sure they won't be seeing the sunrise. If I recall you like getting up early. That still true?"

"Still true. That's a really good idea."

We walked up and joined the group. Being all together again was wonderful. We were still a family, and we picked up right where we left off. Even though Danny, Simon, and I were living together, our busy lives precluded us from spending the kind of time we did when in college. Our other friends were the catalyst we needed to recreate the spirit we had enjoyed together for four years. None of us, I thought, could be happier than at that moment we were back together.

We ended up at a restaurant I had never been to before, mostly because they had a private room that could accommodate us all. Every so often, I would glance over at Joanna, and each time she caught my eye and smiled. Something was going on. I could feel it. *I know things* flashed through my mind. I had the urge to close my eyes and look into the future. Just the thought that I wished to do so initiated a train of inquiry.

Choosing my time destination had never occurred to me. Why would it? It seemed a preposterous concept, but then again so did time travel of any type just a year or so ago. Once the impossible becomes attainable in one venue, it throws the door of possibility wide open. This was something I now needed to consider. Who knows, I thought. Maybe one day I can.

◆◇◆◇◆

JOANNA AND I HAD DECIDED to meet at the student center for breakfast at seven thirty the next morning. I arrived a few minutes early; Joanna was not yet there. As expected, the place was nearly empty. A few dedicated souls were eating breakfast before heading to the library to study; about ninety-nine percent of the student body was still unconscious on this Saturday morning.

Joanna walked in and scanned the room looking for me. The table I had chosen was way in the back where we would be far from anyone else. I could look at this woman forever, I thought, as I waited for her to see me. When she did, her wide smile momentarily halted my breath. Franklin, I thought, after all these years you still don't have a chance of resisting. If Henry were here, he would be laughing.

"Good morning," I said as I stood up to greet her.

"Good morning to you, too," she replied, that smile perhaps even a bit wider.

"Want something to eat?" I asked as she sat.

"I'd rather wait a while if that's OK with you."

"Perfectly fine," I said as I sat down across from her. "Joanna, I have been wondering since yesterday afternoon why you wanted to talk alone. I know you said that you were fine but I'm still a bit concerned."

"I promise you I'm fine. I've just been thinking about you a lot lately."

"Wow, I am honored."

"No, really, I have. I've never told you this but ever since we became friends you have been such a big part of my life. That's one of the reasons I didn't want us to get involved. I was afraid if it didn't work out, I might lose you."

"You could never lose me, Joanna. I don't operate that way. No matter what, I'm your friend for as long as you want me to be your friend."

"What would you think if I told you I was moving to Boston

"What? Really? You're moving to Boston?"

"I asked you what you would think if I did. I haven't decided."

"I would think it was terrific. You know that. Why Boston?"

"My design firm is opening a branch there. You remember our conversation just before graduation when you told Henry and me about the book and Professor Niemeyer. You talked about how everyone's choices make the future. I have thought about that a lot. So when I heard my manager talk about the new office in Boston, I got the strangest feeling that I was supposed to choose to go there. Isn't that crazy? The feeling was so strong. I almost looked around to see if there was someone standing behind me whispering to me."

Here was the universe, at least the one I was in, pulling more strings to direct the outcome. So maybe all those choices we make are not free will at all. Maybe we just think we are making the choices. Now I was completely unsure of everything I thought I had already worked out.

At this moment, it didn't matter. Joanna was coming to Boston. She hadn't yet decided, she said, but it was a done deal. She and I had a future; that was also suddenly crystal clear. I didn't know why I knew all of this, but it was as certain as the tides. Maybe I had already seen it in the future and I simply could not recall the vision. Nevertheless, I knew what was about to happen.

"So do you think I should do it?" she asked me.

"Look, I would love it. But I don't want you to feel that I'm convincing you to do this if you're not sure." I could afford to be magnanimous. All the cards had already been dealt.

"I know it's not your decision to make, Franklin. I would never put that kind of pressure on you. The funny thing is I'm not even sure it's my decision. This whole thing seems to have a life of its own," Joanna concluded.

Little do you know, I thought, as I thanked the universe profusely.

30

The End of the Beginning

AFTER MOST OF OUR FRIENDS HAD SAID their goodbyes on Sunday, Henry corralled me outside the student center.

"First of all, I want to tell you I'm sorry that I have been such a lousy friend. You know I can't help myself when it comes to school. I knew going in that I would need to control my obsessive behavior when it came to studying, but I just haven't been able to do it."

"You're getting a PhD in psychology, Henry. Don't you think you should figure this out?"

"I know, it's like the shoemaker's kids who have no shoes. It's terrible, and it's embarrassing."

"Forget embarrassing. Who cares? It's killing your life. You have to get a handle on this. I'm sure there are lots of people to help you at the university."

My words did not honestly reflect what I knew to be true. Henry didn't want help. He wanted to graduate at the top of his class again. Most people assume that an individual's primary motivation is to actively seek out that which gives him or her the most pleasure or satisfaction. That assumption is incorrect. Above all, a person will always first seek the path that minimizes pain, the option that results in the least discomfort. For Henry, the anxiety of not completing every assignment or maximizing his grades trumped the pain of sitting in his room studying night and day. When will this change? When the equation is reversed; when missing out on the rest of life is more painful than staying in his room and studying. A woman will likely be involved.

"I know, Franklin. And I appreciate your concern. Now catch me up on the rest of your life," he said, effectively closing that line of discussion.

"One of the problems with your best friend never calling you and never answering his phone," I began, "is that you end up having to cover a year's worth of events in a few minutes."

"Look, didn't I already apologize? Enough of the guilt stuff. I'm listening."

I told him all about Maurice Burnside: the time travel to Professor Niemeyer's house, the book, and our weekly conversations.

"Holy crap, Franklin, this is all unbelievable."

I continued with my visit with Doranto Durning and finished with Doranto's proclamation that I and Professor Niemeyer were quite famous. After that last blockbuster of information, Henry was silent. I wasn't certain if he was just stunned by my discussion, or if he thought that this time I had truly gone insane.

"I'm almost afraid to ask you, Franklin. Anything else?"

"Oh, God, yes. I got a visit from Professor Niemeyer in my room."

"What do you mean you got a visit from him? He's dead!"

"Here comes the physics, Henry. Sorry."

"Go ahead. I'll see if can keep from swooning."

Out of respect for my best friend, I kept it brief.

"So you're telling me that there are multiple universes, and somehow that means there's a purpose to our lives? You lost me, but that's all right. I'm sure I'll hear all of this again one of these days. You know, Franklin, I'm amazed how matter-of-fact you are about all of this. It's impressive."

"That's only because you're seeing me as sort of a finished product. Believe me, I've had my ups and downs." At that moment I realized how much I had missed seeing him and sharing all of these events with him. And I also felt bad that I wasn't around to help him get over his anxiety.

"You know the reason I'm so mad that you don't answer your phone, right?" I asked him.

"I do. One of these days I'll get past all of this. It's not that I don't care; you know that. But I will try to do better, I promise."

Danny and Simon walked out of the student center.

"So we going to see you some time or will it be another year?" Danny asked Henry.

"Less than a year, I promise."

"Yeah, well, you know where we are. You are always welcome at our place. Simon and I are hardly ever there anyway. Franklin should be paying double rent," he added looking at me.

"I should, but I won't," I replied.

We walked together to the parking lot, loaded up our cars, and met between them to say our goodbyes.

Henry shook Danny's and Simon's hands, then turned and hugged me. "I'll do better," he said.

"No you won't," I replied. "It's OK. I'll keep calling you and every so often maybe you'll pick up the phone."

The weekend had been a respite for my friends. For me, it had been even more. I had been blessed with a glimpse into my future, one that included Joanna.

My confidence was high. I felt ready for whatever was next. I knew from my visit to the future with Doranto that I was destined to succeed. Failure seemed impossible based on the knowledge I had, at least in this universe. Things were going to work out.

I closed my eyes. The world did not shift. Danny woke me as he parked at our apartment.

"You good?" he asked me.

"I am." And immeasurably grateful.

◆◇◆◇◆

FRANKLIN AND I DID TALK MORE OFTEN following that reunion weekend, much to his surprise. Sometimes Franklin underestimates his friends. He's not the only one who acknowledges his responsibilities.

I wasn't surprised when he eventually told me about Joanna and that a few months after she moved to Boston their relationship changed. I always knew that those two would end up together. For all his talk about seeing the future, Franklin was curiously unable to accurately assess their relationship. It was clear to me all through our college years that Joanna cared deeply for him, more than even the closest of friends would. Whenever I caught her looking at him, I would smile. I have often wondered whether she always knew they would be together and just kept it to herself.

Their wedding was two years later, almost to the day of her announcement of moving to Boston. Even now, when I think about their exchange of vows, I get choked up. Franklin always talks about the universe doing this or that. On that afternoon under an almost cloud-free sky, the universe was in charge. It had long ago decided that Franklin and Joanna were to be one. Franklin's eyes consumed her, wrapped her in a love that everyone in attendance could feel. I watched as whatever force was joining the two of them penetrated the hearts of all in attendance. No one there will ever forget that moment.

Over the following months, Franklin and I talked a good deal about the future. He insisted that he had to explain to me the quantum physics that Professor Niemeyer taught him, so finally one day I agreed. I admit I never quite understood the idea of everything being just a probability, so I just nodded a lot as he talked. But when he got to the part about choices creating reality, he got my attention.

"Henry, making the 'right' choice is impossible," Franklin told me. "The outcome of any specific choice is unknowable. It will be influenced by the billions of other choices made simultaneously by countless others, so there is no way to know if one is better than another." As Franklin often does, he invoked an analogy to illustrate his point. "Imagine you are riding the Tube in London. At every stop you exit the train and someone you don't know randomly assigns you to either get back on the same train or transfer to another train. There is no plan, no overall strategy. Just one random choice after another. You could not possibly predict at the outset of your journey where you would find yourself at any particular time."

Franklin stopped to let me absorb what he had just told me. When I finally nodded indicating that I understood—sort of—he continued.

"Henry, do you see what this means? You don't have to worry about every decision. Once you accept that there is no way to know which is the right choice, the pressure is off. It's immensely liberating."

My best friend was telling me to stop worrying, and he was giving me the tool to do just that. Now whenever I find myself struggling with a choice or decision, I recall his explanation. Franklin's words remain one of the best gifts I have ever received.

Although he and Joanna were extremely happy together, I could tell that Franklin was becoming frustrated with his situation.

"Henry, I'm still waiting," he told me.

"For what?" I asked.

"Something," he answered. "I haven't gone anywhere, in time I mean, for a while now. No Professor Niemeyer, nothing. I even called Govinda last month to see if he had any new dreams or any indication about anything."

"What did he say?"

"He told me to be patient. That's like telling me to be taller. You know patience is not my strong suit."

"I'm sure Joanna tells you the same."

"She does. Joanna is the most patient person I have ever met. Unfortunately, it's not rubbing off."

"I thought you could see the future."

"I have seen the future."

"So what's the problem?"

"There is always that tiny seed of doubt."

Franklin had no cause for concern. The transition was already underway.

PART THREE

Transition

31

In Flight

JOANNA LURCHED UP FROM her recumbent position in our king-sized bed, which was enough to make me do the same.

"What, what is it?" My heart was pounding as my eyes searched the darkness, the only illumination from the few rays of light from the streetlamp in front of our house stealing between the slats of the wooden blinds. I saw nothing and heard no one.

Joanna's silence quickly became uncontrolled laughter. It was a minute before she could even utter a word.

"He dropped it!" Her fit of hilarity continued.

"What? Tell me," I asked as I rapidly transitioned from deep sleep to fully alert.

"The bouillabaisse. On my dress, in our bed, the clams. They were everywhere!" Joanna could still not corral her laughter. After a minute or so, she was able to squeeze out a sentence.

"I was dreaming a bouillabaisse nightmare." She began to laugh again. "Crazy."

"And you tell me my dreams are bizarre. Double standard here, no?"

"No. Your dreams *are* bizarre, Franklin. Mine are just dreams, and this one was very funny." She lay down next to me, took my face in her hands, and gently kissed my lips.

"I adore you," she whispered, then turned away, pulled the covers over her shoulder, and laid her head on her pillow.

"That's it?" I asked.

"Shush, go back to sleep." And that's exactly what she did.

I did not. Joanna could wake from a dream, linger for a moment or two, and then immediately return to that place where quiet minds go when not required to be alert. My wife's hysterical nightmare had nudged my nearly always-on brain back into action. Like the toddler accidentally awakened, there was no quick way to get me back into sleep mode.

During such moments, I lie in bed and pray that sleep will return. It's not that I worry about getting insufficient rest for the following day's demands. It's the dreams I crave. My dreams, the ones Joanna labels bizarre. They aren't bizarre to me. I hadn't had one yet tonight—most nights I am good for a couple—so if I could fall back asleep, there was still plenty of time before morning to fit one in.

I fluffed my pillow, carefully massaged the down filling back towards the center, and laid my head on the small mound I had created. Joanna had long since returned to her usual restful slumber. I listened closely to her breathing, already the slow and steady cadence of sleep's deepest level. Its rhythm became my rhythm, not just the rhythm of my breath but also the rhythm of my being. Soon it came.

I was on a beach I did not recognize. The cool breeze and the heavy cumulus clouds obscured a late-day sun; the setting convinced me that summer was already gone and fall was in the air. I was a bit chilled, clad in only a polo shirt and shorts, no shoes or socks.

At first, I was certain I was alone—just the sun, the sand, the waves, and I. That was until I heard the faint sounds that I quickly recognized as men talking. The sounds were coming from behind me, but I could see nothing except the grasses blowing on the tops of sand dunes. I stood motionless, straining to hear what they were saying, but their language was unrecognizable.

Suddenly the grasses melted away, revealing row after row of armored men. In their hands were weapons, but they were not guns. They were shields and clubs. Their headgear was made of metal, and they wore breastplates. This was an ancient army of thousands and thousands of soldiers, yet I was certain I was in the present. I turned and looked out over the water. A few sailboats gracefully navigated the still calm sea. An oil tanker was visible just before the horizon. I noted a passenger jet at cruising altitude slowly making its way from west to east through the afternoon sky. To my right was today, but to my left was sometime very, very long ago.

I glanced down the beach and made out a shape in motion. As it came closer, I realized it was a woman, a young woman. She had long, thick, jet black hair that framed azure eyes. Her body was lithe and athletic and her skin radiant. She was exquisite to behold. The breeze intermittently blew her hair across her face; then as if ordered to, it receded so that her features remained unobscured. It was obvious that I was her target. I remained motionless as she approached me. Her smile was brilliant, and the look in those vibrantly blue eyes was unmistakable. It was the look of love—deep, familiar, and permanent love.

"I am my beloved's, and my beloved is mine," she whispered. She took my right hand in hers and with it caressed her cheek. Then she pulled me to her, wrapped both arms around my neck, her lips inches from my own. She turned my face towards the ocean and began to kiss me.

I held her as tightly as I could and began to cry. I could hear the ancient army approaching, their voices becoming louder. Though I could not understand the words, I knew they were words of death and destruction, and I began to sob even louder.

"Why are you so afraid?" she asked in golden voice. "Don't you know I would never let anything happen to you?"

And with that, we rose together into the air, as if gravity had suddenly been extinguished. It felt so right, as if I should always have been able to rise off of the earth at my whim.

"Look down," she said. I did as she instructed. The ancient army was gone. All I could see were the dunes and the ocean.

"Where did they go?"

"Where you wished that they would go." She kissed me once more on my cheek. I heard "I love you," but I was not sure if those words had come from my lips or hers.

"Can I always feel this way?" I asked.

"Yes, of course," I heard, or maybe just thought.

Then she was gone, but my flight continued. My movement through the clouds was blissful. Nothing intruded on the peace that enveloped me. My euphoria, however, was short-lived. Without warning, I began to fall rapidly, as if whatever power source had permitted my flight was abruptly extinguished. I tried to call for help, but I was unable to make words. All I could do was utter weak cries as I accelerated downward.

Something pulled me from this scene of panic, across a definite divide, to the tranquility of my bed. Joanna was gently tugging my arm.

"You were whimpering in your sleep again, Franklin. Are you all right, sweetheart?"

"I'm fine," I told her, though my heart was still racing.

"How was your flying tonight?"

"You can always tell, can't you? It was lovely, until I fell from the sky."

"You must take me with you one night. As long as you promise me we'll stay airborne."

"I give you my word that I will. I think I just need a bit more practice and then I'll have it. We should probably wait until then for you to join me. The falling part isn't nearly as much fun."

Tonight's was not the first of dreams in which I was in flight. Over the past year, they had become more frequent. Usually I was in a reclining seated position, and for some reason, I always flew facing backward. In those portions of my dreams, I was enveloped in an aura of sublime peace. Always the sky was blue, dotted by light and elegant clouds. If I were tasked to defend heaven, those dreams would be my evidence.

The clock read 4:45 a.m. Too early to get up, I thought, and attempted to get back to sleep yet again. After a short period of tossing and turning, I surrendered. As I quietly left the still dark bedroom, I sought out the silhouette of my beautiful, sweet Joanna. I could hear that familiar cadence of her breath, confirming that she had—as usual—returned to blissful unconsciousness.

Oscar, our golden retriever, raised his head as I walked into the kitchen. He looked at me as if to say, "Don't you know it's still nighttime?" Soon his long fluffy tail began to wag. No matter the time, he was always happy to see me, and I equally happy to see him. I nodded my head towards the door. Oscar stood, clearly understanding my signal that despite the darkness, we were going outside.

Sunrise was still about an hour away. For me, no time of day was better for reflection. Our street was silent. Automobiles that would be whizzing by in just a couple of hours remained quiescent. Street lights intermittently illuminated a neighbor's fence or basketball hoop. The rest of the visible world remained in darkness. Oscar stopped at each of his friends' houses, his nose in the air, attempting to detect if his playmate was out and about. "It's just you and me, pup," I told him reading his mind. "Your buddies are still asleep."

"Somewhere I can fly," I thought again, as Oscar and I walked side by side. Dream flight felt as natural as a stroll. When I would awaken only to realize those utopian airborne moments were not real, my feeling that I could fly did not dissipate along with the rest of the imagery. Dream flight felt like practice; I felt confident that soon I would master it. Joanna was well aware of this persistent fantastical belief. She was also aware that a part of me was convinced that one day Franklin Rock would indeed take flight in the non-dream world.

I have learned to listen to the silent voice that intermittently arises from a place I have yet been unable to locate. I cannot describe it, even to Joanna. It is as if I have some internal protector who makes himself known only when required, when I am about to make an error or need a quick decision about which move to make. He is continually monitoring my activity, protecting me, directing me. And every so often the voice teases me with a thought, like the ability to fly.

Perhaps, I considered, everyone has a silent protector. This is not an easy topic to broach with a stranger, or even a friend, so the answer remains unknown to me. It has a schizophrenic ring to it, I admit, but it is not mental illness. It is instead the ultimate mental health. To be able to instantly summon reliable help and advice is a gift. The trick is to know when it's the true silent voice or a machination of the conscious mind. In the latter situation, we fabricate the voice and supply it with the answer we want to hear, confusing that with the silent voice of wisdom.

I have learned to distinguish the two. Joanna, on the other hand, hears only a single voice. I am unsure how she does this. Rarely does she experience doubt; she simply plucks the answer from her reservoir of options and never looks back. As her husband, it is remarkable to observe. To her this is routine; it is the way she has been since adolescence. Regret is a word that cannot be found in her personal lexicon. Friends have often asked me how she does it. "Grace," I answer, with no better explanation available.

"What do you think, Oscar?" I asked my pal. He raised his head and his eyes met mine. "Think I will fly one day?" I stopped and bent to pet him. "You don't care about that. I probably shouldn't either."

By the time we returned home the sun was beginning to brighten the horizon. The house was quiet. It was still early and I was certain Joanna was still asleep. Oscar followed me into my study. I picked up the book I was reading, *Time and Again* by Jack Finney, sat back in my office chair, and began to read. I smiled as I heard the familiar thud of Oscar collapsing onto the hardwood floor into his coiled rest position next to me.

Finney's book had been recommended to me by my good friend and former roommate Simon. "You have got to read that book," he told me. "It's about time travel. Right up your alley." The premise of the book is that the protagonist enters a secret government program and learns how to go back in time merely by altering his environment and thoughts. Although it was fiction, I wondered while reading it if the author knew more than he let on.

As I sat back in the chair contemplating this question, I felt the familiar shift.

32

No Excuses

"WHERE ARE YOU GOING TONIGHT?" I heard, turning towards the direction of the voice. My father was standing directly across from me. He was wearing a white shirt, tie removed, his hair neatly combed and his thick-lensed, black-rimmed glasses just a bit cockeyed, as I recalled them to often be. I felt the lump immediately form in my throat. Other than for that brief sequence when I time-traveled back to my home as a very young child, I hadn't seen my father in the many years since he passed away. I looked around. I was in the kitchen of my childhood home. Everything was as I remembered it, only smaller and more compact.

"Hi Dad," I said, barely able to get the words out.

"You all right, Franklin?" His smile now morphed into a look of concern.

I took a breath and righted myself. This wasn't the first time I had arrived at a destination and been taken by surprise. I had learned to perform a quick assessment, to compose myself, and to appropriately adapt to the situation. Still, this was my father. My shock must have shown.

"Yes, I'm fine."

"I asked you where you are going. Jeff's house?" he repeated, referencing one of my two best friends.

"Not sure. I haven't decided. What are you and Mom doing?" I asked in return.

"I'm watching the ball game," he answered, indicating to me that it was late spring or summer in which I had landed. My dad watched baseball pretty much every night of the season. As a teenager I was far too busy with my friends; I rarely watched with him. When he became ill, I was in the throes of adolescence. After I lost him, I lamented the fact that I had not spent time with him during those previous years, and, worse, that we barely spoke, and when we did, that I wasn't especially kind.

Here's your chance, the silent voice told me.

"Can I watch with you?" I asked him.

"You want to watch the ball game with me?" he replied, his voice rising, making certain that he had heard me correctly.

"Yeah, if that's OK."

"Of course it's OK. C'mon, we can watch in the den. Want something to eat?"

Chocolate ice cream. That's what my mother and I would eat when we watched a crime show together. It still sounded good.

"Dad, you want some ice cream, like Mom and I have when we watch together?"

"Sure. She never offers me any," he commented, and I was pretty certain it wasn't a joke.

We got our snack and turned on the game. About two innings in I went for it.

"Dad, can I tell you something?"

"Sure, Franklin. What's on your mind?"

I reminded myself that my father was talking to a sixteen-year-old, not an adult, so I chose my words carefully.

"Sorry I haven't been talking to you and mom much. You know it's not because I'm mad or anything."

"I know that," he said, now turning both his body and his attention towards me. "I do miss you when you don't. You're growing up and before you know it you'll be off to college."

He had no idea he would be gone before that day occurred.

"Anyway, I'm sorry and I'm going to try to do better. Maybe we should start doing more stuff together," I suggested.

"So what has brought on this sudden change of attitude? When I ask you to help me in the yard or to go to the store with me, you never say yes."

"I know, I should. I will. I was thinking today about all the stuff we used to do together when I was a little kid. Like ice skating, having a catch. That was all fun."

"Franklin, what made you think of that? You sure everything is all right with you? Is there something bothering you?"

"No, I was just thinking that I missed some of those things. I thought it would be fun to do some stuff together since like you said I will be leaving for college in a couple of years." *Or more correctly you will be leaving me forever,* I thought, fighting the tears from forming.

"Anytime you want to do something you just tell me, Franklin. That would be great. Just hearing that you want to do this makes me very happy. You know a father doesn't love his big kids any less than when they were little."

"I know that, Dad. And a big kid doesn't stop loving his father, either. I'm just sorry I haven't been that nice to you."

"It's OK, Franklin. You don't have to worry. Mom and I know how you feel, no matter how much of a rotten teenager you are. Now that I've got you talking to me, can I ask you a few questions?"

"Sure," I answered.

"Have you thought about what college you might want to go to?"

Many years had passed since I had applied to college. I wouldn't have known as a sixteen-year-old sophomore in high school what college I would be attending, but grown-up Franklin sitting in front of my father was well aware of the outcome.

"Probably one of the small schools, I think. I don't want to go to a very big university," I told him.

"That sounds like a good idea. Smaller classes, right?"

"Yeah, plus you get to know the professors better." *Like Professor Charles Niemeyer.*

"Any idea what you want to study?"

"No, not really."

My father paused. I assumed that he was deciding on whether to forge ahead with a line of questioning.

"When you were young, Franklin, it was clear to your mother and me that you were different. You weren't like other kids. You seemed to have an idea of what you were going to do when you grew up. As you got older, that sort of waned. How about now? Any ideas?"

"You mean what I want to study?" I asked, hoping this was going to be more simple than I feared.

"No, Franklin. I mean what you are going to do with your life."

What am I planning to do with my life? What a question for him to ask his time-traveling son who is well aware of his future. How remarkable for me to be having this conversation with him with all I knew about both of our futures.

"I'm not sure yet," I responded. Not the truth of course, but I didn't think that answer technically broke my commitment of total honesty.

"Do you remember the dreams you had as a little boy?"

Oh, God. "What dreams?" I couldn't see any way a conversation about my visions would work out well.

"I wondered if you would remember them as you got older. I guess not. Let's just say you had quite the imagination. Anyway, don't worry if you don't know what you want to do. It's impossible to know the future. You know the saying, 'Man plans and God laughs.'"

No kidding, I thought. Irony was quickly filling the room, squeezing out the oxygen. "I've heard it. I guess it's true," I told him.

"Oh, it's true, son." I could see him reflecting on his own plans, and I was well aware that they had been dashed many years earlier. He had once told me that he had planned to go to medical school. After two years of college, he abruptly left to go to work. I never learned the details.

"Dad, you once told me you were going to go to medical school. What happened?"

"For one thing, money."

"You couldn't afford it?" I asked naively.

"You know in those days there was a lot of pressure to find any way possible to make a living. I guess I could have eventually done it, but once I started to work, the time just never seemed right to try."

"Are you sorry you never went?" I asked him.

"I thought about it off and on for a long time, but my generation was different, Franklin. We didn't dwell on what could have been. Everyone was sort of in the same boat if you know what I mean. We just did what we had to do and didn't think much about it. I did wonder if I would have enjoyed being a doctor. Who knows?"

"I'm sorry that it didn't work out for you, Dad," I told him, realizing that may have sounded a bit too adult for my sixteen-year-old self to have said. I could tell by the way he wrinkled his forehead that the same thought had occurred to him.

"Thanks, Franklin. That's very nice of you to say. But don't worry about me. Everything has worked out fine. And here I am having a wonderful talk with my favorite son."

"Your only son," I added, playing along with one of his old routines.

The sound of cheers from the TV got his attention. "The bums let in another run" was the last thing I heard before I felt the shift.

◆◇◆◇◆

As I OPENED MY EYES, now back in my study, I wasn't sure if I was going to cry or smile. For so long I had regretted losing my father and having wasted those precious years before he died. I was surly, rarely kind, and always distant. He loved me, that I knew, but I was too much of a selfish teenager to have returned his affection.

When I began to time travel I was always frightened. Where would I land, would I get back safely, what would happen while I was out of my natural time? It was all so new that I had not entertained the possibility of any upside. My visit with my father reminded me that in every situation, no matter how apparently bleak, there are unexpected pluses.

Joanna knocked and opened the door of my study.

"You got up early. Couldn't sleep, flyboy?" she asked playfully.

"Joanna, I saw my father."

"In a dream?"

"No, I was with him. In my house. I was sixteen. I told him I was sorry, Joanna. I told him I loved him. He was so happy," I told her with now moist eyes. "It was wonderful."

"Oh, Franklin, that is so sweet. You must be so grateful," she said as she walked over and put her hand on mine. "Did this happen last night?"

"No, just now. I couldn't go back to sleep so I got up and took Oscar for a walk. When I got back I was reading, closed my eyes for a moment, and there I was."

"You're a lucky boy, Franklin Rock. People don't get to go back and undo what they've done, or not done. Why do you suppose you got to do that?"

I thought for a moment. "No excuses."

"What do you mean, no excuses?"

"I mean that as much as possible, the issues in my life are being resolved. This mission thing is for real, Joanna. So there can't be any excuses for me not to fulfill my responsibilities. I think that's why. I feel so lucky. My dad. I got to see my dad. Wow!" I finished, holding my head in my grateful hands.

"Speaking of responsibilities, I need you to help me in the kitchen. There's a full dishwasher and we have a pile of laundry to do. Let's have some breakfast and we can get this stuff done, unless you end up zipping off to another time." She took my hand and led me into the kitchen. We sat together at the table over coffee.

"It's time for me to start, Joanna," I told my lovely wife.

"If you're referring to the dishes, they aren't going anywhere. You can finish your coffee."

"Very funny. I mean my work. It's time. I just don't know where to begin."

"You know a lot more about all of this than me, Franklin. But I can tell you one thing. So far you haven't had to do much searching. What was that saying you always had?"

"Let it come to you," I responded.

"So why would you think it would be any different now?"

"I don't know. It would seem that at some point I have to be proactive, don't you think?"

"So far you haven't. I think I'd just wait a bit longer. It's that patience thing, Franklin. You still need a bit more work, I'd say."

Patience. Something Joanna had in abundant supply and I was still struggling to possess. Working at the hospital had helped. When I was a nursing assistant, I recall spending many hours waiting for patients to return from a test or procedure before I could finish my work. Now as the Director of Patient Services at the hospital, my range of responsibilities had markedly expanded. Instead of waiting for patients, I was now often waiting for staff to get back to me about all sorts of issues. When I would complain to Joanna, she would just roll her eyes.

"Until you learn to quiet yourself a bit, you're just going to get more and more upset. It's not healthy, Franklin, and it's not necessary."

"So for the thousandth time, you are suggesting I be more patient," I said with a bit of an attitude.

"Just proof that you are a slow-learner, my love. I would have thought you would have gotten it after the first one hundred," she said as she leaned over and kissed my cheek. "Really, dear, you will be much happier. And it's not that hard."

"For you."

"True. But you have made progress. You had zero patience when we first met. Just try harder."

Just try harder. Try harder to accept ignorance. Try harder to tolerate injustice. Try harder to ignore violence. No doubt Joanna was right. She was not recommending that I ignore those things. Her point, made to me repeatedly, was that if I wanted to be effective, I needed to be more patient. As usual from my exquisite wife, wise counsel.

Just as I finished the dishes I received a call from the hospital. Seems an incident had occurred between two of the staff in our department. I had no early morning meetings but was scheduled for a late afternoon executive group conference, so I had planned to go to the hospital a bit later than normal. From the tone of the call, I realized that plan was now out the window. I dressed and headed to work.

From what I could deduce from the call, a recent but still unannounced decision had been somehow prematurely uncovered and initiated a departmental skirmish. I had decided to elevate one of the supervisors to a more senior position. Problem was, although more qualified for the position, she was junior in tenure to another one of the supervisors. When word got out that the more junior of the two was to be moved into the position over the longer-tenured, factions rapidly formed and the joust was upon us. By the time I arrived, other members of the department were hiding under their desks lest they become collateral damage.

"Please ask Becky to come to my office," I asked my assistant. A few minutes later she arrived.

"Hi, Becky. Please sit down," I said, pointing to the chair in front of my desk. She sat silently.

"First of all, I want to tell you that you are very important to me. I have great respect and admiration for you," I began. "Plus, I like you," I added with a smile. Becky smiled; she knew it was true.

"Second, I am also sorry you found out about the promotion the way you did. I had planned to talk with you tomorrow after I had gotten everything arranged with HR."

She remained silent but nodded to acknowledge my apology.

"I was thinking that you could fill me in on what happened, how you feel about it, really anything you want. That sound OK to you?"

"Yes, I appreciate that, Franklin. You know I've been working in the hospital for almost ten years now, six in this department. I believe I have done a very good job. I take my work very seriously. I'm always on time, I'm never late, I always get my work done, right?"

"Absolutely," I answered.

"When I heard that Lois got the promotion I was pretty upset. I don't want to tell you how I found out."

"You don't have to tell me," I interrupted. "I would never ask you."

"Thanks, I appreciate that. I don't want to get anyone into trouble. Anyway, like I said I've been working here for a long time, a lot longer than Lois. I like Lois, and I guess I'm happy for her in a way, but it just doesn't seem fair. I kind of feel like why did I bother to work so hard if I'm just going to get passed over?"

Becky paused, waiting to see if it was all right for her to continue.

"What else could I have done? That's the other part I don't understand. I mean, you never once told me I was doing something wrong or that there was a problem. Can you see why I feel this way?"

I waited to see if she was done or just taking a break. After a few seconds, it became clear that it was my turn.

"First let me say you did nothing wrong, which is why I never told you that you had. I try to tell you how much I appreciate all you do, and if I haven't done that enough, I apologize."

"No, you do, which is why I was so surprised. You've always been very kind and complimentary. That's why I like working in your department. You make all of us feel appreciated."

"You are appreciated. So let me see if I can address some of your concerns. Only one person could get the promotion. So how did I choose? I didn't pick Lois because I like her better, or because she works harder or is smarter. I chose her because of her experience with the legal team. The person in this position will be working with the hospital and outside lawyers on a regular basis. That is something Lois has done and you haven't.

"Now as to your question of why you should work hard. Becky, the reason any of us should do so is not because of the promise of reward or promotion. It's because it generates self-respect." Maurice Burnside was in his easy chair telling me the same.

"You do what you do because you are a person of great integrity. You hold yourself to a high standard. I cannot imagine—and I'm sure neither could you—that you would ever purposely do less than your best just to make a point or to demonstrate dissatisfaction with something. To do so would just diminish you in everyone's eyes, most importantly your own. That's a primary reason why I have so much respect for you.

"There will be more promotions, and when you are the right fit—which for sure you will be sooner than later—I will be calling you with the good news.

"One more thing, if I may. You said you were happy for Lois. You should be. Ever notice that when we celebrate the good luck or success of another, it makes us feel good? Why is that? It's because everyone feels better when they act in a kind and caring manner. No one feels good when they are bitter.

"You're a good person, Becky. I know it, Lois knows it, everyone knows it. Show Lois that you are happy for her, and watch your star rise. Your colleagues will be even more impressed with you than they are now."

Her eyes had become tear-filled. I reached over and handed her a tissue.

"You all right?" I asked.

"Yes." Becky righted herself, took a deep breath, and continued.

"Thank you, Franklin. I mean it. Your kindness is so sweet. I am sorry that I caused a fuss. I shouldn't have. I believe you that my time will come, and your word is good enough for me. This might sound a bit crazy, but I am happier now that I work here even though I didn't get the new job. You make it a great place."

Becky stood up. "Is it OK if I give you a hug?" She asked. I walked around to the front of my desk.

"Who could ever refuse a hug?" I answered.

"I'm going to give one to Lois right now. I feel so much better. Thank you again," she told me as she headed out of my office. She paused, turned back to me, then added, "How did you just do that?"

33

Moonlighting

I HAD NO IDEA THAT BECKY would share our conversation with so many people, both within and outside our department. Two of my fellow department directors came into my office the next day. They wanted to know how I managed not only to diffuse the situation between Becky and Lois, but had them end up closer than ever, and the rest of the staff ebullient.

"You've become a star around here," one of them told me. "You should know that Becky has told everyone that you're some kind of magician. She said when she came to your office she was furious and thinking of quitting, and by the time she left, she told everyone she'd never work anywhere else as long as you were her boss."

"That's very flattering," I told him for lack of anything else to say. What the big deal was I didn't know. All I did was listen to Becky, tell her the truth about how I felt and why I did what I did, and that was pretty much it. Seemingly nothing that anyone else couldn't do.

"Would you be willing to help me when I have a similar problem, which I can guarantee I will?" he then asked me.

"Of course," I told him.

"Franklin," the other of my colleagues added, "You're going to get a lot of similar requests from all over the hospital. The word is out."

"Why do you say that?" I asked her.

"Because you just managed to diffuse a situation between two employees, women no less—I say that only because you're a man—and in the end have everyone loving you. Believe me, Franklin, you will be a busy guy putting out fires for other managers."

Sure enough, I received about a half dozen calls from other department managers over the next several days. Could I teach them what I did? Would I write something up to help them? Is it all right if they call when they have a problem?

As I walked to my car after work the following Friday evening, I reflected on the entire episode. No matter how much I dissected the event, it seemed to me to be no more than a straightforward employee issue. I could not imagine why it had generated such attention. My daydreaming was interrupted by loud voices emanating from the parking garage one level below the one I was currently on. As I was about to unlock my car door, I heard what I thought was a short scream, then silence. I waited to see if I would hear it again. At first, there was nothing, then the sound of scuffling.

Slowly I walked down the ramp, and when I rounded the corner to the lower floor, I peeked between the railing and the concrete wall. In the far corner, I could see two men and a woman. One of the men was holding the woman against the back of a red station wagon. The other was holding something in his hand. At first, I could not determine what it was until he turned slightly to his right and I had a view in profile. A gun! I pulled back just enough to make sure I could not be seen but still have a view of them.

The man without the gun was trying to pull a bag off of the woman's shoulder. I had seen enough to assume it was a robbery. I quickly turned, ran up the ramp to the emergency blue telephone, and pushed the button.

"Yes, can I help you?" the woman asked.

"A woman is being robbed at gunpoint on B2," I rapidly told her.

"OK, don't try to intervene. Someone will be there in a minute."

I quietly returned to my previous spot to see what was happening. The man without the gun was rifling through the woman's purse. The one with the gun still had it pointed at the woman as he watched his accomplice throwing things out of the purse, in search of money I presumed.

"That's all I have," I heard the woman say. The one who had the purse was stuffing something into his pants, then threw the purse down. Both of them turned to see the arriving headlights, then ran towards the staircase. As they opened the door to the stairwell, two police officers, guns drawn, appeared.

"Drop the weapon!" one of the officers said. The men started to turn away from the staircase just as a second police car pulled up onto the ramp.

"Drop it now!" the officer repeated. The man did as commanded, and both of them put their hands in the air. I watched as the police quickly had both men on the ground in handcuffs. I could see that, fortunately, the woman had not been harmed. I walked towards the scene. One of the officers saw me and approached me. "Are you the one who called this in?" he asked me.

"Yes, officer. I heard the commotion and went to check it out. As soon as I realized what was happening, I called on the emergency phone."

"What's your name, sir?"

"Franklin Rock."

"Do you think you could come with us to the station to give a statement? It will save both of us time."

"Sure, officer."

Other than TV shows and movies, I had never been privy to a crime investigation. I watched the suspects go through the usual registration—or whatever police call it—and some interrogation. One of the detectives asked me to fill out a form, which I did. He asked me a few questions which I answered, then said I was free to go.

"Do you mind if I stay a few minutes?" I asked. For some reason, I was finding the whole process fascinating.

"Sure. Have you spoken with the woman who was assaulted?"

"No, sir."

"She was asking who it was who called for help. She's very grateful. Want to meet her?"

"I would."

The two of us walked around the corner to a group of small offices. He stopped at one of the doors.

"Ms. Boyd, this is the man who called for help." He turned to me. "Sorry, I forgot your name."

"Franklin Rock."

"I know you wanted to meet him," the detective added.

Ms. Boyd looked a bit shaken but otherwise all right. I recognized her. I was pretty sure she worked as a nurse in the recovery room.

"Mr. Rock," she began, "I know who you are. All my co-workers were talking about you just the other day. You're the one who was so nice to Becky Withers, right?"

I laughed. "Yes, that's me. But more importantly, are you all right, Ms. Boyd?"

"Yes, I think so. But it was very frightening."

"I'm sure. You're a nurse, right?"

"Yes! How did you know? Oh, silly question. You probably know just about everyone in the hospital."

"Not everyone, although I'd like to. Recovery room, right?"

"Yes, that's right. For going on fifteen years," she said proudly.

"Let's hope you're here at least another fifteen, and that this is the first and last problem like this you ever have."

"Amen, Mr. Rock. And Mr. Rock, thank you so much for saving me. I don't know what would have happened if you hadn't been there."

I could see the possibilities flashing through her mind.

"Well, I was, so don't even think about it. I'm just so glad I could help."

"God bless you, Mr. Rock. God bless you."

I left her and headed back to the front. As I prepared to leave the building, I saw the two men who had accosted Ms. Boyd, handcuffed, seated in chairs, just inside one of the detective's offices. Our eyes met.

"So you're the guy who caught us," I could see them thinking, as I was simultaneously thinking, "So you're the two assholes who assaulted that lovely woman." I looked a bit closer. One of them lowered his eyes to the floor. The other continued to look at me. His eyes were talking. Remorse: he was sorry. As has happened so many times over the years, my silent voice assured me that my assessment was correct.

Eighteen to twenty was my guess at their ages. Why had they attempted to rob that woman? Who were they? What was their story, or rather what was each of their stories? What choices had been made in their lives to have arrived at that moment of the crime? What other previous choices by many others had put them at that scene at that particular time? It was as if I was about to view a movie in reverse, following the characters back to some earlier point in the narrative.

The detective who had been questioning them got up and left the room. As he walked towards his desk, I approached him.

"Excuse me. I'm Franklin Rock. I'm the one who witnessed the crime and called the police."

"Good job, Mr. Rock. Can I help you?"

"I know this is going to sound a little crazy, but would it be all right for me to talk with the two of them?" I pointed towards the two assailants.

"Why would you want to do that?" the detective asked.

"They're young, and they look like they realize they did a stupid thing. I work in the hospital. I'm not a lawyer."

The detective looked at his colleague who nodded. "You can talk with them for a couple of minutes until I finish the paperwork."

My heart rate was markedly faster as I approached the door. Both had their heads down and were silent. Now that I was closer, I could see that one was a year or two older than the other.

"Would you mind if I talked to you two for a minute?" I asked. Both heads rose simultaneously as if connected.

"Who are you?" the older one asked.

"Hey, you're the guy we saw with the police in the garage," the younger one said.

"You sure?" the older one asked.

"Yeah, I'm sure. Right, mister? That was you?"

"Yes, that was me," I answered.

"So what do you want?" the older one asked again.

"I just want to understand a few things," I responded.

"Like what? Billy, don't say anything to this guy," he warned.

"Look, I am not a cop or a lawyer. I won't say anything to them, I promise," I tried to assure them.

"Yeah, so why are you so interested in us?"

I looked at Billy. "You're Billy. What's your name?" I asked the older one who had so far done all the talking.

"Anthony."

"Are you guys related?" I asked.

"Cousins," Billy answered.

"You do look a bit alike," I said. "How old are you two?"

"I'm seventeen," Billy said.

"Nineteen," Anthony said.

"You two been arrested before?" I asked.

"I thought you wasn't a cop or lawyer," Anthony said. "Why do you want to know?"

"I'm just trying to find out something about you guys. Maybe I can help you," I offered, the words exiting before I had had a chance to consider them.

"Like how?" Billy asked.

"I'm not sure. But maybe if we talk some more I can figure that out."

"No, this is my first time," Billy answered and looked at Anthony.

"Second. First time was for possession."

"Why did you try to steal that woman's purse?" I asked, getting right to the heart of the matter.

Billy looked again at his older cousin. We all waited. When Anthony declined to reply, Billy spoke.

"For my mom," Billy said without waiting for Anthony's approval.

"What do you mean?" I followed up.

"She's addicted to H. We ain't got no money. So Anthony said we needed to help her." Billy looked gratefully at Anthony.

I looked directly at Anthony. He simply nodded.

Knowledge changes everything. So now instead of one victim, we had three: Ms. Boyd, Anthony, and Billy. Ms. Boyd, thankfully, would be all right, but these two young men were facing prison time and a deep hole from which they might never climb out. How Billy's mother got to where she was, well, that was the result of another cluster of choices made by her and many others, possibly going back a generation. A mess for sure.

"Look, you two know you just did something very stupid. Thank God you didn't hurt her. Still, armed robbery. That's a big deal. What were you thinking?"

"We didn't have bullets in the gun," Billy replied. "We weren't going to shoot her."

"I'm not sure that makes any difference," I told him.

Anthony turned to me. "Thinking? Man, we can't afford to think. My aunt, this is my mom's sister. We don't get her what she needs, she dies. Simple as that. What would you have us do?"

"How about get an education and a job? That would probably be a better long-term solution."

"Yeah, well, it's too late for that. We both had to leave school, really just to stay alive. It's easy when you wear a suit to work and have a fancy job. You don't know shit," he finished as he looked away.

"You might be surprised by what I know," I told him. "I'm willing to bet I know a lot more about life than you do."

"How's that?" Anthony asked me.

"Suppose I were to tell you that just about everything you think you know about the world and about life is pretty much wrong."

"How do you know what I know?" Anthony continued.

"You're sitting handcuffed in a police station. It's a pretty good indication that you don't know enough to have kept you and Billy out of here."

"So you gonna teach us what we need to know, Mr. Genius?"

"If you want me to, I will. Let's just suppose I could arrange for you to stay out of jail. Maybe I can get you probation with the agreement that you work in my hospital. I'd see to it that you also get paid. If you do what's asked, I will also find a way to get you both an education. Would you be willing to do whatever public service a judge tells you to do? Would you promise to give up all drugs? Would you promise never to assault another person? And you will need to make good with the woman you tried to rob. Whatever she needs, you will do. Agree?"

"Sure," Anthony responded without checking with Billy. "You think you can do all that?"

"I can get you the jobs, I know that. I don't know about the other stuff. I've never actually tried. But I have a feeling I can do it. And if you two give me your word that you will hold up your end of the deal, I will give it my best shot."

"We will. We promise," Billy answered immediately.

"We will," Anthony agreed.

"Why are you willing to do this for us?" Anthony then asked.

"Not sure. It just seems like the right thing to do," I told him.

As I got up to leave, Anthony stopped me.

"Mister, we don't even know your name."

"Sorry. I'm Franklin Rock."

"Mr. Franklin Rock, if you could do what you just said, I will make sure that Billy and I do what you tell us to do. I mean it. I never wanted to get to this," Anthony confessed, tears now visible on his cheek. "Billy is like my little brother." He turned to him. "Sorry, Billy. I'm so sorry." Anthony put his arm around his cousin and looked up to me. "Could be our lucky day, little 'bro," he told Billy.

After prolonged discussion with the DA's office and the judge, Anthony and Billy eventually got probation and about a million hours of community service. They were lucky the woman they assaulted was a saint. Once she believed that they were honestly sorry and sworn to never again engage in any criminal activity, she forgave them. She did more than that. She appeared before the judge and asked him to allow the boys a chance at life. Then she arranged for both of them to get a GED. Turns out Ms. Boyd's oldest daughter worked for the superintendent of schools. Anthony had been right; it had been their lucky day.

Billy and Anthony came to work part-time in the hospital. Each time they saw me they would wave and smile and mouth the words "thank you". Finally one day I stopped in the hallway and told them that they had thanked me enough by holding up their end of the bargain.

If the Becky and Lois story wasn't enough, the tale of Anthony and Billy made me a hospital icon. When I went to the cafeteria for lunch, the foodservice team fell over themselves making me special meals. Housekeeping insisted on cleaning my office so often that I had to shoo them away. It was all very kind, but way over the top.

Weeks after the entire episode had been resolved, I received a call from a detective from the precinct where I had talked to the boys.

"Mr. Rock?" the caller asked.

"Yes, this is Franklin Rock."

"Mr. Rock, this is Detective Phil Olsen. I met you when you were here after the attempted robbery a few months ago. I was the one you asked if you could talk with the two suspects, remember?"

I hadn't known his name but I could see his face.

"Oh, yes. Hi Detective." Had something else come up? My heart began to beat a bit faster.

"Everything is fine. We were all pretty impressed with what you did for those boys. Any chance you could come down to the precinct tomorrow afternoon? The captain would like to talk with you about possibly helping us out with something. We would all appreciate it. At the least, we could thank you in person."

That was certainly unexpected, I thought. My curiosity was piqued.

"Sure. What time?" I asked the Detective.

"Is three good for you? We won't keep you long."

"Should I bring a lawyer?" I asked, mostly in jest.

"I hope that's a joke, Mr. Rock. We could use your help. We don't need any more lawyers around here."

So at three o'clock the next afternoon, I headed over to the police station. When in response to the officer at the front desk I answered that my name was Franklin Rock, every head in the room turned to look.

"So you're the famous Franklin Rock. Pleasure to meet you. I'll take you back to Captain Pulaski's office."

Seated behind the desk was a very fit fifty-something-year-old man, full head of salt-and-pepper hair, black-framed glasses, and deep blue eyes. Captain Pulaski was a caricature of a television precinct captain. He rose as I entered and extended his hand.

"Franklin Rock," I announced as we shook.

"I know who you are, Mr. Rock. Thanks for coming. Let me get the others." He picked up his phone. "Francis, can you please have Detectives Olds and Olsen come into my office? Tell them Mr. Rock is here."

Less than a minute later, both detectives entered, introduced themselves, and took seats across from me.

Captain Pulaski began. "Mr. Rock…"

"Please call me Franklin," I interrupted.

"Franklin, we first want to tell you how impressed we all are with how you helped those boys. These kids have it rough. It's no excuse to commit crimes, but it's rare for a stranger to reach out and help them. But what impressed us all was how you turned that situation around so quickly. Can I ask, how did you get those boys to respond to you?"

I didn't want to admit to them that I had no idea.

"Most of the time I just sort of evaluate the situation and go with my instinct. Not sure what else to tell you."

"It's a hell of an instinct," Detective Olsen said. "I'm glad you asked me if you could talk with them. The funny thing is that normally I would say no. Something about you caused me to let my guard down a bit. Didn't I tell you that, Captain?"

"You did. And for some reason, I didn't suspend you for it," Captain Pulaski answered. "Anyway, Franklin, we think you could help us. You had a way with those boys. If you could bring that same talent to others, we think it would make a big difference. We'd have to figure out how often you're willing to come, what we could pay, that sort of stuff. But I'm sure all of that could be easily done. Judging how satisfying that episode was for you, the detectives and I thought you might like to give it a go."

Let it come to you.

Both detectives were smiling at me and had moved ever slightly towards the edge of their chairs, awaiting my response. Every so often, the universe throws out a challenge: try jumping over this, it says. You can choose to try or to pass. Passing wasn't in my bones.

"Captain, that sounds great to me. I just hope I don't let you all down. I've never done this sort of work before. Maybe I just got lucky," I told him with true humility.

"Could be," Captain Pulaski replied. "I don't think so, but what do we have to lose? If you're game, so are we. You two agree?" he asked turning to Detectives Olds and Olsen.

"Absolutely," Detective Olsen responded.

"Yup," Detective Olds confirmed.

What I had just assumed was a one-time random event involving a saint of a woman and two young, foolish but good-hearted criminals became the next vehicle for fulfilling my mission. People made choices, switches were thrown, and I was off on a new track. As simple as that.

34

Police Work

Detective Derrick Olds, all two hundred and fifty-five pounds of whatever it was that made him effectively immovable, motioned me into his small office.

"In a nutshell, unfaithful wife reconsiders, begs husband for forgiveness and dumps her lover, who in a jealous rage, breaks into her house and threatens the wife and her two daughters. The husband is upstairs, hears the commotion, runs down the stairs, tackles and then attempts to strangle the ex-lover to death. Screaming wife runs outside, and power company workers who happen to be working on electric lines right in front of the house rush in and drag the husband off of the guy just in time. Uniformed officers arrive, subdue the husband, and arrest him and the ex-lover. And here we are."

"And now here I am. But I'm not quite sure why."

"Because the husband is a city councilman. He's a really good guy, Franklin. And who could blame him for what he did? So we need you to fix it."

"What am I fixing?"

"You're fixing everything. His marriage, his life, his future. It's what you do, Franklin."

"So you want me to get rid of his rage and put a campaign-winning smile back on his face, and make sure that he doesn't hurt anyone else, and that would include his wife who just cheated on him. Right?"

"You got it, Franklin. Go work your magic."

The councilman looked terrible. He was breathing rapidly. His thinning black hair was glued to the dried sweat on his forehead. The back of his head was resting on the short sidewall across from the detective's office, his arms hanging limply on his thighs, his feet touching with his knees slightly parted.

"Hello, Councilman. My name is Franklin Rock." His eyes looked up at me as his head remained fixed in place, still resting on the wall. Two aluminum chairs sat empty across the hall from Detective Olds' office. I pointed towards the chairs. "Would you mind if we sat over there?"

The councilman willed his body up from the chair. Everything rose in unison, except his chin, which seemed to have not yet received the signal to do so from his brain. Finally, he raised his head and regarded me for a few seconds. "Mr. Rock, you are obviously not a detective. Are you from the DA's office?"

"No, sir, I am not."

"Are you a lawyer? Did someone call you to come?"

"No, not a lawyer, either. The only one who called me was Detective Olds. He thought I might be able to help you."

"I'm not sure I understand. Who exactly are you?"

"I help the police sometimes."

"Help with what?"

"Situations that need to be fixed, where no one gets hurt, and good people are spared unnecessary pain."

"You're kidding, right? Detective Olds!" The councilman shouted across the room.

Detective Olds turned at the sound of his name and walked across the hallway. "Yes, Seth. What do you need?"

"Not to be rude, Derrick, but who exactly is this guy?"

"Franklin Rock. Give him a chance, Seth. I think he can help. Look, you almost killed that guy tonight. This isn't nothing. I can't just let you go home."

Councilman Terry took a deep breath followed by a long sigh. "All right. I'm sorry, Mr. Rock."

"Please call me Franklin." Once again I motioned towards the two chairs. We sat.

"OK, Franklin, I'm listening."

"Why did you want to hurt him?"

"Who? You mean my wife's lover? I didn't want to hurt him—I wanted to kill him!"

"OK, so why did you want to kill him?" I asked again.

"Why? Why did I want to kill him? He tried to hurt them. He could have killed them! What was I supposed to do? Just let him try again?"

This shouldn't be too difficult, I thought, making sure not to smile. Although I found this conversation amusing, I preferred that no one else knew it. It's difficult to explain to people how I can find situations like this one, where life and death seem to be in play, funny. It's not the possible outcome I find funny. Murder is not funny. Violence of any kind is not funny. What's funny, at least to me, is this game of life that we all play. It's ridiculous that anyone wishes to harm anyone else. There's simply no gain in that move.

"Was I just supposed to ignore the fact that some guy was about to hurt my family, Franklin?" The councilman's raised voice refocused my attention. "I am not a madman. But I am also not about to let some asshole go after them. Any man would have done the same thing. Am I wrong? "

"From your vantage point, the choice was simple. Either I hurt him, or he hurts them, and 'them' in this case are those closest to you."

"One of them at least. My wife is now another issue. If it were just her, I might have felt differently."

"I don't think so. I'm sure you felt anger and humiliation and a lot of pain, but I'm also certain that you did not wish to see your wife hurt."

"How come you're so sure?"

"Because you tried to kill the man who was threatening her. That's a pretty good clue."

Councilman Terry smiled. "Good point."

"So you still love her. And how does that make you feel?"

"Like an idiot, like a moron. What's wrong with me? She betrayed me, and as you said, humiliated me. My heart hurts. And I feel so stupid." Councilman Terry's eyes began to tear.

"First of all, Councilman, you are hardly an idiot or a moron."

"Really? You could have fooled me. No, Franklin, I am an idiot. I should have known. I guess I just didn't want to believe it was possible."

"You can never be an idiot for loving someone, no matter their behavior. You can never be an idiot if someone hurts you or takes advantage of you. That would be *their* problem, not yours."

"You don't believe that. No one believes that."

"I do believe that. I am certain it is correct, Councilman."

"You can't go through life letting people take advantage of you. You'll never get anywhere if you do."

"Where is it you want to get?"

"It's a figure of speech. You know, get ahead, be successful."

"You mean become a councilman?"

"Funny. I mean successful. Run a business, become a professional, a lawyer, or a doctor. Or yes, a politician. At least one who wins elections. Let people step on you and you go nowhere. My dad taught me that. 'Don't let anyone take advantage of you, Seth. You stand up for yourself,' he would tell me. And he was right."

"With all respect to your father, Councilman, he was wrong. I'm sure he loved you and wanted to make sure that no one hurt you, but the truth is that the best way to make sure that no one hurts you is to understand that no one can. Unless you give them the power to do so."

"You sound like a psychiatrist or a psychologist. So that's what you are."

"No, actually I'm neither."

"So what are you? And how come you're so sure that you're correct?"

"If I tell you tonight that I think you are a jerk and that I dislike you, you might just tell me to bleep off and you'd ignore me. I mean nothing to you. Now instead let's say your daughter or your wife—before this episode—says the same thing. Those same words would probably hurt a good deal more. But why? They're the same words. You choose to make them mean more when they come from those you love or respect. You give that power to those people and deny it to me."

"So you're telling me that we get to decide if something hurts."

"Exactly. And if you don't give anyone that power, no one can hurt you."

"And it's that simple?"

"It's that simple."

"What about the scumbag who was sleeping with my wife and then tried to hurt her. What should I have done?"

"You had to intercede. But stopping a lunatic is not the same as deciding that you have to step on others to prevent them from stepping on you. Beating the crap out of him—enough to prevent him from hurting your wife and daughters—was just fine. But he has no other power over you, nor does your wife unless you give it to them."

"You make me sound omnipotent."

"You are. We all are. But we're not quite done. Let's get back to the scumbag. What do you want to happen to him? Think for a second before you answer," I instructed him.

He did. For a short while, he said nothing, but it was evident that his thoughts were evolving.

"You know my initial reaction was to hurt him, castrate him, maybe worse. But I'm gonna guess that is not the correct answer, is it, Franklin?"

"You tell me, Councilman."

He paused. "I'm also going to guess that somehow forgiveness is involved."

"It always is. Now you have to tell me why."

"I don't know. It's the Christian thing to do. Turn the other cheek? Honestly, that's not how I feel."

"I'm not surprised that's not how you feel at the moment. It's what most people would say. Now tell me how *you* feel while you contemplate his demise. Are you at peace? Is your pulse slow and steady? Are you filled with joy?"

"Ha, of course not. Those are not peaceful thoughts," he replied with a smirk.

"Wouldn't you prefer peaceful thoughts? Wouldn't you prefer to be relaxed, at ease, without anger and angst? Have you ever felt great when you were angry or enraged?"

"So you're telling me to let go because it will make me feel better. You know that's easier said than done."

"Yes, I am telling you to let go because you will feel better. So will everyone around you, and that will only add to your good feeling. Yes, it's easier said than done, but each time you do so, it gets easier and easier. And before you know it, that becomes your natural reaction. Like for just about learning anything, practice works."

"Your world sounds so simple, Franklin."

"I don't know if simple is the right word. But I know that our world is not nearly as complicated as we make it."

"Maybe not for you. The rest of us probably wouldn't agree. Sometimes life seems so difficult. What is it that you know that we don't?"

"That the world is not what it seems to be. And when you understand how the world works, you learn that there is no need to worry. Everything works out. I give you my word."

"How the world works. So I assume most of us haven't figured that out?"

"Correct, most of us have not figured that out."

Councilman Terry leaned back in his chair, every muscle simultaneously releasing its tension. He looked directly at me, now sporting a small smile. "You know, Franklin Rock, I'm not sure why, but I feel better. I know this sounds ridiculous, but for some reason, I believe that everything you just told me is true."

"And you feel like someone just stopped pressing your shoulders into the ground."

"I do," he said, pulling both shoulders back and expanding his chest to simulate his release. "That's exactly how I feel." Councilman Terry looked up and saw Detective Olds standing across the hall.

"Derrick, I don't know if you were listening to this guy. Just hours ago, I found out that my wife was cheating on me. I nearly strangled the bastard. I admit I wanted to kill him." The councilman took a deep breath, then continued. "Now, I don't want to hurt anyone anymore. Crazy, right?"

Councilman Terry turned to me. "I have no idea how I will deal with my wife or the press for that matter. But I feel a whole lot better. How did you do that?"

"You know, Councilman, I'm not sure. But curiously it seems to work out this way just about every time."

Detective Olds laughed. "Of course it does, Franklin. Why do you think we always call you? You know what we say around here after you leave? We say the perp just got Rocked."

I left the two of them to complete whatever police work was required before the Councilman could be released and begin to put his life back together. A short conversation wasn't going to solve all of his issues, but I knew that his course would at least be easier now than if I had not intervened. "When you begin to worry more about other people than yourself, when you place their troubles ahead of your own, the burdens of your own life instantly lighten." Maurice Burnside's words always followed the successful resolution of a case. As had become my custom, I looked over my shoulder and mouthed the words 'Thank you, Maurice,' hoping he was watching.

A plethora of cases had found their way to me over the months I worked with Detective Olds and his colleagues. I enjoyed the challenge presented by each. It was humbling to watch the transformation and to watch the tears of sorrow become tears of joy and gratitude. But did I want to continue?

Derrick had been watching me. "Am I going to lose my greatest resource, Franklin?"

"Why do you ask, Derrick?"

"Because, Franklin, you were a long way away just now, and whenever I see you like that my heart rate and blood pressure begin to rise. You won't do this forever, that I know."

Maybe Derrick saw something. It's certainly happened before. One day, for no reason I could ever discern, a switch is thrown—just as Professor Niemeyer explained. New track, new adventure.

35

Closing In

DERRICK BEGGED ME TO STAY, and so I did. Derrick Olds is my friend. For some people, friends are an accoutrement, like a purse or a pair of earrings, called upon to fit a specific occasion or situation. Maybe a particular friend has a skill you sometimes need, like fixing your car or computer.

I knew two women, as close as sisters for twenty years, until one day, one of them seemingly said or did the wrong thing, and in that singular moment offended the other. Instantaneously—I nearly added the word almost just before instantaneously, until I recalled just how fascinatingly sudden it was—the offended woman banished the offender completely and permanently from her life. Just like that, it was over, forever. No matter that their husbands and children felt a real loss—and I cannot fathom that they did not as well—some mysterious line had been crossed.

Where or what that line was baffled me. What could have occurred to have so abruptly terminated that relationship to the point that no words were ever spoken between them again? Did one steal from the other, or make advances on the other's husband, or deliver an insult that would have made a stripper blush? Seemingly none of the above. It was as if the offended had been patiently waiting for just the right moment, just the right offense, to sweep down and sever the cord of connection. Like the love affair that begins with explosive passion but from day one has no chance of evolving into forever intimacy, this friendship was doomed from the start. Only the time and place waited to be revealed.

True, committed friendship is a sweeping metaphor for life, and love, and God, and all good things that mankind has ever generated from Adam's first breath. Its color runs true and through to the core of each member. It is no veneer, able to be stripped away with minimal effort. Real friends are like appendages. They become a part of you.

A friend for me is not something one needs, but rather something one is. Friendship keeps me anchored to Earth and the responsibilities I embrace. Derrick Olds is my friend; I would not abruptly walk away from him.

"You are well aware that I am perpetually petrified by your leaving," Derrick told me just the other day.

"C'mon, Derrick, you would be fine without me. I haven't been here all that long and you managed to have a pretty successful precinct before I arrived. Why is it so important to you that I stay?"

"Because you're cut from a different cloth, that's why. Everyone around here wants to just cuff, arrest, and ship the suspect off to jail. Tolerate nothing, lock 'em up, next case. As if that has worked. Jesus, the prisons are jammed. I have known for so long that this cannot be the best solution. No one seemed interested in finding another way. I was so damn frustrated every day. And then into my precinct walks Franklin Rock, like manna from heaven. 'Lord, you heard me!' I thought."

The blood flooded into my face, the heat and color arriving simultaneously. "Derrick, please. I am nothing special."

"Nothing special? Are you kidding? You have no idea how special you are, Franklin. Did I say manna from heaven? No, that is far too simple. You are like the Force, you, know, from Star Wars. 'May the Force be with you.' You don't have any idea, do you?"

I did. Govinda had told me pretty much the same thing, as had others. But how does one admit this? It seems nothing short of unbridled hubris, dangerous to even contemplate, a Greek tragedy waiting to unfold. No, I dared not dwell on the thought for more than a moment, not before, not now. Maurice Burnside's words of caution about taking oneself too seriously remained a fixed part of my psyche. What a debt I owed that man.

Derrick tried to claim me as his own, but in short order, every officer in the precinct called on me.

"Rock can get anything out of anybody, Derrick," his colleagues would tell him. "The guy is weird, but he is amazing. I don't bet against him anymore."

And that's exactly what they were doing: betting on me. It began when Detective Olds promised his chief that I would succeed in a robbery case where no one could figure out where the stolen merchandise was hidden.

"Chief, let Franklin speak with the guy. What do you have to lose? No one here is getting anywhere." The chief relented, and Derrick tossed me into the interrogation room with the suspect.

"I'm Franklin Rock." I introduced myself as was my custom.

"Who the hell cares?" came the response.

"You should."

"Yeah, and why is that?"

"Because I am all that stands between you and a lot of time in jail."

The suspect, a thirty-three-year-old man, just laughed. "Really? Kiss my butt, asshole."

I said nothing. I just looked at him. For twenty uninterrupted minutes. As I had anticipated, short, rapid visions raced through my mind.

"OK, so you're good at staring contests. Listen, just tell me what you want, so I can say no, and we can both move on."

I did not respond and continued to sit silently and motionless. Sure enough, the remainder of what I needed to see arrived over the next few minutes.

I abruptly began. "I've got what I need."

"What the hell are you talking about? You don't know crap. And I'm not telling you anything."

"No need. As I said, I already know everything. And when I tell the cops and the district attorney what I know, you will go to prison for about twenty years. Have a nice day."

As I got up to leave the room, he grabbed my arm. "Listen, I don't know who you are but I think you are full of crap. Prove to me that you know anything."

"I don't need to do that. I'm not the one in trouble. Now please kindly let me go or I'll have to get Detective Olds to pry you off of me, and I promise you that will hurt a great deal."

His hands and feet were now in motion. I knew this would not take much longer.

"What's your name again? Frank?"

"Franklin."

"Look, Franklin, I'm pretty sure you are full of it."

"I'm not full of it. I know all about your past activities."

He was moving in his chair, drying his sweaty palms on his thighs. "So you tell them everything you know about the robbery. Big deal."

"Oh, it's not the robbery I found the most interesting. I must admit that I don't know what you did with the jewels, so that, unfortunately, I can't tell them. It's the other stuff you've done. Far more incriminating than the location of stolen merchandise."

He leaned forward, now on the edge of the chair. Beads of sweat hung tenuously from each side of his forehead.

"Look, you seem like a good guy, Franklin. How about if I tell them where I've hidden the stuff? And in return, we stop there. Will you do that? I never hurt anyone on purpose, I swear. I'm not a violent guy. Please!"

Game over.

◆◇◆◇◆

AND SO THE LEGEND OF FRANKLIN ROCK, secret weapon, only deepened, as did the betting. Derrick offered to share his considerable winnings with me, but on obvious ethical grounds, I declined. I didn't even let him buy me dinner.

Although I helped solve my share of crimes, I preferred to focus on what started the whole thing. More and more I asked to spend my time helping people, both victims and perpetrators like Anthony and Billy, the two who had started my mini-career with the police. I have been asked why I waste my time with the criminals. The question itself implies a lack of understanding. Those who commit the crimes remain part of the play, participants in the same story we share. To leave them out is foolish. The world doesn't come with extra pieces, like a child's build-it-yourself construction set. Every person is a part of the story and none can be ignored. To fix the world is to repair every one of us. And so the criminals got my attention.

Each day a broken part appeared, and each day I did my best to mend it. While Derrick's colleagues fought among themselves for my assistance, I could feel the evolution. My skills were maturing. This talent I had was a power, just as Govinda had predicted, and I was responsible to use it well. Each troubled soul they brought to me I owned during those moments we were together, and I needed to leave them better than I found them. Rather than a job or a burden, it became my sustenance. There were times the chore seemed unconquerable. It was at those times that I would hear the voice of my former nurse colleague, Nancy Sturdivant, in my head. "They are all God's children, Franklin."

I never gave up. I never left before I found success. Maybe it wasn't perfect success or permanent success. But one hundred percent of the time the whole—and by that I mean the entire universe of the crime—was at least in some small way better after my involvement than before I had intervened. I can say that because I would not cease in my efforts until that statement was true.

Nevertheless, I knew I would not be Derrick's go-to guy forever. Something more was to be my fate; this was a certainty. Until then I would spend my days—and nights—doing what I could. To be chosen, I frequently reminded myself, is to be ready and responsible. Maurice Burnside would have been very disappointed in me if I wasn't both.

36

One Last Success

Lara held Anna upside down, suspended by the black shoe that barely clung to the doll's foot. With her free arm, she pushed open the unlatched screen door and hurried into the front yard. To and fro she walked, head down, between the station wagon and the front door. "Where is it?" she wondered aloud. Her eyes were glued to the ground in search of Anna's beret.

"What are you looking for, child?" the woman asked. Lara's eyes moved rapidly upwards and met those of the large lady with the gray-streaked black hair.

"Anna's hat," she replied.

"Is this Anna?" the woman asked, pointing at the doll. "May I hold her for a moment?" Lara hesitated. "Oh, I won't hurt her, my dear. Here, let me fix her shoe before it falls off." The large woman lifted the doll from Lara's hand and placed the doll's shoe securely on her foot.

"There, that's better. Now you won't lose her shoe *and* her hat. " The woman returned the doll to Lara. "Now tell me, what does her hat look like?"

"It's black and soft and floppy and it fits just right on Anna's head. And it makes her look beautiful," she added.

"May I help you look?" the large woman asked.

"OK, I guess so."

"Come, we will look together," the woman said, and quickly took Lara's free hand in her own. Lara noticed how much rougher the woman's hand was than her own mother's, which was always so soft and warm. "Keep your eyes on the ground, dear. You don't want to miss it."

Lara and the woman walked together, hand in hand, as Lara made sure to keep her head down and her eyes peeled for Anna's lost hat. After some time Lara looked up. She was no longer in her front yard. Lara was confused. Probably they had walked around the corner, she thought.

"This isn't my street. I have to go home now."

"But we haven't found Anna's hat yet. Best we keep looking, don't you think?" The woman tightened her grip on Lara's hand.

"Ow, you're hurting me." Lara looked up into the woman's face. The woman was no longer looking at Lara. She didn't answer.

"Please, I need to go home."

Still no response. The large woman was now pulling Lara at a faster pace. "Be still, child. We will go home later."

"I want to go home now!" Lara yelled, tears now welling up in her small blue eyes. The large woman ignored her plea. Her grip tightened, pulling Lara towards an old-model filthy Chevrolet Impala. When they reached the car, the large woman opened the passenger door and pushed Lara into the seat. She quickly slammed the door, hurried around to the driver's side, opened the door, got in, and in seconds the two were driving out of Lara's neighborhood.

Two teenage boys were skateboarding down the street. The filthy Chevrolet swerved to miss them. They both noticed the screaming child struggling to free herself from the driver's grip.

◆◇◆◇◆

I LOOKED UP FROM my tablet. Over the past thirty minutes I had been catching up on the news, the stock market overvaluation, a planned private rocket launch to Mars, and discovered that I did not recognize the names of any of the current five highest scorers in the NBA. Joanna's radio had interrupted the broadcast for some breaking news story. I looked up and listened as I had become accustomed to doing when it was clear something untoward had occurred.

A young girl was missing. Her mother had thought she was in the house, and having not heard or seen her for a short time began to look for the girl. When it was clear that she was nowhere to be found, she contacted the authorities. The police arrived and quickly canvased the neighborhood for anyone who had seen anything. Two boys had noticed a car speeding from the girl's neighborhood with a crying child that seemed to fit the description of the little girl.

"What kind of world is this?" I turned towards my wife, awaiting her response.

"You didn't say anything, Franklin."

"I didn't?"

"No darling, you didn't. But I have a pretty good idea what you were thinking."

It was not uncommon for me to assume my internal thoughts were vocalized. Long ago I realized that I had difficulty separating the silent from the shared.

"I've got to go," I told Joanna.

"I already knew that, Franklin. Dare I ask how you are traveling?"

Joanna's question, though intended as a joke, was not unreasonable, nor unexpected. The dreams of flight had become even more frequent—and more real—of late, and I had shared them with her.

I settled in behind the wheel of my car and dialed up Detective Olds.

"Olds," the detective answered as he lifted the receiver.

"Hi Derrick, it's Franklin."

"Franklin! You know, I was just telling the Captain that I wanted to call you and ask for your help, but I had promised not to anymore. Are you just calling to say hi?"

"Nice try. You know why I'm calling. And you knew I would."

"Kids, Franklin. You can't resist. Yeah, I was pretty sure I'd hear from you. Are you on the way?"

"Yes. But if you tell me what you know maybe we can speed this up."

"Honestly, at this point, not more than you have probably heard on the news. Some woman snatched a five-year-old, presumably from her front yard, and drove off. Two kids saw her speed out of the neighborhood. Have a description of the car, but no plate."

"Are the parents together, separated, divorced?"

"Together. So far sounds like a great family. Dad was at work, flew home when his wife called him. Both are frantic. Doesn't sound like a domestic case to me."

"Both parents work?"

"No, just the dad."

"What does he do, Derrick?"

"You mean for a job"?

"No, during commercials of a football game. Of course for a job!"

"I don't know. Want me to find out?"

"That would help," I answered, a bit too abruptly I realized immediately after my response.

"Fine, I'll call you back in a minute. You know, all of that work you claim to be doing on that patience problem of yours doesn't seem to be working."

"Sorry, Derrick. The thought of that little girl…Hurry, please."

Within two minutes, I pressed the green answer button on my mobile phone.

"He's a lawyer, Franklin. Works for a small firm downtown."

"Do you know anything about his law firm? Who they represent? Anything like that?" I asked.

"I'll get that checked out right now and get back to you," Detective Olds responded. "You're thinking the father has something to do with this?"

"If you mean the father had his daughter taken, absolutely not. Do I think he's at the root of the issue? Yes. I'm going to guess his firm does family law, and that the father is a divorce lawyer," I told Derrick. "I could be completely wrong on that," I added as a somewhat feeble attempt to maintain some degree of humility. I was about ninety percent sure I was on the money—I had already glimpsed part of the outcome—but Derrick didn't need to know that. "Is the father at the house?" I asked.

"Yes, both he and the wife. Detective Lugerner is with them."

"Call Detective Lugerner and tell him I'm on my way. I don't think this will take very long. I'm pretty confident that we'll have the child home soon. And then I'll fix the other problem."

Just after I arrived at the home, Detective Lugerner introduced me to the husband and wife.

"John Hancock," the husband said as we shook hands. My head jerked up when I heard his name.

"I know, I get the same reaction from everyone. This is my wife, Arlene."

"I'm not sure what Detective Lugerner has told you about who I am and what I do," I began.

"He said you help the police solve crimes," Arlene Hancock told me. "That's all."

"At least that's what I try to do," I answered.

"Don't listen to that, ma'am," Detective Lugerner interjected. "He's amazingly good at this."

"Mr. Hancock, can I speak with you privately?" I asked, turning to the husband. "I will talk with you next, Mrs. Hancock. I prefer to speak with one person at a time."

I followed Mr. Hancock to a small library down the hall from the living room. We sat directly across from each other in matching upholstered chairs.

"Mr. Hancock. If you tell me the truth, I will have your daughter back safely in no time."

"Of course," he answered.

"Please tell me the name of the woman you are representing in a custody battle. The one you're having the affair with."

John Hancock's face instantly turned sunburned red. I watched him sigh. "Jennifer Lipton. But there is no way she could have anything to do with this."

"I'm quite sure that's incorrect. But why do you say that?"

"She's a wonderful person. It's impossible."

"Have you met her husband?"

"Yes, he seems like a nice guy. You don't think that he is involved, do you?"

"I'm sure he's involved. Why and how I can't say without more information, but for sure he is. Do they have children?"

"Yes, two. A son twelve, a daughter five."

"Your daughter, what's her name?" I asked.

"Lara. Oh, God, Mr. Rock, please find her and bring her back."

"We will. Lara is also five?" I asked him.

"Yes."

"Did Ms. Lipton—Jennifer—tell you if her husband was faithful? Any possibility he was also having an affair?"

"She thought he had had more than one. He'd often be gone on business trips and wouldn't call her for days at a time. So she was suspicious. According to Jennifer, after the first couple of years, their marriage was horrible. Seems like neither of them was very happy."

"Would Jennifer know the name of any of those women her husband was fooling around with?"

"I could ask her," he answered.

"Call her right now," I insisted.

He did, and six hours later Lara was home, her doll Anna in tow. Jennifer Lipton's husband had fallen in with a woman whose brother was involved in a drug ring. When he decided to end the relationship, the woman was livid. He had promised to marry her, support her, buy her all manner of things. Seems she was a gold digger. She had left another man for him, assuming—incorrectly—that he was wealthy. When her brother heard what had happened, he too was livid. They cleverly searched for and identified the deepest pockets in this loosely linked group: John Hancock. The two of them then concocted a convoluted plan to kidnap young Lara and blackmail John Hancock. The jilted woman—and her brother— would at least feel that they had gotten compensation for her "loss."

Detective Lugerner and I calmly explained all of this to a distraught but relieved John Hancock back in the study while his wife soothed little Lara.

"Who was the woman who took the child?" he asked.

"Some low-life involved with the drug ring. They probably traded her drugs for doing the dirty work," Detective Lugerner explained.

A few hours later, after Lara was in her bed, I sat down with the Hancocks. I looked over at the husband. "I believe you should begin," I suggested.

Mr. Hancock admitted to his indiscretion. As I had anticipated, Arlene Hancock showed no great surprise. Infidelity is rarely a secret. Even when it seems to be, it's almost always more denial than ignorance. I then explained to Arlene Hancock the web of involvement that led to Lara's kidnapping. Mrs. Hancock's mouth stayed open as I wound through the convoluted tale.

"Arlene, I cannot tell you how sorry I am," John Hancock pleaded through a now steady stream of tears. "Not just Lara. All of it. I know what I did was terrible. Believe me, I am embarrassed and sad beyond words. I cannot believe I did this to you."

I turned to Arlene Hancock. "Your marriage isn't a failure, and I suggest neither of you looks for fault. I can guarantee you it's everywhere. Life is all about learning, and the most important thing to learn is love.

You two can for sure go on and have a wonderful relationship, but to do so, you have to be willing to ignore the past. Those who hang onto the past have no future. You may never have had the foundation of a great relationship. Build one now. Learn to climb into the other's head and see the world the way your spouse does. Each of our opinions about another person's observable actions is irrelevant. Only if you view that action through the other's eyes does it have any meaning. Don't judge; praise. And don't keep score."

No one said a word. I continued.

"I have a certain gift," I told them. "I can see the future; that's how we got Lara back so quickly."

Husband and wife exchanged a startled look. Good, I thought, their first shared moment of their new relationship.

"It's not that big a deal actually, since the future, just like the past, has already happened. But that's a conversation for another time. I promise you both, you will be together and happy for a very long time if you are both willing to walk away from the past and start again today." It's easy to make declaratory statements when you have seen the future.

Both were now sobbing uncontrollably.

"Will you give me another chance, Arlene?" John Hancock asked between gasps of breath.

Arlene nodded. John walked over to her and wrapped her in his arms, their tears now mixing on each other's cheeks. Neither looked up as I left the room.

My car phone rang.

"Franklin, it's Derrick. I don't know how you figured that out. Beautiful man, beautiful. Just wanted to let you know the neighborhood kids ID'd the woman who grabbed the child. Crazy case. Thanks, man."

"Glad it worked out, Derrick. Don't call me, I'll try not to call you."

"Hey, I might not get you to help too often, but we're still brothers," Derrick told me. "You can't get rid of me."

"It's never been my plan to try. Stay well, brother."

As I drove home to Joanna I reflected on this episode. Most times it's just a small slice of the future that I am permitted to see, just enough to direct me. As in this case, I saw a vague outline of the protagonists, a glimpse of a law office, a haggard woman dragging a child. Sometimes I feel like I'm cheating, as if I have seen the answer sheet before the exam is given.

I have assumed for some time now that a career change was on the horizon. My silent voice was occasionally whispering and teasing. For sure I was fixing things, but these police adventures seemed more an appetizer than an entree.

Joanna was in the kitchen when I arrived home.

"Success?" she asked, turning towards me, her hands expertly chopping vegetables.

"Success," I confirmed. "Very strange turn of events."

"You can fill me in over dinner. Want to check the fish in the oven for me, love?" she asked.

Together we finished preparing dinner, and with two glasses of wine poured, we were ready to eat.

"Thanks for making this and waiting for me," I told my beautiful wife.

"My pleasure. It's the least I can do while you're out rescuing a small child."

We clinked our glasses in a toast to Lara and a bit more tranquility and joy in the world.

"I think I know what I'm going to do next," I said.

"OK. Want to share?"

"I want to write. I think that's the best venue to continue my efforts."

"Your mission," Joanna specified.

"OK, my mission, though you know I don't like calling it that."

"You might not like it, but that's what it is," Joanna insisted. "Books, stories? What are you going to write?"

"Not sure. I'll figure that out. Joanna, I'm afraid to say this but here goes. You know I know things."

Rolled eyes spoke. "God, Franklin, yes, I know. It's not necessary to keep repeating that. It's annoying, love."

I laughed. "I didn't say it to annoy you, and I'm sorry. I just said it because I know that it's the next step. Once I start writing…"

"It will come to you," Joanna finished my thought.

"Right. I think the next part will come to me. Look, you're the one that convinced me to be patient and let it happen. You were right."

"You may know things, Franklin, but don't forget that I am *always* right."

"I would never be so foolish as to forget that."

"Have any ideas what you're going to write about?"

"I have a few."

"All right, Hemingway…" she began.

I interrupted her. "You don't want me to be Hemingway. He wasn't the happiest guy."

"Fine, writer man. Let's clean up." Joanna put down the plate she was holding, wiped her mouth on her napkin, and kissed me. "I've never slept with a writer before," she whispered.

37

The Game

"Joanna, this one was intense."

"Darling, they are all intense. Now must I hear about last night's dream or can I get on with something in the real world?" She caught my frown. "Oh, yes, forgive me. Your dream world is also a real world. Did I get that right?"

My wife did not await my response and continued flipping through the three high-gloss magazines perched on her bent knees. At that moment, like so many others, I felt incredibly blessed. I love her voice—every word she utters is like the favorite phrase of a best-loved melody. I adore her perfectly-crafted, long, slender fingers, my hand determined to hold hers whenever she is near. No kiss on her lips is ordinary, and after all these years together, I still become woozy when she lets my lips linger on hers for even a few moments. How immensely wonderful life is when one is so fortunate to have another to cherish as I do my lovely Joanna.

Still, my dreams remain a source of eye-rolling for my elegant wife. It's not that she dismisses them. Rather, she regards them as my province, not hers. Other worlds and universes, and Time as a proper noun, hold no special place in her life as they do in mine. She is respectful, I think, as another wife might be of her husband's fascination with sports statistics or the intricacies of the internal combustion engine.

"There were bad guys. I'm not sure what the crime was, but I was in hot pursuit."

Joanna never looked up from the gardening magazine that had leap-frogged the other two to command her attention. "Bad guys. Got it," she said, just to confirm that she would indeed indulge me once again.

"I was trying to stop them before they could harm someone. I was airborne, usual position, seated facing backward. This time flight felt turbulent; I did not feel comfortable. I was confused by this state, and I tried to turn around to face forward, but I could not seem to master that move. I kept going and could see the would-be perpetrators far below me. They suddenly stopped, and so did I. Hovering was short-lived. I began, as usual, to drop like a stone. But this time, as I neared the ground, I did not awaken in panic as I always do."

"While whimpering like a lost puppy," Joanna added, finally looking up at me with her sweet smile. "Not that I mind, love, but it is a little wimpy."

I ignored her tender jab and continued. "This time I somehow took control—I have no idea how—and abruptly slowed my descent. I can only describe my sudden change in awareness as an airborne epiphany, like the toddler who suddenly realizes he can right himself just before taking a tumble. I had learned to control the free-fall. I gently lighted on the ground, so excited by this event that I forgot why I had been flying in the first place. It was is if the faceless perpetrators served only as the fox enticing the hounds."

I waited for a response. "Joanna?"

"Oh, that's it? She lifted her eyes from the page. "I assumed there was more."

"Yes, there is much more," I said and continued despite my love's disingenuous response. "I once again flung myself skyward, and sure enough I was soon aloft. But this time I was unconcerned, unconstrained by the knowledge I had previously possessed that eventually, inevitably, I would plummet towards earth. I felt so free, Joanna, so incredibly powerful and dynamic. And I was flying facing forward for the first time in one of my dreams. That feeling you had when you first realized that you could ride a bike without assistance, that was the feeling that now overwhelmed me. I had done it!"

I walked over to Joanna's side of the bed, sat, and leaned towards her so that my face was a foot from hers.

"This is huge, Joanna. I know you think I make too much of this. Something is happening, though. I am so certain that I am in some kind of transition, preparing for something."

Joanna placed the magazines to her left on the bed, sat just a bit more upright, and looked me squarely in the eyes. "First of all, yes, I think you are a bit bizarre, but that doesn't mean I don't believe you, or in you. I love you, and I know you feel this with all of your being. I'm just not as curious as you. I accept this as part of whatever our lives are to be. That's just who I am. You doubt, you seek, you question, you search. Not me. I just accept. If you are to do something fabulous, then I'm with you. It just won't make me swoon or cheer. That in no way minimizes its importance to you or even its importance to the universe. I accept, and that makes me very peaceful."

If her beauty was not enough to knock me out, her serenity would finish the job. She who is in harmony with all things is my wife.

"Why God decided to give you to me is a mystery. I must have been very good in a prior life."

"How do you know it wasn't me who was so deserving as to get you?" Joanna responded, her wonderfully soft hands now cradling mine. She paused and moved her hands to lift my chin until our eyes were inches apart. Hers were smiling. "I'm sure you are right. I'm the gift, you lucky boy. Now I'm going to read for a few more minutes and then I'm going to bed. I'll have to sleep fast just in case I am once again awakened by my flying, whimpering husband."

◆◇◆◇◆

NIGHT HAD BROUGHT WITH IT a brilliant moon-lit sky and a light spring breeze, perfect for Oscar's and my intended short walk around the block. My neighbors had long since drawn their curtains and doused most of their lights; the neighborhood was mine. Every few houses, I encountered a new fragrance, mostly pleasant like my favorite honeysuckle; others not so much, such as the trash that overflowed from a dented topless metal can. I looked down at Oscar. Every foot we traveled was a source of new olfactory knowledge about his world. He would ignore the honeysuckle and cherish the garbage lying just to my right as I passed by. Something for everyone and everything.

Just one street and a few hundred yards from my house was a large fenced garden. Here, I knew from experience, I would find just the right composition of scents, the sweetness and the fullness of a wide array of floral fragrances. The garden sat upon the crest of a small hill, fronted by a wide grassy bank, plenty large enough for one to stretch out and take in the beauty of God's sky above. That is what I did. The moon's light limited the visible stars, but I knew they were there despite the camouflage. What we see is so little of what there is. For many of us, what we see is not only all we know but what we insist must be all there is to know. If only such naiveté were merely charming. Unfortunately for mankind, it's a frighteningly small step from naiveté to ignorance, and ignorance begets havoc.

As I took in the night's sky, my thoughts returned to my previous night's dream. Flight. I had experienced real, forward flight. Crazy thinking I told myself. These were just dreams. I can't fly, and I was not deluded enough to attempt to leap off a building and assume I would stay airborne. But my internal words belied what I can only describe as a deeper truth. While today I could not fly, the sense that somehow flight would become for me a reality eclipsed the logic and reason I had been trained to respect. Wishful thinking, childhood fantasy, imagination run amok; I considered them all. Always I returned to that deeper truth, that inner knowledge, that this was no fantasy. Flight would be mine, I was convinced, but I was also certain that keeping this to myself, for the time being, was the best strategy.

After some time of staring straight up into the moon's offering, my eyes craved darkness. I briefly allowed them to fall closed, but I knew if I did not force myself to rise, I would fall fast asleep. I made my way back home and silently crept into bed next to my peacefully sleeping bride, then slid close enough to smell her and feel her short breaths on the back of my arm as I rested it against her pillow. Soon I felt the muscles of my face, torso, and extremities simultaneously release. Sleep came quickly, followed by the dream.

An unfamiliar and confusing scene confronted me. I was in a brightly-lit and noisy room. In front of me was a large crowd seated and clapping. To both my right and left were men and women, each of us approximately two arms' lengths apart, all facing the crowd. I peered behind me. Some sort of electronic scoreboard covered the back wall, and I scanned its content. My name was illuminated, as were the names of others who I deduced must be those individuals on either side of me. A tall dark-haired thin man with a microphone—I would estimate he was maybe forty years old—entered from the right, waving to the crowd. Now I understood: we were contestants.

In front of each of us contestants lay a bin full of bricks. Just in front of the bricks was a platform approximately six feet square. Above each platform, a standard traffic light was suspended—red, amber, and green in descending order. I looked to my right and left. Each of the others faced the same scene—bricks, platform, traffic light. No one was moving. Every contestant was simply staring straight ahead.

The emcee raised the microphone to his mouth and began. "Welcome, ladies and gentlemen. As you can see, we're just about ready to go. Check the board and choose your favorite. All right, lights down, and here we go!"

A huge television screen descended from the ceiling just in front of my fellow contestants and me, and a silent movie began. The initial scene was a replica of the live scene of which I was now a part. Bricks, platform, and traffic light were all there, but the players on the screen were not us. A completely different cast was starring in this film. This was a tutorial of sorts; we were to learn the game from the movie.

On the screen, the suspended traffic light changed colors in reverse— from red to amber and then to green. At the green light, each contestant began stacking the bricks on his or her platform as high and as fast as he or she was able, frantically attempting to stay ahead of the others. We watched as the stacks rapidly grew. The goal of the competition appeared to be to build the tallest stack.

The camera then focused on a single contestant, a woman of average build with short brown hair. Her arms flew from bin to platform, stacking brick after brick. Her breathing was rapid, her face flushed. After a minute or so, the camera turned its lens on the traffic light in front of her, and we saw it change from green to amber. At the moment she noticed the change in the color of the light, she quickly increased her stacking speed, now working with critical urgency. When the light then turned to red, her face froze, and she vanished.

The scene moved over to that of another contestant, and the same sequence of events we had just witnessed for the brown-haired woman was repeated. One by one, in no special order, we witnessed the same precise sequence of events for each contestant. As the light turned green the stacking began and continued until the light turned amber, at which point the contestant sped up the stacking, frantically trying to grow the stack before the light turned red. And when it did the image of that contestant immediately disappeared. We had no idea which contestant won, if any, or where they went after their scene concluded.

The screen in front of us vanished and the room lights were again bright. The large, now exuberant crowd was directly across from us. All of the contestants were still in the same line, still with the bins of bricks and platforms before us. Our turn had arrived. As his or her light turned green, I watched each of my fellow contestants, one after another, begin to stack bricks onto the platform as fast as possible. And just as in the film we had watched, eventually each of their traffic lights turned amber, then red, and, then just like that each of them was gone.

I was the final contestant in our group. I watched my traffic light, anticipating its illumination. Just as I prepared to begin furiously stacking in the same manner as those before me at the appearance of the green light, I heard a voice I thought I recognized. The voice said, "Franklin, is there something else you might do with those bricks?"

I look around and at first I saw no one; all of my fellow contestants who had preceded me were gone. I turned and looked behind me and for the first time became aware that there was another line of would-be contestants, queued up just as we had been, awaiting their turn. As soon as my turn was completed, they would step forward, be shown the silent movie, and then begin their stacking. Green light, amber light, red light—gone. Again I heard that voice. "Franklin, is there something else you might do with those bricks? Is there more that you haven't seen?"

I surveyed my surroundings. I gazed above me and saw row upon row of contestants; the same was now visible below me. Everywhere I looked in every direction there were lines of contestants, thousands upon thousands, all of us in some multidimensional array.

My focus returned to the platform in front of me, and my eyes landed on what was a just barely visible notch in two of the sides of the platform. I had not noticed these before. When my traffic light turned green, instead of beginning to stack the bricks, I placed a brick at each of these notches: both bricks fit perfectly. It was then that I saw that the bricks also had subtle notches on both ends, which explained the precise fit of the bricks and the platform. I placed a second brick on either side adjacent to the first two, their notches also matching seamlessly.

As soon as those bricks were joined, a faint but visible blue beam began to emanate from the free edge of the last brick on each side. The bricks themselves then became translucent, filled internally with a rich, blue hue. The peripheral blue beam continued from the last brick I had placed, inviting me to add another brick to extend this developing blue path. Brick after brick, the blue beam grew from both the right and left ends of the line of bricks, and simultaneously each additional brick transformed into a translucent blue hue, just as those initial bricks had done. The twin blue beams did not fan off randomly; a specific pattern was emerging.

Within seconds the blue beams exponentially proliferated, so that soon a plethora of blue beams emanated from my line of bricks to uncountable others, and from each of them to even more uncountable others until everywhere I looked I witnessed a starburst pattern of blue beams. Other contestants had seen the same proliferation of blue beams linking my platform to my neighbors, and they too began to link the notches in the bricks before them to their platforms. And just like mine, their blue beams began to link to thousands of their neighbors. What seemed like millions of us were now connected by ever-growing paths of warm, inviting blue beams.

I began to feel unstable and noticed that the entire scene of which I was a part was now wobbling, as if our universe of contestants was about to tip over. I rushed to place bricks at the corner of this universe, and as I did, others observed what I was doing and began to do the same. Soon the wobbling lessened, and I saw that we were now high off the ground, resting on a new bedrock of bricks being put down by innumerable contestants.

Suddenly I felt a surge of panic—the traffic light! I had forgotten all about it and frantically looked up to check its color. My green light was still illuminated and had grown geometrically in size and now dwarfed the red and amber lights. The green light emanating from my traffic light illuminated the infinite web of brick pathways now linking the infinite contestants. This light, that blended exquisitely with the blueness of the beams, was embracing and indescribably peaceful. I was enveloped in its warmth, and as I looked around it was clear that my fellow contestants now felt that same serenity.

"Franklin, I hope it was me to whom you were repeating, 'I love you.'"

Joanna's lovely eyes were just above mine as I re-entered the world we shared, and for a moment I could see that other world that I had just left deep within them. "Of course, darling, it's always you," among millions of others, I added silently. "Did I wake you? Was I whimpering again?"

"No, I think you were saying 'mm' as if you were savoring something delicious." Joanna looked at me with stern but laughing eyes and added, "And it had better been either food or me."

"Want to hear about it?" I asked the love of my life, already slowly but inexorably tuning me out now that I was safe and awake.

"Tomorrow, love. It's the middle of the night, and most normal people prefer to sleep instead of chat about dreams." And with that, she returned to peaceful slumber.

As usual, I was not able to follow her example. My dream, though fading fast from my consciousness, left me confused. Was the deep and satisfying peace I had just experienced merely wishful thinking? Or was it something to be pursued? And if so, was that merely the optimism of the dreamer, or the required labor of a chosen one?

I stared at the ceiling of our bedroom and watched the fan rotate counter-clockwise over and over again. Its rhythm and uninterrupted low-level hum calmed me, and at some time I fell back to sleep and remained that way, dreamless, until a warm, gentle and loving touch awakened me. Daylight illuminated Joanna as she softly whispered, "Wake up, dream boy. Time for the real world."

38

A Meeting of the Minds

DREAMS.

Mine have been an integral part of my life. I remember almost all of them. I'm not aware of what percentage of the population can recall any of their dreams, but to recall all of them I knew to be unusual. In college, I had studied the psychologist Carl Jung. Professor Jung had spent his life interpreting dreams for patients and written many scholarly articles and books. I often wondered what it would have been like to discuss my dreams with him, the acknowledged expert of experts.

Might it be possible for me to visit Professor Jung in his time? For quite a while I had been contemplating the possibility of targeted destination time travel. All of my "trips" had been to somewhere specific and, as it became obvious in retrospect, for a distinct purpose. Who or what was making those decisions I had no idea, but a likely candidate was my unconscious. So perhaps it would not be a great leap to have my conscious self participate in the choosing of destinations.

Could I make it happen? If so, how? Where would I begin? Often fiction is the preface to the real. Jack Finney's book, *Time and Again,* the one I had been reading just before I visited my father, again came to mind. Perhaps it was my unconscious that had taken me back to see my father in response to the suggestion from the book that submersing oneself in another time could transport one to that chosen setting. No other reason was apparent for the temporal relationship of my reading and the event. It was certainly worth another try.

The next evening, I sat in my office with the lights dimmed. From the bookshelf behind me, I plucked one of Jung's texts and began to read.

I imagined myself in front of him, discussing his work with him, and seeking his counsel. No shift occurred, but I soon fell asleep for a very brief period. I felt my mind rinsed clean, as if my brain was attempting to remove any potential impediment to my attempt. After reading a few more pages, I once again closed my eyes, and this time the world shifted. I reopened them, and there he was.

"Hello, Professor Jung."

"Have we met?" he inquired.

"No, sir, we have not."

"And you are?"

"My name is Franklin Rock."

"I believe I might have heard your name somewhere before." His pensive look confirmed a rapid search of his memories. "It does sound vaguely familiar. No matter. You are American, yes? Where are you from?"

"I am American, and I am from another time."

His look made it clear he did not tolerate foolishness. "You are telling me the truth, I hope."

"I am, sir."

Jung's eyes scanned me, took in my clothing, my demeanor, every aspect of a person as he had expertly learned to do as a psychiatrist.

"You may be telling me the truth, young man. Tell me, then, from when have you come?"

"2020."

"My goodness. How is the world doing?"

"There are still the usual problems."

"Such as?" Professor Jung inquired.

"Violence, for one. Cruelty, for another. Hate. Intolerance. The same as in every generation."

"May I call you Franklin?" he asked.

"Of course."

"I am going to assume you have chosen to come here and did not just land in my library accidentally."

"Yes, sir. You are the first person whom I have visited intentionally. I mean, this is the first time I have been able to choose where in time I wished to go."

"You know," Professor Jung told me, "I once asked Herr Professor Einstein about time travel. He was doubtful."

"Albert Einstein? You knew him?"

"I know him. He is still alive, but for you, he would be gone a good many years. We are both, I'm afraid, nearing the end. I am a bit older than Professor Einstein, I think, by a few years."

"Can I ask you how old you are now, Professor?"

"I am seventy-six, so in that case, he must be seventy-two or seventy-three. It has been many years since I have seen him. You seem very interested in him."

"I am. It is his discovery that has allowed me to understand how I can travel in time," I explained.

"Tell me about that," Professor Jung asked.

"I'll try to explain it as best I can. I hope your friend Einstein will forgive my simplification of his theory," I said. Jung smiled. "All of time exists simultaneously. Past and present of course have already occurred or are occurring now. But even the future has already happened. Professor Einstein once wrote—and I am paraphrasing—that for believing physicists, the past, present, and future are only stubborn illusions. Every moment of time lives on for eternity in its specific location in what he termed 'space-time'. If that weren't the case it would be impossible to move in time. There would be no place to go. And I wouldn't be here talking with you," I added with a smile, then paused for a response.

"Go on," Professor Jung encouraged me.

"I have read some of your work. Not all, I confess. But I did notice in one of your publications where you referenced the possibility that something you saw in the unconscious may be occurring somewhere else. Is that right?"

"Yes, Franklin. I have had the sense on more than one occasion that time, as we typically know it, is incompletely understood. So it seems that I was correct at least in that assumption."

"You were, Professor." Again I paused.

"It's fine, Franklin, please continue. I am enjoying this a great deal."

"I also recall from your writings that you have an interest in the paranormal. I think there was even an episode with Dr. Freud where you predicted something would happen in a cabinet in the room you were in."

"You did your homework, I see. Yes, that also is true. I thought Freud was going to pass out after the episode you describe. We heard a loud noise in a large cabinet in his study, or maybe my library. I don't recall where we were. I told him that was a manifestation of the paranormal based on a disagreement we had just had. He rebuffed me, at which point I possessed the sudden knowledge that the same sound would occur again and told him so. Immediately after I made the prediction it happened as I had said it would. Freud was stunned to silence."

"Did you know how this knowledge had come to you?" I asked him.

"No idea at all. But I am going to assume that you are about to tell me that I had had an insight into the future," Professor Jung concluded.

"Exactly. To me, that is an example of how sometimes we can access the future. You would probably credit the unconscious with that access."

"I probably would, yes."

"Professor, I have been to both the past and the future on numerous occasions, so I know that this occurs."

Jung leaned back in his chair. "Why?" he asked me.

"Are you asking me if I know why I time travel, or why I end up in a specific place at a specific time?"

"Answering the latter will explain the former, I presume. Have you been able to discern a reason?"

"I think I have. Each time I have traveled somewhere—the past far more often than the future—I have learned something. Sometimes it's to demonstrate a skill or talent I have. Sometimes it's to explain a feeling or phenomenon I have witnessed. In the case of the future, I'm pretty certain that it was to let me see at least part of the finished product so I know how to solve a problem, like a crime. Other times I think it was just to focus me on what I'm supposed to do."

"What are you supposed to do?" he immediately asked.

"Believe it or not, I'm supposed to fix the world," I told him with a confidence no different than if he had asked my weight.

"What tools do you possess to accomplish this great feat?"

For a second I wasn't certain if he was mocking me. The look on my face was sufficient for this extremely experienced reader of human words and movements to understand my concern.

"No, Franklin, I am not doubting or making fun of you. My question is legitimate. I'm going to assume you have some tools at your disposal. I had to develop tools to be able to interpret dreams. No one goes to war without weapons."

"I know things," I said, and before I could continue he sat up, looked directly at me, and said, "As do I."

"So sorry, Professor, I didn't mean…"

He cut me off before I could finish. "Again you misunderstand me. I am not belittling you. I am merely stating that we share what you might call a talent or gift. To know things, things about the unconscious in my case, or time, and maybe the unconscious as well in yours, is powerful indeed. Unfortunately, as I am sure you already know, or if not you will soon discover, knowing things that others don't can be problematic. You will be ostracized, ridiculed, overlooked, as I was. I assume you are aware of this?" he asked, his voice rising.

"I am. Believe me, I'm not looking forward to more of it as I proceed. You're probably going to recommend that I ignore it and just keep following my path. I believe that is what you did."

"That is what I did. That is what I continue to do, as you must."

"That's my plan. I'm afraid I will have to grow thicker skin."

"Unfortunately, you will. But it will all be worth it if you stay the course and follow the truth. Now, where were we? I believe there was something else you were about to tell me," he said presciently.

"I have visions," I blurted out.

"You do, do you? Is that why you came to see me?"

"Yes, sir, that is why I wanted to meet you."

"And can I assume you also have dreams that interest you?"

"You may. I learned long ago to pay attention to them. I had studied you a bit in college, so I knew that for you dreams were not suppressed sexual issues as they were for Dr. Freud but much more manifestations by the unconscious of current events in one's life."

"Well stated, Franklin. Dreams are expressions of the unconscious in an attempt to deal with the conscious world. My disagreement with Freud cost me our friendship. Tell me about your dreams, please."

"I have had dreams you might describe as emanating from the collective unconscious. These involve armies and violence, things like that. Plus I have many that to me at least reflect my own challenges. I am fortunate to remember many of my dreams and as I said I pay close attention to them. I also have very real time-travel visions. That's probably the wrong term because they are actual events. I go to those different places in time."

"You physically go to those times in the past and the future? Do you simply vanish from your present? I assume that would not go unnoticed and might be difficult to explain."

"That's the strangest part. I never go anywhere physically. My body stays put; it's just my mind that travels. But believe me, Professor Jung, these are quite real."

"I too have both dreams and visions, Franklin. The visions, as I have just learned from you, are more likely brief glimpses of a future that, as you describe, has already happened. That is so interesting and explains a lot. Dreams emanate from the unconscious. Undoubtedly there is some relationship between the two. I need to give that more thought," he said, now looking out the window of his library and no longer at me.

"Can I ask you something else, Professor Jung?"

"You may," he responded as he turned back towards me.

"You have said that you felt that you had a destiny. I think you said you knew you had a very specific fate. What did you mean by that? How did it work out? Did you feel trapped? Do you believe in free will?"

"Slow down, Franklin. That's a lot to cover. Let's start with the destiny question. You want to know if our lives are fated to turn out as they do. You likely have had some experience that has prompted that inquiry. Yes?"

"I have always felt pushed in a specific direction. When I have tried to deviate from whatever path has been chosen for me I am always blocked. It's as if some force drags me back from my desired course."

"Interesting," he said. "I too am sure I was assigned a specific destiny. Unlike you, I did not spend much time fighting it. My path was apparent and I accepted it. Perhaps the difference between us is related more to our cultural differences and the gap in time than to our personalities. I don't know you well enough yet to make that determination, but I don't view it as germane. As to the question of how it has worked out, I would rephrase it as could I have done better? Who knows? That's part of the mystery, isn't it? I have no idea if it worked out; I have nothing to compare it with. None of us gets to try out different destinies. It has worked out as it has; that is all I can know. And no, I have never felt trapped. How can one feel trapped and simultaneously believe in fate or destiny? Those two ideas are incompatible. Do you see that?"

I nodded.

"Free will is another question. You have an opinion?"

"Honestly, I'm not sure."

"Want to know what I think?" Professor Jung asked.

"Please."

"We will likely never know. And it doesn't matter one whiff."

"Why do you say that?" I asked, my surprise surely evident.

"Think about it, Franklin. Either way, your behavior would be identical, as it would be for everyone else. If there is free will, then choices matter. If not, if there is no free will and it is simply a myth that has been perpetuated for centuries, you will never know, because you will assume that the decision you think you just made led to the eventual outcome. It is behavior we need to be concerned with, especially you, my friend, if you plan to fix the world. Free will or not, you will still be required to deal with the resulting behavior. I would suggest you not devote another minute to the question."

Now I knew why I had come to see him.

"Why are we here, Professor? Is there a purpose to each of our lives? And what about death?"

"How long do you have with me, Franklin? These are not small issues you raise. But they are two of my favorite areas for discussion. Did you already know that?" he asked me.

"Not exactly, but I assumed that might be the case. You had mentioned the concept of human purpose in your writings. You talk about finding the true self, communication with the collective unconscious, those sorts of things."

"Among others. I assume you have an opinion on this as well. So far you've had one for nearly every question you have posed," he said with a smile that reassured me that he was enjoying our discussion.

"I do. But I'm anxious to hear your views on both of these."

"You are referring to the hereafter, I assume?" he inquired.

"Yes, partially. I think I read that you didn't believe in a heaven filled with pleasure and milk and honey and so on," I stated.

"I think I also said that I have no idea what happens after death, if anything. But you seem to believe something does."

"I can't believe we go through all this learning, really an entire lifetime of learning, for nothing. I mean, every human has a similar history; only the details change. That seems strange to me if there is no point to it all."

"Do you believe, as you phrased it, that there is a point to it all?"

"Yes, but I'm afraid it may sound a bit crazy," I said sheepishly.

"You're talking to Carl Jung, Franklin. I have been accused by many of talking crazy for my whole life. Rest assured that I will not think any less of you. I may not share your conclusion but I will not judge you."

"Thank you, Professor. I think we will have other jobs to do wherever we go after death. I can't explain what that would entail or why we will do this. It just seems that this education we go through, all the events and relationships in our lives, cannot be for nothing. It's only near the end of our lives that most of us have figured out anything. It would be such a waste to not put that knowledge to some use. That makes no sense to me."

"I have thought along similar lines, Franklin. This life, I feel confident to say, is only part of our total existence. We will just have to see. Can I ask you a question now?"

"Of course. I certainly have asked you enough."

"How do you know you're supposed to fix the world?"

"It's a long story. I had a mentor. His name was Professor Niemeyer."

Professor Jung eyed me carefully. "Would that be Charles Niemeyer?" he asked.

"You know him?" I asked, incredulous that Professor Niemeyer was making yet another appearance.

"I have met him on more than one occasion. Interesting gentleman. Very intelligent. I ran into him at several meetings over the years. I haven't seen him for a very long time."

"What kind of meetings were they, if I may ask, Professor?"

"These were conferences focused on the content and interpretation of dreams. The reason I remember him is that he repeatedly asked many of us who were lecturing whether we thought dreams could be actual events in another dimension or something along those lines. His point, I think, was that dreams might not be merely fantastical expressions from our unconscious, that they might be real in some context. That created a lasting memory for me. First, the concept was one I had not entertained. Plus he was not so gently ridiculed by some in attendance. Once upon a time, I had been the recipient of a similar response, so it struck a chord with me. So he is from your time, I take it?"

"I think so." Professor Jung had me questioning Professor Niemeyer's origin.

"Now I can guess where I might have heard your name, Franklin. It could have been from Charles Niemeyer."

"Why would he have mentioned me? I wasn't even alive yet."

"Weren't you?" the wise Professor asked. "If as you say, and Herr Einstein claims, all time has always existed, then you were indeed alive."

That concept had not occurred to me. It is not only the past that remains alive. The future is already alive in the past. What more am I missing?

"Do you recall in what context he mentioned me, Professor?"

"Sorry, Franklin, I don't. I just can't recall."

"Professor Niemeyer died recently. I mean, in my time recently."

Professor Jung looked directly at me with a kind but piercing gaze. "You can't believe that, either."

"Are you asking me if I believe that people die? No, Professor, not in the classic concept of death. It's back to the Einstein thing. Since all moments exist forever in their fixed place in space-time, no one ever really dies. Their earthly story may have ended at some point, but they are never dead. At least that's what I think. What do you believe?"

"For me, death is not very important. Your explanation is interesting and seems reasonable," he told me. "I know that the concept most people have of death cannot be all there is. That became clear to me during my extensive research on cultures and history. You know, Franklin, for me the precise explanation—physics, chemistry, whatever—has never been of much concern. I simply know what is. Why interests me less than it does you."

"Do you have time for one more?" I asked him.

"Yes. This has been great fun for me."

"Why is there so much violence in the world?"

"Ah, that is a good one. I have written a fair amount about this. To be brief, it arises I believe out of a failure to reconcile issues within the unconscious. Failure to address the shadow side of our personality allows our unresolved issues of fear, shame, and inadequacy to surface, and so we project these personal weaknesses onto others. Sometimes this drives one to violence. When an entire group collectively suffers from this, mass-scale violence can erupt."

"Do you think violence can be conquered, Professor?"

"I would tell you, Franklin, that so far it has not been, and I fear it may never be. But I would also tell you that it is not impossible that it could be. No one who has committed violence is ever free. The burden remains forever; violence will eventually destroy the soul." He paused. "Perhaps this is one way in which you could fix the world," he added with a smile. "Now that would indeed be something."

I could feel the earth begin to move. The familiar shift was almost upon me.

"I am so very grateful to you, Professor Jung," I said hurriedly. "Sadly I am about to leave now."

"You can feel it? Fascinating. It's been a pleasure. I hope to see you again one day, Franklin Rock. Go fix your world. I'm sure it could use your help."

39

A Short Story

"YOU WON'T BELIEVE WHERE I went last night," I told Joanna as she awoke the next morning.

"After all of our years together, what do you think you could possibly tell me that I would not believe?"

"I spent time with Carl Jung."

"The famous psychiatrist?"

"Yes. It was fascinating."

"So you had a dream about Carl Jung. What part of that is so incredible, love? You have dreams every night."

"No, Joanna. It wasn't a dream. I saw him, I was with him in his library in his home."

"How did you end up there?"

"That's the best part. I time-traveled to see him intentionally. I made it happen," I explained, then related the full sequence of events.

"I wish you could take me with you on some of these, Franklin."

"Maybe someday, my love. Anywhere I am with you is always where I prefer to be."

"You are a sweet man," Joanna said as she fluffed her pillow. She stopped, looked up, and said, "Write me a story, Franklin."

"What?"

"You heard me. Aren't you planning to be a full-time author? Write me something."

"About what?"

"Something cute, not too long. Just something fun. Think you can do that?"

"I'd better be able to or this new plan of mine will be pretty short-lived."

"You have until dinner," Joanna added.

"Oh, c'mon. That's not fair. What's the rush?"

"If you are going to do this, then you're going to have to write every day, and not just a few words. So let's see what you've got. So by dinner. Better get going, love."

Settled in my office at my computer, I prepared to take on her challenge. Sweet, something cute but not too long. Ten minutes went by and nothing. Zero. Empty. Go back to something you know, I thought. College essays! Henry and I had read scores of them while serving on the college admissions committee as seniors. Most were wretched, but occasionally there was a good one. What would I write about today if I were trying to impress an admissions officer? A story for sure. People love stories, even college admissions officers. Those are the only essays I still remember.

For the entire afternoon, I kept my butt in my chair, typing away. Once the idea came to me, the rest was relatively easy. Fiction is fun. When you find you have painted yourself into a metaphorical corner somewhere in the story, all you have to do is draw a door on the wall behind you and step through it. If you're clever enough it's hard to get too stuck.

By six p.m. I had finished and even had a chance to do a quick edit. Joanna was in the kitchen, a glass of white wine in hand.

"Hi," I said, catching her by surprise.

"You have escaped, I see. How's it going?" she asked.

"Done, at least enough to read it to you."

"What did you decide to write about?" Joanna asked as she took a sip of her wine.

"Remember when Henry and I were on the admissions committee as seniors? We read a lot of essays. So I thought I would pretend I was a high school senior writing a college admissions essay."

"That could be fun. I guess I'll be the judge of that," she added with a smile.

"You will. Ready?"

"Let me just refill my wine." Thirty seconds later she had. "OK, I'm ready. Let's see what you've got."

◆◇◆◇◆

Everyone knew that Jack would be the class valedictorian. He had the halo effect working to perfection. Every A was his unless he somehow managed to snatch defeat from the jaws of victory. And honestly, this was an impossibility. The kid never wavered, never had a bad day, and was unfailingly prepared.

Academics was not his only strong suit. Just as every subject gave way to his mastery, so did his peers. He was never arrogant—his parents would never have allowed that. When Jack arrived, all eyes turned to him. Attention was diverted, anticipation replaced conversation. Jack was always in command.

I, on the other hand, never succumbed to the magic. You see, Jack is my identical twin brother. The Jack all the other students and faculty see daily is not the only Jack. Oh no, there is another Jack, the one that I have shared a life and a room with for seventeen years. Jack's aura of perfection is more like a thin laminate. Just beneath that surface of invincibility lies something far more vulnerable. I alone knew this truth, knew that this paragon of adolescence possessed an easily-pierced Achilles heel.

Laura Coates. That's not her real name—it would be unkind to reveal that on a college essay. My brother drooled over Laura Coates. If she were within a hundred yards, he would know. His heart would race, breathing accelerate, and a barely noticeable tremor would appear in both hands. God forbid she came closer and looked at him, or, worse, spoke to him. When that occurred, I feared for his consciousness, and so I would immediately position myself behind him in preparation for his imminent collapse. He's my brother; I didn't wish to see him crack his skull open.

"Jack, c'mon. She's just a girl."

"Just a girl? Are you kidding? She is beautiful! Don't tell me you don't think so, Joey."

"Yeah, she's a babe. I get it. But you act like she has some superpower and that you will disintegrate if she even breathes on you. It's pathetic."

So went our frequent conversations about Laura Coates. I knew I had to take matters into my own hands if he were ever to be free of her paralyzing spell. Although I have historically been the second banana to his starring role, I have never felt jealous or resentful. It's hard to be Jack, and honestly way more fun to be Joey. Jack takes the first wave, which has made my path far easier and markedly less stressful. And for that, I am grateful to my brother. Let's just say it works out fine for both of us.

So how was I to save my poor brother from his self-inflicted terror? Naturally, you, the reader, is now assuming that as the identical twin brother I will merely pretend I am Jack, woo and conquer Laura Coates, and then simply invite my astonished and immeasurably grateful twin brother to replace me and live happily ever after with the girl of his dreams. I had no intention of replacing my brother. Too simple, and frankly inelegant.

I was certain that my brother was never going to find the testosterone to make this romance happen. And I was pretty sure that Laura was not the type to coax him out of his shell. She probably liked him, but I could not count on her approaching him and saying, "Oh, Jack, no need to feel so shy. I find you quite handsome and interesting, and I plan on marrying you and having something between three and five beautiful children with you."

This question consumed me for days. Like many brilliant ideas, the solution came to me at the end of a dream. Honestly, it was so ingenious, so fantastic, that when I fully awoke for a moment I thought it must be too good to be true. Minutes later wakefulness had replaced my stupor, and I realized that my idea was indeed brilliant and achievable.

Homecoming was but a few weeks away. As part of the weekend's festivities, our small town came out in sizable numbers for the Saturday afternoon family events. The Chamber of Commerce sponsored an old-time picnic replete with games of yesteryear. Water balloon toss, piggyback competitions, carrying an egg on a spoon; you get the idea. Teams were drawn up randomly by the committee overseeing the event.

Marvin Waterston is the president of the Chamber of Commerce. He is also my uncle. After school one afternoon I wandered over to his law office on Manchester and presented myself to his secretary, Mrs. Kornweiler.

"Joey, or is it Jack? I still cannot tell you two apart."

"Hello, Mrs. Kornweiler. You got it right. I'm Joey."

"I assume you want to see your uncle, correct?"

"Correct, if he's not too busy."

"He's a lawyer, Joey, how busy can he be? He's not exactly saving lives. Hold on. Let's see what he's doing." She rose out of her chair and turned around, the door to Uncle Marvin's office but a step away. She beckoned me towards the door.

"Thanks, Mrs. Kornweiler," I said gratefully. I entered my uncle's office.

It would be pretty clear to any sighted person that this was the office of an attorney. Typical dark wood bookshelves lined the walls filled with those legal books with the leather bindings you always see on the lawyer TV shows.

"Joey, come on in. Everything OK?"

"Yes, everything is fine. But I could use a little help with kind of a silly problem."

Uncle Marvin smiled. "I would much rather it be a silly problem than a real one. So what's the problem?"

I explained my twin brother's dilemma with Laura Coates. Uncle Marvin listened attentively while reclining in his lawyerly brown leather lounger, a caricature of his profession.

"And you have an idea and I can be of assistance. I assume that is why you are here."

"Yes, sir." I proceeded to reveal the details of my plan.

Five minutes later Uncle Marvin was leaning forward, shaking my hand, and with a huge grin, looked at me and said, "I just hope that Jack appreciates what a great brother he has. The alternative is that he will want to strangle you. Could go either way, don't you think?"

We lost the Friday night football game to our archrival, Martin Van Buren High School. Fortunately, football failure is hardly unknown in our community, and everyone quickly rallied for Saturday's festivities. Once all of the plentiful food was consumed by the masses, the games began.

You might recall I mentioned a few paragraphs above that teams were randomly assigned for the afternoon's games. That is unless your uncle is president of the Chamber of Commerce and ruler of the day. My brother, the borderline psychotic when it came to a certain local lady, and that certain local lady, the adorable Laura Coates, were mysteriously assigned to the same team. With Uncle Marvin's assistance, I didn't stop there. I had made sure that one leg from each of this duo would be strapped together and challenged to make their way from start to finish in the three-legged bag race.

"Joey, you have got to do something!" a viciously perspiring twin shrieked when the three-legged teams were announced. "I can't do this. I'll have a heart attack or stroke or worse!"

"What's worse?" I replied to my stricken sibling.

"It's not funny, Joey."

"It's very funny, Jack. In your state of panic you have lost your sense of humor."

While now motionless as well as breathless, at least Jack was still standing. I put my arm around my brother. "Jack, this is the best thing that could happen. Take a breath; enjoy this. Look, she's smiling at you. I think she is excited that you are her partner. Now, please, don't embarrass your family and your ancestors. Get over there, strap 'em up, and go win this thing. And if you can find a way to stop sweating like a wild boar, I'm sure Laura would appreciate it."

I gave him one last hug and sent him on his way.

Jack survived and he and Laura became an item. Jack will undoubtedly be class valedictorian. He will attend some Ivy League school, and sadly we will be separated for the first time in our lives. I'm fine with that, although I do worry what will happen when the next Laura Coates enters his life and I am not around to catch him when he falls. Like a parent for a child, an identical twin's thoughts are never far from his other half.

◆◇◆◇◆

"So?"

"Just what I ordered. Sweet and cute. Well done, husband," Joanna told me, then put her arms around me and kissed me.

"Think I can do this?" I asked.

"Of course. You just have to work at it."

"What's next?" I asked.

"Dinner."

"Clever. What do you think I should write next?"

Joanna put down her glass and looked at me. "Isn't the whole point to write things that are going to make a difference? Are you still planning on fixing the world?"

"I am," I answered.

"Well, there's no shortage of disaster in the world. Read a newspaper. Watch the news for an hour. Just make a list."

Simple but brilliant. Make a list. Over the next few weeks, I did just that. I swiftly filled a page and decided I had enough to get started.

The pen is mightier than the sword. Let's hope the Englishman who wrote that was correct.

40

Violence

"I'VE DECIDED WHAT I NEED TO tackle first," I told Joanna as she was finishing putting things away in her office. Foolishly, I awaited some recognition that she had heard me.

"I'm listening, dear. Unlike men, women can do more than one thing at a time."

"Violence. It's number one on that list you had suggested I compile."

"And what are you planning to say about it?"

"That it needs to end. Violence always diminishes us," I boldly told her.

"I understand how you feel, Franklin, but that's just not practical. Violence has been a part of human history forever and it will always be a part of human history. That's just the way we are. Correction: it's just the way men are. If there were only women on this earth, we wouldn't be having this discussion."

"Sorry, darling, but that's not correct. Not the 'if there were only women' part. That may be right. But I don't buy that violence is forever. You recall that I know things."

Joanna smiled and leaned closer to me. "I am well aware that you know things. But not everything, darling."

"I'll meet you upstairs. I'm going to take Oscar for a quick walk."

My buddy and I headed out the door. "You think I should write about violence, pup?" I asked him. He turned to me, realized I had nothing to give him, and returned to sniffing the grass along the sidewalk. I could think of no subject more important to address. Solely because something has been a particular way up until the present did not mean it must be so for eternity. Here was my first major challenge. I could not imagine shrinking from it. I must do what I can to end violence.

We had made our way back to the house by the time my internal argument had concluded. "Goodnight, Oscar. You're still the best dog," I assured him, and left him in his favorite sleeping spot.

By the time I got into bed, Joanna was out. I rested my head on my pillow and sleep rapidly followed. Soon after the dream began.

I was on a familiar beach. The late-day sky was also familiar; the scene identical to one I had experienced in a previous dream. Just as I had before, I heard the sounds of soldiers before I saw them. All were again armed with shields and clubs. The army, thousands strong, began to approach. My back was to the water; there was no escape. Swords were drawn as they descended on me, an enormity of warriors seemingly focused on a single enemy. Suddenly I felt the coolness of steel on my back, certain that this was the end of me.

She arrived on a brisk breeze, scooped me up, and into the air we ascended. This was the same magnificent woman from my previous dream, and she had arrived in the split second before my certain doom. Once again she cradled me like a child, and once again she whispered into my ear: "I am my beloved's and my beloved is mine."

"Who are you?" I asked.

"Who do you think I am?" she replied.

"Are you God?"

"If you wish me to be. Are you still frightened, Franklin?"

"No, I am not. Not with you. Can I ask you a question?"

"Of course," she responded with a voice as sweet as honey.

"Why am I here? Why did you save me?"

"You would not have been harmed," she assured me.

"But the sword! I felt it!"

"Only so that you would know what it would feel like to another."

"Why would I need to know that?" I asked.

"So that you will do whatever is needed to prevent that from happening to someone else," she answered.

"Why do some people want to harm others?"

"Why do you think they do?"

I paused in thought before continuing. "Because they are angry, or alone, or frightened."

"Do you believe that some people are intrinsically evil?"

"I don't want to think so. But maybe I am wrong. Maybe pure evil is real. Is it?"

"No. That is merely an excuse," she told me.

"For what?"

"For human failure. Don't let them fail, Franklin, and you can have what you wish."

"I wish for peace, and kindness, and love.

"Do you recall that I once asked you why everyone wouldn't want it as much as you?"

"I do. You were that voice?"

"I am that voice."

With those words, she vanished. I was suddenly alone and sobbing.

"Sweetheart, wake up. It's all right."

As the familiar sensation of being dragged from one set to another abated, my half-opened eyes brought Joanna into focus.

"Oh my God, Joanna. It was the same dream I've had before. Do you remember the one with the ancient army?"

"No. Sorry, love. There are so many," she replied gently so as to not disappoint.

I retold the dream and included every word the voice shared with me. By the time I finished, the expression on Joanna's face had changed. No longer did she view me as a pathetic victim of a child's nightmare. "What do you think this means?" my wife asked.

"It's a dream about violence," I answered. "An army of thousands of soldiers was attacking me. I was completely unarmed and alone. I could hear their shouts of hate and see their insanely virulent eyes anxious to destroy me. And when I thought I would die, Joanna, when I felt that sword slicing into my back, violence became so real for me. Violence is abhorrent, a terrible, awful thing. It should not exist in our world. It is the darkness beyond darkness, the vilest element in creation."

My clear-thinking, mentally tough, no-nonsense love looked me squarely in the eyes and said, "Then you must do all that you can to defeat it, Franklin."

41

Peculiar

"DID YOU INVITE US HERE TO ASK us for money?" J Bob questioned as we sat around our kitchen table. "Now that I'm thinking about it, probably not, since you included me."

"Nope, not for money. If I did, it would probably be the last time I saw any of you," I responded.

"Damn right," Danny added.

My college friends had arrived only a few hours earlier, and already we had taken up where we had left off. Joanna knew these guys as well as I did, and she adored them and their wives. It was her idea to get us all together. Friendships molded at a young age are irreplaceable. They are relationships at their purest.

"We haven't seen them in a while, and we always have a great time," she had begun one evening a couple of months ago. I suspected that wasn't all she had in mind.

"True, but you have another agenda."

"Hardly an agenda. Franklin, these are the people who know you best. You have confided in each other for years. I just thought it would be good for you to spend time with them. Won't it be nice to share your thoughts and plans with people you know won't judge you?"

"They won't judge me? They will be the first to judge me! J Bob will look for any possible way to humiliate me, and the others will jump right in."

"Are you concerned about that?" Joanna asked, her tone indicating that I might have been serious.

"No, dear, that's the fun part. Then I get to insult them right back. I'm pretty sure that will never change. Some parts of us never grow up," I added.

"That's a boy thing, Franklin. Women grow up, every single last drop of us."

Now, two months later, my closest friends were all gathered around our kitchen table. Comfort food for the soul.

"So what's your plan, Mr. Fixit?"

Immediately I glanced over at Joanna. My body language was meant to confirm my prediction that they would be making fun of me right from the start. Joanna responded with a slight shoulder shrug.

"Thanks, J Bob. That is so clever. Did you get help on coming up with that one, maybe from a six-year-old in your neighborhood?"

"Boys?" J Bob consulted Danny and Simon.

"I thought it was pretty good." Danny looked over at Simon.

"Pretty good," Simon added with a head nod.

"Everybody done commenting yet? Good, then I can answer J Bob's question. I do have a plan. I'm going to start writing full-time."

"That's how you're planning to fix the world? With a blog? C'mon, Franklin, you're kidding."

"No Danny, I am not kidding, and thanks for the encouragement."

"So are you asking us what we think of that idea?" he continued.

"I wasn't planning on it. But it's already pretty clear what you think."

"We all thought you had had a dream, or maybe you even saw the future, something that would tell you what you should do. I think you're telling us you're pretty much clueless," Simon concluded.

"He's clueless but happy," Henry finally spoke.

"So you finally say something, and that's your defense of me?" Henry loved these gentle jousts, especially when I was on the receiving end.

Dinner was a combination of delicious food and light banter about a variety of topics. Everyone was tired from traveling, so we made it an early night.

After coffee the next morning, Joanna made a suggestion. "Why don't we go for a hike? There are some great trails through the woods near the river. I'm sure I'm not the only one who wants to get some fresh air."

Thirty minutes later we were on the Silver Mine trail, a three-mile loop through a forest of towering trees, separated enough so that a good deal of dappled sunlight highlighted the varied foliage. Humidity was low and the temperature just right for a light jacket. Shortly after we began, like liquids of different specific gravity, we separated into two groups, women in the front, men behind.

I caught up on the lives of my friends. Just as people choose their pets to reflect their personality, my doctor friends had similarly chosen their careers. Danny, always in control and never in doubt, had become a surgeon. Simon chose internal medicine, where he could employ his keen intellect to simultaneously juggle different options as he rapidly sorted the clues until he eventually arrived at the correct diagnosis.

J Bob snagged a PhD in molecular genetics. He was now on the cutting edge of medical innovations. Thankfully, none of that changed who he was. I don't think we have ever had a conversation where at least one of us was not at some point laughing. "True," he told me when I repeated that to him. "Unfortunately, it's always you who is laughing. I can't recall anything you've ever said that is funny."

Henry had concluded his own PhD in psychology, as expected once again finishing as the top student in his class. Multiple academic articles and a textbook already bore his name. My friends were an impressive group.

After about a mile, Simon took my arm to stop me and allowed Henry, Danny, and J Bob to separate from the two of us.

"Let them go ahead," he said to me.

"You want to talk."

"If you don't mind."

"Something's bothering you, Simon."

"I think I'm having a bit of an existential dilemma."

"That sounds a bit ominous. Any idea why?"

"After medical school and residency I thought, OK, the hard part is behind me. But after all that I'm not exactly feeling psyched about things."

"Everything OK with Jennifer?" Simon and Jennifer had been married for almost five years. I would have been surprised if that were the issue.

"No, that's great. Although I think Jennifer is concerned that I'm a bit down."

"I'm also going to assume this is not directly related to work."

"Not really. That's fine. I'm probably going to make a few changes, but that's not what's bothering me."

"I'm pretty sure I know what is, Simon. Can I take a shot?"

"Sure."

"After all the education, all of the time, you wake up every morning and think, this is it?"

"Exactly! I feel guilty. I mean, I'm really lucky. All of us are really lucky. So what's the matter with me, Franklin?"

"Same thing that's the matter with lots of people."

"Which is?"

"A lot of us grow up thinking that there is a specific road map we should follow. Work hard in school, get a good job, maybe have a family. All of those things are for sure important and valuable. But then one day maybe you've done all of that and you still wake up feeling the way you feel now. The question you are asking yourself, and just about everyone at some point is asking themselves, is what's the point?"

"Is there one?" Simon asked me.

"What do you think?"

"I have begun to believe that there isn't. One thing about being a doctor, you get to see all types of people with all sorts of issues. You see good people get very sick. Last month, a twenty-eight-year-old woman who just had her second baby showed up in the clinic with a very aggressive breast cancer. It's incredibly sad, so unfair. We used to have a saying in the emergency room: you can't kill dirt. Terrible people survive and wonderful people get awful diseases. It's hard to believe there's a point when that sort of stuff happens."

"That's only true if the number of days someone lives determines the success or failure of a life. Meaning if someone dies at twenty-eight, it's automatically a tragedy, a failed life. I don't believe that."

"I'm not saying that it would be a failed life. But it would be a tragedy, don't you think?"

"Only if you are certain that all there is to a life is the time we spend here on earth."

"So you're talking about heaven, an afterlife. I don't believe any of that. I mean, in that case, you're just hoping that there is something else. It's kind of betting on something that is at the minimum unknown. What evidence is there anyway? Sorry, that's not something that I can embrace."

His words sounded like mine years before when I was talking with Maurice Burnside. I was now on the other side of the argument.

"I can't give you any hard evidence. I've traveled into the future, but not that far," I said with a smile. "But I do think there are clues. For example, don't you find it a bit peculiar that generation after generation goes through the same progression in life? You have done pretty much the same thing as your parents, and they did the same thing as their parents, and on and on. Nothing changes except the setting in which it occurs. It's like we never collectively learn anything."

"That's just the way life is," Simon responded. "I'm not sure I see where you're going with this."

"Exactly, that's the way life is. Why is it that way? Why is each of us required to go through the same steps as those who lived before? Why can't we just have someone tell us when we're young what is going to happen to us as we advance through our lives? Why is it necessary to individually repeat all the mistakes, suffer all the heartbreak, experience all the joys? The process never changes. As the famous quote from the Bible says, there is nothing new under the sun. Each of us repeats what has come before. When you stop and think about that, it's peculiar. We just accept it, like you said, as the way life is. But the truth is it could be another way. Our world could be different. That's a clue."

"How is that a clue?"

"You agree that we each repeat the same stories and events that humans have acted out through eons, right?"

"Yes."

"And you would agree that each of us needs to personally experience relationships, adversity, stuff like that?"

"Of course," Simon responded. "You can't simply read something to understand the emotions and all of the repercussions."

"That's my point. We each have to go through the experience because it's the only way to learn about love, hate, sorrow, joy, and so on. But why do we have to learn those things? That is the clue. I think we have to learn all of those things to get prepared for what's next, which of course implies that there is a next. That is the purpose as I see it: we are here to learn and get prepared for what's next. And when you do that, you are well on your way to fulfilling purpose. It gives us a reason to participate in all of the stuff we go through each and every day."

"So the way you see it the experience of life is required because without it we would not be prepared for what comes next. But if you are wrong and there is no next, then none of what we do makes any difference.

We might as well sit around all day and smoke pot. If there is no over-all theme or purpose to life, we might as well just go for what makes us feel good."

"Agree. But all of the evidence says otherwise. All of the relationships we make, the coincidences that we encounter daily, all of the magic of the world speaks to another truth. Plus—and I know this is not exactly scientific—we can feel that there's something more. We just know it in our bones."

"I want to believe what you tell me, but I'm a science guy. I need proof."

Time to channel Maurice Burnside yet again. "Proof is everywhere. How about this? How come we are stupid when we're young and smart when we're old? Wouldn't it make more sense for the opposite to be true? If we knew more when we were young, we wouldn't do all of the foolish, dangerous things teenagers do. By the time we're wise, there are rela-tively few years remaining. How does that make sense in your view of the world?" I asked him.

"Versus your view in which it would make perfect sense. We would continually learn until the end, and then be best prepared for what's next," Simon deduced.

"I think that's a pretty good clue."

"So the point of every day then is to progress, to move forward towards the next phase."

"Bingo. Every day, every action and activity, and especially every inter-action with another person; they're all important. They are, as you just said, moving you forward to where you need to be to fulfill your purpose. You're here learning and experiencing individually because you have a specific purpose. I won't say it's a unique purpose—my guess is that what each of us must learn has a certain commonality—but it is yours to achieve. I'm not one to say that God has put you here and you are unique and yada yada yada. I have no idea if that is true or not. It doesn't matter. I just know each of has what I would call a potential purpose. You can choose to achieve it or not. That's up to each of us. But there is a reason to try, that's for sure."

"You believe, I assume, that all moments are learning moments, good or bad," Simon said, now committed to following the concept through to its logical conclusion.

"Yes, for sure. Instead of waking each morning, thinking is this all there is, each of us should be excited about what the day will bring. As much as we wish it were not true, the distasteful is no less important than the uplifting. Sadness is of no less value than happiness. A bad day still has value, at least equal to or perhaps of more value than the day where everything goes right. Everything counts."

"You believe this. I mean you're not just trying to make me feel better?"

"Of course I'm trying to make you feel better. You're my friend. But everything I just told you I believe to be true. I know it's true."

"You know things, I recall."

"I do, Simon, and I'm going to assume you're not making fun of me like Joanna does."

"No, I'm not. I'm serious. I know you know things, and I'm really glad that you do. In just a few minutes of walking in this beautiful forest, you have flipped my view of my life. I get it. When you stop and think about life, I agree. It is peculiar, and it does imply a purpose. How come everyone doesn't know this?" Simon asked me as we started walking again.

"There is a lot people don't know. Sorry; that's not true. People do know a lot. Most people are smarter than you think. They've just been taught a bunch of crap about the world."

"And you're planning to correct that?"

"I'm sure as hell going to try. We have had enough conflict, and anger, and hate, and certainly way too much violence. All because—and I'm sure about this Simon—that people have misunderstood why we're here. Don't you think that could change everything?"

"Everything, Franklin. Absolutely everything." Simon stopped and looked at me. "Holy crap, Franklin. You are going to fix the world."

"You think?"

"I do. Maybe one day I can help you," he added as we once again began walking.

"Nothing would make me happier."

"Now I understand why you want to be a writer. You're hoping your ideas will catch on."

"Probably wishful thinking, but I've got to start somewhere. People have to be ready to hear it, like you were. By the way, Simon, I'm not surprised that you had come to this point in your life."

"Why do you say that?"

"Because you've always been introspective. Plus you're one of the smartest people I've ever met."

"Hey, did you guys take a nap or something?" I heard Danny yell. The others had reached the end of the path and had been waiting for us.

"Sorry. We're just slow," I said.

"We know that," J Bob said, referring to our intellect.

"Sorry, Einstein," Simon answered.

"Please, do not use Einstein's name in vain," I pleaded.

We headed out to a restaurant to have lunch. As we were just about to go inside Joanna stopped me and allowed the others to enter.

"Everything all right?" she asked me.

"You mean with Simon? You saw us talking, I presume."

"I did. Is he OK?"

"He was having what he called an existential dilemma. But I think I fixed him."

"I'm sure you did. Can I ask what you told him?"

"What we talk about all the time, Joanna. He was looking at his life the wrong way, not understanding why all of his success was not leading to fulfillment. So I explained my view on purpose."

"He's smart. I'm sure he got it immediately," she concluded.

"Immediately. And then he told me he believed that I was going to fix the world."

"He's right, my love. You will."

42

I Had a Dream

"IT CAME TO ME," I told Joanna on Monday evening.

"Are you referencing your famous mantra to let it come to you?" she replied, looking up from the spreadsheet she was deciphering.

"I am. Want to hear about it?" I continued.

"Do I have a choice? No matter what I say you're going to tell me anyway."

"True. I was just being polite."

"Not really, Franklin. Polite is when you ask permission and then respect the response. That wasn't going to happen," she jabbed. "So, my love, please get on with it so I can get back to my work."

"Violence is the number one issue, at least for me. You know how I feel about it, Joanna."

"I do."

"So I need to get this right. As you have reminded me on many occasions, I know things, but not everything."

"Humility is important, as I recall your friend Maurice Burnside taught you. I wish I had gotten to meet him."

"I wish you had, too. I decided who I should talk with about violence."

Joanna looked up from her spreadsheet. "Is this someone alive?"

"Everyone is always alive," I reminded her.

"So I assume you plan on trying to visit someone from the past?"

"I do. Want to guess who?" I challenged her.

"How many guesses do I get?"

"Three."

After taking a brief period to think, Joanna answered. "OK, I have them. Gandhi, Martin Luther King Jr., and Nelson Mandela."

"You are good at this game. My choice is indeed one of the three. Want to go for the win?"

"They would all be good choices. Gandhi was the first of the group, so it could be him. But I'm going to go with someone you are more familiar with. Martin Luther King."

"Ladies and gentlemen, we have a winner."

"When are you going to try to do this?" Joanna asked.

"Probably in a few days. I need to do some homework first. I never know how much time I will have if I'm lucky enough to get there. Best to be prepared."

"He's a great choice, Franklin. He was an amazing man."

"He *is* an amazing man," I corrected her.

"You know when you first explained to me how time works, that every moment lives forever and that we all remain alive in every moment of our lives, I just humored you. Fine, if that's what he wants to think, that's great. But over time you have convinced me. It is so comforting to think like that. It keeps everyone alive."

"It's comforting for me too, Joanna. And it's not just a way to think of things; it's the way things are. Everyone is alive forever."

"Franklin, do you think one day I might be able to join you on one of your trips? I'm serious this time."

"I know you are. I have thought about that. Maybe. It would be wonderful for me if you could. You know there is nowhere I ever want to be more than with you."

"I know. It's very sweet. A bit suffocating, but sweet."

For the next two days, I read as much as I could about Dr. King. I learned about his parents and siblings and his childhood in Atlanta. I could feel my anger and resentment rise as I read about the discrimination his family, and all African-Americans endured. One does not have to have been the direct recipient of hate and bigotry to share the pain of those that have.

What affected me most were his speeches. I could feel the inspiration those in attendance must have felt when hearing his eloquent words. Dr. King brought poetry to public speaking. His words were like a velvet hammer, power without poison. So beautiful. I was certain that I had chosen the right person to talk with. Now it was only a question if I could make it happen.

Wednesday evening I was ready. As I had before I met with Carl Jung, I submerged myself in Dr. King's words. I imagined myself by his side or in front of him at a sermon. My office lights were dimmed; the house was quiet. This time, unlike when I tried to visit Professor Jung, my initial effort was successful. The shift was pronounced.

I was standing at the doorway of a motel room. The door was ajar; I could see inside. An African-American man had his back to me. I had no doubt I was looking at Martin Luther King Jr. He was seated in a chair at a small table, looking down at a book or document.

"Hello," I said while knocking on the partially open door.

He turned. "Yes, can I help you?"

"Dr. King. Hello, sir. Yes, you can. I have come to talk with you."

"And you are?" he asked.

"Franklin Rock, sir," I answered.

"Do you have an appointment? I'm sorry, I don't recall that I had any scheduled meetings this morning."

"No sir, I don't. I hope that is all right. I apologize for coming to see you without one."

"No, that's fine. I have time. Your name again?"

"Franklin Rock. Please call me Franklin."

"All right, Franklin, what can I do for you?"

"Dr. King, I have come to talk with you about violence. I know you have dedicated your life to civil rights, and that you have been committed to a non-violent approach."

"I have, Franklin. But you know I have come to understand why people, specifically my people, sometimes cannot always resist taking a violent swing at their oppressors. I don't like it, I know it is against God's will, but I understand it."

"Why is that? Why did you change your opinion?" I asked him, surprised by this unexpected revelation. Had I chosen to visit the wrong person?

"It's not that I have changed my opinion. Violence is abhorrent. In my speeches, I have often talked about this. Violence is poisonous, not only for the individual who commits the violence but for the entire world and generations to come. It yields a bitter legacy."

"But you can see a time for violence?" I continued.

"It is not that I see a time for violence. What I told you is that I can under-stand it. When we have witnessed riots following yet another episode of degradation and oppression and there is looting, this is often misunder-stood. The man who loots during such a riot often takes things he does not even want. What he wants is the experience of taking. When everything is always taken from you, especially your dignity, it is understandable to want to take something from him who has done the same to you."

"Does it work?"

"You mean does it make one feel better about his situation? It does, but for a very brief time. My issue is that it accomplishes nothing in the long run and distracts from the cause. An otherwise good-hearted, caring white person will look at the looting and see only wanton destruction. He will be distracted from the reason it is occurring, which is the oppres-sion of a people. What I am telling you, Franklin, is that I understand the urge for violence. It is real and genuine and predictable. But violence will always beget hate and hate only begets more hate. Which begets more violence. It is a cycle without end."

"So how does one end violence, Dr. King?"

"Darkness cannot drive out darkness. Only light can drive out darkness."

"I have read those same words from you. Where does the light come from?"

"Surely you know the answer to that, Franklin. The light comes from love. Only love can defeat hate. You seem to have read many of my speeches. Do you recall that I have also said that only love can make a friend of an enemy?"

"Yes, sir, I do. How is it that with all you have been through you manage to still believe that? You have repeated the words of Jesus, to love your enemy as your friend. How is that possible for you?"

"It is not only possible, it is the only way I know, Franklin. Life is about love and kindness. That is what we must learn during our time here on earth. Nothing else matters. Not power, or wealth, or fame, none of it. Only love. We must care for the poor and oppressed, not solely because it is good and right, but also because that is how we learn to love. We must raise up all people and hate none. That is how we reach our goal as God's children. There is no other goal, and there is no other way. Hate and violence are the sworn enemy of love, and it is our duty, each of us, to see that love prevails."

Even in an unplanned conversation with someone he has never met, Dr. King's words were overpowering. I was struggling not to cry. He noticed.

"I see my words are bringing you to tears. But if you are to shed tears from what I tell you, understand that the urge you feel is to weep, not simply to cry. Weeping and crying are words we mistakenly use interchangeably as if equivalents. But they are not equivalents. Cry is what a child does when she skins her knee. To weep is something else entirely. It is an expression of loss for all of humanity. Tears of weeping are the transformation of a revelation that arises from some mysterious place we each harbor but rarely notice. Weeping is a connection to God, Franklin."

Dr. King took his handkerchief from his pocket and handed it to me. "Don't worry. I always have several with me," he said smiling. He allowed me a moment to collect myself. "Now tell me about you, Franklin. Where are you from? Why did you choose to come see me? Without an appointment." Another smile.

Once again I was conflicted. Do I tell him the truth? If my initial assessment was correct, I was in the late nineteen sixties. What would it sound like to tell him he was talking to someone from the next century? The thought of lying to this man, an icon, one of the greatest Americans in history, was unthinkable. Tell the truth, Franklin, Maurice Burnside was whispering to me.

I took a deep breath. "Where I am from is an interesting question. I'm glad you're seated," I began, trying to prepare him for my reveal.

"Now you have piqued my interest. Go ahead, I think I'm ready," he laughed.

"I am..." I paused.

He tilted his head slightly and furrowed his brow. "What could you possibly think you could tell me that requires such obvious consternation?" he asked.

"Dr. King, I have come from the future."

"That is what you hesitated to tell me? Good try, Franklin. Is there more to your joke?"

"I am not joking, sir. Where I live, it is the year 2020. What year are we in here?"

"Franklin, who put you up to this?"

"No one put me up to this, Dr. King. I am honestly from the future. I will explain everything. I will tell you how it is possible, why it is possible, everything. And I will try to prove to you that what I am telling you is the absolute truth. Would you please tell me what year this is?"

"1968."

Oh my God. Dr. King was killed in 1968. "What month?" I asked with great trepidation, afraid that my initial assessment of our location was correct.

"It's April Fools' day, Franklin. That's why I thought this was a joke. And you're telling me that it is not."

April first. He was assassinated on April fourth, 1968, only three days from now. I swallowed hard.

"No, sir, it is not a joke. I would never dishonor you with a lie."

"Can you prove to me that you are indeed from the future? I am no man's fool, Franklin. Time travel is the stuff of science fiction books."

I dove right in. I had anticipated his suspicion about the veracity of my claim. Who wouldn't doubt such a wild pronouncement? And this was no ordinary person; this was Martin Luther King Jr., a giant among men. Before coming I had armed myself with a reply.

"I know that you are familiar with the Apollo space program. On May tenth next year, 1969, Apollo 10 will fly around the moon. It will be commanded by Thomas Stafford. Two months later, Apollo 11 will repeat the same mission, but this time the lunar module will separate from the command module and land on the moon. The date will be July twentieth, 1969. Astronaut Neil Armstrong will step first on the moon and say, 'That's one small step for man, one giant leap for mankind.'"

I could tell he was impressed by the detail I had just given him. His concentration divulged his consideration that what I was telling him could be true.

"Now tell me, who will be the next President of the United States?"

"Richard Nixon."

"Whom does Nixon defeat in the election?"

"Hubert Humphrey," I immediately answered. My confidence was beginning to convince him of my claim to be from the future.

"So Bobby does not win the nomination? I was sure he would."

Should I tell him the truth? He would not live to see the event. Once again, I could not imagine misleading him.

"Robert Kennedy will be assassinated the night he wins the California primary, June sixth."

Dr. King gasped and flung himself against the back of his chair. "No, do not tell me this will happen again!"

I remained silent.

"What is happening to this nation? Bobby Kennedy is a friend of our people. He is the best hope for change in this nation." Dr. King sat forward once again in his chair. "This will lead to even more unrest, and I suspect more violence. Does it, Franklin?"

"Sadly it does."

Dr. King rested his head in his hands and stared down at his desk. Slowly he lifted his eyes to me. "I fear asking you any more questions. Can you tell me any good news?"

"Yes, sir, I can. There will be more civil rights legislation soon. Jim Crow laws in the south will eventually be abolished. Many cities in this country will have African-American mayors. There will be African-American congressmen and congresswomen. There will be African-American governors and African-American leaders of American companies."

"My Lord! How wonderful. Does my dream become reality, that my four children will not be judged by the color of their skin but by the content of their character?"

"I won't mislead you. It's still not perfect in 2020. As you might imagine there are still elements of discrimination, and there is still unequal education and opportunity. But it is much better than in 1968. And one more thing that you will be very happy to hear…"

"Are you going to tell me that a Black man has been elected President?"

"I am going to tell you exactly that. Barack Obama will be elected in 2008 and re-elected in 2012."

"Hallelujah, hallelujah. It will all be worth it. Thank you, Lord, thank you!"

"I can tell you that it was an unbelievably exciting time for America when President Obama was elected. I cannot recall a more emotional night."

"2008. That is forty years from now. Am I alive to witness this great moment?"

Now what? I was afraid our conversation might come to this. I cannot tell him the truth. I cannot be the one to reveal the details of his death. This is not what I came for.

"You can see the future in the past, Franklin," I heard Professor Niemeyer saying, "Choices are made; switches are thrown." Perhaps I am to be the one to tell him.

"Your hesitation has answered my question. No matter, I did not anticipate living until eighty," Dr. King continued. I could see that he was carefully considering his next words, and I knew what they would be.

"You know how long I will live and when and how I will die, don't you Franklin? You must. If you can tell me the date of our moon missions, that Bobby Kennedy will be killed, and that Richard Nixon will be president, you know my fate. Now my decision is whether I should ask you for the details."

I remained silent, but I feared my silence was sufficient evidence that his was not to be a happy ending.

"You are quiet, Franklin. Too quiet. You do not want to be the bearer of bad news. Yet you know the truth, and I must now hear that news. Nothing you can tell me will dissuade me of the goodness of the Lord nor the noble purpose of man. Tell me, Franklin."

"Dr. King, are you sure? Do you need to know your future? Perhaps it is best for each of us not to know."

"Why do you say that, Franklin? Didn't you prepare for this meeting? You told me you've read my speeches. Why did you bother?"

"So that I would not waste your time, so that I would be efficient in my questions," I answered.

"Shouldn't I wish to be efficient with my time, whatever it is I have left? You are only the vehicle, Franklin. God is making this decision."

"On April fourth, you will be shot." I could not go on.

"April fourth of what year?" he insisted.

"April fourth, 1968. I am so, so sorry, Dr. King. I did not come to give you this news." My heart was breaking.

Instead of a cry of grief, I saw only a look of resolute determination. How was this possible?

"Franklin, do not worry. I have had a premonition for a while now that this would be my fate. I did not guess it would be this soon, but I knew it would not be long. There is simply too much hate in the world, too much in this country. But you have told me such wonderful, wonderful news. A Black man as president of the United States. My, my, my. Mine eyes have truly seen the glory of the coming of the Lord."

I had just informed a man that he had but three days to live, yet he was praising the Lord. At that moment in his eyes I saw Maurice Burnside. Mr. Burnside never lost his smile despite all of his tribulations. Now, seated in front of the great Martin Luther King Jr., I was witnessing heroism once again. Why in the world would anyone ever judge another by the color of his skin?

"Dr. King, I have something else to share. I think it will help."

"Franklin, you need to know that I don't fear death. I never have. Our earthly life is but a part of our whole existence. What comes next I cannot say, but there is a next, that is a certainty. So do not be sad for me, and do not feel you must manufacture some other news to lift my heart. You have already lifted it more than you can imagine."

Despite his protest, I continued. "You are familiar of course with Albert Einstein."

"Don't tell me you have met him also," Dr. King said while chuckling.

"I have, but that is not what I was going to tell you. His theory of special relativity has proven that all time exists simultaneously and forever. Meaning that there is no past that is forever dark and a future yet to be revealed. I am proof that the future has already occurred. What this means is that every moment lasts forever in its own special place in time. No moment ever vanishes; each remains alive forever."

Before I could explain the implication of Einstein's discovery, Dr. King did it for me.

"So no one ever really dies. Is that what you were going to tell me?"

"Yes, sir, exactly. We all remain alive in all of the moments of our lives in perpetuity. The past does not vanish. That is how I was able to come to see you."

"God does have a plan, Franklin. He has brought you to me for a reason. Seems that I have almost completed my time on this earth. I am neither surprised nor despondent. I have done what I can do, and I hope that has been enough for God. Tell me, what does God have planned for you?"

"I don't know if it's God, but I know I have a mission."

"And are you aware of what it is?"

"Yes, sir. I am." I took a breath. I was still not completely comfortable with the concept, especially in front of a man as impressive as Martin Luther King.

"Franklin, if you have a mission, I am quite certain it wasn't anything you asked for. Believe me, I never asked to be the voice of my people. Yet here I am."

"I'm supposed to fix the world. That is why I came to see you. To me, violence is the most abhorrent element on this planet, so it seems to me that is where I need to begin. I could think of no one from whom I could learn more. Thank you so much for talking with me. And, Dr. King, please forgive me. I feel terrible for telling you what will occur."

"Franklin, you are mistaken. This has nothing to do with you. This is between me and God. He just wants to make sure I have time to finish my words before I go on to meet him. Just like you, I prefer to be prepared," he said with a smile. "Our time together is growing short. Am I correct?"

"Yes sir, sadly for me it is. It will always be one of the greatest honors of my life to have met you. Thank you from the bottom of my heart. You should know that your words and deeds live on long after you are gone. There will be statues of you everywhere in America, and even a national holiday in your honor."

"That I must admit I could never have imagined. I have been hunted for years, and to know one day I am to be respected and honored for my work is more than any man could ask."

"Thank you for your life," I told him, the words forming themselves.

"You are too kind, Franklin. Let me finish our conversation by confirming that you are correct about violence. Justice must win out over oppression, that is for certain. Do all you can to ensure that is so. But it will mean little if in the end violence prevails. Defeat violence, Franklin. Fix the world for all of those to come. Consider it a special favor to me. God bless you, Franklin Rock."

On April third, two days after our meeting, the day before his heinous murder, Dr. King gave a speech in Memphis. These were his final public words:

*I don't know what will happen now. We've got some diffi-
cult days ahead. But it doesn't matter with me now. Because
I've been to the mountaintop. And I don't mind. Like anybody, I would like to live a long life. Longevity has its place.
But I'm not concerned about that now. I just want to do
God's will. And He's allowed me to go up to the mountain.
And I've looked over. And I've seen the Promised Land. I
may not get there with you. But I want you to know tonight,
that we, as a people, will get to the Promised Land. And I'm
happy, tonight. I'm not worried about anything. I'm not
fearing any man. Mine eyes have seen the glory of the coming of the Lord.*

43

Sum of the Parts

EVERY MAN PUTS HIS PANTS ON one leg at a time, my father used to say. His implication: we are all just humans. After my time with Dr. King, I was no longer convinced that my father was correct. Yes, we all make mistakes, say foolish things, and require food and water to survive. But when one is seated across from a person of such grandeur, a man overflowing with kindness, generosity, humility, and grace, it becomes evident that some rise above.

All men are *created* equal. Every man, woman, and child must be afforded the same opportunities. Each of us should be heard and respected and treated with kindness. It's not just that these things are right and just. These are the basic requirements for a cohesive society.

After that, we are on our own. As Maurice Burnside taught me, respect cannot be given; it must be earned. Earned respect comes from honesty and acquiring that "smell" of integrity he described. It comes from placing the welfare of others ahead of our own. This life we have been granted comes not only with opportunity. It also comes with great personal responsibility. The world will not fix itself.

"Hate begets hate, violence begets violence, and only love can defeat hate." Dr. King's words remained with me. I reread many of his speeches after our meeting. His message was never complicated. Anyone listening understood exactly what he was saying. Every word rang true and made perfect sense. So why, more than fifty years after his death, are we still such a mess?

I already knew the answer to that question.

My contemplation was interrupted by the ringing of my cell phone.

316

I did not recognize the number, and usually, I would ignore the call. "Probably spam," I said to myself until overruled by my inner voice who instructed me to answer.

"Hello."

"Is this Franklin Rock?" a woman's voice asked.

"Who's calling?" I responded, not yet willing to admit the caller had reached me just in case it was a sales call.

"Franklin, this is Lucille Burnside. Do you remember me?"

"Lucille! Of course. Do you think I could ever forget you? It is so good to hear your voice."

It had been years since I had spoken with Lucille Burnside, Maurice's daughter. We had kept in touch after his funeral for a short while, but as so often happens life takes over for both parties and communication lapses.

"It is so nice to hear your voice too, Franklin. I hope you are well."

"I am Lucille, and you?"

"Yes, fine. Now that we are talking I am angry at myself for not keeping in touch."

"As am I, Lucille." I assumed that she was calling for a reason. "Is there something I can help you with?"

"Yes, Franklin, there is. We are going to sell our house. We just don't need so much space anymore. You know how it is. All of the things you accumulate—and never use—end up somewhere in the house, then you have to go through it all. Anyway, I was cleaning out the closet in my father's old room and came across a box with some papers. I found something you should see. Would it be asking too much for you to come to the house one of these days? I would tell you on the phone but I don't understand what it means. Better if you see it for yourself."

If Lucille had ever previously asked me to do anything for her, I would have done so with alacrity. She was the remaining link between her father and me. Lucille never did. Of course she didn't; she was a Burnside. They gave. They did not seek to receive.

As I made my way up the front walk memories flooded my mind. I rang the bell. Lucille and I looked at each other and immediately embraced.

"Franklin, it is so wonderful to see you. It feels like a Monday," she began, "except I forgot the iced tea."

"Lucille, I cannot tell you how happy it makes me to see you."

"Come in, Franklin." From the moment I stepped in the door, I anticipated Maurice Burnside to be seated in his usual spot. His chair was still there, though empty. I looked over at Lucille.

"I know," she said, "I still find myself looking at it and expecting to see him."

He is there, Lucille. The only difference is the date we are looking.

"I am so glad you were able to come, Franklin. When I found the paper I was surprised and confused. Come. I'll show you."

Lucille led the way back to Maurice's old room. The last time I had visited, he was propped up in bed looking frail and exhausted. Today the bed was formally made, not a wrinkle in the bedspread or an indentation in his pillow. No one had been in that bed for many years. Lucille had put a large towel on the bed, I assume to protect the delicate linens from the cardboard box she was lifting from the floor. She placed the box on the towel and motioned for me to come by her side. I did so as she removed the cover off of the box.

"Most of what is in here are old invoices from jobs he had done. I think he told you he mostly did new construction, but he had a nice little side business working on people's houses. I have no idea why he kept all the bills. Maybe these are ones he never got around to sending or maybe the ones people never paid. You know, Franklin, my dad never chased anyone for money. If they paid him, great, and if not, well, he just assumed they couldn't afford to. That was my father, generous to a fault."

"Your father was an exceptional man, Lucille. I only wish I had a chance to spend more time with him."

"You might not have spent that long with him, Franklin, but you had a big effect on him. Here, look at this."

Lucille pulled a manilla envelope out of the box and handed it to me. "I found this inside on top of the bills. I put it in the envelope for you. I wasn't sure if my dad had planned to give it to you."

I pulled out a page of handwritten notes. Immediately I noticed my name in a couple of places. I began to read from the top.

dream??
Franklin was here in my room   didn't know who I was
told him he knew me but he didn't remember   I told him we

talked a lot   still he didn't remember
said something about time and a river in a book he said he
was reading in college
asked if I know Arthur?

About halfway down the page, Maurice had begun another note.

another dream?? don't think so, felt awake very real
Franklin was back with me   asked me again about Arthur
not sure of the name
told him he was going to be famous told him he was going
to do great things
he asked how I knew   told him I was just sure that it was all
true   boy was very excited

Then in large letters near the bottom:

tell Franklin??

"Lucille, do you have any idea when he wrote this?" I asked.

"It had to be near the end. Do you remember how long after your last visit he passed away?"

"I do. I was here last on a Wednesday. He died that Friday night."

"He had asked me to give him a pen and some paper Thursday morning when I went in to see him first thing. So he wrote that sometime Thursday or Friday."

"He said he had the dream twice, so Wednesday and Thursday nights. That makes sense."

"Do you understand what he wrote, Franklin? What do you think those dreams were about?"

Lucille noticed the change in my expression when the answer became clear to me. I could see no reason not to tell her everything. "I do Lucille. If you have time I will explain."

She led me to the kitchen table and we sat.

"It was no accident that I met your dad and that we became close. It's a strange story, but I'm going to ask you to trust me on all of this. Professor Niemeyer—Charles is what your father called him—asked your dad to teach me, really how to become a good person. Charles, like everyone else who ever met your father, knew that he was an exceptional human being. He wanted your father to mold me."

"Why?"

"Before I answer I ask that you understand that I am not one to brag or think too much of myself. Your father made it clear that wasn't acceptable."

"You don't have to tell me that, Franklin. I would never think that of you."

"I have a mission, Lucille. I have been given a great responsibility. Charles Niemeyer knew it. He was my first mentor."

"My dad told me, Franklin. He said you were chosen to do important things."

"When did he tell you this?"

"Only a few hours before he passed. He was very lucid. My father never got confused, even in the final minutes of his life. He was crystal clear when he told me. 'Franklin Rock is going to do great things, Lucille. You just watch,' he told me. And, Franklin, he had that big grin when he said it. You know that one. He was proud of you, just like he was of his children. At least when we weren't doing anything major stupid," she added with a beautiful smile that she had clearly inherited from her father.

"You know what he meant to me, Lucille."

"I do, Franklin. You know if I had been younger, I might have been jealous of your relationship. Good thing I was a grown woman or I might have shooed you away!"

"My dad died when I was young. You and the rest of your family were lucky to have your father so long."

"A gift from the Lord. Don't I know it. I was happy to share him. He might have taught you a lot, Franklin, but you had a mighty impact on him. He loved those Mondays. I think you made him feel like he had a reason to keep going. What did those notes mean?"

We had reached the moment when I had to fill in all the blanks. I needn't have worried about how she would take my revelations. She was Maurice Burnside's daughter.

"Lucille, ever since I was young I have intermittently traveled in time. I don't physically do so. My body remains where it is, but in some way—I still don't know how—my mind travels to other times. I know it sounds crazy, but everything I am telling you is true."

"You forget, Franklin, that I am a believer. I trust you, and I don't think you're crazy. My father and I had talked about some of these things. He told me once when I was already an adult that Professor Niemeyer had explained to him that the world was different than we think, especially time. Please, keep going."

"Although I had time-traveled as a young child, it wasn't until college that I became aware that it was happening. I'm pretty sure I know what your father saw and described in his notes. It wasn't a dream either time."

"What do you mean they weren't dreams? What were they?" Lucille asked, puzzled by my explanation.

"I must have visited him when I was in college." I abruptly stopped. That meant that some of my initial trips, the ones I did not recall, were into the future. Interesting, I thought, but at this time in my life of no relevance. "I'm not quite sure why it was your father who might have been my first destination. I can only guess that it was a preview, sort of like a coming attraction for a movie. Maybe that visit remained somewhere in my memory so that when I met him in the hospital my unconscious drew me to him."

"Who is Arthur?" Lucille asked. "Seems from his notes that my dad didn't know. Why are you smiling, Franklin? Do you know?"

"I do, Lucille. I'm pretty certain your dad misheard. I was likely asking him about Siddhartha, the main character in a book by the same name written by the German author Hermann Hesse. I had been reading that book and was struck by the author's discussion of time. When I mentioned to your father about time and a river I was referring to a passage from the book."

You were there. What you imagined is true. It will happen. That's a promise, and you know you never promise anything you can't deliver.

"Franklin?" I heard Lucille ask me. Her words drew me back.

"I'm sorry, Lucille. I just tied up a long-time loose end." Lucille noticed the quick shiver.

"You cold?" Franklin.

"No. It's just seeing you, your father's notes, being here. All the pieces coming together. Life's amazing, isn't it?"

"Lord knows it is, Franklin. Lord knows it is."

Lucille and I took turns telling each other how wonderful it was to visit and how we promised to keep in touch. As we embraced, I could feel one of her tears on my cheek, and I am certain she felt one of mine on hers.

◆◇◆◇◆

"JOANNA, IT WAS MAGIC," I told my lovely wife on returning home. "And now I know the time has arrived."

"For what?"

"For the real work to begin."

"Why do you feel that way, Franklin?"

"Because today the final thread was pulled tight. The first part of my story has concluded. It's time to start writing those chapters."

"Are you thinking about Professor Niemeyer?" she asked presciently.

"I am, and I am about to see him again."

"How do you know?"

"I know, Joanna."

◆◇◆◇◆

TWO HOURS LATER I was in my office, simultaneously reading and waiting. It had to come, that was for certain. Sure enough, just after I felt the shift, standing in front of me was Professor Charles Niemeyer.

"Good to see you, Franklin."

I looked around and immediately noticed that the set had changed. I was still in my office, but something was different.

"You've moved," Professor Niemeyer explained before I could ask.

"In time, I presume."

He nodded.

"Why?" I asked him.

"Believe it or not I'm not sure, Franklin. Despite your high opinion of me, for which I remain grateful, I cannot explain everything."

"Do you know when we are?"

"Remember when we met after you had been in the future with that older gentleman? What was his name?"

"Doranto Durning," I reminded him. As I said the name, another loop closed. It was my visit with Doranto Durning that Govinda had seen in his dream.

"You must have just figured something out, Franklin. I have seen that look before," Professor Niemeyer correctly surmised. "Anyway, you recall on your way back from that visit that you and I were briefly together in your room. I seem to remember that you were a bit upset with me."

"Oh, I remember."

"You asked me the date then also. Seems when you and I meet—and I'm going to assume this is the way it will be going forward—it will be in-between times."

"In between what times?"

"In between where you are and where I am. Think of it as neutral territory."

"And you don't know why that is?"

"Sorry, Franklin. I don't. But I'm quite sure it doesn't signify anything. It's just the way it works. You should have asked Einstein why when you met him," he said with a smile.

"You know that I met Einstein?"

"Of course. I'm surprised you recall the meeting. It was very early on."

"I don't remember much, Professor. It was a long time ago and very brief. But if I recall he told me he knew who I was."

"Eventually everyone will know who you are, Franklin."

"I believe those were his exact words."

"So tell me, Franklin. Have you made any plans?"

"You know I am writing. Good idea?" I asked.

"Good start. The rest will come."

"As it always has," I said.

"As it always will," he responded.

"Did you know I visited with Carl Jung?"

"No, I did not."

"He knows you or knew you, Professor. He told me you had been vocal at some of the meetings at which he discussed dreams."

"What else did he tell you?"

"That you had an interesting theory on dreams perhaps representing reality in another universe. Since no one had as yet developed the theory of multiple universes, he had no way to evaluate your theory at that time. So is it true, Professor? Are our dreams reality in another universe?"

"As I told you a few minutes ago, Franklin, there is a good deal that I don't know. But it is an interesting theory, don't you agree?"

"I do. Remember how I always used to ask you if I was ready?" I said, changing the subject.

"Of course. I don't believe I ever got that assessment correct."

I laughed. "That was not what I was referring to, but no, I don't think you ever did. I look back and remember how much anxiety I would feel whenever I traveled through time, and how everything you told me seemed so complex."

"And now?"

"Now I am a man on a mission. I'm ready. Before we leave each other—by the way, how do you know when our time together is just about over?"

"Shortly before the shift when we return to our respective times, there is a very subtle movement, like the minimal jump one can notice if paying attention in an old movie just before the reels are changed. You'll know what I mean now that you're aware of it. You were saying?"

"Before we leave each other I do have a question, something I need to understand better. Free will. Yes, no, some, none?"

"First tell me what you understand," he instructed me as he would have in his college seminar.

"We know all of time exists simultaneously and in perpetuity. The future has already happened. So in that scenario, there is no free will. But if our choices do create new universes, then we do have free will. That of course is mitigated by the choices made by countless others. So I'd say we have some, but not nearly as much as most people think," I concluded.

"If this were an oral final, Franklin, I would personally pin the A on your shirt. Well done, and well said," Professor Niemeyer responded looking like a proud parent. "I would add that what you just accurately described turns out to be a blessing. Each of us lives under the illusion that we determine our fate, that the road not taken is not taken by choice. What pressure that puts on humans! Parents fret about the choices they make for their children and the choices their children make for themselves. A fork in the road can be terrifying for many. The flaw lies in believing that making one choice rather than another is crucial to who we are to become and how our life will play out over time. It is impossible to know in advance which road should be taken. The question itself has no meaning."

"When you come to a fork in the road, take it," I said, referencing the famous Yogi Berra quote.

"Turns out Yogi was correct."

"There is no best choice," I said.

"There is no right choice," Professor Niemeyer added.

I noticed a sudden flicker. "That's it!" I proclaimed. "I just saw it!"

"As did I. So now we part for a while. Time to write chapter one, Franklin. Just remember; the first chapter sets the tone for the book. Make it a good one."

44

A Visit With an Old Friend

"HENRY, YOU MIGHT BE INTERESTED TO HEAR that I met one of your favorite psychologists."

"Alive or dead?" Henry answered. "Wait. Let me rephrase the question. Could someone other than you—meaning someone who cannot traverse time as if it were a ski slope—currently be able to have lunch with this person?"

"You are getting quite good at this. The answer is no. You could not currently dine with this person."

"I think this is a pretty easy one. Dreams must be involved. This person must have an opinion on the nature of time. You would only travel to meet someone you had heard of; I can't imagine you researched the history of psychology. So, I am going to go with Carl Jung."

"Well done, Henry!"

"When did you meet Carl Jung?"

"When. Always an interesting question. Are you asking in his time or ours?"

"God, Franklin, does it always have to be this difficult?"

"Sorry, Henry. I was just trying to answer your question. In his time, he was in his seventies, so in the latter part of his career. I assume that is what you're interested in."

"Not really. I just wanted to know if it was recent. See, it's not always so complicated. How does Joanna put up with you?"

I filled Henry in on my discussion with Professor Jung.

"What an interesting man." Henry leaned forward, his demeanor suddenly turned serious. "You have decided that the time has come."

"It has, Henry. As Professor Niemeyer told me—that would be the other day in our time, in case you were wondering—it's time to write chapter one."

"Of the fix-the-world book."

"Correct, the book you saw years ago."

"Joanna told me you also met Martin Luther King."

"I don't recall ever being so affected by a meeting and conversation."

"Does he think you can succeed?"

"You mean find a way to reduce violence? Like Jung, he has his doubts but they both think it's worth a try."

"Franklin, if you could do this…" Henry paused. "If you could find a way to subdue violence that would be the gift of all gifts for our world."

"Look, I am not going to tell you that I know how to accomplish this just yet. Remember, Henry, that book that Professor Niemeyer gave me isn't entitled the man who tried to fix the world or the man who failed to fix the world. The future is on my side." I thought of Doranto Durning. In his time, violence and crime were essentially non-existent.

"You know, Franklin, I was just thinking. It is interesting—even more than that, inexplicable really—why peace is so elusive. Why wouldn't everyone wish for peace?"

"I think, Henry, that it's because the goal of the individual seems to supersede the goal of the society. Peace sounds like a good idea, but not if it means I must sacrifice what I want. It comes back to the purpose of life. If we collectively have the wrong concept of what a human life is about, what our time on this earth is for, then we naturally exhibit behaviors that fit that incorrect conclusion."

"The inclination to fight to get more or to protect what we have."

"Exactly."

"So you're going to try to change that."

"I don't see another path."

"You're going to need a posse, Franklin."

That evening Joanna and I were just finishing dinner when my cell phone, which was on the kitchen counter, began to ring. Joanna was putting away leftovers and could see the screen.

"It's Govinda, Franklin."

"Would you answer it for me, love?" Joanna reached down and did so.

"Govinda, hi. Just letting you know you're on the speaker. Joanna is here."

"Hi, Joanna! Tell you what, Franklin, you can go do something. I'd prefer to talk with Joanna."

Govinda was not completely joking. Everyone loves Joanna. Polite to a fault, generous, fun: she is all of those things. Those enviable traits, however, are not the main reason everyone loves her. Joanna demands nothing from anyone. She is all give and no take. No one ever feels judged; she is always accepting.

"Hi, Govinda. How are you, sweetheart?" Every person in Joanna's life is sweetheart.

"All good, Joanna. I hope Franklin is behaving and not driving you too crazy."

"Most of the time. Here he is. You take care, love." Everyone is also a love.

I picked up the phone, took Govinda off speaker, and headed to my office. "Just you and me now, Govinda. How are you?"

"I'm good, Franklin."

"Let me guess, Govinda; you had another dream."

"Yes, but that's not all. I've been walking around with this sense that something is about to happen. It's been a few days now. Very noticeable."

"And you think I have something to do with it, I assume."

"Oh, for sure. You pop into my mind constantly whenever I feel this. Plus there's the dream. It's the same one where you're in front of a crowd, just like all the others. This time you are holding a book. I can't see the title, but in the dream I seem to recognize it. So I'm thinking it's your book, the one Professor Niemeyer gave you."

If there were even the tiniest shred of doubt that the time was now, Govinda had just erased it.

"Chapter one, Govinda. Professor Niemeyer told me it was time to write the first chapter of that book."

"You saw him?"

"I did. And he cleared up a bunch of those questions you and I have had."

"I look forward to hearing what he had to say. So can I ask you what your plan is?"

"I assume you are asking me how I am going to go about solving the violence problem."

"If that's chapter one, then yes, that's what I'm asking."

"I'm working on it."

"Meaning you currently have no earthly idea."

"Well, maybe not that desperate, but not too far off."

"No time like the present."

"And the past, and the future. I'm thinking we might be able to get some help from all of them," I told Govinda. "I'm pretty sure I'll be calling you soon."

"Anytime, my friend."

I knew what I needed to do next.

Within a few minutes, I was seated in my office chair. Two Einstein volumes now rested in front of me on my desk. I picked up his short treatise on both his special and general theories of relativity. In his own words in the preface to the book, the great man states that "…the work presumes a standard of education corresponding to that of a university matriculation examination and, despite the shortness of the book, a fair amount of patience and force of will on the part of the reader." I was struggling with the material, and with keeping my eyes open, right from the start. Einstein's definition of a university matriculation examination was likely the equivalent of a PhD in physics in today's world. When my eyes fell closed once again I felt the shift.

I was standing before him, this time in a small library that I presumed to be his home office. He looked up. To my surprise, he recognized me instantly. "Franklin Rock. Good to see you again. You're aging well, I'd say."

"Thank you, Professor Einstein. As are you."

"I've looked like an old man for so long it's hard to tell the difference year to year," he laughed.

"What year is it, Professor?"

"1953. And you? Where did you hop off from this time?"

"2020."

"Oh my, that is a trip indeed." He sat back, obviously in thought. "So," he continued, "if I am correct, you should be just about ready to get started."

"I am," I responded, certain that we were referring to the same thing.

"And you came to ask me what?"

"I have an idea about how I might proceed, but I could use your help, sir."

"Let's just talk and see what happens, shall we?"

"Perfect."

"It might be best if I begin," Einstein decided. "Unless I am grossly mistaken, our topic is violence. That is your mission, or at least your initial effort if I recall correctly."

"Yes, sir it is, but how did you know that?"

"Please, Franklin."

I should have known better than to ask.

He continued. "It's 1953 here, Franklin. Only eight years since the war ended, since the incomprehensible loss of life. From the massacre of two-thirds of European Jews and countless others. So it is a particularly good time for me to discuss violence. Did you know I changed my mind on the war?"

I was aware of that fact and acknowledged so with a nod.

"I was a committed pacifist until I saw what Hitler was doing. There's nothing like gross inhumanity to convert a pacifist to someone who wishes with all of his heart to kill those who would perpetrate such heinous acts. I was never happy about the transition."

"Because?"

"Because, Franklin, as I'm sure you know, violence destroys the soul."

"Carl Jung said the same," I told Einstein.

"That remains my conundrum. My physics colleagues and I worry constantly about the conflict between my theory of general relativity and quantum physics. How are they to be reconciled? I continue to work on that even now that I have left the university. But, Franklin, that pales in importance to how one reconciles the scourge of violence and the natural desire to fight evil."

"That is the dilemma, or as you said, the conundrum."

"I am going to surmise that you have an idea of how to do this."

"I do. That's why I'm here. I need to get this right."

"You know, Franklin, I recall telling myself the same as I struggled with the equations for general relativity. Good for you. Tell me your thoughts."

"Just about everyone sees time as the sequential flow of moments, from the past towards the future. You have proven that incorrect, yet hardly anyone knows it, even in my time, sixty-seven years from now. Without that knowledge, correctly understanding how our world works is impossible. If one starts with a faulty assumption, all of the following deductions are going to be wrong."

"I must say, Franklin, that I am surprised and disappointed that even in the next century most people remain ignorant of the nature of time. How is that possible?"

"Most likely because it runs afoul of what they experience every day. It does seem that there is an order to things, that A comes before B. For you, Professor, the leap from the way things seem to be to the way the universe works is not difficult. You are not hindered by the apparent; you have spent your life ignoring the apparent and getting to the truth behind reality. That's not so simple for most people. You are the exception to the rule."

"Tell me, why do you feel that understanding the true nature of time is important to address violence in the world?"

"Because if we can demonstrate that something so essential to life as time is not what it appears to be, that might be the first step to convince the same people that there are other aspects of life that are not what they assume them to be."

"Such as?"

"Such as death. I assume, Professor, that we agree that death is not what people assume it to be."

"Since every moment in time exists eternally, therefore so do each of us. In that very real sense we never die," Einstein concurred.

"We can talk about what happens after death in a minute. If death is not what it appears to be—and we agree it's not—then we have demonstrated that two fundamental concepts that just about everyone believes they understand—time and death—are almost universally misunderstood. So far so good?"

"So far so good. May I?"

"Of course," I replied.

"If time and death are both misunderstood by most people..."

"By just about everyone," I interrupted.

"If time and death are misunderstood—by just about everyone—then it is but a small step to show that life itself—its purpose—is also grossly misunderstood. Is that where you were headed?"

"Exactly, sir. You and I both know that life is not about fame or wealth."

"Fame. It's enjoyable for a short time, and then be careful. I did enjoy the fanfare after my theories were finally proven. It does swell one's head when people are shouting your name as if you are the Messiah. But after a while your privacy is a memory, and there are those who will go to great lengths to knock you from the pedestal you have no desire to be on anyway."

"Still, people seek fame and fortune, and of course power. As you know all too well."

"The images of the millions of murders the Germans committed will never leave me."

"Can I ask you a delicate and personal question?"

"You may."

"Do you hate them, the Germans?"

"I must admit that I do. And I hate myself for that. Because hate, like violence, poisons the soul."

"That, Professor, I believe is why violence has been so intransigent, why we have not seemed to get ahead of it. Violence is the natural human response to violence. Hate begets hate, violence begets violence," I told him, quoting Martin Luther King.

"I'll tell you something else I have learned," Einstein continued. "If you surround people with violent images, they begin to accept it. Worse, they become comfortable with it, used to it. Fill the world with hate and violence, constantly expose people to hate and violence, and you will only get more."

"If instead you expose people to beauty and peace?" I asked.

"You will get more of those, thank God. Is that part of your strategy, Franklin? I think it should be."

"It is."

"So, Franklin, we agree that fame, fortune, and power are not what life is about. And that brings us back to where I think you were headed earlier. The hereafter, correct?"

"It does, but I prefer not to use that term."

"Why does it matter?"

"Maybe you're right; it shouldn't. I worry that the word connotes heaven."

"Why is that a problem?"

"Because, Professor, I believe that what happens after death is not what most people would think of as heaven."

"Interesting. What do you believe?"

"I believe that we will have more work to do after we leave this earth. When you began your thought experiments you looked at nature without preconceptions and uncovered the laws of nature as they are. You were not fooled by time or gravity. I am no Albert Einstein—don't wave me off, I'm not anything close—but I am trying as best as I can, as you did, to read the facts. Here's an example: Why are we foolish when we are young and most wise just before death? That makes no sense from a survival perspective, right? It's completely backward. Here's another: Why must each of us run the same course as everyone who came before? Meaning, why must each of us personally experience the full gamut of human experiences and emotions? It is not enough to read about them. We all recognize that. But why?"

"Because we need to prepare individually for what comes next."

"Because we need to prepare individually for what comes next. Yes, sir, that is what I think the world tells us."

"And if that is true, then it matters not what we gain or what we lose, what we have or what we don't, or how long each of us lives. Once we get it, meaning once we understand what is important to be gleaned from this life, we should be good. In that case, I would prefer to be a slow learner," Einstein closed, with a smile and a wink.

"For sure there is no need to rush," I agreed. "There is much to enjoy in life. And that leads us to the next link in the chain."

"I sense this has something to do with love."

"Yes, Professor, everything to do with love. I believe that we are here to learn empathy, compassion, justice, and most critically love. These are the skills we will need next."

"Violence is the enemy of love. It destroys the soul, as Jung said. So the conclusion is that violence is never warranted, no matter what," Einstein concluded.

"That is where I have landed as well, sir."

"And I am going to assume you are as uncomfortable with that conclusion as I, Franklin?"

"Yes, very uncomfortable. I cannot imagine how anyone would be able to resist violence if a loved one is put at risk. Or how the world could have ignored Hitler. To use your word, it is a nearly impossible conundrum to reconcile."

"Yet if you are correct about the purpose of life—and Franklin, I suspect that you are—then we are left with a conclusion we do not like. I am familiar with this problem. I ran into it again and again as I formulated my relativity theories. A scientist must be willing to accept unpleasant results. Granted, what we are discussing is not pure science. Still, it is compelling. How do you plan to get around this?"

"You mean because I will likely never be able to convince people to abandon violence when it appears that it is justified? Even though if we are correct, it never is."

"Precisely. We should be able to decipher this together, don't you think?"

Albert Einstein had just invited me to solve a problem with him. I could not conceal my appreciation. "Thank you for that compliment, Professor. I would never imagine myself in this position."

"Your humility is endearing, Franklin, but unnecessary. Now let us think."

After a few minutes of silent contemplation, the greatest physicist of the twentieth century spoke. "So, Franklin, what have you come up with?"

"I would first like to hear what you have to say."

"In physics, we do not like exceptions. They generally indicate a fault in the theory. But sometimes there is no getting around it if one is to make any headway. All or nothing is not a great strategy for progress."

"I was thinking along the same lines. Perhaps we don't need to shoot for perfection. Any reduction in violence would help."

"We can get much further than a mere reduction in violence. We can get almost all the way. Only in the most egregious situations would it be acceptable. I say acceptable because it is the individual—and as I think about it more I would say also the society—that suffers the loss of soul when violent. No one wishes to be tormented, and that is what violence yields. So each of us, and all of us collectively, should seek to avoid violence and embrace peace as much as possible. When another Hitler arises, or on a personal level when we or our loved ones are directly threatened, violence at some level might be unavoidable. And I would say that need is likely to diminish over time if you are successful."

"Our goal, then, is to explain that collectively we have misunderstood the world and that our misunderstanding has resulted in unnecessary and undesirable behaviors, of which violence is the most egregious," I thought out loud.

"Well said and accurate, Franklin. You will need many others to assist you. But as I am sure you know, most anything of any value begins with the efforts of a single individual. One person can indeed change the world. It happens all the time."

Professor Einstein swiveled in his chair and looked out his window.

"You know, Franklin, what I see when I look out at the world has changed over the years. I now see eternity. I see every day that has ever existed. Nothing makes one feel part of something greater than under-standing the nature of our universe. We are each a small piece of an inconceivably massive whole, but that does not make us powerless. On the contrary, we are in the most important ways omnipotent." He turned back to face me. "Defeat violence, Franklin."

"I will do all I can."

I noticed the flicker as did Professor Einstein.

"Goodbye, Franklin. We will see each other again I am sure somewhere in space-time."

"I will need your help, Professor."

"And you shall have it," he promised as we both felt the shift.

45

A Jumble of Time

DESPITE PROFESSOR EINSTEIN'S ACCURATE STATEMENT that anything of value begins with a single individual, I was going to need, as Henry put it, a posse. Prepared as I was to be the nidus, real change would take the efforts of many. Just how I would assemble the many was the challenge awaiting a solution.

Franklin Rock: The Man Who Fixed the World. As I had reminded Henry, the title confirmed my eventual success. So just how did I do it? Instinctively I pulled my phone from my pocket as if I could simply Google it and find the answer.

"Joanna!"

"I'm still in the kitchen," she answered.

I raced from my office to find her.

"I figured it out!"

Joanna lifted her eyes from her book on canning and preserving. "Figured what out?"

"How I accomplish my mission."

"You mean defeating violence?"

"Yes, but that's just the first challenge. I mean all of it. Remember Professor Niemeyer's words? 'Franklin, if you pay attention you will find the future in the past.' He told me that on more than one occasion. That's the answer!"

"What's the answer? I'm not quite following you, love."

"Doranto Durning, the man I met in my visit to the future, was just about to take me to the Franklin Rock Museum before I felt the shift signaling my return to the present."

Her pause was brief: she had instantly made the connection. "So you're planning to go there, visit the museum, and learn how you did it. That's your plan, isn't it?"

"Exactly. Want to come? You do love museums."

"Of course. You think it's possible?"

"Everything is possible, Joanna."

"How?"

"I'm not quite sure, but I know it's going to involve Govinda."

"Why Govinda?"

"Because long before I visited Doranto Durning, Govinda had a dream. Although he had no way of knowing it at the time, he somehow played the part of Doranto Durning in his dream and welcomed me to the future. Govinda was the future in the past, Joanna. He's the key."

I left Joanna to her reading and walked over to Oscar. "C'mon, pup." Oscar rose and headed towards the door. As we enjoyed our nighttime walk, my mind covered a lot of ground. Getting to the Franklin Rock Museum was not guaranteed. Although I had managed to visit several great men of the past, I hadn't chosen the time or place of those encounters. I had as yet not even attempted purposeful travel to the future. Even more problematic, I had no real target. All I knew about my trip to the future was that the year I visited was 2095.

"Just have to figure out the details, Oscar," I told my buddy. He looked up at me as if to confirm that I would.

"Govinda, this is Franklin. I need you to call me as soon as you can," was the message I left on his phone early the next morning. Five minutes later he returned my call.

"Your message sounded urgent. You all right?" he asked me.

"I have an idea and I need your help."

"You said that you would be calling me, but I didn't anticipate that it would be this soon."

"Nor did I. When you accused me of having no idea how to move forward—actually I think your words were 'no earthly idea'—you were pretty much correct. Last night it came to me, Govinda," I told him, then explained my strategy.

"So in my dream that I had years ago, you're telling me that I played the part of the man you met in the future? Wow, that is incredible. What was that man's name?"

"Doranto Durning."

"Seriously?"

"Yes. Why?"

"That was my great-grandfather's name, Franklin."

A chill briefly shook me.

"Franklin, are you still there?" Govinda asked after a few seconds of silence.

"Yes, sorry," I responded after absorbing the shock of Govinda's revelation. "That's it, Govinda. That's how I'm going to get there."

"You mean to the Franklin Rock Museum?"

"Yes, through your great-grandfather."

"I don't understand. What does my great-grandfather have to do with traveling to the future?"

"Everything Govinda. If I get to your great-grandfather, I will get to the museum."

"Are you sure?"

"As Maurice Burnside would say, hundred percent."

"How, Franklin? My great-grandfather was born in 1885 and died in the 1940s. I don't see how visiting him helps."

"Look, it's obvious that it is no coincidence that the man I met in the future and your great grandfather had the same name. We agree on that, I'm sure."

"Absolutely, but I don't see the rest of the connection. We're talking over two hundred years between my great-grandfather's birth and your visit to the future. How is this going to work?"

"I just know it will, Govinda," I responded with unwavering certainty. "First, I need to learn about your great-grandfather."

"What do you need to know?"

"Not much. Stuff about his life. Where he lived and what he did."

"That's easy. I still don't see how that is going to get you to the future."

"It will. I can see it."

"You can see yourself at the museum?"

"Sort of."

Then why do you need to go?"

"No, Govinda, it's not like that. It's more like I know that I got there and saw what I needed to see. Can we get together in the next few days? Just bring a picture of your great-grandfather if you have one and whatever information you have about him."

"I don't need a few days, Franklin. I'll gather what you need and get in the car. What's for dinner?"

"Anything you want, as long as I know how to make it. On second thought, Joanna will be very happy to see you and will hopefully chase me from the kitchen. We both may luck out and get something delicious. See you soon. And thanks, my friend."

By sunset, Govinda had arrived.

"Did you bring the photo?" was the first question I asked him as he entered the house.

"Yes. Just curious. Why do you need a photo?"

"I don't need it. I just have a hunch. Can I see it?"

Govinda pulled the photo from his backpack along with a few letters, a yellowed news clipping that I assumed was his great grandfather's obituary and a small pamphlet from a church event.

"Doranto Durning," I said out loud.

"Yes, that's him," Govinda answered.

"He looks exactly like the Doranto Durning I met in the future. Just what I anticipated," I concluded.

"Really? They look the same?"

"They are the same."

"Franklin, are you implying that my great-grandfather was reincarnated?" Govinda asked me with obvious skepticism.

"No. I don't believe in reincarnation. All I can tell you is that your great-grandfather Doranto Durning and the one I met maybe one hundred and fifty years or more after this photo was taken are essentially identical. I don't mean they simply look alike. They are nearly the same person."

Govinda's expression questioned my credulity. "What does that mean, nearly the same person?"

"I'll explain in a minute. Can I see the other stuff you brought?"

Govinda handed me the obituary and the pamphlet. I took a glance at each. His great-grandfather finished high school but did not go on to college. During the Depression, he volunteered at soup kitchens to help the many less fortunate than him. He rose to a prominent position in his community, serving on his church's council and continuing to volunteer in many community organizations.

"Your great-grandfather seems like a wonderful person," I told my friend.

"My grandfather talked about him all the time. I wish I had gotten to meet him."

"You did, Govinda."

"I guess in a way I did. So now what? Have any idea how you're going to turn this information into a trip to the future? How will you know where to go, or I guess just as importantly when to arrive?"

"I won't. It will just happen."

"Oh, c'mon, Franklin. You can't just trust that to be the case. I've got to assume there's more to it than that."

"I don't think so, Govinda. I'm pretty sure I have what I need."

"Are you going to take Joanna?"

"I'm going to try."

"When are you going to attempt this?"

"After we eat, and while you do the dishes," I responded with a grin.

"Hey, I'm happy to clean up. I'll be waiting for you to return. Assuming you do."

I looked at my friend.

"You never know, right? Maybe you could get stranded there."

"Zero chance. We will be back, so make sure you do a good job of cleaning up the kitchen."

"If you succeed, I'll scrub the floor and wash the windows," Govinda volunteered.

After dinner—which my wonderful wife agreeably whipped up so that we need not eat some inferior fare that I might have prepared—the three of us sat in the family room.

"How is this going to work?" Joanna began. "I don't understand how going to meet someone from so long ago is going to instead move us one hundred years into the future."

"Govinda's great-grandfather and the Doranto Durning I met in the future are linked. I believe the more correct way to say it is that they are entangled. Meaning that what one experiences is in some mysterious way automatically experienced by the other. It's the same principle that occurs in quantum physics between two particles. Professor Niemeyer had briefly touched on this despite my aversion at the time to learning it. Now I see why he wanted to teach it to me. I'm pretty certain that if we try to get to

Govinda's great-grandfather we will automatically link to the Doranto Durning of the future."

"Let's say you're right, that the two Dorantos are linked, or entangled. Why wouldn't we just end up in the past with Govinda's great grandfather? How do you know we will end up with the future Doranto instead?" Joanna asked.

"We will."

"Because you know things, I presume."

"Yes, love. I know sometimes that drives you crazy, but I promise you it's true."

"Not that I would necessarily mind if we arrived in the past, Franklin. You know I love history."

"We can go back some other time. This time we need to go forward."

"So what do I have to do?" Joanna asked me as she sat next to me in my office, lights dimmed as usual.

"Not a thing. Just hold my hand."

"We have to be touching for this to work?" she inquired.

"I have no idea. I just love holding your hand," I told her as I leaned over and kissed her cheek.

"You are impossible."

"Impossibly in love, from that day I first saw you freshman year."

I laid the photo of Govinda's great-grandfather on my desk and began to read his obituary out loud. Unlike modern-day obituaries that are often short summaries of the deceased's life, this one was a long, detailed article. It began when Doranto was a young child and covered every one of the man's stops and accomplishments. Govinda's great-grandfather had served in World War I in England working in logistics. From that experience, he was able to land a job working for several companies purchasing supplies. Each of his many volunteer activities was listed as well as his community awards and honors. His wife died several years before him. Govinda's grandfather was one of seven children from their long marriage.

"Close your eyes, Joanna. Let's see if we can make this happen. Oh, and don't be frightened by the shift. It's a bit unnerving the first time you experience it."

Her audible gasp confirmed that Joanna had indeed felt it. Our eyes opened simultaneously.

"Oh my, Franklin! Where are we?"

I looked up. High above us was the familiar dome. We had arrived in the atrium of the building in which Doranto had taken me so long ago.

"Come, Joanna. I think I know where to go. I've been here before."

"What place is this?" she asked me.

"I never actually knew. It's where Doranto took me. We had lunch…" I paused as I scanned our surroundings. "If I'm remembering correctly we had lunch down this hallway. C'mon, let's explore."

I took Joanna's hand and headed along the same route Doranto and I had traversed. Soon the atrium opened up into several large spaces. To our left, I saw the place Doranto and I had sat.

"Did I ever tell you about the turkey sandwich I ate here?" I asked Joanna.

"You're kidding, right?" she responded.

"No, I'm not kidding. Doranto bought me lunch. Just because one time travels doesn't mean he or she doesn't get hungry."

"I can't believe you are talking about a sandwich now."

"I know. Sorry," I laughed. "Let's see if we can find who we came to see."

"You think he will be here?" Joanna asked.

"Oh, he's here somewhere."

"How can you be sure?"

"If he weren't, we wouldn't be here. I just have to figure out how to locate him."

With Joanna in tow, I headed towards the dining area. I scanned the relatively sparse group seated at the numerous tables. "Hmm, I don't see him," I said out loud. "Let's head down another hallway and see what happens."

I was still looking over my shoulder as I turned to head out of the dining area and began to walk.

"Franklin!" I heard from just in front of me. I abruptly stopped and turned to face forward.

"Doranto! It's so good to see you. This is my wife, Joanna."

"I know who she is, Franklin. Why didn't you tell me you had brought her? It is an honor to meet you, Joanna."

"And you, Mr. Durning. I have heard a lot about you."

"Please, call me Doranto. That is very kind, but I'm going to guess that I know even more about you. All wonderful, of course," Doranto quickly added. "Where did you go, Franklin?"

"I'm not sure I understand."

"After we finished lunch I was about to take you to the Franklin Rock Museum. I'm not sure what happened but as we started to exit the building I lost you."

"That was a long time ago, Doranto."

"What do you mean? It was just an hour ago. I looked everywhere."

"It wasn't an hour to me. It was years ago."

"How is that possible?"

As I thought about his question the answer became obvious.

"I should have expected this. It makes all the sense in the world. I had to return to this time to find you and to visit the museum. When else would I have the chance? It's only when we mistakenly think of time as linear that we are surprised by the simultaneous availability of all moments." So obvious, I said to myself. "Can we go to the museum now, Doranto?"

"Of course! It's my distinct pleasure to accompany you two there. I assume Joanna doesn't have elevars either?"

"Correct." Joanna looked at me quizzically. "I'll explain later," I whispered.

"No problem. We can take the HoverRail."

"Is it true you have little crime here, Doranto?" Joanna asked as we whisked silently along in the HoverRail car.

"Essentially none. Or violence. In large part because of your husband." Joanna squeezed my hand.

"Here we are," Doranto announced as we exited.

We were standing in front of another nondescript white building. On the wall to the right of the entrance was the following:

The Franklin Rock Museum. Visitors Welcome.

"My God, Franklin, it's real," Joanna said as she took my hand in both of hers.

"You will need these," Doranto told us as we entered the vestibule. He handed us what looked like super-thin visors that weighed less than a handful of popcorn. "They are for the holograms. You'll hear the sound as if it's coming from inside your head. I'm guessing both will be new experiences for you two."

As we walked through the museum I saw my entire life in review. My parents were alive as holograms; seeing them was thrilling. Every individual who had had any impact on my life was represented. Professor Niemeyer had his own room; his entire life was reviewed as well. While it was all fascinating, I remained focused on a single topic. How had I managed to make it all happen? How had I turned the few into the many?

"Doranto, I came here for a reason."

"I assumed you wanted to see how your life and work were represented."

"No, Doranto. I came to learn how I made it happen."

"You don't know?" he asked with surprise.

"No, I don't. Do you?"

"Of course. Everyone does. How is it even possible that you don't?"

"It's because I haven't done it yet. That's why I needed to come here. I know, it sounds crazy. That's the thing about time, Doranto. The past, present, and future are just a jumble. It seems like there is an order to things, but there isn't. So how did I do it?"

"Let's go to the place where you can see for yourself."

Doranto led us through a couple of hallways lined with photos and testimonials. Some of the names and faces I recognized. Wow, I thought. I met and knew these people?

"I think you'll find what you're looking for here, Franklin."

Just above the entrance to the room Doranto had led us to was the following inscription:

The Words of Franklin Rock

Every case was full of things that I had written in what appeared to be chronological order.

"So looks like that short story I wrote for you had legs," I told Joanna. "It's over there on the wall, under *Early Writings*."

"That's what did it?" I asked Doranto as I turned to face him. "The stuff I wrote?"

"You got the attention of the right people, Franklin. And from there it just exploded. It's funny. Nowadays everything you said seems so obvious. I guess it wasn't in your time."

"Or for centuries before. I am so humbled."

I planned to spend as much time as possible in this room and read as many of my creations as I could. That was not to be. Within a couple of minutes, I noticed the flicker. It didn't matter. The fact that I now knew what I had to do was sufficient.

"We're leaving now, Joanna."

"Why? This is so much fun!"

"It's not our choice. Sorry. That's how this works. Take my hand."

"Is this another ploy?"

"No, I just don't want to take any risk and leave you here," I told her. This time I was serious.

"Doranto, we are about to leave you yet again. Thank you so very much for bringing us here. It has been wonderful to meet you. I will never forget your kindness."

"The honor and pleasure were both mine, Franklin," were the last words we heard before the shift.

◆◇◆◇◆

"WELL?" I ASKED JOANNA as she opened her eyes and confirmed our safe return.

"I don't know what to say. I am so proud of you," Joanna told me and started to cry.

"Please, you'll make me cry, too."

"Franklin, we forgot to see how long it took for you to succeed."

"I already know. It will take a bit. I have a lot to write about. Time is the last thing we need to be concerned with, Joanna."

We stood and embraced. "Quite a love affair we have, don't you think?" I asked her as we separated.

"Quite. Now get to work."

Oscar had wandered into my office as Joanna left. I sat with him on the floor, his long, soft tail wagging rhythmically as I stroked the back of his neck. "The world has so much potential, pup. Time for me to get to fixing it."

I leaned back against the couch, Oscar pressed closely to my side. My eyes drifted closed.

Throngs of people were visible as far as I could see. They were smiling and laughing, waving their arms and swaying to the beat of the music. Behind me on the platform were Joanna, Henry, Govinda, and Lucille Burnside. They too were smiling, waving their arms and swaying with the crowd. I glanced at Joanna; she blew me a kiss. Henry could not suppress his smile.

Govinda approached and embraced me. "You have indeed begun to fix the world, my friend."

"There will always be more to do, Govinda. This is only chapter one," I told him as I opened the book to the table of contents. "For sure there will be many more chapters to write."

I felt a tap on my shoulder. Now standing just behind me was Maurice Burnside.

"I knew you would succeed, Franklin. Didn't I tell you so, Lucille?" Tears were streaming down Lucille Burnside's cheeks. Maurice leaned closer. "Franklin, is this a dream or is this really happening?" he asked.

"Sometimes it's hard to tell," I told him. "But in the end, both are equally real."

And with those words gravity once again released me. As I soared into the clouds, free flight was now mine. The familiar voice returned. "Franklin," it whispered, "now everyone wants it as much as you." I looked down and beheld a world at peace.

Epilogue

"DID YOU EVER IMAGINE WE WOULD see this day?" Joanna asked me.

I smiled at her. "Oh, goodness, of course you did. You could always see it, couldn't you?" she said, answering her own question.

I could, and I did.

A world without violence. Would it last? It could, as long as each new generation learned the truth about time, our world, and the purpose of life, I concluded.

"What's next for you to fix, my love?" Joanna asked me.

"You've seen the list."

"I have, and it's long."

"Have any suggestions?"

"How about we look at it together, after you do the dishes?"

"Hey, c'mon, I just brought violence to its knees."

"What do you think Maurice Burnside would tell you to do?"

I picked up the plates and headed to the sink.

Acknowledgments

As Henry told Franklin, "You're going to need a posse." Perhaps there are individuals who can do it all without assistance. I am not one of them.

First, I thank my wife, Deneen. My initial thought every morning and last before sleep is how fortunate I am that we are husband and wife. Her comments and guidance markedly improved the story—though not nearly as much as her presence has markedly improved my life.

A small group of friends and family members read evolving versions of the manuscript and pointed out deficiencies and errors of both content and grammar. To each of them—David Klein, Saul Pressner, Richard Newman, Robert Goldsmith, William Hard, Larry Bernstein, Daniel Mcnulty, Michael Sokalsky, Larry Siegel, and Todd Johns—I say thank you.

Janice Benight has designed all of my books. I thank her for another wonderful cover and layout, for her wisdom, and for her kindness.

Finally, I thank God—or whoever is in charge—for bringing Franklin Rock to life, and for all of the magic and majesty of our universe. Both are everywhere one looks.

About the Author

Photo by Avi Bender

MARK E. KLEIN is a physician and author. His career has been centered on caring for others, whether they be patients, colleagues, friends, or strangers. He is always a teacher, sometimes of new medical technologies to other physicians from around the nation and the world, other times of the more important issues of life that none of us can avoid. He continues to practice medicine in Washington, DC. *Franklin Rock* is his third book and his first novel.

CPSIA information can be obtained
at www.ICGtesting.com
Printed in the USA
BVHW072041220121
598495BV00007B/64

9 780976 168447